SOMEBODY HAS TO BE THE FIRST

"How many suspicious ... Tracy Greene demanded ...

"Too many to count ... mostly. "Dozens, at least. Why?"

Carol Beseman said, "We've had a death in the Antilympus program that we'd like you to investigate."

"A death? Who? One of the candidates?"

She nodded grimly. "Yes. A botanist, Etsub Beyene. Ethiopian American."

"I know Etsub, yeah. But isn't he . . ."

"On the Moon? Yes. He died in an EVA accident, and we think he might have been murdered."

"Okay," Raimy said slowly, taking all of that in. "What's this got to do with me? Am I . . . what am I, a suspect?"

Carol Beseman looked confused for a moment. "What? How would you . . . No, you're a *cop*. You're the closest thing we have to a *space cop*. Both the Catholic Church and Harvest Moon Industries have agreed to grant us jurisdiction, and your bosses at the CSPD have agreed to a leave of absence."

"To do what?" Raimy asked, still not quite sure he was getting it. Not daring to be sure.

"To investigate a possible homicide," Carol said, now a bit impatiently.

"On the . . . on the Moon?"

"Yes," she said, as though it were the most natural thing in the world.

BOOKS by WIL McCARTHY

Antediluvian

Rich Man's Sky Series

Rich Man's Sky
Poor Man's Sky
Beggar's Sky

The Queendom of Sol Series

The Collapsium
The Wellstone
Lost in Transmission
To Crush the Moon

The Waister Series

Aggressor Six
The Fall of Sirius

Flies from the Amber
Murder in the Solid State
Bloom
Once Upon a Galaxy

To purchase Baen titles in e-book form, please go to
www.baen.com.

POOR MAN'S SKY

✦

WIL McCARTHY

A Baen Books Original

Baen Publishing Enterprises
P.O. Box 1403
Riverdale, NY 10471
www.baen.com

ISBN: 978-1-9821-9316-4

Cover art by Dave Seeley

First printing, January 2023
First mass market printing, January 2024

Distributed by Simon & Schuster
1230 Avenue of the Americas
New York, NY 10020

Library of Congress Control Number: 2022046599

Printed in the United States of America

10 9 8 7 6 5 4 3 2 1

This book is dedicated to the
monks of Saint Benedict's Monastery.

POOR MAN'S SKY

1.1
12 November 2052

✧

Orlov Petrochemical Compressed Gas Cargo Landing Vehicle #14 Lunar Orbit

Andrei Bykhovski had been tied up for sex a time or two, and he had once been in a helicopter crash. His present circumstance was a bit like doing both of these things at the same time. The ground below him was getting bigger and closer and bigger and closer, and he was strapped securely, facedown, arms down, feet down. But instead of a blindfold he had a fogged-up spacesuit visor, dripping with condensation as the water droplets stopped being weightless and started being pulled downward along the clear plastic.

Instead of pillows or flight seat hardware underneath him, he had the metal struts and tanks and pipes of the gas delivery lander, poking up uncomfortably against the padding of his suit like the bars of a miniature jungle gym. And the ground rising up to meet him was the dusty-cratered surface of the Moon, which provided no sense of scale. He'd been strapped to this thing for hours, and he really didn't know if it could land properly with him onboard, and he also couldn't tell how close he was to touchdown. Seconds? Minutes? Another hour? All he could say for sure was that there were craters rolling by, getting slowly bigger as they went.

It helped that he'd put himself in this situation. It helped that he was escaping indentured servitude, in search of sweet freedom. It helped that he was an experienced astronaut, with literally hundreds of EVA hours in his logbook. But his oxygen consumption was high—very high—because he was hyperventilating, because this was way more terrifying than he'd allowed himself to expect. He was tempted to lean on the chin switch that would activate his radio on the emergency channel. He was tempted to call for help, but who could help him? What could they do? What would he even say?

Andrei Bykhovski fell from the sky like a tank of cyanogen, like the tanks of asteroid-harvested carbon-nitrogen gas he'd pulled out of the lander a couple of hours ago, replacing them with his own body weight. He fell from the sky cramped and cramping and half-blinded, thinking this was the dumbest thing he'd ever tried, and also quite possibly the last.

And yet, as bad a day as he was having, he was out here for a reason. He had to remember that, while he panted away his oxygen. Had to remember that Grigory Orlov, by refusing paid shore leave for the workers at Clementine Cislunar Fuel Depot, while also refusing to accept any resignations, had effectively made serfs of them all.

Without breaking any laws! It was intolerable, and somebody had to do something.

Then again, the spasms in Andrei's back and shoulders were also intolerable. He might almost welcome a fatal crash if it meant an end to this. Would it hurt if he died on impact? Would he even know it happened?

The forehead of his helmet was braced across a metal pipe, which hummed as the rocket engines beneath him fired. He couldn't see any flame, any gas belching out of them, but he could feel the deceleration, greater now than when it had first kicked on. Ten minutes ago? One minute? Hovering on the edge of panic, all his internal senses were scrambled, except for pain. His whole world was reduced to this crab-shaped delivery lander, or smaller than that, to the bubble of air inside his fogged-up helmet. To the loops of nylon holding his wrists and ankles, too far down, too far stretched. To the growing sensation of his own weight, against a spindly structure never meant to bear it. A structure meant only to support the weight of a pair of gas cylinders, against the weak pull of Lunar gravity.

If this were a dumber craft, his weight—heavier than the bottles he'd removed—would have thrown the trajectory off entirely. But it was smart enough to find its way, though he did run the very real risk of, at any moment, running out of propellant and simply falling the rest of the way to the Lunar surface. And so his whole life was reduced to this one endless moment, waiting in terror.

But then something changed; he saw shapes drifting by beneath him, black and white and yellow and red. Cylinders and rectangles, casting long shadows in the slanting rays of the sun. Could it be? Was this the St. Joseph of Cupertino Monastery, three degrees of latitude off the Lunar south pole? Had he arrived?

The structures swelled alarmingly as he dropped toward them, then they rotated out of view as the lander made some kind of automated adjustment, and all he knew was that he was falling fast and decelerating hard, and his breathing was so rapid and shallow he felt in real danger of passing out.

And then he could see streaks of dust kicking out from the rocket plumes, and then he could see a long shadow throwing itself beneath him, and then he was in shadow, and then WHAM! The lander touched down with an impact nearly hard enough to break his ribs.

Gasping, he saw stars, and not the good kind. Beneath him, the lander's metal webbing crumpled and then, disorientingly, went still.

For seconds, he did nothing. For seconds more, he tried to breathe, and realized the wind had been knocked out of him. Well, that was one way to stop hyperventilating!

He struggled for breath, and finally caught it.

Struggled to free his hands, and got the right one out of its loop, then the left. Struggled to free a leg, and failed, still gasping. Finally got it out, then fished for a knife and cut the other strap free, hoping he wouldn't slash his suit open in the process. Hoping but not really caring, just needing needing *needing* to be free of this thing. He rolled off the lander, falling slowly in the Lunar gravity. Came down on his side, and just lay there a minute catching and catching and catching his breath.

It occurred to him that he was alive, albeit barely.

It occurred to him that he was free.

It occurred to him that he was probably one of the first hundred people to land on the surface of the Moon. Number ninety? Ninety-five? Something like that.

He had possibly, probably, just made history. This deed of his could well join the October Revolution and the Boston Tea Party in the Go Fuck Yourself Hall of Fame. Better than the Darwin Award he might have earned instead! Better than simply falling off en route and simply becoming a Very Missing Person. Nobody knew he was here. Probably, nobody even knew yet that he was missing, that he wasn't onboard Clementine Cislunar Fuel Depot at all. Fearing spies and snitches, he'd told no one about his plan.

Then he stopped thinking for a while, and just let himself breathe. Then he thought he should maybe turn that chin switch on after all, and let someone at the monastery know they had an uninvited guest. His suit—a bottom-of-the-line General Spacesuit Light Orbital—had no heads-up display or time-to-depletion meter, but the oxygen dial inside his helmet said just under twenty percent. He was still jittery with adrenaline, and at this rate he had maybe thirty minutes of breathable air left.

A 20/80 nitrox mix, it blew in a steady stream onto his visor, and now that he was no longer facing downward, the fog had condensed into droplets and rolled to the edge, soaking into the helmet's padding. It was so cold here, he thought the remaining droplets might soon begin to freeze. Nevertheless, through the visor he could see the gray, dusty Lunar surface, and part of a habitat module.

He decided to stand, which proved rather tricky in Lunar gravity, in a suit designed only for weightlessness. On his third try, he got his feet underneath him. He turned on his radio, and heard nothing. No voice traffic, no conversations, no chatter. This was strange to him, because the emergency channel was actually dozens of private and commercial channels all at once, and Clementine was always alive with chatter. To Andrei, radio silence was a rare and disturbing thing. He wanted to call out a mayday, to let someone know he was here and needed help. That he needed to be taken indoors before his air ran out. That he needed a drink of water and a chance to pee. Hell, he needed a lot of things, but some instinct told him to stay quiet and look around first. In space, no one liked surprises, and he was about to drop a *duratskiy* on the people here.

He turned his body in a wide arc, taking in the monastery and the little valley in which it sat. The sun hung very low in the sky, fully eclipsed by one of the low hills surrounding this cluster of modules, although its position was evident by the light it cast on the edges of other hills. He could see in through some of the habitat windows, and thought for a moment he caught a flicker of movement inside. But no, it was dark in there, with shades pulled down over some of the windows. Through the rest he could make out some shelves and bulkheads, maybe, and some rows of blinking lights. Nothing to suggest this place had a religious function, or any function, really.

Behind the habitats he could see a crew lander of some sort, and a spindly tower, and behind that . . .

Behind that he saw a human figure in a dusty orange spacesuit, bathed in sunlight and climbing down one of those little hills.

Correction: not climbing down, staggering down. The figure held something in one of its hands, like a megaphone or a radar gun, which it presently dropped. The arms went up in apparent distress, as if reaching for something behind the helmet. Reaching and failing. The figure fell to its knees.

"Hey," Andrei said into the radio channel. In English, which he was pretty sure was the language here. "Hey, buddy. Hey! You distress? Hey!"

No answer.

Andrei had no idea how to run in Lunar gravity, but he scrambled and fell, scrambled and bounced, and finally got into a sort of slow-motion loping gait around the habitat modules and toward the human figure.

"Hey! Hey! Mayday! I have EVA emergency!"

After a pause, a male voice came onto the radio. "This is Sierra Juliet Ground Actual. Who's on this channel? What is your position?"

Now panting again, Andrei said, "I am outside your habitat. You have astronaut down! Mayday!"

"Can you render assistance?"

"I don't know his problem. I will bring him to airlock."

Andrei was certain, somehow, that the figure was male.

"Who is this?" the voice repeated. "Are you from Shackleton?"

"I am Andrei Bykhovski, from Clementine Cislunar. I am refugee."

Another pause. "Explain that later. What are you seeing? We don't have any people outside."

As Andrei approached, he could see a fine white spray emerging from the kneeling man's bright orange suit's backpack. Not good.

"*Oranzhevyy* spacesuit," he said. "Orange. Orange spacesuit, venting gas. I'm believing person is male."

No immediate answer. The orange-suited man fell forward onto his faceplate. Andrei skidded awkwardly to a stop, falling forward onto his hands and knees beside the man. He grabbed for him, inspecting the leaking backpack. The gas was venting from somewhere inside the pack, and leaking out through a seam between two plastic cover panels. Andrei didn't know what to do about that. If this were Clementine, he'd be clipping himself to this man and unfurling a rescue bag to seal around the both of them, but that wasn't an option here. He didn't have his tool belt with him. He didn't have anything.

"Sierra Juliet Ground Actual here. We may be missing one of our students. Etsub Beyene, if you're on this channel, please respond."

Then another voice, female: "This is Shackleton Actual, responding to mayday. Can we render assistance?"

"I am taking him to airlock," Andrei said. "Look out of window, please, and tell me where to go. And how to operate controls."

There was, unfortunately, no standardization in space, or not enough. The monastery was built by Harvest Moon Industries, and Andrei had experience only with Orlov Petrochemical's systems, some of which were self-built and some of which came from a different company, Renz

Ventures. Even the labels would be in a foreign alphabet, hard to puzzle out in real time.

He flipped the man over and grabbed a fistful of chest harness, thinking to carry the orange suit like a parcel. But it was heavy, even in Lunar gravity, and much bulkier than his own suit, and his space reflexes were adapted for zero gravity and had no idea what to do here. And he was cold. He fell, and fell again. The man was limp now, and Andrei could see right through his visor to his dark brown face, lips moving in a gasp of horror, his bulging eyes filming over with gray. That couldn't possibly be a good sign. There was no way he was going to get this man into a breathable atmosphere in time.

Still, Andrei wasn't a doctor, so he got to his feet and started dragging, saying, "I believe man has lost consciousness. I am dragging him." Looking ahead of him now, at the collection of flat-bottomed habitat modules, he added, "I see airlock. Yellow door, yes? I bring."

"Acknowledged," said the voice of Sierra Juliet Ground Actual. "Do you have any idea what he was doing out there?"

"Pointing object at sky," Andrei answered. "Maybe laser communication device."

"In the middle of the night?"

Was it the middle of the night shift here? Fine, then, yes, this man had gone outside at night, without a buddy, and apparently without telling anyone. Right when Andrei, an unannounced visitor, was about to arrive? No part of that sounded right. And was it even stranger that an air leak should befall the man at just such a compromising moment? And that he did not call for help when he realized he was in trouble? Something was very, very rotten here.

"*Da*," Andrei said. "Is strange. He will tell you all about it when he wakes up, yes?"

But that was *blya chush' sobach'ya*, fucking bullshit, because Andrei was looking right into the man's bone-gray face as he said this, and he knew in that moment with certainty that this man, this student of the monastery, would never inhale another breath.

Andrei was too late—he'd moved too slowly—and Etsub Beyene was dead.

1.2
13 November
✧
U.S. Olympic Training Center
Colorado Springs, Colorado, USA
Earth Surface

As Raimy ran past a group of people he didn't recognize, a woman's voice called out:

"Raimy Vaught? Can we have a word?"

It took him a couple of seconds to process that, by which time he was twenty meters further down the track. He was running in the field house of the Olympic Training Center, because it was cold and windy and snowing outside, and he didn't dare risk injury by running on the street. He'd done eight kilometers already, and though he'd been left in the dust by the actual Olympians training with him, he was pretty deep in his personal running zone. But okay, once he'd figured out they were talking to him, he slowed, stopped, and turned to face the group of people. There were three of them, and they were all wearing lightweight jackets that were arguably too warm for the nearly room-temperature air in here, but very definitely not warm enough for the snowy weather outside.

"Can we have a word?" the woman repeated. She was white and blonde, and even from a distance Raimy could see she oozed money from every perfect pore. There was actually something vaguely familiar about her, although the woman and man on either side of her were unknown to him.

His camera drones took an interest, their pea-brained AIs spreading the five cameras out to form an ellipse with himself at one focus and the three strangers at the other. This was not particularly remarkable, as (per his contract) the drones followed him around most of the time, capturing and live-streaming nearly everything about his life. Suspended on streams of ionized air, they were small and nearly silent, though hardly unobtrusive.

"Sure," he said, walking back in their direction. "Do I . . . know you?"

"We've never met," she said, "but you're competing for a chance to work alongside me."

The face clicked.

"Carol Beseman?" Wife of Dan Beseman? Wife of the trillionaire founder of Enterprise City, presently residing in low Earth orbit aboard the H.S.F. *Concordia*? Technically the owner of Raimy's camera drones?

"That's right. It's nice to meet you, Detective."

And that was a strange thing for her to call him. It was his rank in the Colorado Springs Police Department, but it had nothing to do with her, and nothing to do with his bid to join the Besemans' Mars colony. If he were in first place for that competition, she might call him "Colonist," which was the title afforded to anyone living in space, or planning to. Since he certainly was *not* winning, though, the applicable title was "Candidate Vaught," or just "Candidate."

But why was she calling him anything at all? It didn't make sense that she was even here, because he was currently number three in the running for the colony's Male Administrator slot, and only the number one would actually get to fly. Raimy might be determined to play this reality-show contest to the bitter end—it was why he was out running almost every day, or in the police station weight room hoisting barbells—but he only had nineteen thousand sponsors and ten million pledged dollars, and any fool could see that was never going to move him into second place, much less first. Like all of the Antilympus colony's hopefuls, he was an overqualified human being who looked great on paper, but that wasn't enough. That wasn't going to cut it, and on a detective's salary, he was never going to afford a private ticket into space, either. So the whole astronaut thing was pretty much a pipe dream. Candidate, indeed.

Why would someone like Carol Beseman take time to visit someone like Raimy Vaught? His minor celebrity status would not impress her; the underdogs and also-rans were of no real concern to the project. At best, Raimy was the understudy to the understudy of the man who would actually land in Antilympus Crater.

"What can I do for you?" he asked, stepping up and offering her a handshake, which she politely accepted.

"You're a certified Navy diver, yes?" said the woman beside Carol Beseman.

"Yes," he said, shifting his gaze and handshake over to her. "Hi. Raimy Vaught."

"Hello," she said. "Tracy Greene."

Tracy's skin was darker than Raimy's own, and there was something hard and impatient about her. The man standing on the other size of Carol Beseman stuck his own hand out and said, "Emil Fonseca, Human Resources. Pleasure to meet you."

"Hi," Raimy said. Then, to Tracy Greene, "I was a diver and a submariner, yes, but that was a long time ago." As his sponsors and followers well knew, he'd gotten out of the Navy as quickly as he could, then gone to law school, become a prosecuting attorney and assistant DA for El Paso County, and then (in a move that confused nearly everyone, including his parents) quit that to join the Colorado Springs Police Department.

"How much total dive time have you logged?" Tracy wanted to know.

"About three hundred hours," he said. "Not much by Navy standards, but I never had a serious accident."

"And you've had basic spacesuit training," she said. It didn't appear to be a question.

"Six hours, yes. As I'm sure you know." All the serious Antilympus contenders had. Once you hit a million dollars in pledges and passed the basic psych and confinement evaluations, you had to go through two weeks of "astronautics training" (cynically referred to as "space camp"), of which the spacesuit training—scary for many people—was one of the centerpieces. It was all really just an excuse to weed out another seventy-five to eighty percent of the candidate pool before putting the survivors up in front of an audience. Four hundred survivors, initially, and now down to just two hundred ninety. Still too many for the fans to follow in any great detail.

Nobody said anything for a moment. Finally, Raimy said to Carol Beseman, "You live in Oregon, right? You look like you just flew here. What's this about?"

"How many suspicious deaths have you investigated?" Tracy Greene demanded.

"Too many to count," he answered honestly. "Dozens, at least. Why?"

Carol Beseman said, "We've had a death in the Antilympus program that we'd like you to investigate."

"A death? Who? One of the candidates?"

She nodded grimly. "Yes. A botanist, Etsub Beyene. Ethiopian American."

"I know Etsub, yeah. But isn't he . . ."

"On the Moon? Yes. Studying low-gravity horticulture at St. Joseph of Cupertino Monastery. He died in an EVA accident, and we think he might have been murdered."

"Okay," Raimy said slowly, taking all of that in. In his line of work, he dealt with death all the time, and liked to think it didn't faze him, although of course it did. He tried not to imagine what it would be like to die in a spacesuit, during "extravehicular activity." Tried and failed—his mind playing out a vivid simulation for him: trying to breathe and not being able to. Not like drowning at all— just a sucking emptiness flattening the walls of Etsub Beyene's lungs together. It must have been awful. "What's this got to do with me? Am I . . . what am I, a suspect?"

Carol Beseman looked confused for a moment. "What? How would you . . . No, you're a *cop*. You're the closest thing we have to a *space cop*. Both the Catholic Church and Harvest Moon Industries have agreed to grant us jurisdiction, and your bosses at the CSPD have agreed to a leave of absence without pay. We'll cover your salary, along with a substantial hazard bonus."

Raimy frowned. "'We,' meaning . . ."

"Myself and my husband, yes."

"Huh."

Raimy was momentarily at a loss for words. All of that seemed quite presumptuous—they'd arranged things with his employer before even talking to him? But the distortion field surrounding Dan Beseman's wealth made almost anything possible. He was a trillionaire—one of the Four Horsemen—rich enough to afford his own robotic Mars colony, and a spaceship big enough to carry a hundred people there.

"To do what?" Raimy asked, still not quite sure he was getting it. Not daring to be sure.

"To investigate a possible homicide," Carol said, now a bit impatiently.

"On the fuc . . . on the Moon?"

"Yes," she said, as though it were the most natural thing in the world.

And that was how Raimy Vaught got a ticket to fly in space after all.

1.3
14 November

✦

Peakview Apartment Complex
Colorado Springs, Colorado, USA
Earth Surface

"My motivation?" said the man on the video screen. "I think everyone watching this knows my motivation. Unlike Earth, space is infinite. The final frontier! And Mars is a complete reboot; living there provides the human race with a second chance. Or third one, if you count what's happening on Luna right now, which, okay, yeah. Fair enough. But to be there, right at the beginning of it, is something really quite amazing. Helping to define what that new world is going to look like, and how it's going to be, um, governed. I mean, the Besemans have already figured out the governance part, for the first few years at least, but, I mean . . ."

The man's face—Raimy Vaught's own face—wavered uncertainly.

Unseen, the interviewer asked, "So, a chance to affect the future?"

17

"Yes."

"Can you unpack that a little? What's your reason for wanting to shape the future in this particular way? For your own personal glory? For the betterment of humankind? To make the world—the *worlds*, plural—conform to your own sense of what they should be?"

"Whoa, hey," said the man, "I just said, I think people get it. I mean, it's all of those things to some extent, but mostly it's the betterment thing. Of humankind, like you said. Yes. In the ... frontier."

Raimy paused the video player, took a sip of cold coffee from the mug he was holding, and sighed. He was in his study, a bookshelf-walled room left over from his days practicing law. He was watching himself on a rollup screen—a short Black man with a shaved head and a weird, self-conscious smile that never seemed to leave his face—and just like every other time, he could barely stand the sound of his own voice. He was really quite bad at unscripted public speaking, and it was just his bad luck to get all the way through law school and into a criminal courtroom before figuring that out. He'd also gotten five years into a marriage with Harriet, who seemed to really *need* him to speak well, especially when they were fighting. But when it mattered, no matter how clear the thoughts were in his head, they seemed to come out half-assed when he spoke them.

Oh, he could write clearly, and read back what he'd written. He could interrogate people and bark orders and recite theories and read suspects their Miranda rights. Hell, he could even discuss the motives of a criminal suspect with the suspect himself, no problem. But if he had to think on his feet, speaking unscripted as his thoughts occurred to him, it didn't go as well. Especially with people looking at him. It somehow hadn't been a problem in the Navy, and not much of one in law school. When he was a prosecuting attorney, though, with lives and justice hanging in the balance, it mattered a lot. And it counted against him even now, in the competition to win a slot at Antilympus Township. He had a lot of relevant skills—really quite a lot—but if he wanted to rake in the pledges he had to look good on video. And he just didn't.

Ah, well. It broke his heart that he'd probably never see that butterscotch sky, looming above the red sands and black-rock cliffs of Antilympus crater. He was a grown man who'd had his heart broken many times, and he knew how to get over it, but right now he was, at best, still in the "bargaining" phase of the grieving process. As such, he would keep on doing whatever it took to keep the dream alive—the dream of space, the dream of *Mars*—and he would keep on feeling the bones-deep ache of it, every day. Third place: God damn.

He skipped the video forward, until he found Etsub Beyene answering the same question. Etsub had the kind of profoundly black skin that was rarely found outside of sub-Saharan Africa, and that alone might have marked him as an immigrant to the U.S., even if not for his accent. The accent was quite Americanized, but carried a lilting quality that Raimy supposed was Ethiopian. Raimy had an ear for accents, partly because of the jobs he'd had and partly just because it interested him: where people had come from and where they had lived. You could tell a lot about a person from their accent, and that was true sometimes even if they tried to conceal it. To Raimy, it sounded like Etsub may have come to America as a teenager, and lived here for a couple of decades since.

On the screen, Etsub said, "Motivations are complex, and I'm reluctant to boil mine down to the level of a sound bite. I know you need an answer to your question, though, so I'll focus on one aspect, which is the idea of bringing life to a dead planet. I find that so profound, I can hardly put it into words."

"Do you mean terraforming?" asked the offscreen interviewer.

"Not exclusively," Etsub said. "I'm a specialist in aquaculture, so I'm talking primarily about that. Specifically, growing plants in a medium that didn't originate on Earth at all. Unlike the Moon, Mars has all the resources living things require, meaning that life on Mars can be made self-sustaining. Terraforming is a part of that, and we're already seeing some exciting developments there, as I'm sure our viewers are aware. The effects of the MSL1 Magsat on the Martian atmosphere have exceeded even the most optimistic projections, and that's just one small machine. There will be other surprises, both positive and negative, in our future. But terraforming is a project of lifetimes, or centuries, so if that were my only motivation, I'd have to be a saint. None of us will live to see that even partially completed. But we can make Mars alive inside the confines of Antilympus Township, and all the other towns that follow after it, and that's more than exciting enough for me to devote my life. More than exciting enough."

Raimy paused the video again, and checked the project rankings. There were still ten applicants for the one and only Male Administrator slot—down from several dozen at the beginning. Anyone with half a brain could be an administrator, which made that slot one of the most competitive in the whole program. But hydroponics was different; you had to actually know something, and if you were bad at your job everyone could see the dead plants as proof. There was only one Male Hydroponics slot, and Etsub Beyene (whose name had not yet been removed from the leaderboard) was number one in the rankings, meaning he was almost definitely going to take the prize. He was Mars-bound even before he'd traveled to Luna, to study the hydroponics systems at "Saint Joe's" for six weeks. With that credential under his belt, he'd've been unstoppable.

The idea made Raimy sad, then angry. Such a waste. Death was always a waste, and a suspicious death doubly so. A murder . . . Well, Raimy had been drawn to the legal profession, and from there to policing itself, by a sort of deep, persistent grief that something like murder could exist at all. What gave anyone that right? Nothing. Justice didn't fix it, or even necessarily deter it, but in an imperfect world, it was the best human beings could strive for.

Drawing another sip from his dead-cold coffee, he hit play again, and watched Etsub nodding in satisfaction at his own answer, unaware that he had, at the time the video was taken, less than two months left to live. Had he made the most of that time? Had he loved someone? Had someone loved him? He didn't make it to Mars, but he did visit the Moon, and that had to have been exciting. What person could honestly say they'd never dreamed of doing that?

With a jolt of something like fear, Raimy remembered that *he* was also headed for the Moon. To the place where Etsub had gasped out his last breath. That simple fact made outer space more real to him than it had ever been before—as real as the dark beneath the ocean. In two days, Raimy would be at Spaceport Paramaribo, in Suriname. The day after that, he'd be on a rocket ship blasting into space. And then in orbit, weightless and surrounded by suffocating vacuum. In space, the sun was murderously hot and the shadows were murderously cold, and (as with the ocean deeps) no quarter was given for mistakes or accidents or equipment failures of any kind. And Raimy was going to be up there for at least a week.

Did it mean something, that the reality of it made him nervous? He'd generally been nervous before a dive, too, hanging out in the torpedo tube while they dogged the hatch behind him, and even more so as the tube began to flood. It was only when he was out in the water, swimming under his own power, that training and reflexes pushed the anxiety away. And even then, he'd keep a close, dispassionate eye on the sub, on his own equipment, and on the equipment he was supposed to be servicing or sabotaging. Always looking for the thing that could kill him.

On the screen, Etsub's face vanished, replaced with that of a frail-looking white woman in her early thirties, bleached blonde by the look of her. Standing on a sunny beach, holding a strand of thick, greenish-brown seaweed while the surf rolled in behind her. She squinted against the sunlight, and the tan outlines on her face suggested she'd rather be wearing sunglasses. Raimy didn't recognize her, but the captions on the screen said *Bridget Tobin: Candidate, Female Hydroponics. 3rd place.*

Raimy did recognize her name, as one of Etsub's fellow students up at St. Joseph of Cupertino Monastery. He paused the video and looked at the current rankings again. In the months since this video was taken, Bridget Tobin had moved up solidly into second place for the Female Hydroponics position. Not quite a ticket to Mars, but close. Raimy wasn't sure how she'd afforded a trip to the Moon or six weeks' lodging at the monastery, but the gambit certainly seemed to be helping.

Pressing play again, Raimy heard the unseen interviewer ask Bridget Tobin about *her* motivations, and he watched her reply, in an Irish accent, "I'm a very determined person. Mars is a grander yoke than any human being has ever taken hold of, and quite frankly there's nobody going to beat me to it. Nobody. It's quite simple: I'll do whatever it takes."

She nodded, also seemingly quite happy with her answer.

Raimy, however, was not happy. He skipped the video back ten seconds, and watched her again, several times.

"I'll do whatever it takes."

"Whatever it takes."

And that was the whole problem, right?

News about the death of Etsub Beyene had been kept quiet so far, but the story of the Clementine defector, Andrei Bykhovski, had gone viral, and then pandemic. He was the subject of serious scholarly analysis, and also of jokes and memes and toonlets that called him "History's first vacuum-back." Nice. And it bothered Raimy that this now-infamous defector, this Russian refugee, Andrei Bykhovski, was somehow there at the scene when Etsub died. Was *alone* at the scene, in fact. The only witness, with a story that made no sense. Of course it bothered him, but Raimy's gut told him that Bykhovski also made no sense as a suspect. Why would history's first vacuum-back kill anyone, much less the first person he saw, in the safe haven he'd just escaped to? No reason. No motive.

But for Bridget Tobin, and hundreds of others like her, the math was very simple: if Etsub Beyene was in her way, she would do whatever it took. Mars was the biggest prize in history, and the people competing for it were some of the most motivated, most capable in the whole human race.

Murders had been committed for much less. Hell, in Raimy's own experience, murders had been committed for pocket change and parking spaces, and simple human spite.

What little evidence Raimy had so far was consistent with this theory. "There was an air-line rupture in Etsub's suit, down inside the backpack," Tracy Greene had told him in a terse phone call that morning. Some Black women spoke to Black men with a certain familiarity, like they were all members of the same big family. There was none of that in Tracy's voice; she was all business, and spoke as though Raimy were the twenty-fifth item on a fifty-item to-do list.

"Bykhovski had no tools with him," Raimy mused,

although the way she rolled over him, it was clear she'd only paused for breath, and not to solicit questions.

"It looks like a braided hose failed catastrophically. An antenna wire was routed alongside it, and that failed, too, which shorted out the radio. The monks at Saint Joe's sent images to General Spacesuit for analysis, but our GS rep says an accident like that is very unlikely, given their quality-control process. Which implies sabotage. We don't know why or when, or by whom, but I suppose that's what you'll be finding out."

But Raimy, who was on his way to the Moon to interview everyone who'd interacted with Etsub in his last few days, figured he already knew why. And while it was poor practice to develop a theory too early in an investigation, it wasn't much of a stretch to think his main suspects were all the other contenders for the Male Hydroponics slot at Antilympus. There were only four such contenders still alive and in the running, one of whom was currently resident in Florida, where Etsub's spacesuit was assembled. One of whom was resident at Transit Point Station in low Earth orbit, which was one of the stops on Raimy's way to Luna. The third of whom was currently on Luna, at Saint Joe's. The fourth one lived in Japan, but was so far behind in the rankings that he'd have to commit *three more murders*, and get away with them, to have a hope of landing on Mars. Raimy felt fine about waiting, and scheduling that particular interview only if none of the rest of them panned out.

No, he had three suspects he liked much better—men with the means and motive and opportunity to sabotage the spacesuit of a rival.

Raimy thought about his own situation. Unless things went really wrong, there would be no need for cops or lawyers in a small, highly motivated community like Antilympus Township. The best he could say was that his experience in both of these jobs gave him a different perspective on the Admin job. Basically, that the two men ahead of him in the queue—the academic bureaucrat and the business mogul—were less grounded in the real world. In fact, he should try to make that point a little better in his online feed! Raimy also rode motorcycles (which was a rare thing in this age), had a pilot's license (just barely), gardened, practiced amateur meteorology, and spoke intermediate-level French. And although he was no Olympian, he was physically among the fittest of the Male Admin contestants, with a resting heart rate of forty-seven bpm even at the high altitude of Colorado Springs. And he'd been a goddamn diver in the goddamn Navy, for real.

And yet, it wasn't enough. None of that was enough to overcome the fame and fortune of his two main rivals, and at this point in his life there was very little he could do to improve or enrich himself any further. Going to the Moon had apparently helped Bridget Tobin, and there was of course a chance it would turn out to help Raimy as well. But probably not, because going to the Moon to *investigate a murder* simply highlighted what a grim, backward skill that really was, in the grand scheme of things. So yeah, if Raimy had the opportunity to sabotage the spacesuit of a rival—world famous billionaire Ian Doerr or world famous astronomer/author/Ivy League dean Tim Long Chang (now the CEO of National Geographic!)—he had to admit he'd be tempted.

And so, with the standard caution to himself about keeping his eyes and mind open, Raimy closed up the rollup, took it off its charging pad, and stuffed it into his flight bag. And with that final item in place, he was officially packed for his journey to outer space.

2.1
14 November
✦
Clementine Cislunar Fuel Depot
Earth-Moon Lagrange Point 1
Cislunar Space

"Earth media has been confirming it: Bykhovski arrived safely," Dona Obata said, cringing ever so slightly at the inevitable response. Dona was not a timid woman by any means—she had once killed a man with her bare hands—but the moods of Grigory Orlov, trillionaire, were volatile, and he was a dangerous man even when calm. Easily the most dangerous of the space industry's Four Horsemen, which made him the most dangerous man in all of cislunar space.

"Where?" Orlov demanded.

"Monastery. Where the lander was programmed to go." That by itself didn't mean much; even if Bykhovski had managed to reprogram the lander for a different destination, where else was there to go? North to the Chinese? Would that be an improvement over life at Clementine?

"Mmm," Orlov said. Not exploding yet, though the line of his jaw was hard and tight. He was in the "upper" observation deck, hanging by the porthole that looked up toward Luna, holding onto nothing. This spoke, silently, to how comfortable he'd become in this environment. There was no microgravity here at L1—there was no gravity at all—and the room was large enough that if he drifted too far from a handhold, he could be stranded in midair for quite some time. He was wearing the gray stretchy pants of a Clementine uniform, but without the top; instead he wore a gray-and-white polo shirt with the Orlov Petrochemical logo embroidered across the back.

When Bykhovski was first reported missing, Orlov's reaction had been a single word: "Regrettable." Because the obvious assumption was that a despondent Bykhovski had simply stepped out the airlock to breathe some vacuum. Dona had warned him, then: "This could be bad for morale." To which he'd said, "Fuck morale." Right there in Operations, where Commander Morozov and Subcommander Voronin and a couple of unimportant functionaries could hear him. To which Dona had replied, in her poor-but-improving Russian, "That a good business strategy, is it? He'll be expensive to replace. Even more expensive if people are moping around about it."

When it turned out Bykhovski's spacesuit was also missing, the conclusion wasn't much different, because what was he doing out there, all alone? Opening his visor, most likely. But radar sweeps turned up nothing, and then it was discovered that one of the Lunar landers had departed on schedule, minus its load of pressurized gas canisters, and Subcommander Voronin had said, "My God, he's on that thing. He's *defecting.*"

"Impossible," Orlov had said. Flatly. Unimpressed.

But Commander Andrei Morozov said, "Bykhovski is one of our best."

"Meaning?"

Nervously then, Morozov said, "It must be possible. He would not attempt such a thing without knowing it was possible."

After a deadly long pause, Orlov said, "Review all security footage." And then he had left the room.

That was five hours ago.

Now, seemingly exothermic with rage, he turned to Dona and said, "How did he do it?"

"It doesn't matter," she said, briefly touching a grab rail on the wall.

He snorted at that, as if amused by her boldness. Dona held no formal rank here on Clementine—just the uneasy position of "girlfriend." She had stolen an RzVz shuttle to get here—also a defector, also a refugee—and everyone here seemed to think she was some sort of spy. Which was exactly correct, though not in the way they probably thought.

"No?" Orlov asked her. "And what does matter?"

Back on Earth he had been, by all accounts, a wife beater. Two times over, actually. He was welcome to try it with Dona, but to his great credit he'd seemed to sense, right from the very beginning, that he couldn't have that kind of relationship with her. Even if he managed to overpower her (which he might or might not), she'd simply kill him in his sleep. And he seemed to get that about her, which she figured was why, ironically, they'd been working out rather well as a couple.

"He's talking," Dona said.

She gave Orlov's anger a few seconds to work its way around that information.

"Unfortunate," he said.

"Very."

She'd actually warned Orlov, more than once, that his cost-cutting measures would bring him grief in the end. She was no businesswoman, but she knew an unstable political situation when she saw one. You take a confined population, already unhappy with their lot, and then take just a little bit more from them, and boom. Revolts, revolutions, strikes, sabotage. She'd seen it in diamond mines and factories, farm collectives and slums and refugee camps all across Africa, where it mostly took on the cloak of tribalism, because that was easier somehow than the simpler truth. Tenants hated their landlords; workers hated their bosses; farmers and ranchers hated the exchanges through which they were forced to sell their output at whatever pittance the government chose to set. For almost ten years it had been Dona's job, more or less, to exploit these frictions as a way of extracting information, or applying useful leverage, for the benefit of a certain European power. But she also knew when she was losing—when she'd lost the trust or the patience of the people she was manipulating. She knew when to cut her losses and run.

Right now was one of those times. When news spread of what Andrei Bykhovski had done, the men and women of Clementine—all forty of them—laid down their tools, crossed their arms, and refused to work. Even knowing that the air they breathed came from asteroid rock. Even knowing that, if the recyclers continued to run, they had maybe a two-month supply before they all suffocated to death. And Dona could not escape.

"Legally, Clementine is a sovereign nation," she told him.

He glared, saying nothing.

Struggling through her limited Russian, liberally substituted with French and English words, she said, or tried to say, "We'll be accused of human rights violations. You're used to running your businesses as transnationals, straddling borders and playing governments off against each other. But here you are the government. There's no one to play or bribe. On Earth, if your workers don't like the deal you're offering them, you simply replace them with cheaper workers from a more desperate country. My love, you have learned the wrong lessons from this."

He looked at her for an uncomfortably long time before answering, "I own mining towns in Siberia, some of them nothing more than a single large building. The workers emerge in their protective gear, they do their work, and then they come back into the building. My building. They make good money, and their food and drink are provided. They have Internet. They grumble about the conditions, but when they go back home, to whatever shit town gave birth to them, they don't stay. They come back to me, again and again. You think this is different?"

"It's similar," she said carefully, touching the grab rail again to stabilize herself. Orlov remained motionless in the air, an angry Buddha. Here at L1 they were most of the way to the Moon; it loomed above the window like a rocky sky. Unlike other places in outer space, the gravity of Earth and Moon balanced perfectly here. There were no microforces pulling him this way or that. He could stay there a hundred years, or launch himself like a missile toward the hatchway, to take some sort of action against the striking workers. She didn't, in any sort of humanitarian sense, care what happened to the workers here, but this was her home now, and she cared about that. She needed this thing to work out, and so did he. So she said, "But what would happen if you didn't let those workers back to their shit towns? And what would happen if they were not peasants at all, but highly trained astronauts? How would that go?"

He didn't answer. As a "belt-tightening measure," he had canceled all shore leave and refused to let anyone out of their contracts early. Their five-year contracts! It made a kind of superficial financial sense, because sending a shuttle on a round trip to Earth and back cost two hundred million dollars, or some even more ungodly number of rubles, which was quite a bit more than these people made in a year. But it made them prisoners.

"It's almost dinner," she said. "Come with me to the mess hall. Eat with the people of Clementine, and see how they look at you."

"I know how they look at me."

In a hard tone, she said, "Well, then you know you're going to have to make some kind of statement. Some kind of concession. If you simply roll back your existing orders, you're going to look weak and encourage more misbehavior. But if you don't . . . I think some of these people are willing to die. Bykhovski certainly was."

Derisively: "Mmm. If labor relations are such a specialty of yours, do you have a recommendation?"

"It isn't," she said, "and I don't. But things have reached a breaking point. Your people are not powerless against you, and the more chance you give them to realize that, the more power you're going to have to concede. Time and speed are of the essence."

He said nothing. For a long time. Eventually he turned his gaze back upward, to the Moon.

"There's also an anomaly," she warned him. Still cautious. "Regarding Bykhovski's landing at the monastery."

"Mmm?"

"Someone was killed. I don't know the circumstances, but Harvest Moon is calling for an investigation."

"Mmm. Useful," he said.

She thought about that, and decided he was right. Anything to keep Bykhovski from looking like a hero. Let him be a blundering coward and fool instead.

"How did he do it?" Orlov asked again.

"Voronin is compiling a full report, with video."

"I see." After another long pause, the trillionaire said, "I will think of something fatherly to say, to get these bastards in line. I'll think of something they value more than I do, and I will say it was always my plan that they should have it, but I'm revealing it early to help assuage their grief, at the loss and disgrace of a beloved comrade. I'll do it in an offhand way, and truthfully, because this issue isn't even my biggest headache."

"No?" she said, surprised. What could be bigger?

He looked up at the Moon for a while, silent and very still, and Dona could see his anger was not cooling. Her sense of such things was finely honed, through years of gathering up-close intelligence on dangerous men and, when necessary, goading them to action. The people of Clementine had made a powerful enemy, and it would take a lot of peace and quiet and hard work to reverse that.

Eventually, he reached into his leg pocket and pulled out a rollup tablet. He opened and locked it, poked briefly at its screen, and handed it to her. This imparted a slight momentum to his body so that, finally, he had to feather-touch one of the grab rails beside the window to hold his position.

"Press 'play,'" he told her darkly.

She did, and a video started up. For several seconds, she didn't know what she was looking at. Gymnastics? An obstacle course? The picture was grainy and dark, and showed a long-limbed figure in fast, whirling motion, vaulting hand-and-foot over stacked rectangular obstacles. With some surprise, she realized the figure didn't have a head. Its arms and legs were identical, and capable of bending unnaturally, and made of shiny gray plastic.

"It's called 'parkourbot,'" Orlov said.

"What am I looking at?" Dona asked, unsure why he was showing this to her.

"Classified footage."

"Of what?"

"An assassin."

She watched the robot flip and tumble, uncanny in its grace and speed. It was outdoors, at night, on some sort of purpose-built course. A casual glance made it look human, but its top and bottom halves were interchangeable. There was no up or down for this robot, and its hands were . . . complex. She could hear human voices in the background, gasping and muttering in amazement as the thing moved around, fluid and deadly.

"Whose?" she asked.

"American. But others have their own versions, including defensive versions that hunt and kill other parkourbots."

"Hmm. Hmm. Why does this worry you?"

"I have heard, through trusted sources, that these robots are being adapted to operate in zero gravity."

She thought about that, but whatever connection he was drawing, she couldn't yet see it. "And?"

Without looking at her, he said, "Renz Ventures is compromised. ESL1 Shade Station is under American control. Your friend Alice Kyeong has seen to that."

"She's not my friend," Dona said.

Ignoring her, Orlov said, "Something happened up there at ESL1. There are strange rumors—conflicting rumors—which I take to be someone's attempt to conceal the truth. They cannot prevent it from leaking, so they hide it in a jumble of stories so bizarre even the tabloids aren't touching them. But is this jumble the work of Renz, or the Americans? The American President, Tina Tompkins, has said nothing publicly about Renz Ventures. She sent her agents in, and took the place over. Now Renz is speaking with the UN about using the ESL1 Shade for weather modification, and Tompkins says nothing. Is she working Renz like a puppet? Harvesting his riches for the

United States of America? Activity patterns at ESL1 have markedly shifted. The machines that build the Shade have stopped operating. Why?

"Please know, that kind of infiltration will not work here. Even if you, yourself, were still secretly in the pocket of an Earthly government, you could not take control of our systems. And we'd put you out the airlock for attempting it."

"You could try," Dona said.

"Don't posture at me, woman. We've done this dance too many times. We would kill you, and you know it."

"What's your point?"

He drew in his breath and let it out—not a sigh, but a yoga-style cleansing breath. "Many countries depend on Orlov Petrochemical, and some on Clementine as well. We control the world's supply of tralphium. All the lights and computers and air conditioners of the world."

"Not all," she said.

"Enough," he said. "We control enough. Not in America or China, perhaps, but they do not like the rest of the world depending on us. Like Renz Ventures, we are a direct threat to the world order they have built, and thus our size and our power puts us in their rifle sights. I am not so reckless as Igbal Renz, and in this sense they fear me less. But this simply places me second on their hit list, and unlike Lawrence Killian or Dan Beseman, I am not beloved. The Earth will not weep if something bad were to happen here. And I have enemies capable of making bad things happen."

"And?" she said, still not sure exactly what he was trying to convey here.

"Because infiltration will not work, I have been expecting someone to send a platoon of space marines to capture this place by force. But they may already know, we are well prepared for that contingency. Marines have their vulnerabilities, which we are able to target precisely. Visors and hoses are easily recognized, yes?"

Dona was well aware of the countermeasure programs, as she was effectively in charge of several of them. But she began to see what Orlov was worried about. "Robots don't need air," she said.

"Exactly. You paint one black and throw it at us. You throw a hundred of them at us, and what can we do? It might as well be a nuke."

It was better than a nuke, she realized. A nuclear explosion—even a small one—would be seen by half the Earth. Everyone would want to know who, and why, and these would be hard secrets to keep. Whereas if classified robots simply killed everyone onboard the station—or killed Orlov and shut off electrical power and started issuing commands to the survivors—the responsible parties could make up any story they liked. And Dona had to agree: that was a bigger problem.

"What do we do about it?" she asked.

"We buy some of these robots ourselves," he said.

"From whom?"

"I don't know yet. Nor for how much. But it will not be cheap, my love. Assuaging the whining of forty asteroid miners will be a rounding error in comparison."

"Then why do you balk? Why are you hiding yourself up here? Take your medicine, Orlov. Speak to your people. Some of them are hard people, yes. Together they could certainly kill me if you ordered it. They could also kill you if they wished to, but they want their jobs here, their lives here. They came here for the same reason I did: because you have built a place that is not for weaklings or half measures or idiots. This may be your place, but it is also theirs. You must acknowledge this. There is no time to waste."

"No time?" he asked, licking his lips. Eyeing her body. Still an angry Buddha, but now also swollen with a bullying sort of lechery. She shouldn't love that, but she did.

"No," she said, with a twinge of regret. But truly, he was out of time, and more than out. Which meant that she was out of time, too.

"Very well," he said, setting aside both lust and anger. "Let us go, a bully emperor and his bitch spy, to speak with these peasants who so concern you. You're correct: they are my people, and they need to be reminded of it."

1.4
17 November

✦

Transit Point Station
Low Earth Orbit

"I didn't kill anyone," a pale-looking man said to Raimy as he floated through the hatch into Transit Point Station. Seriously, the very moment he floated through.

"Later," Raimy said, and reached clumsily for a grab bar. Closing his eyes for a moment, he just tried to work on his breathing. He was wearing a vomit-stained spacesuit with the helmet off, and his face was a sweaty sheen of quivering weightless droplets.

"I know I'm on your list of suspects," the man said, in a sort of generically European accent. Swiss, Raimy thought.

Despite himself, Raimy glanced up.

"You're Geary Notbohm?"

"I am, yes. First officer of this station, and very definitely not a killer."

Raimy tried to care about that, but his stomach and inner ear were having none of it. He was *falling*, damn it.

The room seemed to tumble around him. There was a porthole window in this docking module, through which he could see the little capsule that brought him here, with the blue-white Earth scrolling slowly behind it. Far enough away that it didn't look like "the ground," but like "a planet." The very idea made Raimy's feet tingle with something close to panic.

"I'd leave this one alone for a while," said the Harvest Moon pilot who'd brought Raimy here, whose name was Ling something or other. D. Ling, according to the nametag on the outside of his suit. He came through the hatch behind Raimy, also wearing a helmetless spacesuit. Also covered in vomit—not his own.

"Good lord," said Geary Notbohm, looking the two of them over. "Difficult flight?"

"Uneventful until about twenty minutes ago. Fucker's got two SAS patches on his neck and can't stop puking." To Raimy he said, "Nothing personal, buddy. You never know who's going to get it bad."

Raimy nodded, then immediately regretted it. SAS stood for "space adaptation syndrome," aka motion sickness, and the patches were medicated Band-Aid discs stuck to the skin below his ears. He wasn't sure what was in them, but he could feel it blunting his mind and senses, while doing nothing at all for the nausea or vertigo.

"I had a hard time, too, my first trip up," Geary said, in a kind but weary voice. "Don't go anywhere, please. Don't leave this chamber. I'll go get you a package of barf bags."

And with that, he kicked off from a grab bar and vanished through the docking module's hatch, into the station's main corridor.

"Get some disinfecting wipes, too!" Ling called after him. Then, to nobody in particular, "Jesus Christ. I wasn't even scheduled to fly today."

"Sorry," Raimy told him, for about the twentieth time.

"Not your fault," Ling said, "I'm sorry I called you a fucker." He moved to look out the porthole, blocking Raimy's view of Earth in the process. Was that better or worse? Raimy couldn't decide.

With the blue glow of the planet on his face, Ling continued, "I've seen worse than you, though not very often. If you'd been through a proper zero-gee training course, you'd've known you were vulnerable, and you'd've put a couple of patches on yourself, before we buttoned up your suit. This mission is a rush job. This death on the Moon has a lot of people out of their grooves."

"Yep," Raimy agreed. The story had leaked through every barrier set out for it, and while the news services were reporting it so far only as a rumor, the rumor itself was burning brightly. The fact that Geary Notbohm knew why Raimy was here was not surprising in the least. And although it was way too early to be formulating any theories, Raimy's gut was already telling him that Notbohm had nothing to do with Etsub's death. Not because he'd protested his innocence (who didn't?), but because he'd left Raimy alone on his space station, without one of his own crew members to provide guidance and supervision. People with something to hide didn't generally behave that way. It was thin reasoning—really just an explanation fitted to what his gut was telling him—but nevertheless that was where he was leaning at this too-early moment.

The module was silent for a few seconds, filled only

with the sound of breathing and the hum of fans and equipment. Then Ling said, "You're wasting air. You should turn your suit pack off."

When Raimy only looked at him helplessly, he said, "The dial on your chest. Here."

He reached out and manipulated something on Raimy's suit, and a hissing sound vanished that Raimy hadn't even realized he was hearing.

"Thanks," Raimy said, closing his eyes again in an effort to find some kind of equilibrium.

His suit was different from Ling's. Ling's was yellow and lightweight, a "launch rescue suit" or "flight suit" meant only to protect him in the event of a capsule depressurization, but Raimy hadn't been issued one of those. His was highway-cone orange, and vastly bulkier, because it was meant for extended EVA excursions on the Lunar surface. Same type of suit Etsub had been wearing when he died, and the Harvest Moon technicians had had to install a special seat in the capsule to accommodate it. This was not unusual in itself—HMI launch capsules apparently had six different seat types and dozens of possible interior configurations, all swappable with a few days' notice—but the six other passenger seats were all empty, and that *was* unusual. Other than the pilot, Raimy had had the flight to himself, which was a rather ridiculous waste of resources. Enterprise City, the Antilympus Project, Harvest Moon, and the Catholic Church were all sharing expenses to make that happen, as they all seemed to agree they wanted this matter solved quickly. Presumably so they could move it into the past and forget about it.

❖❖❖

"The Moon is hot, cold, irradiated, and a constant target for micrometeoroids," the chief technology officer of General Spacesuit had said to Raimy, two days ago in Cocoa Beach, Florida. "You have to carry not only the air and water and power you need, but also communications, thermal management, abrasion and impact resistance, and a goo layer to seal any leaks that do happen."

"That didn't help Etsub Beyene," Raimy had observed.

For security reasons, Raimy had no camera drones with him that day, which was a weird feeling. He could speak freely, without worrying how it looked! On the other hand, he wasn't getting much audience cred for what he was doing. He'd spoken into an ordinary glasses cam on his way in, announcing where he was and what he was about to do, and then he'd switched the glasses off and slipped them into his shirt pocket. End of transmission.

"No, it didn't help Beyene," the CTO had said. Raimy couldn't remember his name. John Jones? Sam Smith? Something like that; he had it in his notes. The two of them were looking into the open backpack of the suit Raimy was about to be fitted into. CTO made a big deal out of this—that he was personally overseeing the technicians today, that Raimy would want for nothing while he was here. CTO pointed to a bundle of wires and hoses in the top-left corner of the backpack. "His suit failed right here—one of the very few places in the Heavy Rebreather model with no redundancy, no self-sealing, and no autonomous damage-control features. It would be very difficult to engineer redundant features into this particular location, although we will certainly reassess in light of this incident. But it's awfully suspicious, yeah?

These components are tested to eleven times the actual operating pressure, and no failure like this has ever been recorded, in over two thousand hours of cumulative EVA."

Sardonically, Raimy had asked, "So it's the position of General Spacesuit that Beyene was murdered?"

To which CTO had smoothly replied, "We haven't studied the damaged components firsthand yet, but it's our strong belief that this was a human-mediated failure, rather than a manufacturing or assembly defect. As I said, our quality control processes make that essentially impossible."

"Essentially impossible," Raimy mused, with a cop's skepticism and a lawyer's ear for evidentiary statements.

CTO declined to retract the comment, saying simply, "Everyone who goes to the Moon is processed through this facility, which is under exclusive contract with Harvest Moon Industries. Every suit bound for the Moon passes through eighteen different quality checks and four different fit checks. A defect like that, we would have caught it. One hundred percent."

CTO seemed to genuinely believe what he was saying, so Raimy sighed and answered, "All right, when we're done with my fitting, I want to talk to everyone who ever interacted with Beyene's suit. I mean everyone."

CTO nodded. "Some of the people fitting you are . . . it's some of the same people. Good people, algorithmically vetted and with centuries of collective experience. Please be kind to them, Detective. Every one of them has held dozens of lives in their hands, and this death might as well be one of our own. We don't have anything to hide."

That had been a long day, whose only really memorable

highlight (aside from being closed up in his own personal moon suit) was speaking with a man named Luke Hopken. Hopken was a longtime GS employee with no criminal record, but in his spare time he was also the number four contender for the Male Hydroponics slot at Antilympus. Now number three.

"It's terrible, what happened to Etsub," he'd said, when introduced to Raimy. He was wearing a floral-print polo shirt and a pair of khaki trousers, and looked overdue for a haircut.

Raimy stuck out a spacesuit-gloved hand, which Hopken shook.

"How terrible?" Raimy asked. "How well did you know him?"

"I only met him very briefly when he was here, but of course I watched all of his videos. Studied them, really. He was so far out in front of me. It's like he was perfect. I rarely saw him make a mistake, no matter how much I wanted him to."

"Hmm." Raimy knew the feeling.

It was an awkward moment; Raimy had backed his suit up until the back of it latched onto a gowning rack bolted to the wall. This was a high-bay industrial area, with light streaming in from rows of windows near the ceiling, and the noise of machines all around. Technicians had swiveled his waist connector ring, separating the top and bottom halves of the massive suit, and Raimy was sagging under the weight on his legs. With considerable effort, he wriggled his hands and arms and torso out of the suit's top half, and stood there with his armored pants falling down around his hips, and nothing but loose-weave, 3D-printed "space underwear" between his private parts and the cool air of the factory.

Ignoring the indignity, he asked, "What exactly do you do around here? Hydroponics?"

"In a way," Hopken answered. "I design the fluid management systems that distribute heat from the sunny side to the shady side of your suit. I can see you're struggling under the weight of it, there. It's heavy because it's got a whole circulatory system of water-filled tubes between the inner and outer surfaces."

"Okay," Raimy said, fishing a paper notebook and a ball-point pen out of the back pocket of his actual pants, sitting on a little table beside the gowning rack. "I'm confused. What does that have to do with hydroponics?"

"Common components," Hopken said. "Renz Ventures and Harvest Moon have their own proprietary systems for growing plants—in zero gee for Renz and one-sixth gee for HMI—but we make about ninety percent of the fluid management components they both use, and most of those are the same ones in our suits. That means they can be repaired out of a common pool of spare parts, which is very important for any remote installation."

"Hmm. And you're part of the quality control process for outgoing suits?"

"Only indirectly. I know, my name is on your list there, but what I do is, I sign off on four of the QC processes. I don't perform the tests, but I review and initial the results before a suit can leave the premises."

Raimy made some marks in his notebook.

"So you don't actually touch the suits on their way through here?"

"Not usually, no. And in this case, definitely not."

"But you could? You have access?"

Hopken nodded vigorously at that. "Oh, yeah. Yeah, I'm part of the engineering team. I can drop into the line at any point during manufacture or inspection." Then he stopped, and seemed to think about the implications of what he was saying. But then pressed forward anyway, with, "There's a lot of video surveillance, but it doesn't cover every centimeter of the facility. I mean, I've got my own camera drones, but like you I'm not allowed to bring them on campus here. Nobody's allowed to bring recording devices of any kind. If a person wanted to tamper with a suit, there are places in the line where they could do it and not be seen."

This was very different from the smooth confidence of the CTO, and not a thing most people under suspicion would blab about.

Raimy asked him, "You do realize you're a suspect, right?"

Hopken shrugged. "That's inevitable. That's up to you. I mean, obviously, I've moved up in the Mars rankings, but that's not something I'm happy about. I've been with GS for fifteen years, and that suit you're wearing is kind of my life's work. Hydroponic gardening is one of my hobbies, and I'm good at it, but spacesuits are what I do. I wouldn't . . ."

He paused, and Raimy waited until he continued.

"I wouldn't kill a human being at all, I mean, for anything. And even if I somehow did, I wouldn't do it *that way*. Nobody here would. What we do is . . . You . . . I'm sorry, I don't know your name, but please understand:

what we do here is sacred. Even if we never travel in space ourselves, everything that's going on right now, all that stuff up there"—he gestured upward, toward the metal-trussed ceiling, and the sky beyond it—"starts in places like this, with people like us. Somebody *desecrated* one of our products, but I don't possibly see how it could be one of us."

Hopken sighed, then seemed to busy himself for a moment, looking at the connector valves in the waist ring of Raimy's suit. It was uncomfortably intimate, and uninvited, so Raimy cleared his throat. Hopken looked up, unembarrassed, and said, "The day he was here, Etsub had two reporters with him, and three traveling companions also being fitted. Are you talking to them?"

"Not the reporters," Raimy admitted. "Can you ask someone to provide me with their contact information?"

"Sure."

And although Raimy already knew the answer, he asked, "The reporters were here because camera drones aren't allowed? Your own included?"

"That's right. I think it hurts me in the rankings, too, because my livestream feed is dark most of the time, and my most relevant work is invisible. But yes, these two were from a local press organization; I've seen them in here before. Maybe hired by the Antilympus Project, but not really part of it. They were all over the place, all day long. All six of them were."

"Would these reporters have a motive to kill anyone?" Raimy asked, although it was not really a fair question. In a courtroom, it would be objected to as both hearsay and leading the witness, but Hopken seemed to have a lot to say, and if he was guilty then Raimy wanted to give him enough rope to hang himself. If he was innocent, then his perspective would be useful.

"For what, to boost their viewership? I doubt it."

"You don't know anything about the organization that sent them?"

"No, but I mean, that doesn't really make sense. What would they have to gain?"

"Not like you," Raimy needled.

"No, not like me. I already said, I moved up in the rankings. It doesn't mean I sabotaged a spacesuit, right? That's not enough of an incentive. I wouldn't trade my soul for it."

"Are you religious?"

"Not particularly, but I believe there's something. Souls and whatnot, probably. But even if there weren't, I wouldn't go around killing people. I just wouldn't."

"All right." Raimy made some more marks in his notebook, not really writing anything of consequence. His real notes were all in his head, slowly assembling themselves like puzzle pieces. His memory for this kind of thing was close to photographic, but he found an old-fashioned paper notebook was a useful prop for signaling his attention to the people he was speaking with.

Hopken went on, "The female hydroponicists, Bridget Tobin and Katla Koskinen . . . I talked to both of them pretty extensively when they were here."

"But not to Etsub?"

"Not really, no."

"What about Anming Shui, Etsub's backup? He was here, right?"

"He was. I didn't talk to him."

"Just the women?"

Now Hopken looked slightly embarrassed. "I mean, there was a chance I'd be working alongside one of them. If Etsub and Anming dropped out, and I got my flight status, one of those gals might have been side by side with me, every day for the rest of my life."

"And you wanted to know . . ."

"What they were like, yes. Whether they were pretty, or nice, or I just couldn't stand them, or whatever." He paused, then said, "Is that a crime?"

"No," Raimy said. "Of course not."

That was the first thing Hopken had said that sounded even the slightest bit shifty, but Raimy could understand it well enough. The Antilympus candidates were, all of them, hoping to leave behind all of their Earthly attachments and start fresh, with a pool of just ninety-nine other human beings to choose as friends and lovers, rivals and enemies. Until the second batch of colonists arrived, four years later, those would be literally the only people in the whole world. Given that, Hopken's curiosity was natural enough. He didn't strike Raimy as much of a womanizer, and perhaps that made the stakes even higher.

"All right," Raimy said, "so you talked to them. What were your impressions?"

"Both very serious," Hopken answered. "Very driven. I mean, they were different people, but they both had that . . ."

"Drive?" Raimy suggested.

"Yes. Very driven. But nice enough, both of them. That's how you move up in the rankings, right? If everybody likes you. And honestly, it's not like they would stand to benefit from Estub's death."

Raimy wasn't one hundred percent sure that was true. Obviously, emptying a Male Hydroponicist slot wouldn't magically open up a Female Hydroponicist one. However, Bridget Tobin was apparently a signatory on the recent "gender neutralling" petition, requesting that the roles at Antilympus be divided differently among the sexes, and that nongendered and transgendered persons be allowed to join the competition, so long as they could prove fertility. That didn't make her special; nearly a hundred candidates (mostly in trailing positions) had signed the thing, but if the Besemans actually listened and acted on it, it could mean (for example) that both hydroponics jobs could go to women, as long as a different job slot were assigned to a person capable of generating spermatozoa.

Raimy wasn't sure the Besemans were going to budge about this, and if Bridget Tobin were smart, she wouldn't be, either. The Besemans' old-fashioned and (if you thought about it) rather privacy-invading plan was to bring fifty natural-born heterosexual males and fifty natural-born heterosexual women to Mars and let them work it out, breeding-wise, to create the first generation of true Martians. They seemed really wedded to the idea, and puzzled by the protests and injunctions people had raised against it. Enterprise City and the Antilympus Project were both headquartered in Suriname, where nobody gave a shit, and Dan Beseman himself had been residing in space for well over a year now. So what did protests or foreign-soil injunctions, or even a petition from the candidates themselves, mean to him? He might well be beyond Earthly coercion. Maybe he'd have a change of heart, or Carol would, or maybe somebody would get to them somehow. Or not. Bridget Tobin should in no way be certain enough about it to commit a murder.

But smart people did stupid things sometimes, and Raimy had seen murders committed on thinner hopes than that. People were endlessly disappointing. Bridget Tobin had been in second place for the Female Hydroponics slot as of last week, so in that sense, she did potentially stand to profit from Etsub's death.

"What if they could?" Raimy asked.

"If they could . . . benefit?"

"Yes."

Hopken looked uncomfortable. "I . . . I don't know. I didn't get a, like, a murder vibe from them. Would I? I mean, would murders get committed at all, if people gave off a murder vibe?"

"Probably not," Raimy admitted, although he had certainly gotten some strong murder vibes from suspects after the fact.

Luke Hopken himself was not one of these, at least at this moment. Yes, he had motive. Yes, he had opportunity. Yes, he probably knew the vulnerabilities of a Heavy Rebreather suit as well as any other living person. But he seemed exactly nervous enough and forthcoming enough for a murder suspect who wasn't guilty and wanted to clear his name. Wanted to clear his employer's name, too. Nothing he'd said was inconsistent, or vague, or overly specific. Lots of guilty people would try to flood you with a seamless litany of times and locations, accounting for every minute of their day in a way ordinary people never would. Or they just said yeah, I wasn't there, don't know what you're talking about. If Hopken were guilty, then he was a smooth sociopath indeed, and still one giant leap away from achieving his goal. Right now, Raimy couldn't see it.

And that left Anming Shui, presently resident at St. Joseph of Cupertino Monastery, as Raimy's far-and-away favorite suspect. With Etsub's death, Anming had moved into first place in the Antilympus rankings, and would be going to Mars. *That* was worth killing for, though only if the bastard actually thought he could get away with it. Raimy's mind kept tripping on that point; could *anyone* possibly expect to get away with such a transparent crime? He'd never met Anming, but from the stats he knew the man was unlikely to be that stupid. So yeah, nothing really made sense yet.

"Are you going to solve this?" Hopken asked, with the kind of quiet outrage usually reserved for a victim's family and friends.

"I am," Raimy said. "Yes."

No criminal was perfect. No crime was perfect. If murder had indeed been committed, then the killer had made mistakes and generated evidence that Raimy was very definitely going to find.

Investigating murders was partly a game of cat and mouse, partly a moral crusade of good versus evil, and partly a matter of assembling puzzle pieces until the picture was actually complete. Part of the reason Raimy had signed up for the police academy, throwing away three years of law school and five years as a prosecuting attorney, was because he'd seen too many goddamn botched investigations. Botched by patrolmen, botched by detectives, botched by evidence technicians who'd been dragged out of bed in the middle of the night and wanted nothing more than to crawl back under those covers again. It bothered him, and finally he just couldn't stand it anymore. Finally, he just had to step in and do the damn thing himself. The work suited him better anyway; and, like being in the military, it was not so much a job as an all-consuming way of life. Once a case was assigned to Raimy, that was his life, and God help the guilty.

Hopken added, "Even if one of them did something to the plumbing in that backpack—even if *I* did—the QC overpressure checks would have caught it after the pack was sealed. I don't know. I think whatever happened, happened after the suit left our custody."

The next day, Raimy caught a private jet from Merritt Island, Florida, to Paramaribo, Suriname—a five-hour flight. Not one of Harvest Moon's own jets, but a last-minute charter, complete with *two* personal flight attendants, and no other passengers. His camera drones hovered nervously around him, capturing nothing of importance. After landing, he packed them in their little cases and worked his way through some sort of abbreviated, rich-people customs and immigration where they barely glanced at his passport and seemed to ignore his luggage entirely. For all they knew, it could be full of Cartel bombs and genetically engineered cocaine, but they just waved him right on through. Outside the secure area, he released his drones again. They weren't remarkable; the airport was teeming with them, mostly flying a polite half meter above the crowd's tallest heads. As he made his way to the passenger pickup area, he was met by a young, male limousine escort holding up an e-paper sign that said DET. RAIMY VAUGHT in some fancy-ass copperplate font. The man recognized him on sight, which wasn't difficult, because Raimy was the only bald, Black man dressed in a tan, two-piece Antilympus uniform. With barely a word, the attendant whisked him into a black, double-parked robocar.

From there, things got slower; the city of Paramaribo had roads wholly inadequate to the car and bicycle and truck traffic they carried. Also a *lot* of motorcycle traffic, which was a welcome novelty for Raimy. He used to ride an old Honda CB650 in his twenties, but then manually piloted, non gyro-stabilized bikes had been banned on U.S. roads. He did a bit of track racing after that, just for fun, but it was *expensive*, and getting the bike to and from the track required a trailer and a long drive, so eventually he'd sold off the Honda at a steep loss. The end of that particular era was now five years ago. But Paramaribo was like something out of an old motorcycle magazine's cartoon section; the riders here were flat-out crazy, weaving their way through much slower traffic, often without protective gear of any kind. Raimy figured they must have a high mortality rate; they were dodging swarms of cranky, horn-honking, non-robotic human drivers. But they all seemed to be in an awful hurry, and willing to endure the risk. It amazed Raimy that an up-and-coming industrial nation like Suriname would put up with such chaos, but he supposed America had, too, in its years of stupid-fast growth.

His own limo seemed to have some sort of override capability that could force other cars to brake or swerve when it cut them off. This was frightening at first, like some kind of jump-scare carnival ride, but once Raimy figured out what was going on, he became sort of annoyed about it. Who did this robot think it was? Who did it think *he* was, that its mindless algorithms were willing to inconvenience dozens of other vehicles on his behalf? And how long had this kind of thing been going on? Did Harvest Moon pay off the car manufacturers to include this feature? Had they bought off the whole country of Suriname? Or even the whole world? They certainly had the money, and Raimy had never even heard of such a feature, which told him it was not even remotely available to plebes like himself.

So this is first class, he thought. It was certainly a lot easier than fighting your way through lines and traffic and then cramming into some airline's middle seat. But yeah, during the flight he'd looked up how much it was probably costing HMI to charter a jet for one person, and the answer made him shudder. A five-hour flight, one way, was enough to *buy* a decent robocar, and he couldn't help thinking: if he had so much money that ninety thousand dollars could slip through his fingers unnoticed, wouldn't he, you know, use it to help the poor or something? Of course, that was easy for him to say; his time wasn't particularly valuable. He wasn't needed in multiple places, and he often wasn't needed anywhere at all. And the poor were a bottomless pit that even a trillionaire probably couldn't do much about. If Sir Lawrence Edgar Killian, the CEO and largest shareholder of Harvest Moon

Industries, decided to give away all his money, that would be, what, a hundred and twenty dollars for each person on Earth? Hell, these days that could barely buy you a beat-up old skateboard.

There were, of course, other things money could do for the poor, and truthfully, Killian was already doing a lot of that. Vaccination programs, literacy programs, broadband programs... But as he'd publicly said, probably hundreds of times, his charity bent more toward the long-term future of humanity. To ensuring its long-term survival and, more importantly, "a kind of prosperity we can scarcely dream of right now. The resources of space dwarf those of the Earth, and we don't have to damage our biosphere to extract them." Or words to that effect. Raimy did know that "tralphium" or "heavy helium," pulled from Harvest Moon's polar ice mines, was already providing cleaner energy than the traditional fusile materials found on Earth. Certainly, it was Killian's right to spend his money however he wanted, but it could also be argued that everyone was already directly benefitting from his space operations.

As a person who hoped to live the second half of his life on Mars, and who was raising millions of dollars from donors who probably could be helping the poor with that money, Raimy was hardly in a position to criticize. Still, he felt guilty, because this kind of luxury—uncomfortable though it made him—was something he feared he might miss. Once you'd had a taste of the good stuff, did you start to realize how shitty most people's lives really were, and that you were "most people," and that you were never going to afford an airline seat that didn't make your legs go numb?

The limo attendant rode in what was still politely known as the "driver's seat," but he didn't do much there other than fiddle with the climate controls. He kept it cold, and rather than ask him to turn the temperature up, Raimy (riding in back) rolled down his window and inhaled the rich—if muggy—air of Paramaribo. A lot of this traffic was fossil-fueled, so the scents of the nearby jungles and marshland were overlaid by the old-fashioned reek of gasoline and diesel smog. His drones didn't like the breeze of the open window, though; they eyed him accusingly and settled on various surfaces inside the car.

After twenty minutes or so, the robocar came to a spindly bridge over a wide, blue-brown waterway, and as the pavement carried them up high, Raimy thought, *If this car goes off the bridge I'm going to close the window. Before we hit the water, I'm going to jerk my seatbelt until it locks, and then I'm going to hold my breath. If we hit nose-first, it could break the windshield and flood the car. I'm going to wait until the car is fully submerged, and then I'm going to roll my window back down. The window motor runs on DC current; it should still work underwater. I'm going to keep my seat belt on until the car is fully flooded, and then I'm going to release the latch and swim out. Quickly, before the car has a chance to sink too deep. Then I'm going to swim to the surface, and breathe. Then I'm going to swim to shore.*

It only took him a second or so to go through the whole routine in his head. These were diver's instincts: always know your exit plan. Always. It had saved his life a few times, and in fact this was exactly why he'd quit diving and gone to law school: because if being a Navy diver was that unsafe, then by his extension his best exit plan was to resign from the Navy altogether. The fact that Mars would also be dangerous was something he thought about a lot. But hey, the reward-to-risk ratio was a lot higher there, because he would be one of the first hundred colonists on a brand-new world. Jebediah Springfield or whatever. His children, if he had any, would also be pioneers. And their children after them, et cetera. If he had to pick a single word to describe the feeling, it would be something like *destiny*. Like everything in his life had been a preparation for his shot at this much profounder thing.

Still, the more immediate, less hypothetical dangers he'd be facing on the Moon were a novelty he'd been thinking about this whole trip. He'd never been one to shrink from danger, but he'd also never seriously thought about the Moon as a place he personally wanted to go. Since it didn't have all the ingredients for life, it would always be dependent on someplace else. Also, it didn't have weather or wind or even a sky at all, and these were part of the definition of "world" as far as Raimy was concerned, so what would be the point of going there? But he wasn't going there to live. He wasn't even going to visit. His investigation was tentatively scheduled to last five days, from landing to takeoff.

Whenever he thought about this, which was most of the time, he felt a sort of nervous tension coursing through him. Not fear, exactly, but the heightened alertness that preceded a dive. *Serious business, Raimy. Pay attention. Space is more dangerous than the ocean. More dangerous than anything you've ever done.*

All this reflection happened quickly, while he watched

the water zooming by underneath the bridge. But then the car was angling downward, and then flattening out again, and the bridge was behind them, and Raimy was away from the city and onto the spaceport island itself.

By agreement with the attendant, the limo took Raimy to the Marriott Cielopuerto, the hotel where Etsub had stayed before lifting off. Once there, although tired, he asked to interview any staff who'd come in contact with Etsub or his belongings. Although Raimy had zero jurisdiction in this foreign land, and spoke zero Dutch and minimal Spanish, he was met with total cooperation, as this hotel had some kind of special partnership with Harvest Moon, and they knew he was coming. It was just a pro forma visit, though, because Etsub didn't have the spacesuit with him when he was here, and nobody here had a plausible motive for hurting him anyway. Raimy really just wanted to retrace Etsub's steps, and get a detailed sense of what had transpired in his last few days of life.

Of course, that meant the interviews didn't tell him much. After an hour and a half, he gave up on them and checked himself into his room, then went ahead and got some dinner at the restaurant. Fortunately, Paramaribo, though on the opposite side of the equator from Florida, was actually just two time zones east, so he didn't have to deal with any serious jet lag—just the sort of honest tired that came from spending the morning traveling and the afternoon in police interviews.

After dinner he showered, flipped through a little bit of news, and then spent an hour indulging his secret vice for cartoons. Not Japanese anime but actual cartoon

cartoons. He liked some older stuff from his childhood—
The Simpsons, *Rick and Morty*, stuff like that—but what
he was really into these days was *Chimps and Birds*, which
by any reasonable standard was a children's show. But it
was funny! In some ways it was the funniest thing he'd
ever seen, and so he watched avidly and laughed freely.
He lived in fear that someone at the precinct would
eventually catch him at it, and he'd never hear the end of
it. Or worse, that his Antilympus sponsors would sniff it
out somehow, and never take him seriously again. These
risks didn't keep him away, though. Perhaps he was
addicted.

Unfortunately, the only thing on the show's feed that
he hadn't already seen at least twice was a single twenty-
minute episode. That didn't exactly burn up the evening
for him, so when it was done he sighed and indulged his
other, lesser vice for behind-the-scenes media gossip.
Tonight, he focused for some reason on the Video Reality
Games genre, even though he'd never played a VRG, and
wouldn't admit it to anyone even if he had. Which VRG
voice actors were pansexual? What did the VRG
champions eat? It was pointless drivel, even by the
standards of celebrity gossip, but it allowed him to nearly
forget that tomorrow afternoon he was going to blast off
in an honest-to-God rocket ship.

He went to bed early and slept surprisingly well, but
awoke in a cold sweat at 4:15 A.M., with his heart beating
tap-tap-tap against the wall of his chest, and that was that.
Not fear, exactly, but that heightened state of alertness,
back with a vengeance and quite incompatible with sleep.
Within moments of waking, he could see his whole day

laid out before him: he would shower again, though he didn't really need to. He would make a cup of coffee with the room's little machine. He would get a light breakfast (and more coffee) just as soon as the hotel's restaurant opened, and then he would summon his limousine and head out to the artificial island's long, finger-shaped Eastern Made Peninsula where all the Harvest Moon launch complexes were located. There, he would interview all the people who'd processed Etsub through launch operations, *while they were processing Raimy himself through launch operations*. He'd be buttoned up in his spacesuit again—for real this time—and then he'd be taken up in an elevator and walked into a surface-to-low-Earth-orbit capsule (a "SLEO," as Harvest Moon called them), and strapped into an upward-facing acceleration chair . . .

And so, yeah. In just a few hours, he was doing this, for real.

3.1
17 November

✧

Shackleton Lunar Industrial Station
Lunar South Polar Mineral Territories
Lunar Surface

"Charge torpedo one," said Commander Harb, with all due drama.

Commander Fernanda Harb, a British woman just beginning to form streaks of natural gray in her hair. Not a bad lady to work for, Tania Falstaff thought, but really rather young to be in charge of a moonbase, thank you very much. And Harvest Moon Jumpsuit Yellow was not her color.

"Aye, madam," Tania said back, with drama of her own, and pressed ENTER on her touchdesk's virtual keyboard. "Torpedo one is charging."

There was of course no torpedo—just a dummy payload sitting in Harvest Moon's brand-new mass driver. Ten kilometers long and made of eighty percent indigenous materials, it sat twenty kilometers from here, well away from the base, and from the nearby observatory and monastery.

65

The entire crew of Shackleton Lunar Industrial Station—all eighteen of them—were crammed into the Control Center, jokingly referred to as the Bridge, and the wall displays showed a radar view of the South Polar Mineral Territories, along with radar and camera views of the mass driver itself.

"It's sure to blow," murmured Stephen Chalmers, seated at the console beside her.

It was more than an idle speculation; in order for the dummy payload to reach Earth's atmosphere and burn up as intended, the mass driver's capacitors had to be charged to a hundred percent and then rapidly discharged, each in turn, to zero. Each of the one hundred iron coil magnets had to carry, briefly, a field of 2600 gauss— enough to shred a motorcar or pull the fillings out of God's own teeth. There had been nine catastrophic component failures during dry-fire testing, and only three clean fires since then, and that was without the magnetic eddy stresses of an actual projectile in the tube.

Tania shushed him with a glance. This was a proud moment for Harvest Moon Industries, or was supposed to be at any rate, and she'd already bet Stephen twenty quid about it, so what was there to say? Also, they were on video right now, both livestreamed on the HMI channel and archiving to half a dozen video libraries. The volume of Stephen's voice was low enough she could barely hear it— presumably so the microphones' filters would reject it as background noise—but anyone with a lip reader app could make a good guess what he was saying. Bad form, that. Also, it was his own work he was disparaging, which would not look good if news of it got out.

"Fifty percent charge," Tania reported. Then, a minute later, "Seventy-five percent charge." Then: "One hundred percent charge."

"Status?" Commander Harb demanded.

"All green," Stephen assured her.

"Can you be more specific?" Clearly, she wanted all the juice she could squeeze out of this lemon. The news cycles were of course dominated by the murder of Etsub Beyene, barely four kilometers from here, and something as prosaic as a new launch system would not make much of a ripple. But, her tone seemed to say, let's try, shall we? Let's fill this moment with as many dramatic words as we can. "Call them out by subsystem, please."

"Photovoltaics, green, obviously," Stephen replied. "Charging circuit green, obviously. Capacitors: I have one hundred green, zero yellow, zero red. Induction coils: I have one hundred green, zero yellow, zero red. Payload, green. Aperture magnetic choke, green. Site radar, green. Site camera, green. Area radar, green. Communications green, obviously. My console, built-in test, green. I have zero yellow, any functions. I have zero red, any functions. All functions green, madam."

"Right," Commander Harb said, more smartly than strictly necessary. "Ms. Falstaff, are you ready to fire?"

"Aye, madam," Tania answered. Also with great formality and vigor. She'd been a radar engineer and remote-outpost air traffic controller on four continents, and she'd been told her radio voice was superb, with crisp consonants, and sibilants that didn't hiss the mic. She'd learned the skills as an aircraftman with the RAF, but she'd gone to Cameroon via Doctors Without Borders, and to Antarctica with the British Antarctic Survey, and jumped from there to HMI when the opportunity presented itself. Two years in Paramaribo and then, much to her surprise, a coveted spot on the Moon itself.

"Ms. Falstaff, fire torpedo one." Dutifully, Tania pressed control-F.

"Torpedo one away," she said, before bothering to check if it were true.

The camera views and the K-band site radar were anticlimactic, to say the least. The lights on each coil assembly switched on and off in sequence, one by one, but the whole firing sequence took only eight seconds. There was a hint of a suggestion of a flicker as the payload exited the release aperture, and then nothing. It was like watching a gun being fired, minus the smoke and sparks and definitely minus the bang. The 9 GHz area radar was more encouraging; against a bright, false-color terrain image of the South Polar Mineral Territories (extending from the pole itself to the 85th parallel), the displays showed a little red circle moving upward and north, almost perfectly along the zero meridian line, on a trajectory that would carry it into a very low polar orbit around the Earth. It would never complete its first orbit. A hundred hours from now, it would burn up in the Earth's atmosphere, over the vast expanse of the Pacific Ocean.

"Trajectory is nominal," Tania reported. "Torpedo one is on course for grazing reentry."

She'd installed the radar equipment herself, and customized the software currently generating this display, so her word on the matter was rather definitive. Harb accepted it without comment.

"Payload telemetry also nominal," Stephen added. "All sensors functioning, no acceleration damage."

"I see."

This in itself was a bit of a triumph, as the little dummy probe had to withstand a peak acceleration of 28.7 gee—equivalent to a head-on car crash at highway speed—as it passed through each of the electromagnets. One hundred car crashes, in 8.5 seconds! It spoke to the maturity of Lunar manufacturing, which of course spoke directly to the readiness of Harvest Moon Industries to support a hoped-for wave of colonization. Why, anyone with fifty billion pounds at their disposal could afford their own moonbase as lavish as Saint Joe's own monastery, and there were dozens of people with resources like that, and hundreds of organizations. So far, they weren't biting, but Tania figured that was down to nobody wanting to go first.

"This is a momentous occasion," Commander Harb said, for the benefit of the livestream audience, and for the recordings that would no doubt become important PR assets. Her voice was at once breathy and precise, a staccato of perfectly formed syllables conferring an air of irreproachability to anything she said. "Harvest Moon can now deliver Lunar raw materials to any point in cislunar space, without wasting tons of Lunar-derived propellant in the process. This will drop commodity prices by an order of magnitude, and eventually perhaps by two orders of magnitude, for anything we can supply, which is a long and growing list."

"Making certain people very angry," Stephen muttered.

"Shh," Tania said, although of course he was right. They would soon be seriously undercutting Orlov

Petrochemical's profits on hydrogen, oxygen, iron, calcium, and magnesium. That would still leave Grigory Orlov with monopolies on extraterrestrial carbon and nitrogen and (for now) rare-earth metals, and of course it would lower the cost of the tralphium (or "helium-3") he fed to his fusion reactors on Earth. Which would lower the price of electricity, which should in theory make everyone on Earth happy. But naturally the Americans and the Russians had denounced the mass driver as a weapon of mass destruction, capable of blasting city-block-sized impact craters anywhere on the Earth's surface, and the Chinese (with substantial Lunar assets of their own, clustered mainly around the North Polar Mineral Territories) had threatened to bomb it outright. And yet, here they were, up and running.

"The future of humankind," Commander Harb continued, sounding so over-rehearsed that Tania could barely stand it, "depends on this, and other developments like it, to untether space industry, and space colonization, from their long dependence on Earthly materials. History may well look back on this moment as a turning point, where humans living in space made their first and biggest stride toward real independence."

"Laying it on thiiiiick," Stephen mumbled.

"Shh!"

"Thank you for your attention," Harb concluded, and made a cutting gesture across her throat, letting the AV system know it was time to switch off the cameras. Then, in a more normal voice, she said, "Hopefully somebody pays attention."

"Things have gotten right crazy, ma'am," said Puya

Hebbar. "People's attention is divided, for sure. Ours isn't even the only murder. Someone was killed up on Esley Shade Station as well."

"Gossip and rumors," said Commander Harb.

"Well, something's got them stirred up," Puya insisted, in her singsong voice, which was actually quite lovely. But although Puya Hebbar was brilliant—a PhD rocket scientist and the head of Launch Services for Harvest Moon—she also somehow managed to be both a gossip and a ditz, with her ear to the door of every rumor mill in the solar system. To hear her tell it, Esley Shade Station had been taken over forcibly by the U.S. Space Force, who still maintained an armed presence on board. And Igbal Renz had used the ESL1 Solar Shade as a giant antenna to make contact with an alien civilization, and was planning a crewed interstellar mission to meet them. Oh, and they were also building antimatter bombs up there, and Renz was up to a hundred other things, and so was everyone else in outer space.

But Commander Harb simply said, "Something has them stirred up, yes. And the Americans, generally."

"The Americans can smooch me on the arse and buy me dinner," Stephen muttered.

Tania didn't bother shushing that, because the cameras were off now, and because yes, the Americans *could* smooch him on the arse. Harvest Moon wasn't exactly a British company (it was officially Surinamese, and it hired people from all over the world), but it had British DNA, and the "special relationship" between Blighty and its snotty former colony had never extended past Earth's atmosphere. Oh, the Americans had gotten to the Moon first and never let you forget it, but where were they now? In low Earth orbit, and at ESL1, out between the Earth and Sun, at the very limits of cislunar space. Maybe they would get to Mars, and maybe they wouldn't, but meanwhile they were killing each other for the privilege. And the Moon already in British hands, more or less. Also Chinese hands, for sure, but the Chinese didn't honestly seem to know what to do with the place. Plant flags, fortify positions, all that imperial bullshit. For all their business smarts they had yet to make it *pay*, and to hell with them, anyway. The Moon was big enough for them to fuck right off.

"Keep tracking the payload, all the way in," Commander Harb instructed Tania. Then, to Stephen, "Keep monitoring the payload telemetry. We want to know that it remains functional until it burns."

"Aye, ma'am," Stephen said. "We're storing every bit of telemetry, of course, but I'll keep the simulation running, too, and cut a 3D render of it as we go. Four and a half days—I'll barely sleep."

"Nor I," she said archly.

The phone rang.

"Hello?" said Harb. Not a greeting, but a voice command to the AV system that would put the caller up on screen.

"Good afternoon, Commander," said the caller, Sir Lawrence Edgar Killian. "I see congratulations are in order."

Killian was a familiar face around here, but no less odd for that. That look people get, when they're seventy-nine years old and still stubbornly tearing it up? Bald and wrinkly and stooped at the shoulder, but also tanner and stronger and quicker than you are? That was Sir Lawrence: a sweet old rattlesnake you did *not* try to bullshit. Although he was truthfully looking a bit pallid today.

"Sir Lawrence, always a pleasure," Harb said, with just a little edge of sarcasm. Her voice was slower and thicker now, but still commanding, like a sharpened spoon dripping syrup. "The dummy rock is away, yes, on a nominal trajectory. If all goes well, we may begin commercial shipments to LEO by the end of the month."

"Good, good. If you have champagne, now would be an excellent time."

"We don't, sir, but there might be some vodka lying around, or even some THC."

"Keeping the drug printer busy, then? Well, that's fine. No harm in it. And how are we doing with the other thing?"

"The thorium mining?"

"No," he said, "but all right, what's your update on that?"

To Tania he seemed both cheerful and a bit maudlin, which was also not abnormal. She'd never personally heard him pine for his beloved wife Rosalyn, but his grief for her seemed to infuse his daily life. Perhaps he'd wanted the Moon for her, but she hadn't lived long enough, and so he never quite seemed to have the heart to take it for himself. He'd never been up here, even once.

Harb, sounding miffed, said, "Well I've got two men up at Ingenii Basin, don't I? The robots are doing most of the work, but we'll have a kilogram of pure metal by this time next week. It's quite a big deal."

"Indeed," Sir Lawrence allowed. "Orlov Petrochemical will not be pleased, but this means Dan Beseman's reactor will have fuel, and his township will have heat and light, which should delight him no end. The Antilympus orders are quite aggressive, though. Will we meet them?"

"We will," Harb said, with more certainty than she ought to.

It had taken Bill and Nigel months to find the right spot to dig, and months more to actually dig. There weren't veins of metallic thorium—at least, not that anyone had ever found—but along the northwest rim of the South Pole-Aitken Basin, near the Ingenii Basin on the Lunar farside, there were exposed monazite ripples where it made up more than a tenth of a percent of the regolith by weight, and could be sifted out with a sulfuric acid-leaching process that also yielded up small amounts of valuable rare-Earth metals. It was not the largest deposit on the Moon, nor the richest, but as it was "only" fifteen hundred kilometers north of Shackleton, it was by far the most accessible to Harvest Moon Industries. Tania wasn't technically a geologist or a miner or a metallurgist, but it was impossible to reside here without hearing all about it.

The thorium was wanted for the Antilympus Project— so far the only customer—because they needed reactor fuel to feed the quite substantial power needs of the colony's startup protocol and get them through that first critical winter. But they needed three hundred kilograms of the stuff! Their launch date was fixed by the laws of planetary motion, whereas the output of any mining operation was subject to major fluctuations. Even the harvesting of ice from Faustini Crater, which was basically a frozen lake half a kilometer deep. You'd think you could just cut it up into blocks and truck them wherever you liked, but of course nothing was ever that simple.

"You sound awfully sure," Sir Lawrence observed.

"Yes, well there's a lot of money to be made, and our bonuses are tied to it," Harb said, "So you can rest assured it has my full attention."

"Then assured is exactly how I'll rest," he said drolly.

Allegedly, Sir Lawrence had been a real hardass in the early days, when he was selling off airlines and record companies, tin mines and gravel pits to finance what everyone agreed was a phenomenally risky Lunar mining venture. Every man on "critical path" projects (and they were overwhelmingly men) was subject to his wrath—at least, when he wasn't off racing motorcycles or jumping out of dirigibles. Then they were subject to the wrath of his lieutenants, twice as fierce and ten times as numerous. But those days were over long before Tania was hired. It gave her a bit of survivor's guilt, if you wanted to know the truth, because she'd stepped lightly over the burnt-out husks of a hundred male colleagues to land this plum assignment, and all because, now that things were up and running, Sir Lawrence wanted to pretty up his gender balance. Tania and Fernanda Harb had come up at the same time, and showed up together in all the promotional videos. Puya Hebbar, too, had risen through the ranks with ease, to land in the chair she now occupied. It's not that they weren't qualified, because God knew they were, and then some. No one worked harder or longer than the women of Shackleton! But they were also pretty, and it didn't take a rocket scientist to figure out that was good for recruitment. And Sir Lawrence had never had a harsh word for any of them. Nor for anyone, really—not in a long time.

"Now about that other thing," Sir Lawrence said.

"The SLAP?"

Also known as the Shoemaker Lunar Antenna Park— an observatory under construction a few kilometers past the linear accelerator.

"No," he chuckled, "not that either."

"Three astronomers on site," Harb reported anyway. "We're building the base around them while they work."

"Yes, I know all that. They're our first real customers after the monastery—you think I'm not paying close attention?"

"On the contrary, sir, I'm sure you are."

"I'm talking about the other other thing."

"Malinkin Base?"

"The same."

Commander Harb sighed. "You know it's not a real base they've got. Malinkin Shed is more like it. I know you're excited to have another contract, but they're not our people out there, so I've no real idea what they're up to. A pair of very self-sufficient civil engineers, is all I know. They don't call for help much, and they're not looking to expand their facilities, so until they need transport home it's not really much of our business."

Supposedly, with the Marriott Stars Hotel now operational in low Earth orbit—full of well-heeled guests and booked solid for the next five years—Marriott was contemplating an even more lavish hotel here in the South Polar Mineral Territories, with five-star suites built along the inner surface of a buried dome, with a big round window of clear, starry sky at the top center. Those two blokes, Dwight Bratton and Chie Rongish, were allegedly scouting for a spot suitable for such a large excavation.

"Yes, well, it is our business, actually," Sir Lawrence said, "or at least I'd like it to be. I'd like you to find out as much as you can, without actually coming out and asking them."

"A bit of subterfuge?"

"Just looking ahead. It appears Marriott may be backing out of the project. They're white as ghosts over the cost, and when we showed them something within their price range, I swear they turned a bit green around the edges, like a Nigerian flag. They can't seem to imagine anyone paying to stay in our current production modules, and never mind the students who are doing exactly that over at Saint Joseph's. But if they won't listen to reason, I know a company that's not afraid of a billion-dollar hole in the ground."

Tania, feeling left out of the conversation, said, "Walt Disney? No, just kidding, sir. You're talking about us. Our company."

"Precisely, yes." He seemed to find her humor wearying. Actually, he looked like he was finding everything a bit wearying today.

Harb looked uncomfortable. "A hotel, Sir Lawrence? Are you sure?"

"Not exactly a hotel, my dear. Let's just say I've got a trick up my sleeve."

"More than one trick," she said to him, and not as a compliment. "And more than two sleeves, I think. All right, we shall do your spying, but I won't let it interfere with paying work, sir, I really won't."

"Thank you, Commander. You have my utmost confidence."

"Indeed."

She made the cutting gesture again, and then sat down in her chair, as heavily as Lunar gravity permitted.

To Tania she said, "Well, it appears we have our orders. How much do you know about concrete?"

1.5
17 November

✦

Transit Point Station
Low Earth Orbit

Raimy and Ling waited in the docking module for about ten minutes, and Raimy nearly lost his guts a couple of times there. He didn't, though, and finally Lieutenant Commander Geary Notbohm came back in with a mesh purse containing a plastic-wrapped bundle of blue paper bags, a squeeze bottle of what looked like orange Gatorade, a portable urinal, a handful of moist towelettes, and an orange-and-silver bundle the size of a rolled-up towel.

"Your flight to Luna leaves tomorrow afternoon," Notbohm said, in his maybe-Swiss accent. "Ordinarily someone would assign you a bunk in one of the guest barracks, but in cases like this we recommend you spend the night in the docking module, or in the ship that brought you."

"Not in my ship," Ling said.

"You know, I spent four years in the Navy, mostly

underwater," Raimy told them both. "Never got seasick once."

Notbohm nodded at that. "I'm aware of your record, yes. Nobody is blaming you or thinking less of you, and I will try to ensure these details are not made public. Your subscribers and sponsors need never know. This just happens sometimes, randomly, even to people not prone to other forms of motion sickness. Unpredictable. Nevertheless, the inner walls of this module are ceramic, so there is not much damage your stomach can do. You understand?"

"I do, yes. But there's no need for a cover-up."

"Well, you of course may broadcast whatever you like, but unless your drones are designed for zero gravity, they will not be capable of controlled flight here. You may need to stick them on surfaces, or simply rely on your glasses. I think they will not fly properly on the Moon, either, although I could be wrong."

To Ling, Notbohm said, "Your flight plan says you depart in four hours. You have free run of the station until then. You know your way around, yes?"

It seemed to be a joke; these two knew each other, and Raimy knew the modules of Transit Point Station were arranged in basically a double straight line, pointed downward at the Earth. Learning your way around would take all of five minutes, and Ling had probably been here dozens of times.

But what Ling said was, "Thanks, but I need to keep an eye on my passenger. I'll hang around here for a while."

"Very well," said Notbohm. "No need to say anything if you change your mind."

To Raimy he said, "How should I address you? Candidate? Detective? Mr. Vaught?"

"Raimy is fine."

"Ah. Well, Raimy, as you and I are colleagues I would ask you to call me by my name as well, but it happens that everyone on this station calls me Commander Notbohm, or Lieutenant Commander if they want to be proper. So I think that will do for you as well."

"Got it."

"When you're feeling better, you can come find me, but I do strongly recommend you wait until after the night shift. We keep the same time as Suriname, and when we dim our lights, this will help your body adjust. You will likely feel better in the morning."

"Okay," Raimy said. There didn't seem to be much else to say. The situation was mortifying, and potentially harmful to his competitive ranking, and he pretty much wanted to hide anyway.

He wasn't so sure he liked Lieutenant Commander Notbohm as a person. In Raimy's experience, that level of condescension was rarely compatible with, for example, drinking a beer together, or talking about personal issues. But he had to say, Notbohm had twice left him unsupervised, and seemed comfortable in his role here at the station. He probably wasn't a bad leader, as such things went.

"Try to keep your head still," Ling told him, after Notbohm had gone. "Also close your eyes, or look at something close up, like your hand. This sleeping bag"— he fetched out the orange-and-silver roll, and stuck it to the wall with a square of Velcro and a piece of tape—"can help arrest your movement if you set it up. Also better if we opaque this window." He moved to the porthole and flicked a switch, whereupon the "downward" view, toward Earth, was replaced by a blank whiteness, like a sheet of paper. "You may not notice it right away, but these things should help. Do you want a couple more SAS patches? It sometimes helps if you put them on the inside of your wrist."

"Fine," Raimy said, and was then jealous of the effortless grace with which Ling flicked and floated his way back through the docking hatch and into the SLEO capsule.

"We could grab some of theirs from sickbay," Ling called back over his shoulder, "but it would be a bit rude. I'll be on the ground by midnight, and a refurb crew will stock up all my consumables before this ship flies again."

He rummaged in there for a minute, not quite silently, and then reappeared. "I mean, you've already got a whole pack of their barf bags. Somebody's going to have to pay for that."

"Mmph."

Raimy's first thought was that a package of paper bags couldn't be anywhere near as expensive as a chartered jet, but then his second thought was that he shouldn't be so sure about that. He really didn't understand the economics of space travel. He knew some things were shockingly cheap these days, and others remained shockingly expensive, but he didn't really know which was which. And did it really matter? He would either make it to Mars or he wouldn't, but either way he'd spend almost none of his own money, and even if he did, it wouldn't make a difference. He did know one thing: space was too expensive for people like him. Never mind a trip to the Moon; just a ticket to low Earth orbit—say, a night at the Marriott Stars—would cost him three years' salary.

And yet, here he was. Here he was.

The next thirty minutes were consumed with Raimy wrestling his way out of the bulky spacesuit, stowing it in a locker apparently built for this purpose, retrieving his flight bag from the capsule, and putting on his Antilympus uniform. He then applied the two medicated patches to his wrists, threw up a couple more times, and finally unrolled the strange little sleeping bag Ling had Velcroed to the wall.

"I thought zero gravity was supposed to be relaxing," he complained.

"First day is always worst," Ling assured him. "You know when you move to a new house? Don't know where anything is or how it works? You stagger around for weeks, bumping your head and wondering where you're going to get groceries and haircuts. Space is like that, but the basic physics are also different. It's pretty exhausting. If it helps, I've spent a total of almost four months in space, and most ways it's still harder than being on the ground."

"Why would that help?" Raimy asked, rhetorically. Then, changing the subject, he said, "Would you mind if I recorded you on a glasses cam? For vidcast to my sponsors?"

"Sure, I guess. Try not to throw up."

"Right."

Raimy got out his glasses, held them in front of his face, and started recording.

"This is Raimy Vaught, coming to you from Transit Point Station. By now, most of you are probably familiar with the . . . unfortunate circumstances that brought me here. Rather than belabor any of that, I thought it would be fun to ask my pilot some questions. Meet, uh . . ."

Shit.

"David Ling," Ling said. "Harvest Moon SLEO pilot, first class."

"The yellow launch suit is a giveaway—that's Harvest Moon yellow. Ling is heading back to Earth in a few hours, so he's not even bothering to take the suit off. Right now he's nursing me through a bout of motion sickness, which is embarrassing, because he doesn't seem to be suffering at all. Ling, how many times have you been to space?"

"Oh, I think this might be my twentieth."

"Amazing. It's so routine, these days. And you like your job?"

"Immensely."

"Okay. Good."

Raimy had planned this poorly, and was already almost out of things to say. Struggling, he tried, "I keep looking at that emergency locker over there."

"Um, okay."

"Trying to figure out what's in it. I know I'm supposed to be closing my eyes, but . . ."

"You're excited. That's okay. It'd be weird if you weren't."

The locker was across from Raimy, and transparent, and said EMERGENCY across the top and bottom of the door, in big white letters hemmed by red-and-white-striped banners. If the airlock blew out or the module sprung a leak, Raimy knew he would probably die. Like being in a submarine at depth, there really might not be very much he could do to save himself. But the fact that there was an emergency locker at all implied that, in at least some scenarios, there were possibilities.

He said, "I see an aerosol can, a goo suit, a length of parachute cord with carabiners at both ends, some kind of metal tool, and, I don't know, first aid kits and Mylar blankets and stuff."

Ling seemed suddenly interested. "How do you know what a goo suit is?"

"Navy," Raimy answered.

"Were you a fireman?"

That was what the goo suit had been invented for: escaping from burning buildings. It was basically a ring of solid Nomex with a clear polyimide bag rolled up inside. You slammed it down over your head and let it shoot a sticky, expanding gel around your neck and shoulders. Assuming that didn't kill you, the bag would then inflate, and a little regulator would give you, like, two minutes of decent air to breathe.

"No," Raimy said. "I was a diver. We were testing the concept for a submarine escape drill."

"Oh. Wow. I didn't realize they worked underwater."

"They don't," Raimy said, with a laugh. "I mean, none of us died, but the concept never did get approved. As far as I know, we were the only ones to ever try it. I didn't realize they worked in space."

Ling chuckled and said, "They don't. They generate less than a hundred and fifty millibars of overpressure. That's not enough to damage your lungs, but even filled with pure oxygen it's also not enough to breathe. You'd lose consciousness pretty quick."

"Oh. That sucks. Why is it even here?"

Ling snorted. "Makes people feel better? Weight is paramount onboard a spacecraft, but stations like this just sort of accumulate artifacts, the longer they sit. The new airlocks are all built like this—a dozen copies of that same exact locker. Some of that stuff could save your life, I guess, if you had a buddy with you, but mostly I think it's just superstition. There are all kinds of misconceptions out there. Some people think your body would explode in the vacuum of outer space, which it wouldn't. Some people think you can hold your breath, which you can't. To answer your question about the emergency supplies, I think there's a basic tool kit in there, with screwdrivers and duct tape and such. That big metal thing is an airlock wrench. The spray can is standard-issue patch gel; you spray it on leaks and it expands in there and hardens. I suppose it might be the same stuff as the goo suit. Didn't they teach you any of this in your flight orientations?"

"No. Not yet. I mean, *Concordia* doesn't fly for another three years, and most of the passengers will be in hibernation the whole way. Also I'm, you know, not even a backup at this point, so I'll probably never get the real flight training."

"Hmm. That's heart-wrenching. You put in years of work, just to land in second place?"

"Third, actually."

"Huh. Man. Well, my advice is, don't get yourself in vacuum at all. You don't want to pin your hopes on any of that stuff. The good news is, when you're EVA in a spacesuit, you'll always have a buddy, and when you're indoors . . . Well, if you're indoors and there's a *serious* decompression event, you're probably going to die."

"Yeah, I know. But at least I'll have company."

Ling scoffed at that. "Is that a Navy thing? I don't know what you're used to, but if there's a leak, try to be on the correct side of the hatch, before they're all sealed. On a station this size, decompression accidents tend to be of the 'slow leak' variety, in which case, just do what you're told and you'll be fine."

"Hmm. Good advice."

Raimy had never been in a serious naval accident; the U.S.S. *Jimmy Carter*, decrepit as it was, had never sprung a leak or run aground or struck anything harder than a fish. But he'd trained extensively for underwater emergencies, and that training put the fear in you, sure enough. And he'd been in more than his fair share of close calls while diving. None fatal, thank God, but all of them potentially so. And that kind of thing *really* put the fear in you.

He added, "I'm sure this will all be very interesting to my viewers."

And then Raimy came up empty; for a moment he was unable to think of another question, and by the time the next one did occur to him, he was gripped with self-doubt. The ethics of what he was doing were debatable, because even though he tried to keep a firewall between his publicity activities and his homicide investigations, they did inevitably bleed together, if only in the minds of the people involved. By now, everyone knew why Raimy was here. And on the heels of this came the certainty that he must look awfully stupid in this video, as he so often did. But he had to have something to show for his time here, so he powered through with another few minutes of questions, reassuring himself that he had all night to cut and edit the thing to his liking. Damn it, Raimy had been a good diver and a good student and a better-than-mediocre prosecuting attorney. When he'd put in his time as a CSPD patrolman he'd been good at that, too. Not great, perhaps. but what did it even mean, to be a great patrolman? He'd made detective just as soon as it was administratively possible, and that was really, in a lot of ways, the perfect job for him. He didn't aspire to be a damn video journalist, so why was his whole future hanging on his ability to do exactly that?

Focus on the job, he reminded himself. *Focus on the victim. Find out what happened.*

"Thank you," he said to Ling, and switched off the camera.

An hour after Ling and his capsule departed, Raimy's home in the docking module was visited by a little Asian dude whose nametag said D. NGUYEN, who came to replenish his Gatorade and carry away his used barf bags.

After introducing himself as "Dong," the man—dressed in a jumpsuit of the same eyesore-red as Geary Notbohm—unfurled a white plastic garbage bag and started collecting up the waste.

"Why are they all on the same side of the module?" Raimy asked, pointing to where the barf bags were all clustered, up against the same wall where Ling had hung his sleeping bag. "That's the side away from the Earth, isn't it? I tried letting my car keys float in the center of the module, but after about half an hour they'd settled against that wall. Why are things falling 'up'?"

"You brought car keys to outer space?" Nguyen asked, in an accented voice that was about the right pitch for such a small man.

"Force of habit," Raimy said. "They were in my pocket when I stuffed the uniform in my bag."

Nguyen (whom Raimy's inner thirteen-year-old couldn't bear to think of as "Dong") let out a chuckle at that. "Yeah, force of habit. How much we do from habit, hah? I wish force of smartness was half as strong. Your question: things fall 'up' on this side of the station because it's the high side of the boom. Higher than the center of mass, so orbiting a little too fast for the altitude. Centrifugal force is flinging your stuff outward. Slow, but yeah, a little mosquito-fart acceleration adds up over time. We call it gravity gradient. Same thing on the bottom end; stuff falls down, toward the Earth."

With no sign of disgust, he put Raimy's barf bags in the trash bag and tied the whole thing shut.

"What happens to them now?" Raimy asked.

"They go in a trash balloon."

"Oh. And what does that mean? What happens to the trash balloon?"

"Gets detached from the station when it's full. We lower it on a thousand-meter tether, and drop it off the end. Gravity gradient gives it a nice kick, and atmosphere does the rest."

"It burns up?"

"Eventually. Decaying orbit, maybe a couple months.

Dropping trash balloons also raises our orbit a little, which saves on propellant, so your barf is actually helping us."

Nguyen seemed about to leave, but then he said, "I'm not just the janitor here, you know. I handled that guy's spacesuit, the one who died. Didn't open the backpack, but I helped him in and out of it. Helped him stow it. Just thought you should know."

"I didn't say anything about a backpack," Raimy noted carefully.

"Didn't have to," Nguyen said, with a funny little nod. "Everybody knows. Everybody's talking about it. Air hose in the backpack, probably sabotage. There's lots of people on this station could have got to it. You going to inspect the thing?"

"Yeah."

"Well, you want to look for tool marks. GS don't leave tool marks when they put the thing together. Somebody pries it open, you're going to see scratches where they did it. Tell you what kind of tool they used."

"I know what tool marks are."

"Heh. Yeah, I bet you do. I bet you know a lot of things. Sad to see you up here, people getting murdered and such. Things are getting weird, you know. There were deaths up at Esley Shade Station, too. Hush-hush, no investigation."

"I wouldn't know about that," Raimy said.

"Other weird stuff, too," Nguyen persisted. "I seen a stealth spaceship once, like a lens passing in front of the Earth. Not quite invisible, but man. Close enough to throw a wrench at it. I was out in a spacesuit at the time, about crapped my diaper. I wrote a report. Who's up here with stealth spaceships? Cartels? Chinese? It don't make sense."

"I wouldn't know about that either," Raimy said. "Did your partner see it?"

"No partner that day. Emergency repair, big hurry. But it happened."

"No, I believe you," Raimy said, meaning it. The Navy was full of strange sightings that nobody ever could explain. Maybe Nguyen had seen a stealthed spaceship and maybe he hadn't, but he saw *something*, or he sure wouldn't have put his credibility on the line by filing a report.

"About that backpack," he said. "What kind of sabotage should I be looking for?"

"Heh. Tool marks. You want a metal-braided air hose to fail, you're going to have to nick it. The braid is made of little wires, right? And if they fail when the hose explodes, the broken ends will look stretched, like taffy. You might need a microscope. But if they're *nicked*, you'll see a flat end, cut through. Tell you right away if it was an accident."

"Huh. Okay. Why are you telling me this?"

"Why not? You want to catch the guy, right?"

"Yeah. I do."

And that was all the two of them had to say to each other.

After Nguyen was gone, Raimy spent an uneasy night alone in the docking module. There was the occasional bustle of people passing by in the corridor, and of course Raimy had network access, so he could look at all his usual incoming feeds and post some short updates to his outgoing ones. So he wasn't really all that alone. But with no spaceship docked on the other side of the outer hatch, he was uncomfortably aware of being almost completely surrounded by the vacuum of space.

Ling's pep talk had been sobering, but in some ways it was a familiar sensation, not really all that different from being on a submarine. In fact, in some ways it was actually safer, because the pressure difference was much lower. At operating depth, the inward pressure on a submarine hull could be thirty atmospheres or more, and if you sprung a leak and lost buoyancy, that pressure would climb until it crushed the hull like a paper cup. All hands lost in an instant, their mortal remains plummeting forever into the dark and cold. By contrast, the air pressure pushing outward on the walls of this module was only about 0.5 atmospheres. And yes, it really was possible for a space module to leak without failing explosively. So he was aware of the danger with a professional sort of nervousness, without being afraid *per se*.

And yet, he was in here by himself, sick and dazed and out of his element. Notbohm had good reasons for leaving him alone in here, but he also couldn't shake the idea that there was something punitive about it, almost as though he'd been thrown in the brig. He was, after all, here to determine if anyone on board was a murderer who needed to spend the rest of his or her life in prison, and he definitely got the feeling Notbohm resented it.

"What is the expression, rise and shine?" Notbohm said by way of greeting, with the blue-white light of "morning" streaming in from the hallway. "Did you sleep?"

"Some," Raimy told him. "Not much. I talked to one of your men for a while, though."

"Is your stomach feeling better?"

"Maybe halfway better," Raimy admitted. "But I'm well enough to work."

"Would you like breakfast?"

"Ugh. No. Maybe later. The truth is, I've never been much of a breakfast eater. Lunch is my big meal."

"Ah. Well then we'll be sure you get a good one. Nutritious and easy to digest."

"I would love some coffee, though. Do you have that here?"

"We do," Notbohm said, "though I'm afraid it's only instant. Will that do? On a rough stomach?"

"It will, thank you." Fortunately, coffee had never been rough on Raimy's stomach, and he could definitely use the pick-me-up. He wasn't crazy about instant, but what else could you expect on a space station? "I take it black."

Nodding, Notbohm pulled a rollup from one of the many pockets in his eyesore-red jumpsuit. Without bothering to unroll it, he pressed a button and spoke into one end, saying "Notbohm, here. Paul, if you're still in the galley, would you please bring a bulb of black coffee to Dock Five, please?"

The words rang out on a loudspeaker, apparently station-wide.

"Oh, jeez," Raimy said, "you don't have to—"

"It's no trouble," Notbohm insisted. "We were told to give you everything you needed, and I intend just that."

"Well, thank you. In the meantime, I'd really like to retrace Etsub's steps, and those of his spacesuit."

"We will do that," Notbohm said. "Would you like to start with the H.S.F. *Concordia*?"

Raimy's heart skipped a beat. He hadn't exactly forgotten that Dan Beseman's Mars ship was docked to Transit Point Station, just a few modules away, but in the press of other business he'd put it out of mind. Other than glimpsing it through the SLEO's front window on the way in, Raimy hadn't honestly expected to get to see the thing.

"Etsub visited the Mars ship?"

"He did. All four of them did. You don't follow their feeds? Beseman is quite accommodating when any of his candidates are onboard. We can go right now, if you like."

The sheer excitement of that did wonders for Raimy's motion sickness. However, he chuckled and said, "After coffee."

Soon, a young man appeared in the hatchway, wearing what Raimy now figured was Transit Point red. He was Caucasian, about thirty, with a beard and bun that seemed out of place here. He moved with confidence, though, slinging his body through zero gee like he'd been born to it.

"Coffee," he said, holding up a dark-colored squeeze bottle.

"For our guest," Notbohm said, nodding sideways toward Raimy, who accepted the bottle gratefully. After a quick, tiny sip to test the temperature, he took a long pull on it, and felt immediately more human.

"That all?" the young man asked. Amusingly, the nametag on his jumpsuit actually said P. YOUNG. He seemed happy enough to help, but Raimy got the distinct impression that fetching coffee wasn't in his job description.

"Yes, thank you," Notbohm said.

And just like that, the kid was gone.

"Shall we?" Notbohm asked.

Without bothering to answer, Raimy kicked lightly off the wall, floating headfirst out into the hallway, where he awkwardly turned his body and arrested his motion with his feet. Well, mostly arrested, and with a lot of arm-flailing. The movement barely made him queasy at all, though, so he figured he was finally starting to adapt.

TPS's "hallway" or "tower" or "boom" was long, composed of modules that also had other purposes, so that when he looked "down," in the Earthward direction, he could see bunk beds and equipment racks fading off into the distance, for more than a hundred meters. The sight made his feet tingle with acrophobia, but his stomach and his inner ear held firm.

In the other direction, "up," the station was shorter and more functional, with staggered docking-module hatches on the walls, leading up toward a big hatch at the hallway's end, or the tower's top. Rectangular, with rounded corners, like you'd see on a submarine.

In a real sense, Mars was on the other side of that doorway.

"Jesus," he muttered under his breath.

"I see you know the way," Notbohm said, amicably enough. Then, seeing the look on Raimy's face, he added, "Someday, perhaps, you and I will have berths on that ship. Not this time, I think, but maybe when it comes back."

To that, Raimy couldn't help saying, "Unless Anming Shui also gets murdered. Then you're all set."

Notbohm seemed offended at that, which was hardly surprising. Needling suspects was impolite, but could be effective in getting guilty people to reveal themselves. Raimy didn't think it particularly likely that Notbohm had done the deed, but old habits died hard.

"I understand you have a job to do," Notbohm said with some irritation. "I understand I am a suspect for this crime. I understand protesting my innocence means very little to you or your investigation. But please do not speak to me like that on my own station. We're cooperating, but please do not undermine my authority in the exercise of yours, hmm?"

"Fair enough," Raimy said, but did not go so far as apologizing. "Are you leading the way?"

"You go on ahead. You appear quite eager."

Raimy didn't need to be told twice. Switching on his glasses cam, he found a grab rail and launched himself, with more enthusiasm than skill, toward that pill-shaped portal.

1.6
18 November
✦
H.S.F. *Concordia*
Low Earth Orbit

Raimy shouldn't have been surprised that the pill-shaped hatchway opened straight through into *Concordia*'s bridge. The Mars ship was docked nose-down to the top of Transit Point, and the nose was where the bridge was located on every spaceship he'd ever heard of. Still, it was weird to swing through and see Dan Beseman, the trillionaire, strapped into the pilot's seat and working touch screens right beside Raimy's head.

"Hi," Beseman said, absently and without looking up. "You must be our detective."

Beseman was facing down toward the Earth, and Raimy's sense of direction did a little flip-flop so that "down" was the direction Beseman's feet were pointing. He fought back a moment of queasiness.

"I'm Raimy Vaught. Do . . . I shake your hand?"

"I would say so," Beseman agreed, now looking Raimy in the eye. "I paid half the cost of your passage. How do you do?"

"A little motion sickness, but otherwise fine," Raimy said. "Working the case."

They shook hands. Beseman's handshake was firm, but not too firm, about like Raimy's own. A lot of cops and businessmen were given to what Raimy called "cop handshake," which involved grabbing the other person's hand too close to the fingers and then squeezing too hard. The result was not only borderline painful, but also made the victim feel like they had somehow screwed something up. Like they could not fully master even something as simple as a handshake. It was a dick move, and spoke (Raimy believed) to some inherent insecurity on the part of the perpetrator. Beseman didn't seem to need to assert himself that way.

"How's the coffee?" Beseman asked, nodding toward Raimy's squeeze bottle.

"Not bad," Raimy said, and almost meant it.

"I see you're in third place for the admin slot," Beseman said. "That's impressive, considering the size of the initial applicant pool. You've got a lot of interesting experience."

"Thank you," Raimy answered, and was disappointed that he couldn't keep a touch of resignation out of his voice. He should be lighthearted and casual right now, as he was recording for posterity, and maybe also being recorded by cameras here on *Concordia*. Or else he should be deadly serious, out of respect for Etsub, or splitting the difference somehow.

"Am I on livestream live right now?" he couldn't help asking. He wanted, as best he could, to control his image and messaging. His own glasses were in RECORD mode, and Geary Notbohm wasn't wearing any, but still he might be live on the Antilympus feeds right now. With several 24/7 vidstreams to feed, the Antilympus Project fell back on a lot of live video from here. Weirdly, the streams also carried a lot of content from the Marriott Stars Hotel in low Earth orbit, which had nothing to do with Mars but which had also been built by Enterprise City LLC, and so had some of the same design DNA. Also videos from Spaceport Paramaribo.

"Right now?" Beseman said. "No, I don't think so. They're showing an exterior view of the ship on the main feed, and launch videos on the secondary. Our subscribers seem to have a bottomless appetite for launch videos. Especially the ones carrying material up here to *Concordia*, which happens almost daily."

"The ship's not built from extraterrestrial materials," Raimy said. It was something he knew—that anyone closely following the project knew—but here and now it still surprised him, that such a large structure would be shipped up, piece by piece, through the gravity and atmosphere of Earth.

Beseman seemed to take his meaning, and said, "We're certainly doing our best to use as many Lunar and asteroidal materials as possible, but the factories of Renz Ventures and Harvest Moon are still pretty limited in the range of goods they can produce, so about a third of the total mass comes from Earthly suppliers. Mostly ones we own or control, but there are some outliers. A surprising amount of stuff from Germany and Sweden, for example. You can find out more on our website, if you're interested."

"Thank you. I might do that." Then: "It's really quite a pleasure to meet you in person. This whole project is your doing. I feel . . . I mean, I've seen you on TV so much . . ."

"I understand," Beseman said. "Truthfully, you have me at a disadvantage. All I know about you is what it says in your project dossier."

"Ah. You don't follow my feed?"

A dumb question, but Beseman answered without apology, "There are still hundreds of feeds, Mr. Vaught. I don't even follow the leaderboard. Also, my attention is easily split, so I try to stay away from certain kind of distractions. You probably know something about that."

"Excuse me?"

Beseman snorted, looking him over. "You're a fidgeter, much like myself. Also, you're barely forty years old, and you've already had three different careers, and you're trying out for a fourth."

Raimy wasn't sure whether to be offended or what. He was diagnosed with attention deficit hyperactivity disorder by the Navy Recruit Training Command when he was nineteen, and had declined medication or biofeedback for it.

"Hell, son," the psychiatric corpsman had said to him at the time. "Half the people come through here got issues of one kind or another. Navy'd be out of business without ADHD. But it won't go in your record."

No one had ever mentioned it to Raimy again, and he himself had never breathed a word of it, even to his parents. Even to his ex-wife, or the four serious girlfriends he'd had over the course of his life. Back in the twenties and thirties it had been fashionable to talk about brain problems and brain medications in public—even in places that kept an indelible, searchable record. But the privacy pendulum had long since swung the other way, because that information really did get misused by employers and advertisers and amoral artificial intelligences. So on the occasions when Raimy thought about it at all, it was with vague embarrassment, as if the diagnosis were a personal failing. To have *Dan frigging Beseman* call him on it, on video and in front of Geary Notbohm, rocked him a bit.

"Oh, relax," Beseman said, seeing his expression. "You're among friends. Heck, you and I might be coworkers in a couple of years." He took a breath, seeming to realize he'd overstepped. Then he looked around and spread his arms, showing off the cockpit of his spaceship, which everyone knew doubled as his office when he was off the Earth's surface.

"I'm guessing you've seen this before," he said. "Does it look different in person?"

"Bigger than I thought," Raimy said.

And that was true; there were four seats in here, but they were spaced farther apart than Raimy had imagined, and the windows were bigger—looking down the tower of Transit Point Station to the round Earth below. Raimy refused to feel vertigo. The largeness of the cockpit actually helped with this, especially when he steadied himself on a grab bar.

The cockpit's manual flight controls looked about like you'd expect, but the touch screens all around them were larger and more numerous than seemed necessary, or wise. The place looked almost as much like a stock exchange as it did a spaceship. And Dan Beseman was smaller than expected—probably ten centimeters shorter than Raimy, and twenty kilograms lighter—which just made the cockpit seem that much bigger.

"It's roomy," Beseman agreed. "Eight of us will be awake the whole trip, and that sense of interior space is vital. We also need a nice, broad aerodynamic profile for entry into the Martian atmosphere."

The cockpit of the interplanetary ship was, of course, also the cockpit of the landing craft that would actually detach from the ship and carry a hundred people down to the planet's surface. People were increasingly accustomed to space-built spaceships looking un-aerodynamic, but the front third of *Concordia* looked like a classic conical space capsule, scaled up to gargantuan size.

"Of course," Beseman went on, "we also need to keep the mass budget very tight, so this is literally as big as we can make it and still meet our launch window. It's as big *and* as small as it can possibly be."

"Everything is optimized," said Notbohm.

"Yeah," Beseman agreed. "Totally. People ask why it's taking so long to build. That's why. Some component design comes in a bit too large or a bit too heavy, and either it goes back to the drawing board or else everything around it needs to be adjusted." He paused a moment, and then said, "I know you're on the clock here, but would you like to see how the controls work?"

That answer was obviously yes, so Beseman spent the next five minutes showing Raimy the basics of interplanetary piloting, and then another five showing him the landing and relaunch sequences. The explanations were quite complicated, and yet also vague and contradictory in places, because of course Beseman was an Administrator, not a Pilot. Still, Raimy envied him. He got to sit here every day, playing astronaut.

Then the absurdity of that thought caught up to Raimy. He envied a trillionaire who had his own private space program and his own private Mars colony? Really? The Buck Rogers stuff was obviously reserved for the people who could afford it, and who were quite accustomed to other people's envy. If Raimy ever got to Mars, it would be to work his ass off, and in the meantime he was only here because he had a job to do. Also paid for by Beseman.

"Can you give me the same tour you gave Etsub Beyene?" he asked, perhaps a bit rudely. "It's important for me to retrace his steps."

"You think he left a trail of clues?" Beseman asked.

"Yes, sir, I do. Everyone does, and if someone killed him, then *their* trail intersects with his, probably multiple times."

"Ah. And you follow it right to them."

"Exactly. And it's not like there's a whole world of possibilities, either. Beyene passed through a series of choke points, where his position was known and his activities were memorable in some way. Maybe 'trail' is the wrong word; everyone involved has got a *story*. Or, you know, I've been thinking about it almost like a pyramid, that gets narrower the higher you go."

"With a tiny little monastery at the top," Beseman mused. He seemed to think that over for a couple of seconds, then finally said, "Well, good. You know your business. Now, this has been a nice break for me, talking to you, but I'm actually quite busy here, and if I remember it was Geary who gave Mr. Beyene that tour. Geary? Would you mind?"

"Not at all, Dan."

Raimy felt another jolt of envy at that, because Notbohm was on a first-name basis with the head of the Antilympus Project. Living on board the same space station! And yet, he was still only second in line for that Hydroponics slot. Which told Raimy that the guy now in the number one slot, Anming Shui, must be *really* impressive. Raimy had toyed with the idea of interviewing Shui by video link, along with other suspects, just to get an idea of their general character, but had decided against it. For one thing, it went against CSPD regulations to ask murder-related questions over a remote audio or video link, and although Raimy wasn't here on CSPD business, it still seemed a good policy. Second, and more importantly, the information content of a face-to-face chat was so very much higher, and he wanted to keep his suspects in the dark until he could make that happen.

"Well, come on," Notbohm said, kicking off toward the hatchway at the back of the cockpit.

Raimy followed, looking around at everything, and honestly unsure how much of his curiosity was driven by Etsub Beyene, and how much by self-interest. In Colorado Springs he let his attention wander wherever it liked, with some confidence that the information he was taking in would, sooner or later, "feed the monster" and help him solve whatever case he was working on. Here and now, though, he couldn't entirely trust his own motives. Maybe Carol Beseman had made a mistake in selecting him for this job. But even if that were true, here he was, de facto. Etsub and his family deserved justice, and it was only imperfect Raimy Vaught who could find it for them.

First stop on the tour was the flight deck, where the other four acceleration chairs were located. There were no controls in here, other than a couple of video screens and a climate control console, but the walls were all storage lockers, so it was less roomy in here, even though the outside of the ship was actually wider at this point. You could see the conical shape of the landing craft in the shape of this room, which visibly widened toward the back end (or bottom end, when it was sitting on the planet's surface, or its top end, relative to the Earth right now).

"Flight deck," Notbohm said. "Where the Flight Medical and Flight Engineering teams sit during acceleration events. Up there"—he pointed back toward the cockpit—"is for Dan and Carol, and the two pilots." He laughed, then added, "They serve no function up there, except owning the ship. They save the second-best seats in the house for themselves. Must be nice, ah?"

"Yeah," Raimy agreed. Then: "Did Etsub do anything here? Did he sit in any of the seats? Work any controls?"

"He had the same tour I'm giving you. You may sit in a chair if you like, but Etsub Beyene did not. I did not observe anything suspicious during his time here, and quite frankly, his spacesuit was never onboard *Concordia*, so no one here could have tampered with it."

That irritated Raimy, who said, "Let me worry about the investigation, all right? I don't know which details are important here, and neither do you. Did Etsub talk to anyone while he was on the ship?"

"Other than myself and his fellow travelers? Only Dan and his assistant. All of the shipwrights were otherwise engaged." He paused a moment, then said, "Do you have what you need here? Shall we continue?"

"Please."

Notbohm then led him into a wider, more obviously tapering chamber, with eight . . . oversized bunk beds? . . . ringing the walls in an octagon pattern. Four were open and empty. Three were closed off by sliding fanfold doors. One stood open, and had a sleeping bag stuck to one surface, and various documents and photographs, mirrors and mesh bags stuck everywhere else.

"Crew quarters," Notbohm said. "Each cabin is three meters by two by two, except the outer wall is curved, following the contour of the hull. In microgravity that's a lot of space. It's actually larger than my own cabin on TPS, which is itself quite roomy. In here"—he pointed to the central area, between the cabins—"there will be a kind of fold-out surface that can be used as a table or work area." He pointed to other features: "That's the toilet room. That's the shower room. Both operational, as of last month. This makes the ship a lot more independent of the station, although it will be quite some time before *Concordia* has its own solar arrays. A treadmill will be mounted *here*, and a trampoline *there*. You'd strap into these with bungee cords, if you understand."

"It looks a lot more finished than I've seen it," Raimy said, although he was admittedly way behind in following the progress of the ship's construction.

But Notbohm simply said, "The interior is coming

together more quickly, now that the plumbing is in place, and the outer hull sealed around it."

"Ah. And what did Etsub do while he was in here?"

"Nothing," Notbohm said. Then, after a moment: "Actually, that's not quite true. One of his female companions, Katla Koskinen, said something to him, and he pushed her slightly. In a friendly way, it seemed to me, but she didn't like it."

"In what way didn't she like it?"

"Well, I suppose she seemed to be in a not very good mood. But their male companion, Anming, said something to her, that apparently made her feel better."

"You don't recall what they said?"

"I didn't hear it over the sound of the air vents. They weren't speaking loudly."

"I see. And what did the other woman, Bridget Tobin, do at that time? Anything?"

"Nothing that I can recall. You should understand, these four people were clearly friends. They hovered close together, and spoke mainly to each other, as friends do. Does that help?"

"I don't know. Maybe."

Next they entered a long, narrow, cylindrical tunnel lined with small doors. Notbohm said, "This is the forward cargo hold. These hatches open up into sixteen different airtight compartments, all of which have much larger hatches on the ship's exterior. Everything is accessible from outside and in, and each compartment is capable of serving as an airlock in emergencies."

"What kind of emergencies?" Raimy asked, thinking of submarine escape drills and other risky diving ops.

"Well, for example, if the lander comes down in the wrong spot, and a hundred people have to camp out while the rovers shuttle them to Antilympus. Or if there's a survivable crash, or an unforeseen weather event."

"I see." Raimy tried to digest that information as a cop, not an astronaut. "And no emergencies have happened?"

"Not yet."

"So, what kinds of things are stored here?"

Notbohm thumped a fist against one of the doors, which sounded like the lid of a metal ice chest. "At the moment, not very much. A reactor without fuel, a rover without engines. Some inflatable emergency shelters. Spare parts for some of the ship's more critical components."

"Ah." Raimy had seen one of those shelters during his training, but hadn't really understood what it was for.

"Eventually it will hold a year's supply of food, along with each passenger's spacesuit, clothing allotment, and personal effects."

"They don't wear their spacesuits in transit?" Raimy asked, surprised. The passengers, all ninety-two of them, were supposed to be placed in "squirrel hibernation" while still on the Earth's surface, and not revived until they were safely on the surface of Mars. That made logistical sense—basically treating them as cargo, rather than as ninety-two bored, hungry generators of carbon dioxide and poop. But he'd always imagined them buttoned up safely in their suits, protected against sudden decompression.

"They don't," Notbohm agreed. "You'll see."

The next chamber was taller and wider than the ones

before it, and very clearly a work in progress. The white walls, though covered in brackets and pipes and bundles of brightly colored cable, held only a single rectangular box, its longest axis projecting out into the room like a coffin. Three technicians hovered around the box, barely looking up as Raimy and Notbohm floated into view. They were all wearing khaki pants, and two of them—both female—wore matching jackets, zipped partway up over pale, pastel-blue T-shirts. The third technician—male— wore the T-shirt without the jacket.

These were Antilympus uniforms. Raimy's was clean and new-looking, but on these three technicians the garments were streaked with ground-in dust and lubricants, and had a faded, many-times-laundered look about them. Like they'd been lived in, and worked in, for months. With another quiver of jealousy Raimy realized these were probably three of the lead candidates for the four Engineering slots. Already here on the job, cementing and locking their lead. Who could touch them, when they were already here? By implication, Raimy's own losing position was probably locked in as well. He didn't have the resources to buy his way in, or the skills or the charm to convince other people to buy it for him. And yet, he did know that some of the leaderboard positions— maybe even engineering positions—were held by men and women of modest means. It wasn't out of the question for them to reach Mars. Just, perhaps, out of the question for Raimy himself.

"Hibernation pod," Notbohm said, pointing at the box. "Obviously there will be a lot more of these in the future. This one is the prototype. Second-generation prototype, actually. When the techs are happy with it, they'll turn it over to the medical team, and when *they* are happy, Dan and Miyuki will begin ordering the components for the other ninety-one."

"Miyuki?"

"Dan's assistant. That's her," he said, pointing to one of the women, who looked up and smiled briefly, before returning to the conversation she was having.

"That's very hands-on," Raimy observed, surprised that a trillionaire, or even a trillionaire's assistant, would be involved in that kind of day-to-day minutia.

"Indeed," Notbohm agreed. Then to Miyuki he said, "Do you mind if I open it for him?"

"No, go ahead," Miyuki said, looking up again. She seemed to notice Raimy for the first time. "Oh, you're that detective. Ranier Vaught?"

"Raimy."

She pushed off gently from the hibernation pod, drifting toward Raimy and Notbohm. "Sorry, we get so many people coming through here. I'm Miyuki Ishibashi. Very pleased to meet you. I'm glad you were able to drop what you were doing and go all the way to the Moon for us."

"It seemed important," Raimy said.

"Yes. That poor man."

She reached out to grasp Raimy's hand, which had the secondary effect of arresting her motion.

"Did you know him?" Raimy asked.

"Only from his video feeds," she said. "I didn't know any of them—the ones on the Moon right now, I only met them very briefly. But I admire what they were trying to do. It's not the easiest journey, and that monastery can't be a very comfortable place to stay."

"Have you ever been to the Moon?"

"Me? No."

"You sound disapproving," Raimy said.

She responded with an impatient half-smile. "Of the Moon? Perhaps. I don't think it's any secret I'm a Mars chauvinist. It's a better place, isn't it, for some lucky few of us to finish out our lives. Maybe you. Maybe me. Maybe Geary, here."

Probably you, Raimy thought. *Almost definitely*.

"Indeed," Notbohm said again. Then he pointed at the cubicle, which on its long sides was bare metal covered in tubes and wires, and on its short end was transparent, with a shiny brass handle. "These pods will be shipped up from Earth in groups of eight, each with a sleeping passenger inside, and locked into their places along the wall. Once the ship is landed and docked at Antilympus, the medical team will open the drawer..."

The two engineers got out of Notbohm's way, deferentially it seemed, and hovered back along the wall where the hibernation pod was attached.

"Thank you," he said to them, a bit absently, then pulled on the brass handle, which not only folded down the transparent door, but also rolled out a metal tray, like you'd see in a morgue. "...Which provides access to the body. The, uh, patient, or colonist. Any in-flight medical anomalies can be treated right here as they happen, but most people will remain in their pods until after landing. Revived a few at a time and sent to their apartments in the township, to begin their new lives. You see? A very convenient way to travel, for those lucky enough. And yes, the cubicle is airtight, and locks automatically in an emergency condition. So it's all quite safe."

"Wow," Raimy said. At the time he'd signed up for the program, these details were still TBD—to be determined. Now it seemed like things were falling together quickly. More quickly than necessary, if the flight itself was still three years away.

As if reading his thoughts, Miyuki Ishibashi said, "Our goal is to have the ship and crew all flight-ready at least twelve months before the Hohmann transfer window opens."

Then, at Raimy's blank look, she added, "When Mars is aligned for a minimum-energy transit."

"Ah." Raimy knew it was a nine-month flight, and knew it was only possible every twenty-six months. Now he knew there was a special name for it. Probably a good word for him to know, although he'd just gone on video record showing his ignorance of it.

Pointing at the hibernation pod, he asked the two of them, "What did Etsub think of this thing? He was going to climb inside one and hibernate all the way to Mars. Did he share any feelings about that?"

"Excitement," Miyuki said.

"Healthy caution," Notbohm added.

"Yes," Miyuki corrected, "cautious excitement. He figured he was really going, so he wanted to know everything. Not just the equipment; he wanted to know everything that was going to happen between now and launch. He asked a lot of questions about the boost engine's fueling process."

"Like what?"

"Like how it was going, and why it was taking so long."

"And why is it?"

"To push a ship this big with chemical rockets," Notbohm said, "takes a lot of chemical. We receive fuel and oxidizer shipments from Clementine every week, and still it will be another six months before even just the lander is fueled. Twelve months beyond that for the interplanetary booster itself. And that's assuming steady production from Clementine, which is frankly showing signs of labor unrest. You know about the defector?"

"He's one of my chief suspects," Raimy said, although that wasn't strictly true. Raimy had still not come up with a plausible scenario where that made sense.

"Ah, yes. I expect he would be. But surely he's..." Notbohm's voice trailed away for a moment, probably remembering that he, too, was still a suspect. "Well, I've never met the man."

After a pause, he resumed with, "HMI just got its mass driver online, so if their testing continues to go well, we might actually start receiving propellant shipments from Luna as well, possibly in just a month or two. That's quite exciting, and not something we'd anticipated in our mission planning. If it works out, we may be able to pull the fueling schedule in slightly. But that also depends on many factors."

"And if you make that schedule, the ship will just be parked here in orbit, fully fueled, for a whole year?" Raimy asked.

He realized this was actually pretty good video he was taking. He'd been an Antilympus candidate for eighteen months, and had beaten out a horde of competitors to get this far, but it was only the primary and backup candidates who got actual flight training, and even for them most of that training was still in the future. So there was a lot Raimy didn't know. Probably the same was true for his viewers, so asking cop questions might just be good journalism.

"More than fully fueled, in fact," Notbohm said. "There is excess fuel and oxidizer in the tanks—what we call 'margin'—to account for minor leaks and course changes. Specifically, we have ten percent margin in each of the booster's tanks, plus a little bit we call 'residge,' which is what remains trapped in the plumbing after the engines have shut down. That's about one percent of the total. The lander has twenty percent margin and about 0.5 percent residge. Fortunately, landing under the influence of gravity makes it easier to squeeze out those last few drops. But in another sense it will be less than fully fueled; there's something called 'ullage,' which is the dead space above the propellants in the tank. It is very difficult to fill a tank more than about ninety-eight percent full, and in zero gravity it's best to plan for about ninety-five percent. So, the tanks need to be oversized by that amount."

"Interesting," Raimy said, meaning it. But then, more suspiciously, "I thought your background was in hydroponics."

"My background is in plumbing for aerospace applications, including hydroponics."

"Ah."

"The tour stops here, by the way. That hatch"—Notbohm pointed at a round door in the center of the room's far end, which was itself a large circle—"leads to a service tunnel through the center of the fuel tanks, which can be used to access certain components of the landing engine. But it's tight in there, and there is nothing to see. And past that point is an airlock. The interplanetary booster and the aft cargo hold are not accessible without a spacesuit. Etsub Beyene did not go back there, so I assume you also will not. But I will take you if you like."

"It sounds like that would be complicated," Raimy agreed, "and unnecessary. I appreciate the offer, though."

"I'm happy to cooperate," Notbohm said.

Raimy then asked, "What did Anming Shui do on this tour? How did he seem?"

Jealous, perhaps? Murderous, perhaps?

"Just quiet," Notbohm said.

"Yeah," Miyuki agreed, "I didn't really get much of a read on him. Good English, but a really bad accent, and a quiet voice that makes him hard to hear."

"Hmm. And the others?"

"Both women seemed quite distracted," Notbohm said. "Though I couldn't tell you what about."

"I see. Thank you."

After a pause, Miyuki asked, "Have you developed any theories about what happened to Etsub?"

Raimy shrugged. "Too early to say. I'm still retracing his steps and gathering information, which can be a slow process."

"The evidence you need is on the Moon," Notbohm said confidently. "Not here. But speaking of retracing steps, there is something you may want to replicate: when he was here, Etsub Beyene climbed inside that hibernation pod. Are you claustrophobic?"

"I spent three years onboard an attack sub," Raimy told him. And then, when Notbohm looked back at him with incomprehension, Raimy added, "That means no, I'm definitely not."

4.1
18 November
✧

St. Joseph of Cupertino Monastery
South Polar Mineral Territories
Lunar Surface

Father Bertram Meagher
St. Benedict's Monastery
1012 Monastery Rd.
Snowmass, CO, USA
Earth

Dear Bertram,

Per your request, I leave off both the "est" and the "my", leaving only bare salutation to the job of expressing how direly your presence is missed here on the south tip of Lune. Bad enough to hear that skyward transport of our eight additional brothers hath been delayed again— indefinitely this time?—whose absence even now leaves us daily shorthanded and busy as hymenoptera. Bad enough, yes! Do we not need our engineer? Our banker? Our adjunct theosophy professor? Right now we have

Brother Groppel doing the books and Brother Me leading prayers. Engineering is done also by Groppel, and by Purcell, and when they are beggared for answers, they beg Harvest Moon. Which *costs*, Bert. Nothing free here in Heaven, and so I have even pressed our Russkie defector into service for certain technical matters, and yes I know it may be legally and politically unwise, but we had (for example) a leaky cyanogen valve that endangered our ability to produce both foods and medicines—made direr of course by the arrival of said Russkie in place of our overdue cyanogen shipment, leaving us short of the carbon and nitrogen you Earthlings take for granted.

Bad enough, all of that. But you? Really? Ticker trouble is nothing to play around with, so if you're permanently grounded for health reasons, do please then stay on the permanent ground. However, (a) this leaves your prior (me) without an abbot (you), which as a side effect makes this place a mere priory, and not the grand Abbey of our dreams. They say telling God your plans is the surest way to make him laugh, but still, I had hoped the thing I gave my life for might actually be the thing itself. Ah, well. I hope retirement agrees with you.

Also and more importantly, (b) you and I shall never be face to face or shoulder to shoulder again? Seriously? Your traitor heart is breaking my own, and I have never been more in need of your counsel than now. This ghastly Beyene extinction strains the fabric of our community, and I—I??—am supposed to carry others to carry on? I had thought, more than once, that the first death here might come soon enough to shock, for the dangers of this place cannot be overstated or under-feared. But never have I suspected that shuffled mortal coil would be of a student in our care.

We were doing it, Bert! Teaching the future as we build it: the church a central player in the world again, as in bygone times when we nursed the knowledge of a fallen age. It used to mean something, a monastery education, and it was meaning something again. As in that yore they came to us, unbidden and uncajoled, drawn by the advertisement of our mere existence. All are welcome, if they can only find their way! Antilympus may be a beauty contest (indeed, notice how attractive are the leading contenders, each and every!), but whoever wins it will be looking Hereward for example. Mars bearing forever the imprint of our teaching, echoed down through the ages yet to come! And although it's of lesser import, the written history of Mars may well remember us, too. That's the promise of our endeavor, of which Etsub Beyene's death makes flinders and mocks. What shall they now remember? The gasps of a dying man who surely would have been one of their own.

The guilt is unfathomable, more so because it may not be happenstance, but murder. Beware the ides! Oh, God, what have I done? What have I allowed to be done? If this be some error of ours, or mine, then how are we (or I) to find and correct it? How, especially, without your help? Am I to weather this with only your letters for company? Is this really our fate, that a homicide detective should be en route here in your stead? Very well, very well, but there are names in vain I struggle not to say.

In answer to your query, yes, our safety inspections have been twice as thorough as the absurdity they already

were. Every suit and seal, every hatch and bolt. I have
walked around the monastery's exterior with an oxygen
detector, noting the gas flux from every module.
Everything leaks a bit, inevitably, because the sealing
gaskets are made of atoms, and so is the gas that slithers
out between them. But everything appears to be in order;
the flux is low in every spot I've checked. Ditto for solar
radiation leaking in; we can't keep out one hundred
percent, but hopefully enough that it won't be the first
thing that kills us.

It's sweet of you to worry about us but, needless to
repeat, I am twice as worried about you. Your Lunar
dreams are more dashed than ours, and your health in
jeopardy to boot. I would bring you soup and blankets if
I could, but alas I am as remote from you as any two
humans ever were. Be well, please.

Brother Michael Jablonski de la Lune

Brother Michael Jablonski
St. Joseph of Cupertino Monastery
Luna

Michael,

As always, such florid letters, from such a bland fellow
as yourself, never cease to surprise. Of all your flights of
fancy, though, I'm most puzzled by this idea that I'm
stronger than you, and have some fountain of wisdom that
you're somehow lacking. You're a rock, my friend, and I
don't necessarily mean that in a good way. Certainty can
be either a blessing or a curse; for the most part you
channel it well, but if it makes you certain of an outcome

you deserve, and then something different happens, you don't get to fall all to pieces. Things never have worked that way—least of all with you.

I am quite sorry about this misfortune. Still, how much disaster has befallen our monasteries over the millennia? How many have been sacked and torched, their lay workers carried off into slavery? How many were dissolved by legal fiat, with their lands and goods expropriated by greedy governments? Did you think this was the first murder ever committed on monastery grounds? I assure you, it's not. We endure.

I'm sorry you have to go this alone. I really did want to be there, and I tell you I actually imagined my own grave would be the first you dug. But for heaven's sake, Mike, you would've had to be strong then, too. God helps those who help themselves, and he seems to have a particular fondness for the passionate. That man who stood up to Pope David about the mission of the Church? Be him. You have ten men looking to you for guidance, and three living students for whose grief you're the logical spiritual counselor. And this man, Andrei Bykhovski, who came to us for sanctuary—are you going to show him this hand-wringing instead? Mars *will* remember what you teach, and I'll trust you to keep that in mind while you do the things that need doing.

"Retirement" is an ugly word, by the way. It may please you to hear I'm technically still the abbot of Saint Joe for as long as I want to be. You talk about written history a lot, and although it's vain, I do want my name in there, if only as a footnote to the deeds you and the boys are accomplishing firsthand. Also, your worries about me are misplaced. Not only can I fetch my own soup and blankets, I can even admit there's a part of me that's relieved to be staying here on Earth. I miss you, too. I miss all of you, but I'm having fresh-caught trout for supper tonight, on a patio with a gorgeous mountain view. It will be cold, yes, but I've got a hat and scarf, and fresh air to breathe. And if this heart stops beating tomorrow, then I will go to an even finer place, where all good souls will eventually reunite.

> With Love and Kindness,
> Fr. Bertram Meagher, MDiv

1.7
18 November
✛
H.S.F. *Pony Express*
Cislunar Space

RECORDED TRANSCRIPT: RAIMYVAUGHT&
OFFICIAL&INTERVIEW-EDUARDOHALLADAY
(UNEDITED-DRAFT).MP6

VAUGHT: Are we officially underway, now? Can I ask
you some questions?

HALLADAY: We're in coast phase, yes, so I have some
time. Is this about the murder?

VAUGHT: This is an official inquiry, yes. My glasses
are recording. Do you have coffee here, by the way?

HALLADAY: I don't. Sorry. I've got Tang and
Gatorade and beef bouillon, if you want.

VAUGHT: Ah. Not just now, thank you. And for the
record, no one's even ascertained yet, whether a murder
has been committed.

HALLADAY: You kidding me? You Mars people are
bugfuck crazy. I'm surprised it took this long for one of
you to get offed. I was his pilot, too, by the way. He sat
right where you're sitting right now. Full of fucking

enthusiasm. Going to the Moon! To learn even more about plants! Do you want to know what I think about Etsub Beyene?

VAUGHT: Please.

HALLADAY: He was definitely murdered, and not for personal reasons.

VAUGHT: What makes you say that?

HALLADAY: Okay, one: because everybody liked him. I liked him. Guy like that just lights up a room, you know? You ask most people how they're doing, they say fine. Doing fine, thank you. We can all give a better response than that, but we don't, even when we've got all the time in the world. But I asked Etsub that question, and he talked for two minutes about what a great day he was having, and then he asked about me, with what I'd call sincere interest. Mind you, he'd spent all day cooped up in here, with me and three other people, so that great day was all in his head, fabricated from indigenous materials. You see what I'm saying? I don't see anyone hating on that, much less hating enough to kill it.

Two: because the Antilympus Project takes about half its donations in noncash forms. Bonds, shares, options, real estate, boats . . . It costs money to liquidate an asset, so people pledge their assets intact, right? But that means the value can fluctuate. And if you add up the real value of the Antilympus Project, it went up almost six percent the day Etsub died, and stayed there.

VAUGHT: How do you know this?

HALLADAY: I have a lot of time on my hands, and free network access. I read news, study patterns, compile reports. Call it a hobby.

VAUGHT: Huh. Okay. And why does ... why do you think that number went up?

HALLADAY: I don't know. Etsub's death affected the markets in some particular way. I don't understand chaos math, but I do know people profited from his death, and not just the fuckers in line behind him. You think they didn't know that? You think some AI hadn't worked that out in advance?

VAUGHT: Are you saying he was killed by an AI?

HALLADAY: Somebody did the math, is what I'm saying. Somebody profited.

VAUGHT: How about the other passengers on that trip? Were any of them behaving strangely?

HALLADAY: Hard to say. I didn't know them. People tend to be bored and preoccupied on this trip, and the SpaceNet fees are pricey if you're not a Harvest Moon employee. So, it's not like people are glued to their devices. There's a lot of napping, and a lot of looking out the windows.

VAUGHT: Did anyone seem nervous?

HALLADAY: Everyone's nervous in outer space. You're nervous. That's just common sense. But I get what you're asking, and the answer is no. Nobody was twirling their mustache and cackling. I don't know who killed your boy.

VAUGHT: But you're sure someone did.

HALLADAY: Absolutely. Sabotage.

VAUGHT: I see. Could it have happened here?

HALLADAY: Anything's possible, but look around you. There's no privacy. There's a tool kit in that locker over there, but could you get to it without someone noticing? I would say not.

VAUGHT: So what do you think happened?

HALLADAY: I wouldn't know, boss. These moon suits are complicated. Have you talked to General Spacesuit?

VAUGHT: I have.

HALLADAY: Well, it's whatever they say happened. I'm sorry I can't be more help than that.

VAUGHT: On the contrary. Your insight is very helpful.

HALLADAY: Are we through here? I actually do have work to do. You can ask me more questions later if you need to.

VAUGHT: I'll do that. And if you think of anything else . . .

HALLADAY: Right. Will do.

RECORDED TRANSCRIPT: RAIMYVAUGHT& PERSONAL&CALL-SHONDAVAUGHT(UNEDITED-DRAFT).MP6

SHONDAVAUGHT: Raimy, is that you?

RAIMYVAUGHT: Hi, Momma. Yep, it's me. Can you see me?

SHONDAVAUGHT: I can now. Are you floating? Are you in zero gravity?

RAIMYVAUGHT: That's right. I'm on my way to the Moon now. We'll land at Shackleton Base, near the south pole, tomorrow evening.

SHONDAVAUGHT: Well, I guess you finally made it to outer space.

RAIMYVAUGHT: Yeah, I guess I did.

SHONDAVAUGHT: I always told you, you could accomplish anything you put your mind to.

RAIMYVAUGHT: I didn't really accomplish this. It just sort of happened.

SHONDAVAUGHT: Not true. You were the only person in the whole world qualified to do this thing. Does that just happen randomly, to just anyone? People manifest the things they work toward. If you don't make it to Mars on the first trip, it's only because other people are actualizing, too.

RAIMYVAUGHT: All right, Momma.

SHONDAVAUGHT: Oh, don't you patronize me. Don't you even. What does that girlfriend think?

RAIMYVAUGHT: Deb? She moved back to Oregon a while ago. And I don't think she'd've been too excited about anything space-related.

SHONDAVAUGHT: Aw. I thought she understood you.

RAIMYVAUGHT: That was the problem: she did. I loved Mars more than I loved her, and what kind of woman would put up with that? I don't blame her a bit.

SHONDAVAUGHT: Well, I do. It's her loss, baby. Does she think she can do better? I guess she'll find that out.

RAIMYVAUGHT: Look, Momma, you don't want to burn your Drip Feed allowance talking about my love life. Every second of this call is costing you a dollar twenty.

SHONDAVAUGHT: Which I don't understand. I pay my Internet, don't I? I haven't paid to make a phone call in forty years.

RAIMYVAUGHT: We're not on the Internet right now, Momma. The voice packets have to hop through a SpaceNet gateway, which is a totally different network, with a different, um, protocol. The regular Internet can't handle these long distances, speed-of-light delays, relativity and stuff. You should text if you want to get in touch with me. Or turn off your video. Here, I'll turn mine off.

SHONDAVAUGHT: You'll do no such thing. I want to see my boy's face at a time like this. I also want you to show me what you're seeing. Can you wave that rollup around for me?

RAIMYVAUGHT: Fine. Fine. This is the inside of the ship.

SHONDAVAUGHT: Big!

RAIMYVAUGHT: It's built to carry up to eight passengers, plus the pilot. Here he is, by the way.

HALLADAY: Hello.

RAIMYVAUGHT: This is the bow lock, which connects the ship to a docking port on a space station. I entered the ship through this door, when it docked to Transit Point. And this porthole . . . looks forward along our trajectory.

SHONDAVAUGHT: Where's the Moon?

RAIMYVAUGHT: Over here. Can you . . . ? We're pointing at the place the Moon is going to be tomorrow. Where it is right now is . . . Can you see that?

SHONDAVAUGHT: Yes. Yes, I can. My baby, you're really headed there, aren't you?

RAIMYVAUGHT: I really am. And thiiiis . . . is the side lock, which is where we'll exit when we land. It has, well as you can see it has its own porthole, and if you look thiiiis way, you can see part of the Earth.

SHONDAVAUGHT: Amazing. It's so small!

RAIMYVAUGHT: And getting smaller by the hour.

SHONDAVAUGHT: Cover it up for me, with your hand.

RAIMYVAUGHT: What?

SHONDAVAUGHT: Just do it. Indulge me.

RAIMYVAUGHT: Like this?

SHONDAVAUGHT: A little to the . . . yes. Like that. You've got all of history in your hand, Raimy. Everything that ever was.

RAIMYVAUGHT: Nearly everything. There are over a hundred people living in space at the moment.

SHONDAVAUGHT: Don't you lawyer me. I'm trying to make a point.

RAIMYVAUGHT: Sorry.

SHONDAVAUGHT: Now cover up the Moon.

RAIMYVAUGHT: It's too big for that. Momma, I'm really concerned about your budget, here. If you want to keep talking, can you text me? Please?

SHONDAVAUGHT: All right, all right. I love you!

RAIMYVAUGHT: I love you too, Momma. Take care of yourself.

RECORDED TRANSCRIPT: RAIMYVAUGHT& PERSONAL&CALL-TRACYGREENE(UNEDITED-DRAFT).MP6

GREENE: Mr. Vaught? Hi, Tracy Greene, here.

VAUGHT: Hello, Ms. Greene. What can I do for you?

GREENE: I'm just calling to see how you're doing.

VAUGHT: You can tell Mrs. Beseman the investigation is progressing. I've sped my way through about sixty hours of drone and glasses-cam footage, from every Mars candidate who might possibly be a suspect. So far I haven't found anything suspicious, but I'm only about halfway through. The biggest problem I see here is that we haven't got the raw camera data. These are edited feeds, and I wouldn't expect them to preserve much in the way of suspicious activity. I've also got more interview footage to review, but that's even less likely to tell us anything. Obviously, the most important things for me to do are visit the crime scene, examine the physical evidence, and speak to the prime suspects. It's actually very unusual for that not to have happened by now.

GREENE: I'm aware of all that. I meant, how you're doing on a personal level.

VAUGHT: Oh. Really? That surprises me.

GREENE: Does it?

VAUGHT: Well, um. Meaning no offense, but you haven't struck me as the concerned type.

GREENE: Ah. Well, I guess it may look that way sometimes.

VAUGHT: To answer your question, I'm professionally frustrated, that I currently have access to only low-value evidence.

GREENE: I'm not asking you for a report, Raimy. I'm asking how you're doing.

VAUGHT: Okay. Doing fine. Doing fine.... No, scratch that. Scratch that. I'm better than fine, and also worse, I guess. This is a very unstructured, very exciting environment, so I'm having a hard time concentrating on my work. Etsub considered this trip a stepping-stone to Mars, and I'll confess I'm having some thoughts like that myself. And I'm concerned it's distracting me, when he deserves my best work. So I'm trying not to be too excited.

GREENE: Hmm. Sounds like you've got a lot going on. Why . . . If you don't mind my asking, why do you want to go to Mars so badly?

VAUGHT: Ma'am, I would think you, of all people, would understand.

GREENE: Can you speak to me like a normal person? Please? People's motivations are not always obvious, and I'm honestly curious.

VAUGHT: Didn't you ever look up at the sky, and see that red dot? And just think, that place is as real as the place I'm standing right now. A whole world, as old as Earth, with mountains and ice caps and weather and soil. Didn't you ever just want to *be* there? I did. From a very early age. When Beseman announced the Antilympus competition, I thought, why not me? I still think that.

GREENE: Are you a restless person?

VAUGHT: I don't know. Would I need to be? Beseman says I've had a lot of jobs, and he's not wrong about that.

GREENE: Yeah, I wondered about that. Why'd you quit being a lawyer?

VAUGHT: A lot of reasons. A lot, really. I didn't like the courtroom part of it, for one thing. It put me on the spot a lot, and I didn't like that.

GREENE: You're not on the spot as a police officer? Surely you still have to testify in court.

VAUGHT: I do. Yes, I do, but it's not the same. Anyway, if we're speaking like normal people, how are you doing?

GREENE: Frazzled, actually. Tired. I should apologize for the way I've been treating you, but it's likely to keep happening, as a consequence of the job. Mrs. Beseman's schedule is very demanding, and there's only one of me. So if I need information from you . . .

VAUGHT: You need it immediately. I get it. But this isn't a business call, right?

GREENE: No. Is that stupid?

VAUGHT: No, not stupid, but you've caught me off guard. I'm not quite sure what to think.

GREENE: Can you tell me what it's like in outer space?

VAUGHT: Well, it's no joke, I can tell you that. I'm in what I would call a heightened state of alertness, surrounded by vacuum. And as you can see, the ship is very small, even with just two of us onboard. I really can't quite imagine what a full flight must be like. But on this trip I'm seeing a lot more than I would as a popsicle onboard *Concordia*, so if that were my first trip to space, I'd be missing out on a lot. It's very . . . sensory.

GREENE: You're probably not going to Mars, you know.

VAUGHT: I'm aware of that, yes. Neither are you, right? You're not one of the applicants.

GREENE: Nope. I've got a five-day Marriott Stars vacation planned for the day after Carol leaves, but that's all the outer space I'm ever going to need. I've got no interest spending the rest of my life indoors.

VAUGHT: Nah, most people don't.

GREENE: I wish I could, you know, take you out to dinner.

VAUGHT: Um . . . oh. Well. That surprises me. I had the impression you didn't like me. Is that why you're calling?

GREENE. I can't, though. I won't be in Colorado Springs again anytime soon, unless Carol decides to go back for some reason. My time is really not my own. Very little of it, anyway, and it's impossible to socialize. Her friends aren't my friends, and my friends have forgotten my damn name. People like you are my only... This is stupid, isn't it.

VAUGHT: No. It's nice you thought of me.

GREENE: Your pilot is probably sitting right there, listening to every word.

VAUGHT: I've got my pips in right now, so he can't hear you. But every word *I* say, yes.

GREENE: Well, it's not going to happen right away, just so you know. Dinner or anything. I'm just saying. Carol's going to Mars, and you're not.

VAUGHT: I'm not sure I'm following what you're saying here.

GREENE: I'm saying someday. Someday. That's all. You and I will be on the same planet, and I won't be on Carol's leash.

VAUGHT: I see. Well, you've ... given me something to think about.

GREENE: I know you're not free to talk.

VAUGHT: That's true.

GREENE: Oh, jeez. This is embarrassing. I didn't mean to put you on the spot like that. I'm not sure what I'm ...

VAUGHT: It's fine. I appreciate the thought.

GREENE: Wow, this *is* stupid. I just wanted to see you. I wanted to talk when it wasn't on Carol's time. I've been thinking about you. I probably should have said that first. But now I'm starting to feel a bit mortified. I'm glad you're doing okay. I'm going to hang up now.

VAUGHT: You don't have to.

GREENE: I think I do.

VAUGHT: Okay, well . . . thank you for calling?

GREENE: Oh, God.

<DISCONNECT>

<PAUSE>

VAUGHT: Wow.

RECORDED TRANSCRIPT: RAIMYVAUGHT& PERSONAL&INTERVIEW-EDUARDOHALLADAY (UNEDITED-DRAFT).MP6

VAUGHT: Well, I'm on my way to the Moon now, courtesy of this man right here, Eduardo Halladay, a cislunar ferry pilot for Harvest Moon Industries.

HALLADAY: Hi. Pleasure. You're actually the third Antilympus competitor to interview me in the past two months, so I'll make an effort to say something original.

VAUGHT: That means the pressure's on me to *ask* something original. But first, the basics: by the time we reach the Lunar surface, we'll have been in transit for a little over two days. Can you talk a bit about that?

HALLADAY: Sure, yeah. It's what we call a DISTL 50 trajectory, which stands for direct injection, straight to Lunar surface, fifty hours. Basically that means we go straight from Transit Point to Saint Joe, without ever establishing a high Earth orbit or Lunar orbit. It's the fastest fuel-efficient way to make the trip, or the most fuel-efficient fast way if you prefer. For a very brief time, Renz Ventures was shuttling people between TPS and

Lunar orbit, on ion-powered slow ferries that took almost a month. That was technically more mass-efficient, but it relied on tanks of xenon shipped up from Paramaribo, so it was expensive as well as slow. Harvest Moon uses hydrogen and oxygen mined from the Moon itself, so in one sense our chemical propellants are basically free.

VAUGHT: Free if you have a trillion dollars' worth of Lunar infrastructure to extract it.

HALLADAY: Precisely. It's a competitive advantage no one else can match. The irony is, when we leave the Lunar surface, we have to bring enough fuel with us to make it all the way back. Otherwise we'd be refueling at TPS, and paying whatever Orlov Petrochemical cares to charge us. Sir Lawrence is a firm believer that we should make profits for ourselves, and not for Grigory Orlov, but it's wasteful of Lunar water resources, which are not infinite. Vast, but not infinite. That's why the new mass driver is so important; it lets us ship raw materials using only electricity, which is also free.

VAUGHT: If you have the infrastructure, yeah. Fascinating. And how long have you been flying spaceships? When was the last time you were on Earth?

HALLADAY: That's two separate questions, boss. I was actually on Earth about a year ago, for nearly a month, but that was my first time in a while. I'm one of two pilots currently flying this route, and I've been doing it off and on since Shackleton first opened for business five years ago. Does it get old? You bet. Believe me, the thrill of being in space wears off pretty quickly, like thrills do. But I like my job, if that's what you're asking, and I'm making a fuckload of money compared to anything else I could be doing. I have no plans to retire anytime soon.

VAUGHT: Can you say that again without "fuckload"?

HALLADAY: A lot of money.

VAUGHT: Can you say the whole thing again?

HALLADAY: What whole thing? How far back do you want me to go?

VAUGHT: Never mind, I'll just bleep you. Do you have your own quarters at Shackleton?

HALLADAY: And at Transit Point, yes, although I share that one with one of the SLEO pilots. I'm also alone on this ship a lot of the time, when it's hauling cargo instead of people. So this is my quarters, too.

VAUGHT: Does that get lonely?

HALLADAY: Not really. In space you spend a lot of time cheeked up against your fellow man, so it's nice to be on a nearly empty flight for a couple days. Instead of a bus driver, I get to be a long-haul trucker. Remember truck drivers?

VAUGHT: My father was one.

HALLADAY: Really? Mine, too. Took it hard when they went robotic.

VAUGHT: Mine too. It's half the reason I joined the Navy, to get away from all that negative energy.

HALLADAY: I hear you, boss. I hear that very clearly.

VAUGHT: What did you do before this?

HALLADAY: I was the pilot for Sir Lawrence's personal jet. I begged him for this job, and he said okay. Fuck, though, he didn't look happy about it. A really good personal pilot is hard to find.

VAUGHT: Can you . . . Never mind. I'll bleep it out.

HALLADAY: I didn't realize you guys ran such clean feeds.

VAUGHT: Not all of us. But I do try to minimize anything that might make a sponsor switch me off.

HALLADAY: Oh. Sorry, I didn't realize.

VAUGHT: How do you pass the time on these trips? Those are nice AR glasses, and I see you a lot of the time, just staring into them. What do you read?

HALLADAY: News, mostly.

VAUGHT: All day?

HALLADAY: Maybe three to four hours a day. There's a lot of content out there, and it makes me feel knowledgeable and connected. People can lose touch up here if they're not careful.

VAUGHT: How much of that news feels personal to you in your life up here?

HALLADAY: Depends. During the blockade of Suriname, everything mattered. I wasn't sure if I was going to get sent home in a hurry, or marooned out here forever, or what.

VAUGHT: And now?

HALLADAY: Now it varies. Even in space, nothing happens in a vacuum, pun intended. Oil prices affect launch costs, which affect how much it costs me to buy fresh fruit. The war? It looks like the Cartels lost, but I don't think anyone believes they'll stay gone, and that affects all kinds of things. And there are always rumors about what's going on up here, but you have to paw through some sketchy sources to get that stuff.

VAUGHT: I met a guy who swears he saw an invisible spaceship.

HALLADAY: More than one.

VAUGHT: More than one spaceship?

HALLADAY: More than one guy. I know two who say they've seen it, and one more who swears too loudly that he hasn't. There's a lot of strange stuff happens up here, and all of it connects back down to Earth in one way or another. The Horsemen talk about breaking free, but even Antilympus is dependent on regular surface traffic. And the governments have people everywhere: Clementine, ESL1, Shackleton... Nobody's independent, and nobody's free.

VAUGHT: So, I mean, for example, what is the news telling you today?

HALLADAY: Well, supposedly somebody discovered antigravity, which could either put us out of a job up here, or make things way better. Except it's bullshit, because that would be hard to suppress, and it'd be big news on more than just *Rumor Mill* and *Zeitgeist*. Given the level of chatter, I think *something* happened, but nobody knows exactly what. Also, the Americans are cutting their emissions ceiling again, which is going to play hell with the economy and maybe cost Tina Tompkins the election. But there's an exemption for launch services operating out of the U.S., so it won't affect Harvest Moon directly.

VAUGHT: Interesting. Given how much free time your job affords, you may be more in touch than the average Earthman.

HALLADAY: I like to think so. Yeah, I like to think that.

VAUGHT: Well, there you have it, dear viewers. A day in the life of a real spaceman.

5.1
19 November

✦

H.S.F. *Concordia*
Moored to Transit Point Station
Low Earth Orbit

"Explain it to me again," Beseman was saying.

"I've explained it to you," Miyuki said wearily, "Several times."

"Refresh my memory. I've got an interview tomorrow, and I can't seem to hold onto the details for very long."

She sighed. They were in the octagonal crew quarters of the Mars ship, theoretically inspecting the functioning of all the recently rewired switches and touch screens. But in fact, they were at the end of a long day, and basically just hanging out in their respective quarters, with the fanfold doors open so they could see each other and talk. In zero gee it didn't matter that the beds were padded, rather than simply flat polymer slabs, but it seemed like a luxury just the same, and Miyuki was tempted to crawl into her sleeping bag and call it a night. But as always, there was more to do.

Beseman, in the berth opposite Miyuki's, was doing

zero-gravity push-ups—something he did to "get his blood moving." As physical exercise it wasn't worth much, but when he was tired it seemed to help him think.

At issue: she had placed, with his consent, an electromagnet at the L1 position between Mars and the Sun. Not a gigantic electromagnet, just a surplus one from an unneeded fusion reactor, with a little ion engine to keep it in place. It wasn't hard to do at all. Its purpose was the same as the tower magnets around a moonbase: to deflect radiation from the solar wind and keep it from striking the planet's surface. In theory, the people of Antilympus would be partially protected from solar radiation even when they were away from the township. Even when they were on mountaintops far above the top of the sensible atmosphere! In theory, the atmosphere would be protected, too; that one little electromagnet could slow the rate at which solar protons knocked Martian gas particles off into the eternal void.

"You told me it would take millions of years to change the atmosphere," Beseman said.

"I said it would immediately slow the rate of erosion," she answered. "But it would take millions of years for lithosphere outgassing to make a noticeable pressure difference. That's still true."

"How could it still be true?"

"The surface pressure of the atmosphere hasn't changed. Only the density."

Tiredly, resignedly, she retrieved her rollup from a leg pocket and pulled up her viewgraphs on the subject. She held up the most critical diagram: the Before and After cutaway of the Martian atmosphere.

Beseman waved her away. He'd seen it already, many times, but stubbornly refused to understand it. Miyuki had seen this behavior from him before, but it never failed to surprise and disappoint. Though self-taught, Beseman knew an awful lot about space science, and about the particle entanglement that ran his quantum computing servers, and about hundreds of other things besides. But he was no physicist, or even really an engineer, and his brain could sometimes just run up against a barrier of incuriosity and proceed no further. At times this had actually served him well, because he never believed people when they said something was impossible, and he had pushed some amazing developments because of it. But at other times it was simply a liability, and he knew it.

Miyuki was, in theory, Beseman's personal assistant, little more than a secretary. But his global marketplace company, Enterprise City, was too vast and complex for one person to run, and his side hustle—the Antilympus Project—was deeply technical in every possible way. And Miyuki *was* a physicist, and an experienced manager of large projects, so in practice, she actually had more power and access and public exposure than the company's vice presidents. And more chance of actually going to Mars, which was why she'd taken the job.

"The size of the atmosphere has shrunk," she said, pointing again to the diagram on her rollup. "We're not sure why, but it has something to do with reduced excitation of atoms in the thermosphere. That's here, between the stratosphere and the exosphere."

"Mmph," he said, grumpily continuing his push-ups.

"It's difficult to tell without a probe drop, but it doesn't appear the exosphere itself is affected."

"But the lower layers are," he said. "Right down to the ground."

"Yes."

The effect had unfolded over a period of months, and had nearly stabilized by the time anyone noticed, nine weeks ago. Now, they were all scrambling to measure and explain. The United Nations was up in arms about it, although Miyuki wasn't sure who they thought had been harmed, or why it was any of their business.

"The air density is higher," Beseman said.

"Right. Because you have the same number of gas molecules in a smaller volume."

"It's a *lot* higher."

"Shockingly so," she agreed. "Twenty-eight percent, as measured by the weather station at Antilympus. That's twenty-eight percent of fuck-all, but still a surprising result."

"And we did that. *You* did that."

"The press thinks you did it," she said, without envy. "So does the UN Security Council."

"I'll tell *Mars Today* it was your project."

"There were dozens of people involved," she said. "The magsat wasn't my idea, and literally no one anticipated this result."

"You made it happen," he said.

And that much was true. He hadn't really cared one way or the other, but with one hundred percent surplus equipment, the cost was so absurdly low that he'd had no reason to object. So she went ahead and did it.

"You sound tired," he added.

"I am," she agreed.

She and Beseman were more than work friends. Sharing close quarters for months at a time, they were as emotionally and logistically entangled as any two harried business partners ever were. If things went well for Miyuki then they might end up on Mars together, too. Fellow administrators of Antilympus Township, coworkers forevermore.

But she never forgot that he held the power to terminate her employment on a moment's notice. He'd done it before; there'd been two assistants before Miyuki—both terminated in exactly that way. They'd been given generous severance packages and such, but when the rug was pulled out from under you like that, a bit of money didn't really address the injury. Beseman could be that way: a charging bull, given to snap decisions. Not cruel, certainly, but sometimes heedless of the impact he had on people's lives. Miyuki was far more qualified than either Linda Calhoun or Bob Fun had ever been, and she liked to think she had more "grit" as well. She was certainly a lot better at navigating Beseman's moods. And yet, he could still fire her! He could!

This theoretically wouldn't affect her standing in the Antilympus Project, because (again, theoretically) Beseman did not play favorites. However, she'd be out of his inner circle, and back on Earth with everyone else, and she knew damn well the magic aura that surrounded her would quickly dissipate, and her sponsors would drift away to other candidates. She had negotiated a golden-parachute deal in case that ever did happen, but again, could money address such an incalculable harm? She wanted Mars! She had always wanted Mars! Losing her berth on *Concordia* and at Antilympus was simply not an acceptable risk. So obviously she did not want to find out what would happen if Beseman lost faith in her, and so she made sure not to let that happen. This did not stop them from being friends, though, and good ones.

"I'm married," Beseman would say, with grave annoyance, whenever some nosy blogger asked leering questions about their special relationship. "*Doctor* Miyuki Ishibashi is a colleague."

It was the smart thing to say, for any number of reasons, but it also underscored the fact that he really did seem to love Carol quite a bit, and to miss her when they were apart. Which was often. That was an asymmetric relationship of a different sort; he'd married Carol while they were both still in college, before all the money happened. She owned half of everything—literally everything—and so if she ever got unhappy enough to divorce him, she had the power to bring down his whole empire, and to mothball the Antilympus Project forever. But he seemed to enjoy keeping her happy, and also keeping her as close as circumstances permitted.

He'd brought her up to the ship twice already—and himself down to the surface multiple times, at exorbitant cost each time—just so they could be together. Miyuki respected that, even if it meant she had to move back into Transit Point Station for a few days to give the two of them some privacy. In fact, Carol was due here in three days, so Miyuki was going to have to block out some time in her schedule for that.

Beseman continued his push-ups for another several seconds, then finally rested. Finally looked at the diagram Miyuki was holding up.

There were no windows in the crew quarters. That was partly for safety reasons and partly because there was nowhere to put them without stretching the whole thing vertically and thus adding mass to the ship. But it was also nice. The view of Earth rolling by underneath you was always spectacular from the cockpit, but Miyuki truthfully got tired of it sometimes. It was hard to look away from, and yet the ever-changing vistas—blue and green and brown and white and dead-black—took too much attention and mental energy to pay attention to. It also still caused her vertigo sometimes, looking "down" at the planet through the cockpit windows. At the end of a long day it was nice to get away from all of that, and just be.

"Tell me why the pressure isn't different," he said.

She pointed to an equation at the top of the chart: $P = \rho g h$.

"Air pressure depends on three things: density, gravity, and the height of the air column above the point you're measuring. The density went up, and gravity didn't change, but the height of the air column shrank. It's like a teeter-totter: one side goes down, the other goes up, but in a very constrained way. We're not adding gas to the atmosphere, just pulling it in a little closer. It's called isobaric compression."

"But it affects the weather."

"Yes. We're seeing twice as much cloud formation in Hellas Basin, and warmer temperatures."

"Slightly warmer," he said.

"Right. About four degrees. Which doesn't make sense, by the way, because temperature is on the other side of that teeter-totter. It should have increased a lot more, as the volume decreased."

Hellas Basin was a monstrous impact crater in the surface of Mars, and Antilympus was a smaller impact crater near its northern rim. The lowest point on Mars, and the site of a cluster of twenty habitat modules arranged around a central glass dome. Antilympus Township. Current population: zero, unless you counted robots. But that's where, four years from now, a hundred human beings would be living out their dreams.

Even a small planet like Mars was ridiculously immense by human standards, and its atmosphere—a wispy mass of mostly CO_2, bombarded by cosmic rays and churning with weather and suspended mineral fines—was too complex a system for Miyuki, by herself, to model even approximately. Nor did she have the spare manpower right now to set a team on the task. And yet, Mars' surface temperature had barely moved, and the temperature of the upper atmosphere had actually dropped. So where had all that energy gone? Where had it come from in the first place? How had a fifty-kilowatt electromagnet done all this? She could not say with any confidence what was going on in there, and at the moment, neither could anyone else. "Isobaric compression with a proportional increase in convecto-radiative cooling" was all pop-astronomer and Antilympus candidate Tim Long Chang had to say about it. Which was pretty much gibberish, and simply meant he didn't know either, and was a blowhard besides, though a likable one.

Miyuki herself suspected a shift in van der Waals forces between the gas molecules, with consequent deviations from ideal gas behavior, but that was just a guess. Tim Long Chang had disagreed wildly when she posted her suspicions online, and the two of them had had a colorful public argument about it. *Van der Waals forces don't operate in sparse atmospheres*, he insisted, while offering no better explanation himself. One opinion that had cropped up several times in the comments section—simplistic but hard to argue with—was that the cold rock of Mars itself provided such a vast heat sink that the atmosphere *couldn't* heat up.

Anyway, for whatever reason, the atmosphere had nestled in closer to the planet. Not just measurably closer, but really significantly closer. And now all those things—the cosmic rays, the dust storms, the clouds and frost and sublimation—were happening in a smaller volume. Average wind speeds—not only at Antilympus but at every weather station planetwide—were about ten percent lower than they had been, and peak wind speeds were down by almost half. There also seemed to be changes in the surface itself, with the dust fines being less prone to lifting off the surface as the wind blew across them.

It was an immense shift, achieved at negligible cost, and although Miyuki would never say so out loud, she was awestruck to have played any part in it.

"And we can't do this, like, ten times harder than we are?" Beseman asked.

"I don't think so," she said. "As it stands, we're deflecting almost half the charged particles that would've hit the planet. So it's conceivable we could double this effect, but even that's uncertain, because we don't really know what's going on. The dynamics are very complex."

"And it's not the start of some kind of cascade phenomenon that will terraform the planet?"

"No. You're reading too many tabloids."

"Okay, that's what I figured. I like your teeter-totter analogy. It's simple, and I'm going to use it."

"Please do," she said.

He squinted at her chart for several seconds, clearly formulating what he was going to say to the interviewer. "The fact is," he tried, "we've taken the most Earthlike planet in the solar system, and made it a little bit more so. The first step in terraforming, and all the more interesting because that's not what we set out to do. If we start really thinking about it, what other quick fixes can we come up with? We don't really know, but already the conditions at Antilympus are approaching what you'd see at, say, 1.5 times the height of Mount Everest here on Earth."

"Don't say that last part," she advised. "That's not really true."

"Okay, what's the actual number?"

"Depends how you define it," she said.

Beseman didn't like that answer, so he ignored it and said, "Pure oxygen isn't breathable below one hundred thirty millibars."

"That's true," Miyuki said, "but millibars are a unit of pressure. We're talking about density." Also, Mars had almost no free oxygen, and even at Antilympus the air pressure was a tenth that much.

"Way ahead of you," Beseman said. Having halted his push-ups and let go of his berth, he was now drifting out of it, and very slowly downward toward the "floor" of the crew quarters. Or upward, away from the Earth. "But if we the increase the density, then there'd be more air molecules to breathe. Regardless of pressure."

"It doesn't work that way," she said. "Unless you're willing to breathe a gas that . . ." She trailed off, thinking about van der Waals forces again. If the gas molecules were stickier, that would drive up the density and drive down the pressure. Or drive up the density while holding the temperature and pressure constant. "Hmm."

"See?" he said. "We've reduced the effective elevation of Antilympus, by quite a bit."

"I don't know," she said, cautiously. "I don't think we should be framing it that way. Isn't the truth dramatic enough?"

"I don't know," he said. "What's the truth?"

"I don't know," she admitted.

"Exactly. I'm going to say 1.5, and nobody can honestly tell me that's wrong."

Miyuki paused a moment, and then said, "Fine." The iffyness of his point was not worth fighting about. "On a different subject, we've got twelve loads of *Concordia* parts waiting down at Paramaribo, sealed and ready. Do you want to go over the launch schedules?"

"No," he said, suddenly looking as tired as she felt. "I really don't. Have you eaten?"

"Not for a while," she said. "But I think I'm too tired."

The two of them had long ago lost track of what time zone they were supposed to be in, and simply ate and slept when their bodies demanded it. It was easy for people to say that "an army of workers" were responsible for all of

Beseman's miracles. This was true, of course, both literally and figuratively. But it was also true, and usually overlooked, that nobody worked harder than Beseman himself, with Miyuki coming in a close second. They worked hundred-hour weeks together, each doing the work of five or ten normal employees, for the simple reason that if they didn't, the company and the Antilympus Project would fall apart, and nobody would be colonizing Mars in their lifetimes. Let the UN suck on that.

"You look done," he agreed. "You should get some sleep."

"You too," she advised.

"I will, soon. But first I'm going down to TPS for a meal and maybe a round of *Call of Valor*."

But instead, Beseman's phone rang. He cast a surprised glance at Miyuki, because this happened maybe once every ten days. First of all, anyone who worked directly under Beseman knew not to try and get ahold of him that way. Instead, they would update the appropriate shared documents, which Beseman checked obsessively. If a call were really necessary, he would spot it in the documents and typically get back to that person within a few hours. Ergo, anyone trying to call him either wasn't a direct report, or else had a genuine emergency on their hands. For the nonemergencies, Beseman had two layers of round-the-clock secretarial buffer that would shuttle any concern to an appropriate underling, and when all else failed, the call would normally go to Miyuki. If the receptionists passed the call directly to him, that meant it was *really* important.

The tan Antilympus uniforms had excellent leg pockets, and Beseman withdrew his phone from one of these and pressed a button. The thing was fifty percent faux-antique (a fourth-generation smartphone design from the early thirties that "did everything a phone should ever need to, thank you very much") and fifty percent bleeding-edge (a rubberized intercept case with a built-in "unbreakable or we're all dead anyway" quantum-encryption firewall). Holding it to his ear, he said, "Beseman. What do you need?"

He paused. Miyuki could hear a male voice on the other end of the line, vaguely distorted in that tinny SpaceNet way that said the signal was highly compressed, and coming from a long way off.

"Seriously?" Beseman said. Then, to Miyuki: "It's Igbal Renz."

That surprised her. Other than his official communications with the United Nations, Renz hadn't been heard from by anyone, in months. The most reclusive of the Horsemen, he was holed up tight at ESL1 Shade Station, 1.5 million kilometers sunward of the Earth, on the very outer boundary of cislunar space. If rumors were to be believed, he had even refused calls from the Nobel Prize committee!

Apparently it surprised Beseman as well, because the next thing he said was, "We haven't spoken in, what, five years? You've got . . ."

But then the disdain on his face drained away, replaced with keen interest and mild alarm.

"You *what*? Uh huh. Uh huh. Oh, I see. Well . . ."

He looked across the crew chamber at Miyuki, and

said, "I'm going to take this one in private. Can you stay out of the cockpit for twenty minutes?"

Too tired to even really wonder what was going on, Miyuki said, "No problem."

He left, and closed the hatch behind him, and Miyuki unstowed her sleeping bag, slithered into it, and was gone, gone, gone.

1.8
21 November
✦
H.S.F. *Pony Express*
Cislunar Space

The Lunar approach and landing were somewhat frightening to Raimy, despite Halladay's repeated assurance that it was going "nominally," and was in any case painfully routine. The EOLS capsule ("Earth Orbit to Lunar Surface" or "eeyoll," if you really wanted to abbreviate) was, for fuck's sake, pointed nose-down toward the surface of the Moon, which seemed to rush by faster and faster with each passing minute. Raimy wasn't clear on why the capsule was moving sideways over the terrain rather than simply diving down toward it, but he supposed they were still technically in orbit—just an orbit that would soon intersect the ground.

"You'd better get your helmet on," Halladay said, retrieving his own from the rack underneath his seat and latching it in place over the suit's aluminum neck collar.

Raimy didn't like the sound of that, but he did as he was told, fumbling for his own helmet, and managed to put it on and latch it into place without losing it to weightlessness. It was annoying; he was in excellent physical shape, and he could do the CSPD combat handgun course in his sleep, with a near-perfect score. And yet, his space reflexes needed a lot of work. At least he'd stopped barfing.

Halladay's suit was the same bulky GS Heavy Rebreather design as Raimy's, in the same eyeball-searing orange color. Against the whites and blacks and chromes of the spaceship interior, it looked like serious business indeed. Safer than *not* wearing one, but it also underscored the very real danger they were in.

Raimy told himself: *This is nothing. You once swam three hundred vertical meters from the escape lock of a submarine, wearing nothing but a dive skin and a goo suit.* But he was in control, then. Not a passenger.

"Your boy Andrei Bykhovski, the defector, had a much rougher time of it," Halladay said, looking at Raimy's discomfort with obvious amusement.

"My boy?" Raimy asked, catching perhaps a whiff of racism there.

"Your suspect. Whatever you want to call him. Now *that's* a ride I wouldn't want to take, strapped to that fucking gas lander, oh my God. I wonder what the hell he was running from. Or who."

"He's not high on the suspect list," Raimy said, then silently kicked himself for revealing it to someone who, after all, had interacted with the victim himself. The victim *and* his spacesuit. In front of three witnesses, in a tiny ship with zero privacy, but still. There were *so many* people who could have had a hand in Etsub Beyene's death. People with opportunity and perhaps even means, but no clear motive that Raimy could see. Not yet. But that's how some investigations were. And yeah, sometimes the obvious motives pointed to the wrong people, and you eventually caught the actual perp without ever figuring out why he did it. Maybe Beyene said something that Halladay didn't like, or that somebody didn't. Maybe Antilympus had nothing to do with it.

Still, it was hard to keep his mind on such things, with the God Damn Moon scrolling by above his head. "Are you going to point us right side up anytime soon?" he asked, more nervously than he would have liked.

But Halladay was already doing it, and then, as the ship rotated around to its new orientation, Raimy could no longer see the ground. And that turned out to be actually a little worse, because it let him fear the thing he couldn't see. His startle reflex was triggered every time the main engine fired, which was often. The acceleration of it (or deceleration, he supposed) pressed him into his seat like the hand of God.

And yet it was also better, because at one point after the engine cut out for the fourth or fifth time, the sense of acceleration continued, and the ship felt oddly quiet, with only the hum of fans and the faint *tick-tick* of cooling metal, somewhere behind one of the padded wall panels.

Halladay's running commentary with Shackleton ground control changed character as well. Instead of "Sierra Lima two-five on approach," or "Sierra Lima two-five requesting ground clearance," he said, "Sierra Lima two-five reporting zero velocity, zero power."

And instead of something like "Roger two-five. Sierra

Lima Ground reporting clear dropway surface," the (female, and very British) voice of Ground was saying, "Copy you down, two-five. Welcome back."

"Did we land?" Raimy asked, hardly believing it.

"Gentle as a kiss," Halladay confirmed. Then: "Ground, do you have escort for my passenger?"

To which Ground replied, "Confirmed: two students en route from Saint Joe. They should be here by the time you've cycled your locks."

"Roger that. Depressurizing the module now." Then, to Raimy, "God's sakes, man, look out the window. You're on the Moon!"

But Raimy couldn't see the ground, even when he craned his neck inside the massive spacesuit helmet. "Can I unlatch my safety harness?"

"Sure," Halladay said, still flipping switches and reading indicators. Apparently, setting down softly on the Lunar surface and turning off the motor didn't mean he was done piloting.

Raimy was startled by a sort of grinding, gurgling noise, which he had just enough astronautics experience to recognize as the sound of a vacuum pump, yanking the air out of the EOLS and stuffing it back into a storage tank. He could feel the spacesuit stiffening and ballooning around him, and for a moment he felt the same sense of panic he always did as a diver, when the water closed over his head and he had to force himself to take that first critical breath from his regulator. But now, as then, the feeling lasted only a moment, and then he was in familiar territory, breathing normally as the needle of the "external pressure" gauge inside his helmet crept slowly down.

Halladay had told him the cycle would take fifteen minutes to complete, although it could be done much faster in emergencies. But Raimy could see this was one of those asymptotic, diminishing-returns situations, as the pressure dropped by fully fifty percent in the first half minute, and only then started to slow down.

The arm of his suit felt stiff now, like a partially inflated motorcycle tire, but its cunningly designed joints slid and pivoted and rotated so smoothly that he had no trouble moving his hand to the release button at the center of his five-point harness. The glove of the suit was similarly complex; he could feel the pressure inside it pushing his hand out flat, splaying and straightening the fingers, but he could also feel the joint pneumatics pushing in the other direction, so that he easily balled his fingers, with only the pointer extended, and released the harness. It was, in a way, like wearing an articulated steel glove, or controlling a spider robot with one of those thingies that fit over your fingers. He had to give credit to General Spacesuit, because as strange as it was to move in this suit, it wasn't *that* strange. He felt like he knew exactly how to do it.

Throwing off his harness was interesting, because he wasn't in zero gravity anymore, but neither was he back on Earth. No, he was at 0.165 gee, where things behaved almost exactly as though they were underwater. Standing up in his suit was like trying to stand on the bottom of a swimming pool with his scuba gear on and his buoyancy compensator deflated. Totally doable, and not really that alien a sensation.

He took his first step cautiously, and his second with

greater confidence, and then he was at the window, looking out at the flat, gray surface of the Moon and, fifty meters off, a portion of a habitat module casting very long shadows down onto the soil.

"You'll get a better view from the other side," Halladay told him.

"I feel like the Michelin Man," Raimy observed.

"Yeah, these suits are balloony in vacuum. Keep you safe from the harsh outdoors, though. It's very hot in the sun, which never sets here. It's also very cold in the shade, and as you'll see, there's shade everywhere. Without the suit's circulation system, the shadow of a tiny hill could freeze you to death."

"Yeah, the guy at GS told me the suit was full of water."

"That's right, and a little propylene glycol to keep it from freezing. Your drink tube is hooked up to the same system."

Raimy hadn't tried his drink tube yet, but he did so now. It had a beefier version of the "bite valve" you saw on wearable canteens, and the water that came out of it was warm—skin temperature, maybe—and it felt very slightly syrupy against his tongue, and tasted very faintly of salt, or unsweetened Gatorade. It tasted just fine.

The view from the window on the EOLS' other side was indeed better: he could see more of the moonbase— several different modules, an antenna tower, and some spindly-tall solar panels that absolutely could not have stood up like that on Earth.

"It's bigger than I expected," he said.

"Shackleton? Yeah, it sprawls a bit. It's an advertisement."

"For Lunar settlement?"

"Yup. It has to include at least one of every different module type, plus a lot of interior space. It's a lot less crowded inside than Transit Point, I'll tell you that."

Raimy had seen the place many times on video, but he realized now it was one of those things like the White House or the Grand Canyon, where photographs simply couldn't convey the scale of the thing. Any frame wide enough to admit the whole complex would also inherently shrink it.

"I wish we were going in there," he said. "I'd like to see it."

"You will on your way out," Halladay said. "It's on my itinerary."

"Oh, are you my return pilot as well?"

Halladay nodded inside his helmet. "Yup, you and the three students. Their stint is nearly up, so they'll all be heading back to Earth when you're done with them. Etsub's body is coming, too."

Raimy tried not to react to that. Tried and mostly succeeded, but Jesus, whose idea was that? Putting him in a small ship with his three main suspects, plus the victim? He supposed it wasn't that different than sharing the monastery with them, which was also a bad idea, but kind of inherently unavoidable. Of course, on the other hand, a trip from the Moon back to Transit Point Station cost tens of millions of dollars, and the reentry trip from there back to Paramaribo was only slightly cheaper. Raimy couldn't expect an endless supply of empty spaceships rolled out for him alone.

"Huh. Okay. Well."

"Be awkward if one of them was guilty, huh? You going to put handcuffs over a spacesuit?"

Annoyed now, Raimy said, "I really can't discuss it, Captain."

But it would be awkward, yes. Raimy's personal effects included not only his CSPD badge (which of course meant nothing out here) and handcuffs, but also a selection of different sizes of zip tie, in case he needed to get creative. Notably absent was his service revolver, as Harvest Moon, the Antilympus Project, Transit Point Station and the Catholic Church had unanimously decreed that there would be no deadly weapons involved in this venture. Everyone seemed to be presuming that the suspect, if caught, would simply cooperate. And a great many murderers did, yes. But others tried to run, a few tried to fight, and a worrying number went out of their way to get shot by the police rather than apprehended intact.

Raimy wished those people knew that the shot that dropped them had only about a twenty percent chance of actually killing them, and they would simply wind up handcuffed to a hospital bed. Still caught, still guilty, and with injuries that might never fully heal. Modern police training discouraged the old "double tap to the center of mass," and a standard-issue service revolver these days was loaded with low-grain .38 rubber-coat ammunition. Deadlier stuff could be droned in with a few minutes' lead time, if the cops were facing a particularly tough customer, but Raimy had never done that. In fact, like most American police, Raimy had never actually fired a shot in the course of his duty. And if he ever did, he'd be aiming for the buttocks or the solar plexus, not the heart.

"How's the suit feeling?" Halladay asked, after a few minutes of quiet. Not with any real concern—just making conversation.

"Fine," Raimy said, still looking out at the moonbase, and the gray Lunar landscape around it. "It's actually... It's somehow stiffer *and* more flexible than I was expecting. Like the stiffness doesn't matter. I thought it would feel like the inside of a tire, but it's more like having a whole stack of tires around your arm."

"That's a good way to describe it," Halladay agreed. "And believe me, these third-gen suits are a big improvement over what we used to have."

"Well, lucky me."

Another period of silence. Raimy did not get tired of looking out that window. He was a real astronaut, now, and he was going to get the most out of that.

He saw the helmets first, rising above the crest of a low hill, and by the time he figured out what he was looking at, the arms and torsos had appeared as well.

"I see two people out there," he reported.

There were no heat shimmers, no atmospheric haze, so the scene looked vaguely fake somehow as the two figures cleared the hill, their orange spacesuits brightly lit on one side and brightly shadowed on the other. Here at the Moon's south pole, the sun was permanently just above the horizon.

"That will be your escort," Halladay said. "Let's switch your radio over to the Saint Joe channel."

The control was a little knob on Raimy's left forearm, and had four positions: HMI, PRIVATE, GENERAL, and EMERGENCY. It was currently set to HMI.

"Private?"

"Yes. Or general, but then all this chatter will be cluttering up both channels. Private is for the monastery and observatory. HMI is for Harvest Moon business only, which we're arguably no longer doing."

"How is Emergency different from General?"

"Higher power, and duplex override. It'll wake up radios that are turned off, and it will suppress any chatter that might interfere with your signal. Look, don't worry about it. These all go out over the same frequency—it's just ones and zeroes on the network."

Halladay turned the knob on his own suit, and went silent.

Raimy did likewise, and immediately heard a female voice on the channel, saying, "... positive visual contact. Eduardo, is that you?"

"Affirmative, Katla," said Halladay's voice. "Sierra Lima two-five is currently depressurizing. You are safe to approach."

"Roger that."

"Who's that with you?" Halladay asked.

"Tobin."

"Roger that. Hello, Katla and Tobin. I have a passenger for you."

"Roger that."

"You need a call sign," Halladay said to Raimy. "Preferably two to three syllables, so it's easy to understand. Most people use their first or last name, but I would not recommend using 'Vaught.' Too easy to get lost in the noise."

"Raimy is fine."

"Roger that. Katla, Tobin, this is Raimy."

"Tobin here," said a second female voice. "Hello. Welcome to Luna."

"Thanks," Raimy said.

"Hi. Katla here. We're standing by. Estimated time to hatch open?"

"Four minutes."

"Oh, bother," said Katla. "Why didn't you depressurize on the way down?"

"I used to," Halladay said to her. "*Mayflower* still does, but you really kind of have to trust your luck for that. If something goes wrong, you've got less time and fewer options for dealing with it. I keep telling her, her precious schedule is not worth someone's life."

"Doesn't a pressurized landing increase the risk of a depressurization injury?"

"Only if we crash really hard. In which case, you know, we've got worse problems. So, you know, shut up. You can wait a couple minutes."

"Roger that," Katla said. "Brother Michael says 'love the airlock,' and I kind of get what he means. There's a lot of waiting around in this business."

"Roger that."

Halladay was silent for a few seconds, then added, in a tone of greater concern, "How are people holding up over there?"

"Oh, about like you'd think," Katla replied. "Tense. Sad. Jumpy. It's a lot to take in, and with Bykhovski hanging around, it's all quite chaotic."

"No one knows what to do with a defector," Halladay agreed.

"Or a dead body," Katla said.

She was obviously Katla Koskinen, the number one candidate for the Female Hydroponics slot at Antilympus. Raimy had seen her on video, of course, and right now he could only see her face through two helmet visors and a triple-paned window. And her voice was somewhat distorted by the radio, but still, she came across as a smooth, confident person. She did not sound tense or sad. Maybe a little bit jumpy. She did, however, sound Northern European. Raimy wasn't confident he could distinguish a Finnish accent—especially one as slight as hers—but her dossier said she was a Finnish citizen who had spent most of her adult years abroad.

"Roger that."

As far as Raimy could tell, his pressure gauge was at dead-nuts zero, but the timer over the side hatch was still gamely counting down. Finally, it also reached zero, and a band of gently glowing red around the hatchway switched to green.

"Depressurization sequence complete," Halladay said. He moved to the hatch and turned its wheel, silently releasing whatever clamps or latches were holding it. The band of light turned white, and the hatch swung outward, revealing a little platform with handrails and ladder rungs leading down to the actual fucking Moon.

"After you, Raimy."

Raimy did not need to be asked twice. He grabbed his now-inflated flight bag, threw it over his shoulder, and got his butt out there. Then he turned to face the ladder and climbed down, carefully but not slowly. The EOLS capsule sat on top of a fuel tank ten meters tall, so the ladder had thirty rungs on it, which Raimy took one by one. Then one small step, just like Armstrong said, and he was on the surface. For real. Mars might be a daydream, but this was not.

"I'm down," he said, stepping away from the ladder to make room for Halladay.

Raimy took in a deep breath of spacesuit air, and slowly exhaled it. He had wanted to be an astronaut ever since he was seven years old, obsessively watching NASA TV while crewed spacecraft docked at the International Space Station, and while those crews horsed around in zero gravity. He'd joined the Navy because it was a lot like joining Starfleet, and he'd become a diver and a submariner because he didn't have pilot reflexes, and that was as close as he figured he'd ever get to being an astronaut. When Dan Beseman had first announced the Antilympus Project, Raimy had gone ahead and signed up, along with a hundred million other people around the world. But he'd actually made it through that brutal first cut that reduced the applicant pool to just fifty thousand. And then like a greased pig he'd slithered effortlessly through the psych evaluation, and the physical testing, and then the second cut. And then he'd gotten some sponsors and actually started climbing in the rankings, all the way to third place, and it seemed like he might actually go the distance. Like he might actually spend the rest of his life under the butterscotch skies of Mars!

But nah. It had always been a crazy dream, and he'd been a fool to let hope get the better of him. Raimy wouldn't make the first expedition, and if National Geographic's Tim Long Chang had anything to say about it, Raimy wouldn't be on the second one, either. And if there ever was a third expedition, Raimy would be in his fifties, and would he really have waited that long to start his life? No. By then, surely, he'd have a new wife and some kids and a riding lawnmower, and anyway some younger, stronger, more charismatic guy would have sidled up and edged into first place. Raimy knew he was good—really good—but on a planetary scale he simply wasn't the best, and never would be.

And yet, here he was, standing on the surface of the Moon.

He turned to look at his escorts whose spacesuit nametags said K. KOSKINEN and B. TOBIN. "Hi."

"Hello," said Tobin, with a little wave. Bridget Tobin. Raimy had seen her on video as well, but through her helmet visor he would not have recognized her. Space had puffed up both her cheeks and her hair, which was held back from her face with a band of broad white elastic. Her accent was unmistakably Irish.

"I've seen you both on video," Raimy said to them. "And on the leaderboards. I'd guess one of you is definitely going to Mars."

What he didn't say—didn't *need* to say—was that they were both murder suspects, so one of them might well be going to prison while the other one went to Mars. Except that like Eduardo Halladay, they didn't really seem have a motive, barring personal grudges he didn't yet know about.

If his investigation didn't pan out here on the Moon, he could follow up with Earthly witnesses to find out more about those relationships. It was another way this whole thing was wrong and backwards, because Etsub Beyene had been dead for nearly a week, and Raimy still knew next to nothing. And it would be at least another week before he set foot on Earth again. He didn't like it. He could almost *feel* the trail going cold. But it occurred to him that he could ask Tracy Greene to hire a few private investigators, to chase down some of those Earth-type questions in his absence. That could work.

"I've seen you, too," said Bridget Tobin.

After a pause, Raimy told her, "Thank you for not saying it."

"Saying what?"

"That I'm *not* going to Mars."

"Oh, you never know. Truly. Unexpected things happen every day."

"Eduardo here. I'm coming down."

"The path below you is clear," said Katla. "We're watching."

Indeed, both women riveted their attention on Halladay as he closed the hatch behind him and clambered down the ladder in his bulky orange suit. It didn't take him long to reach the bottom.

"Safely down," he said.

"Copy that," Katla agreed. "We'll escort you as far as the Shackleton airlock. Do you need us to stand by while you cycle?"

"Affirmative. There are no HMI personnel currently on EVA, so I'm out here alone."

"Roger that. More waiting around."

They followed Halladay toward the nearest module of the moonbase, which included an airlock clearly marked out in black and yellow chevrons. Raimy tried to walk more or less normally, bounding from one foot to the other in the low gravity, but he noticed he was the only one doing that. Eduardo, Katla, and Tobin were all doing a sort of bunny hop. Raimy tried it, and it was in fact easier. It looked rather silly, truth be told, but took less energy and attention to maintain his balance, so he went with it.

Yellow dome lights flashed around the airlock when Halladay opened it up, and extinguished again when he trundled in and closed it behind him.

"I'm in," he said. "Commencing pressurization sequence."

"Raimy, you need to stand back from the door," Katla said. "If it fails during pressurization, it's going to blow off of there like a cannon."

"Ah," Raimy said, hopping out of the way. "Is that an actual safety protocol?"

"Yes."

"And you're strict about that?"

Socially, it was the wrong thing to say, given that Beyene's death might still have been an accident. Beyene was outside alone, which was a definite breach of protocol. And of course Andrei Bykhovski had arrived on Luna in just about the unsafest way possible, which just showed how insensitive Raimy was being. But he was in cop mode now, gathering up information. He wasn't here to make friends.

But Bridget Tobin answered, "There's just not much room for error up here, Detective. Etsub shouldn't have been out there alone. If he'd had an escort, there might have been time to get him to an airlock, or set up an emergency tent, or something."

"No," Katla said. "It wouldn't have made a difference. That air hose was gone. He was dead in sixty seconds. Unconscious after thirty."

"You seem awfully sure," Raimy observed. But he knew what she meant. The same kind of thing was true in diving accidents: once the guy breathed water, he was pretty much dead beyond saving, even if the body took a little while to catch up.

"It's my professional opinion," Katla said.

And then they were quiet for a while, until Tobin finally said, "You know, Raimy, you don't need to hang around here by the airlock with us. Long as you stay within fifty meters, you can hop around and throw rocks and stuff. You're on the fookin' Moon."

"I'm here to do a job," Raimy stated flatly, in his best professional tone.

"Yeah? Well, you're not doing it right now."

Thinking about that, Raimy said, "This might actually be a good time to start my interviews."

On an open channel, he would of course try to stay away from incriminating details. Later on he would question them both privately, to see if their stories matched up; this would be more like the kind of questioning that happened at the actual scene of a crime: What happened? Where were you standing? Superficial stuff, but it provided a framework for more detailed questioning later on.

But Tobin countered, "Aw, don't be an arsehole. Play around for a minute of your life. How angry will you be, someday on your deathbed, thinking all the things you should've done and didn't? Here, I'll even come with you. See? Boing! Boing! Look at me go."

She hopped away, making longer and higher arcs, and then started throwing her hands up and bending her knees, to increase her altitude and hang time. The results were impressive; without seeming to try very hard, and despite the massive spacesuit weighing her down, she got almost a meter off the ground, and spent nearly two seconds in the air. Or in the vacuum, or whatever.

Raimy was extremely reluctant to screw around, when other people were paying hundreds of millions of dollars for him to be here. Also for safety reasons, and because it was undignified, and because Etsub Beyene was dead. But still very tempting, yes.

"You're going to crack your helmet," he told her.

"Am I? Boing! Boing!"

"It would take a lot more than that," Katla observed. Katla, who worried about an airlock door blowing out for no reason.

Tobin stopped jumping and said, "You think people will survive on Mars if they don't have fun? For the rest of their lives? I'm activating my helmet cam. I'm recording you for the Antilympus feeds. Hello, everyone. This is Bridget Tobin, coming to you from outside Shackleton Lunar Industrial Station. And this is Raimy Vaught, an administration candidate from . . . Colorado, is it?"

"Colorado Springs, yes."

"Raimy was just explaining the importance of play in maintaining a healthy work environment, on and off the Earth. Isn't that right?"

There was something infectious about her attitude, and
Raimy would indeed have been tempted to jump around
with her if she hadn't switched on her damned camera.
But she had, so what he said was, "Ms. Tobin, a man is
dead, and I'm here to figure out why. There is certainly a
time and a place for recreation, yes, but this isn't it. Not
for me."

"Oh," said Tobin, her bounce slowing. "You go and play
that card. We loved Etsub, you know. Very close friends,
all of us. I've been crying every day and every night. But
I'll tell you, that man knew how to have a good time. It
doesn't honor him if we mope around."

"I'm not here to honor him," Raimy said, with such
seriousness that he sounded like an asshole even to
himself. And because he'd already blown his chance to
have fun, he went ahead and switched on his own suit
camera and said, "I'm here to investigate the circumstances
of his death, which are quite bizarre. Where were you
when it happened? Turn your camera off, please; this is
an ongoing investigation."

Tobin was silent for ten full seconds, before saying,
"It's like that, is it? All right, I'm sorry. Truly. I've never
known how to act when someone dies. They don't exactly
teach you that in school. Maybe *your* school they do.
Detective school, or, you know." She paused another
moment, and then said, "It was three o'clock in the
morning, sir. I was asleep, and I stayed asleep even when
Bykhovski's emergency call came through. I didn't wake
up until the monks started getting their spacesuits on.
There was a lot of shouting and general chaos. Nobody
knew what was happening. Bykhovski basically appeared

out of nowhere, and he wasn't really making sense. Not to me, not then."

"What happened after that?"

"Giancarlo and Michael went outside. Those are two of the monks. And then they came back in, with Bykhovski and Etsub. We still weren't sure he was dead. Hamblin got Etsub's helmet off and shocked him with the suit defibrillator. Breathed in his mouth and all that. Bykhovski was just standing around. They were both just filthy, all covered in moondust, which is a carcinogen. It was getting everywhere, and all I could say was, what the hell was he doing outside? Bykhovski had his own helmet off by then, and I was asking him. What was he doing outside? Why was he out there in the middle of the night? This bloke just dropped out of the sky, and I'm expecting him to know what's happening. I didn't even ask who he was. It was . . . I've . . . You've never seen such pandemonium. That's when I started crying."

"It was absolute chaos," Katla agreed. "It took us hours to piece together any sort of picture."

"Were you also asleep?" Raimy asked her.

"Yes," she said. "Very. But unlike Bridget, I woke up when the emergency message came through. They did a rapid cycle in and out of the airlock, but even so it took a long time to get Etsub inside. I made tea while we were waiting."

"You made tea?"

"That's what the monks call it. It's actually just ground-up roots and caffeine, but I was pressing mugs of it into people's hands. Here, drink this, drink this. We need everyone alert."

"Was that a smart thing to do?"

She laughed humorlessly. "In retrospect, no. It only added to the chaos. People were spilling it, and setting their mugs down in random places, and needing to urinate."

And then Raimy asked one of his least favorite but most effective witnesses questions: "When did you start crying?"

"Not right away," she answered. "I was trying to get a story out of Bykhovski. Brother Michael and I. When he told us how he got there, Michael's first thought was that he'd landed on Etsub. He kept asking the question different ways. But that didn't make sense to me."

"Why not?"

She paused for a long moment, then cleared her throat and said, "I don't know. It just didn't fit. There was no visible damage to Etsub's suit, for a first thing."

At that point, Halladay broke in, saying, "Eduardo here. Pressurization cycle complete. Thank you for standing by."

"Roger that," said Katla. "Mind if we get on our way?"

"Please do. Nice to see you."

"And you."

To Raimy, Katla said, "Can we hold this questioning for later?"

"Of course."

And Tobin said, "It's four kilometers to the monastery. If we turn off the cameras, will you bounce a little? For the benefit of your future self?"

1.9
21 November
♦

St. Joseph of Cupertino Monastery
South Polar Mineral Territories
Lunar Surface

The walk to "Saint Joe" was interesting but uneventful, and yes, Raimy did do some bouncing, and throw a couple of rocks much farther than he would have thought possible. It was fun. It was also interesting, because they didn't curve or hook or drop the way they would on Earth, but just flew out of his hand in a perfect parabolic arc. And this didn't in any way detract from the (ahem!) gravity of the situation up here, because he was just following along behind his escorts, trying to keep up as his ankles got tired of bunny-hopping along.

He went back to bounding foot-to-foot, and then experimented with a rather ridiculous gait that involved tucking his butt in and sneaking his legs way out in front of him, one after the other, like Jack Skellington in *The Nightmare Before Christmas*. That one worked surprisingly well, so he finished the last third of the hike that way.

They were walking along a dirt road between low hills, in a kind of gray, twilight fairyland of long, deep shadows. Light, dark, light, dark, as if they were walking through one of those old 2D barcodes. The road itself was not too different from the surrounding land, except that it seemed to have been cut into the soil a few centimeters and then crushed flat. A bulldozer and a steamroller, maybe.

"Why is the road necessary?" he asked the two women.

To which Katla answered, "Katla here. Please announce your call sign when beginning a conversation. The road is so we don't get lost. It's actually quite easy to get turned around out here; every time you come out, the sun is hovering over a different spot on the horizon. The shadows move; the land almost seems to change shape."

"Raimy here. Don't you have GPS? Or something like it?"

"Something like it, yes. Triangulation between Shackleton and the monastery used to be rather inaccurate, but now, with the South Lunar Antenna Park just over the horizon, it's good enough that Harvest Moon started handing out little handheld navigation units with, they claim, sub-meter accuracy. But it's one more thing to carry, and we don't need it, just walking back and forth like this. We have the road."

"Ah."

"Tobin here. The road is also for dust management. Fresh moondust is like asbestos, absolutely awful in the lungs, and hard on equipment, too. But if it's been driven over repeatedly, that tends to smooth out the grains. We do the same thing for plant-growth medium, which is mostly Lunar regolith. Before we bring that stuff inside, it gets rolled in a tumbler for eight hours to make it safe to handle. On Mars you have wind forces doing the same thing, but there's no wind here. The grains are extremely sharp. I can show you under the microscope, if you like."

"Sure, maybe," Raimy said noncommittally. Before anything like that, he was going to use that microscope to examine a hose braid for tool marks. And ask every person in that monastery every question he could think of, until he figured out how and why Etsub died.

Nobody had anything to say after that. A few minutes later, the three of them branched off the main road, down a sort of driveway of similar construction, marked by a painted metal sign that read:

ST. JOSEPH OF CUPERTINO
BENEDICTINE COMMUNITY HOUSES
ALL ARE WELCOME.

From there, it was another several hundred meters, up and over and down a slight incline, before the monastery itself came into view. It was much smaller than Shackleton Lunar Industrial Station, but still larger than Raimy expected. It consisted of three house-sized modules and ten or twelve that were the size of shipping containers.

The first surprise—and it did come as a genuine shock to Raimy—was that Etsub Beyene's body was lying right out there beside the airlock, wrapped up in reflective Mylar and black nylon cord. Raimy didn't have to ask what it was, or who. He didn't have to ask why it was there, either, because obviously there were no facilities inside for storing a corpse, and also because the body wouldn't decay out here in hard vacuum. It might conceivably freeze if a shadow moved across it for more than a few hours, and in the slanting sunlight it might mummify a little faster, but none of that should be a problem. One of the monks was a medical doctor and had already performed a detailed postmortem examination, so unless Raimy decided a full autopsy was called for, the body was essentially ready for burial or cremation, or whatever. Leaving it out like this was a sensible, if grisly, solution.

Tobin looked away from it as she passed, but Katla Koskinen did a strange little prayer thing, touching two fingers to the lower part of her helmet's faceplate, and then pointing them at Etsub, as if tapping some invisible surface in the space between them. She muttered something that the noise rejection algorithm didn't quite pass through, but Raimy thought it might have been "ashes."

The second surprise happened inside the airlock module itself. Raimy and Katla and Tobin went inside and shut the door behind them, and then sat on benches along the wall for fifteen minutes of pressurization sequence. No one said very much. Even Tobin seemed to have misplaced her exuberance.

Raimy watched as the hard, green cylinder of his flight bag slowly shriveled into the polymer bag it had been in transit. It was dusty, he saw, and so were all three spacesuits—from heels to knees especially, but really all over. It seemed to be stuck to them by static electricity.

There was a glass-doored emergency locker in here, much like the one in the airlock at Transit Point, and with a similar assortment of emergency supplies. Rope, hammer, duct tape, goo suit, spray foam, tool kit, first aid kit. This last item struck him as the least useful, because how were you supposed to administer first aid to someone in a spacesuit?

"Raimy here. What's the safety protocol inside the airlock?" he asked.

"For you?" Tobin said. "Stay put and don't touch anything."

"What about for you?"

"Same thing, mostly, unless there's a problem. There's another airlock 'round the back of the complex, so if this one fails, that one's the backup. Most things have a backup."

Katla added, "Until Etsub died, there'd never been an emergency here. As you can imagine, it's a tightly run place. Brother Michael holds regular safety drills, but where to begin? There are so many things that can happen."

Raimy thought about that for a long time.

Once the module was pressurized, they stepped through into what Katla called "the gowning lock," where their suits were showered down with jets of soapy water and then jets of clean, and then jets of air to dry them.

Now cleared of visible dust, the women began removing each other's spacesuits, first taking off the helmet and putting it on a shelf with a dozen other helmets, and then unlatching and pulling off the torso or "coat," which was then hung on a rack with a dozen other bulky suit torsos. This reduced the two of them to rather skimpy camisoles— the infamous 3D-printed "space underwear"—about which they did not seem self-conscious in the slightest. Their last names were stitched in above the breasts. Tobin then helped Raimy out of his own helmet and coat, and then all three of them were wriggling out of their pants, revealing thin, tight boxer briefs of dark gray print-weave.

The air in here smelled almost exactly like the inside of a shooting range: a hot mixture of sulfur, brass, sweat, and machine oil. The light came from yellow-white electroluminescent fixtures in the walls and ceiling. The floor was a metal grating over smooth plate steel, cold against Raimy's thin, 3D-printed socks.

The next surprise was that after wriggling out of their spacesuits, Tobin and Katla went right on undressing, pulling off their space underwear and stuffing it in a little chamber by the inner hatch.

Seeing his look, Tobin said, "Oh, be a pervert, why don't ya. Come on, you're covered in moondust. T-shirt off. Briefs off. Socks off. Into the laundry lock, all of it. You can pick them up after evening prayers."

Until that moment, Raimy hadn't thought of Tobin, or Katla, as anything other than astronauts and Antilympus hopefuls, and of course as suspects he needed to rule out in order to close this case.

But okay, yeah, they were also women. Physically fit, beautiful, and entirely naked.

As a gentleman, he wasn't about to gawk or ogle their naked bodies, but there just wasn't a ton of space in here, and once he'd stripped off his own underwear it was nearly impossible to get it into the laundry lock without his gaze sliding once or twice across areas where it didn't belong. And his brain—his male primate brain, raised on a steady diet of sexualized TV programs and occasional Internet porn—couldn't help evaluating what it saw.

Katla Koskinen was the shorter of the two, with the top of her head coming to about the height of Raimy's eyeline. The hair on her head was chestnut brown and cut in a short bob, probably to keep it out of her eyes when she moved around. The rest of her body, though, was hairless and weirdly smooth. Her body was thin and muscled, with something approaching washboard abs, and her small, pink nipples provided little contrast against the skin of her smallish breasts, so that the overall effect was a bit like looking at a plastic action figure. The way she carried herself amidst this mutual nudity was matter-of-fact; she did not appear to give one shit about Raimy's body or Raimy's gaze, or her own imperfections on display.

Bridget Tobin was different: bleach-blonde and curvy, compact but with an outer layer of visible softness. Her pubic hair (which he really did try not to look at!) was light brown and lightly groomed, her nipples red and prominent, her buttocks round and tipped upward by the flare of her hips. A spray of freckles decorated her chest and arms and face, and she seemed to animate her body with a kind of energy that some women just had and others just didn't. Sensual, yeah. She was also unembarrassed at being naked in front of a naked male stranger, but instead of a blank facial expression she wore a faint smirk of amusement. *Well, fellah, here we are.*

The effect on Raimy was immediate and involuntary: half a boner, right there in the gowning area, not a meter and a half from two naked women. Tobin saw it, too, and caught him looking at her, and her smile became a little warmer and a little more embarrassed. Not for herself, but for him. *Sorry about the close quarters.*

"We need to shower again," Katla said flatly. She worked the controls again, and a spray of soapy water rained down on them.

Tobin squawked in amused dismay; the water was chilly, and it had the rapid effect of killing Raimy's boner and making her own nipples stand up sharply at attention. Raimy tried not to see that, tried harder not to log it in his spank bank, and failed on both counts.

"Oh, that cold always gets me," she said. "Brr."

"Scrub your body," Katla instructed, neither amused nor unamused. "Particularly your hair."

To which Tobin said, "I think he knows how to take a shower, love."

"Get on with it," Katla insisted. "You have fifteen seconds."

Soon, the soapy water was replaced with clean, which ran for perhaps another twenty seconds before trickling to a stop.

"That was quick," Raimy observed.

"It's not to remove your oil and stink," Tobin said, now huddling her arms across her breasts. "Just the moondust."

Katla, moving to open the inner hatch, said, "You came in contact with the outside of your spacesuit, which was contaminated. A little bit gets inside the habitat, no matter what we do, but the showers help. We'll find you a handkerchief; you're going to notice some discomfort in all your mucous membranes."

Then she opened the hatch, and stepped through into what looked like a pretty normal dressing room, with two benches running along it and with clothes hooks and rectangular niches along the walls.

"Come on," Katla said.

Raimy thought it gentlemanly to let Tobin go in front of him, then realized it simply afforded him a better look at her buttocks. Which was not helping. The very last thing he wanted to be was forty years old, single, and lecherous.

Ruefully, he followed Tobin through the hatch and then closed it behind him and dogged it shut. The mechanism was similar to what you'd see on a submarine, or on Transit Point Station for that matter, so there was no point making one of the women reach past him to work it.

Katla and Tobin had towels and space underwear waiting for them in the cubbies. They dried and dressed, and then zipped themselves up in mustard-yellow Harvest Moon coveralls and slippers. For Raimy the process was more involved, as his HMI-issued towel and extra set of underwear, along with his Antilympus uniform, were wadded up in his HMI-issued duffel bag, whose zipper appeared to be jammed. After he'd sat down and fussed with it for a full minute, Tobin came over and peered at it, leaning over Raimy's naked body in the process.

"You've got dust in the teeth," she said. "Did you drop this or something?"

"No," Raimy said, but then wondered if, during his bouncing and rock-throwing experiments, he'd let it drag on the ground, or else kicked some loose regolith up onto it.

"Let me get some silicone spray. Wait here."

This last part appeared to be a joke, as the spray was on a high shelf just a few meters away, and where exactly was he going to go? Unable to get his brain off the sexual track, he watched the slow-motion jiggle of her bosom as she craned upward to grab the spray bottle, then finally gave up and jumped for it. There really was something about the way she moved. Or maybe it was pheromones or something, but he felt an unmistakable attraction. For a goddamn murder suspect.

She came back and leaned over Raimy's nakedness again, then blasted three good squirts from the spray bottle onto the zipper of Raimy's bag.

"Try it now," she said.

Impatiently, Katla said, "Will you two hurry up? Bridget, give him your towel or something. I'm going inside."

True to her word, she opened up the innermost hatch of the three-chambered airlock module, slipped through it, and closed it behind her. Leaving a naked Raimy alone with a fully dressed Tobin.

He couldn't help clearing his throat.

"It's all right," Tobin said vaguely.

Raimy and Tobin both put their weight into the zipper, and after a couple of good tugs, they got it moving. After a couple more, they got it all the way open. And Tobin was still leaning over him.

For some reason, he cleared his throat again.

"Well," she said, "I'll leave you to it, then, and see you on the other side."

Dressed in his tan Antilympus uniform, Raimy soon entered the monastery proper, through a great vaulted space that looked like the inside of a church. Tobin was there, along with two men in honest-to-God monk robes, and a third one in yellow HMI coveralls. Another monk was busy at the back of the room, going over surfaces with a feather duster that appeared to be made of actual feathers.

"You good?" Tobin asked.

"Fine, thank you."

She then said, "May I introduce Brother Michael?"

One of the monks reached out for a handshake. He seemed to be about Raimy's age, though it was difficult to tell for sure, as his blond hair was buzz-cut short enough to blur the edges of his graying temples. There was a physical sturdiness about him that made him look more like a cop or a military man than a religious one.

"Hello, Detective. Welcome to Saint Joe."

Brother Michael's rural-Canadian voice might have been a bit jarring, but he spoke softly and mildly.

"Are you in charge here?" Raimy asked.

"I'm the prior, yes. Technically we have an abbot, my boss, but he's still on Earth. Maybe permanently. So, yes." He paused and then said, "You've had a long trip. Do you need to refresh?"

"No," Raimy said. "I mean, later. If you've got a bunk for me, I guess I'd like to drop my bag off, but my ride is scheduled to leave here in five days. I'd like to get right to work if that's all right."

"Better than all right," Brother Michael agreed. "We're all very eager for progress on this matter. And in that humble spirit, may I introduce your two chief suspects?" With a low sweep of his left hand, he indicated the monk standing beside him. "This is Andrei Bykhovski, our defector. And *this*"—he indicated the jumpsuited figure to his right—"is hydroponicist Anming Shui."

"Hi," said both men, their voices amiable enough, although neither one offered to shake hands. And right away Raimy was thrown off his game, because the only one of these men who seemed even remotely dangerous was Michael. And what the hell kind of motive could *he* have?

"I arrive without clothing," Bykhovski was saying. "They give me this robes until they can figure out where I go. But I am liking it here. Life is short and I am not so good with romance, so I am thinking maybe I stay. Take a vow to become Brother Andrei, if they allow it. Or perhaps I go back to Clementine if demands are met."

Raimy had been given a private apartment (or "cell") with surprisingly thick, surprisingly soundproof walls, and he and Bykhovski were seated in chairs. Bykhovski in his monk's habit, Raimy with his glasses on, recording the interview. Bykhovski seemed collegial, helpful, even eager. He'd watched Etsub die, and it seemed to have had a profound effect on him. Between that and his daring escape from Clementine Cislunar Fuel Depot, he had a lot to say.

"What demands are those?"

Bykhovski seemed to weigh the question, as though his life or his future depended on it. He answered carefully, "Orlov Petrochemical is hiring people to work in space, and is paying good . . . *zarplata*. Slarry? Salary? I think this is word. But life is hard in the space habitat. You cannot go for walk. You cannot order pizza, or go to downtown and look at people going by. Is difficult. And Orlov does not tell people until they arrive, that they cannot go home. Orlov guarantees not to charge for transportation back to Earth when employment ends, so people think, hey, this is good deal. But if there is wedding or funeral on Earth, or if you just need shore leave, Orlov will charge you for this. More money than you are making. There is no way to get home unless you quit, and then there is no completion bonus, which is most of pay. And Orlov has been saying now, that quitting must even be approved by management. So people are trapped."

"Indentured servitude?"

Bykhovski shrugged, his face betraying only apology. "I do not know these words, but I think probably you are right. People are working for money they cannot spend, in place they cannot leave. I have made demand for Orlov and Clementine to change this policy. Maybe they will do this, and maybe I will decide to go back there to get my money. Or maybe they kill me for crossing them. We will see. I defected without knowing future, because situation is bad."

Startled and unsettled by that answer, Raimy asked, "Do you seriously think Orlov Petrochemical would have you killed?"

Bykhovski nodded and, without apparent alarm, said, "*Da*, I know is possible. Grigory Orlov is his father's son, yes? Reputation for bad things happening to his enemies. They fall from high places or ingest poison. Cars hit them on corner of street. Bears attack them in the night. Yes, bears! If Orlov is not ordering these deaths, then others do this to try and please him. I make powerful enemy when I come here."

This was all news to Raimy, who had thought Russian gangsters were mostly a thing of the past, and even then mostly imaginary. As far as he knew, Clementine Cislunar Fuel Depot was a small operation, involving a few dozen people at most, but its parent company was a Fortune 500 multinational that delivered fusion power to billions of people. It would never have occurred to Raimy that murder might be a part of their business plan. But yeah, okay, Jesus. Other lawyers and cops were always telling him he wasn't cynical enough, and at times like this he believed them. Bykhovski seemed credible, and honestly afraid, although he hid it well.

Carefully, without leading the witness, Raimy asked, "Do you think that has any bearing on Etsub Beyene's death?"

Bykhovski frowned at that, and seemed to think it over for a bitter moment before answering, "Orlov has long reach, but I think he will not do something to this place of religion. Bad for business, I am thinking. This is why I defect here, to monastery. Not to Harvest Moon, yes? Not to Transit Point especially. I think about going to other Horseman, Igbal Renz at ESL1, but how do I get there? They are not customer of Clementine. So I come here. As for Etsub Beyene, I do not think he is on shit list of Grigory Orlov. What does Grigory care if Black man is going . . . I am sorry, may I say Black man? I do not mean offense."

"You can say whatever you like," Raimy assured him. *You're the suspect. Have at it.*

"Yes, well why does Orlov mind if Black man is going

on Danny Beseman's Mars ship, or in Lawrence Killian's moonbase, or anywhere he likes? Wherever he goes, Etsub is burning fuel that is purchased from Clementine. Etsub is famous, yes? Etsub tells people that traveling in space is good thing. He is free salesman for Grigory Orlov, not somebody who is wanted to die."

"Somebody may have wanted him dead, though," Raimy said. "Why do you think he was outside when you landed?"

Bykhovski looked down at his feet for a moment, and when he looked back up at Raimy, his face was heavy with guilt.

"I am thinking this may be my fault. Before leaving Clementine I am sending secret message to monastery with laser. SOS, and my projected arrival time. Nothing more. I do not know if anyone will hear me, I am just trying things. But maybe Etsub is outside with communication laser, pointing at Clementine for some reason? Or he has left a detector outside? Because he is in communication with someone. He has some . . . side hustle? Is this correct? And someone else has side hustle as well, and so they are talking. Many strange things happen in space these days. Maybe he mistakes me for this person? If he is receiving my message and he is not telling anyone else, then he goes back inside, and he quietly comes back out at the time I say. He does not have information of me. He does not know human being is strapped to cargo lander, in need of rescue. If he thinks this, he would be telling Brother Michael. So he thinks something else is coming on this lander from Clementine. Something he does not want other people to know about."

"Like what?"

"Who can say? Drugs? Thumb drive full of *kompromat*? Panties of female admirer? If it is information, it is something they do not dare to transmit even by laser. If it is physical object, then . . . I do not know. I have nothing but speculation. I do not know why Etsub is out there waiting for this lander, unless he thinks he will take something off of it. Something meant for him. But instead there is only me. And so he is confused when he sees me. Confused when he dies. Very sad, to end his life that way."

"But he was still alive when you landed, and if your story is accurate, he died almost immediately afterward. That's *very* suspicious timing. How do you explain that?"

Bykhovski's guilty expression was tempered now with a kind of consternation, as if Raimy were asking him to explain a rainstorm or a bolt of lightning. "I understand why I am suspect. Yes? I arrive, and Etsub dies. It cannot be coincidence, and so you are thinking I have done something to spacesuit. I would think this also, if I sit where you are sitting. But I am *knowing* I did not do anything. It is very strange, yes. I am spending my nights thinking about how this could happen. I have only theory, no facts. Do you want theory?"

"Please."

"Etsub is on top of hill when I see him, next to solar collection tower. Most of Saint Joe is in shadow of this hill, because sun is behind it. This much I see with my own eyes. I descend into this shadow as I am landing. Etsub has climbed himself up into full sunlight, and I am wondering about thermal shock. I am astronaut; I know spacesuit is designed to withstand this, but somehow Etsub's suit is . . . defective? He sees me land, and maybe he is confused or alarmed by seeing this, and he is wanting to run down hill. So he boosts his oxygen, and because of defect and thermal stress, the hose is breaking. I see him fall, also. I'm thinking he falls because his air is cut off, but maybe he falls first, and this is shaking the hose which is under stress, and *then* hose is breaking. It could be lot of things."

Raimy thought that over, and finally said, "So you don't think he was murdered?"

Bykhovski held up his hands a bit, as if warding off waist-level danger. "Goodness, no. I think General Spacesuit is wanting us to think this, because they do not want to say their suit has failed. Harvest Moon wants us to think this, because otherwise they must admit Moon is not yet safe place for people to live. Enterprise City, too. Same reason. Nobody wants this death to be accident."

"But couldn't someone have sabotaged the hose?"

Bykhovski spread his hands. "Who? When? Hose is tested in factory, yes? Before backpack is sealed, and again *after* backpack is sealed. Who can damage hose inside of backpack? But they do not test this exact combination of rising temperature, rising pressure, and that the backpack is on someone who is running and falling. Suit is *smertel'naya lovushka*. A trap. Or . . . lemon? Do you say this? We will see if more people are dying from this, or if it is fluke. Mister Vaught, I am sorry you come all this way for nothing, but cause of Etsub's death is back on Earth, not here."

1.10
21 November
✧
St. Joseph of Cupertino Monastery
South Polar Mineral Territories
Lunar Surface

Next to be interviewed was Brother Michael, who (along with another monk named Giancarlo) had been first on the scene after Etsub's death.

"Do you mind if I record?" Raimy asked him.

"It's not against the rules," Michael responded, somewhat cryptically.

"All right, switching on."

Although Raimy had taken hundreds of statements in his ten years as a cop, he didn't feel entirely certain how to proceed with this one. He'd never met a monk before, much less in a monastery, much less on the goddamn Moon. He was a guest here, at the indulgence of the Catholic Church, and did not want to give offense to the people supplying his oxygen, or create some kind of interplanetary incident. Especially he did not want to do anything that might indirectly slow down the Antilympus Project. But he needed to do his job.

"Tell me what happened," he said, more carefully than he ordinarily might.

Michael leaned back in his chair, looking suddenly deep in thought. He stayed that way for uncomfortably long—fifteen seconds at least—before answering, "When a novice takes his vows and joins a monastery, it's not just poverty and charity he's agreeing to. It's a till-death-do-us-part type of situation, where he expects never to leave except briefly, for visits to his family and such. In the same vein, when the Church commissions a monastery—even a humble priory like this one—it's to build a legacy that endures for centuries. Trust me, this isn't lightly done. Saint Joseph's is a place where death and life were always meant to intertwine, as a portion (however tiny) of God's great tapestry. But murder is never part of the design; it cuts a thread mid-course, destroying the weave of every fiber that touches it. We're not equipped for that. Here, as everywhere else, it comes as an awful shock."

"So, you think Etsub Beyene was murdered?"

"I do. In a past life I was a worker bee in the Transportation Safety Board, which is the Canadian government agency that studies airplane crashes. I'm well familiar with the way small failures can stack up into big ones. Every plane crash is exceedingly improbable, did you know that?"

"No. I suppose that's a relief."

"It's mostly pilot error," Michael continued, "but it's quite difficult to crash a plane these days unless you really want to, so a lot of cases wind up being ruled as suicides, or murder-suicides, where the pilot simply flies the plane into the ground. Sabotage is the next leading cause. The same general factors apply to spacesuits. General Spacesuit has a near monopoly on environment suits, for good reason, because they've made it harder and harder to have an accident. This is of grave concern to anyone whose life depends on it. That includes myself and everyone here, but it also includes GS, which is a kind of person, with a kind of mortality at stake. Their engineers tell me they can't come up with a plausible sequence of events—however absurd—that could lead to this result, and I believe them. If there were a flaw in their design, they'd be quite motivated to recall and correct every suit in circulation, because another such failure would end them, as surely as the first one ended Etsub. So yes, I believe that suit was sabotaged, although even on that point GS admits to being stumped. How and when? It must have been cunning, to avoid detection by their quality assurance procedures, so their process needs correction in any case. I'm told you'll be looking for tool marks tomorrow, and I'm quite happy to assist you with it, assuming I'm not myself a suspect."

He spoke slowly and with a kind of restrained energy, like a dog who knows he's on a leash. Or like a doctor who, with great care, dumbs down every thought and word to where he figures you can understand it. It made Raimy wonder how Brother Michael might speak in his truly unguarded moments. But of course, telling him to relax would be pointless. Nobody was ever relaxed when Raimy was grilling them, and he supposed this included every person he'd ever loved, or whoever loved him. "Lawyer mode," his friends called it, although it worked just as well for policing. For daily life, not so much.

"No one's been ruled out at this point," Raimy told him. "Everyone here is a suspect. But for that reason, I guess I can't be too choosy about who's doing what. So yes, I'd appreciate the help, please and thank you. Now, back to my question: What happened that night? Where were you?"

To which Michael answered, "Like everyone except Etsub, I was in bed. We don't keep a night watch here, and our schedule is such that any man who comes to us a night owl becomes, in short order, an early bird. I was quite asleep when Andrei started shouting on the emergency channel. Andrei, whom we didn't know and weren't expecting. We didn't know we had a man outside, so my first thought was that something was happening over the hill at Moonbase Larry. Sorry, at Shackleton Lunar Industrial Station. I didn't think it was our emergency at all, but I dutifully got up and went to my battle station in the radio room, where I saw the position estimate for Andrei's transmission. Right here in the valley. So I got on the radio, still with no idea what was going on, and talked Andrei through a quick checklist. It was soon apparent that he was not dragging an injured man, but rather a corpse, so I judged it safer for myself and Giancarlo to cycle out through the airlock rather than trust Andrei, in his agitated state, to work the emergency ingress cycle by himself. I didn't even know if he could read the labels."

"Cycling out through the airlock, and then back in, takes quite a bit of time," Raimy said. "You must have been confident Etsub was dead."

"If that's the word, yes. I considered blowing the

explosive bolts on the outer hatch to get us out there fast, and then dragging Etsub around to the emergency airlock on the other side of the complex. But that would also be quite risky, and impossible to undo. At any rate, Andrei had described Etsub's air leak and facial features in exquisite detail, and such things don't occur halfway. In a statistical sense, it seemed unlikely we could save him. By then Andrei had read us Etsub's name tag, and we confirmed that Etsub was not inside the monastery. I still had no idea what had happened, or why Andrei was there. I still assumed he'd come over from Shackleton, because where else could he have come from? But we know all the people over there, and they all have better English than Andrei. And Andrei kept saying he was from Clementine and that he was out of air, which I didn't understand. So in my confusion, I was mainly concerned that we not compound whatever accident had befallen them out there. Once it was clear Andrei didn't have a leak of his own, Geo and I did an emergency egress, two-minute decompression, and brought Andrei and Etsub in for an emergency recompression, also two minutes."

"A bounce dive," Raimy said—a term from his Navy days. With scuba gear running a normal air mix, you could avoid decompression sickness if you got deep fast, did your business fast, and then ascended before the pressure really had a chance to pack nitrogen into your bloodstream.

Michael nodded vigorously. "Exactly, yes! Albeit a reverse bounce, from high pressure to low and back, but I see you understand our intention. I begin to glimpse why the Horsemen have put this investigation in your hands."

"So, you're out and in in four minutes."

"Call it four and a half, but yes. And by then, Andrei was getting rather frantic about his own air supply, so we let him remove his helmet right there in the airlock. Although it was exceedingly crowded in there, we took Etsub's helmet off as well, and then we all went straight through into the habitat without showering. Covered in particulates."

Raimy asked, "If you knew Etsub was dead, why did you bring him inside?"

Rather than answering immediately, Michael asked, "May I call you by your first name?"

"Sure. It's Raimy."

"Yes. Well, Raimy, try to understand. Etsub was a human being, and under our care. There was a slight chance we could do something for him, and we were certainly going to try. Once we'd laid him down on the chapel floor, Giancarlo hit the suit's defibrillator and then immediately started mouth-to-mouth resuscitation, until Hamblin showed up and took over. He's our doctor—a foot-bone surgeon pressed into more general service—and he gave it a good twenty minutes before calling the time of death. Etsub was a friend to many of us here—a remarkable man, who'd've been very welcome to remain here on Luna, if his eyes weren't so solidly locked on Mars. The idea of leaving him outside simply wouldn't have occurred to us."

"He's outside now," Raimy pointed out.

Michael spread his hands. "He was in here for days, Raimy. We became concerned about decomposition, and made an ugly choice to prevent an even uglier outcome.

Look, I'm sure we'll handle our next emergency more sensibly, with a script derived from this one, but there was a logic to our actions."

"I didn't mean to offend."

"You haven't."

Changing directions, Raimy said, "I'd like to hear more about your time as a crash investigator."

To which Michael said, "Not much to tell. At the time, it seemed a good use of my education, though a bit depressing. I wanted to help people, and indirectly the TSB does that, by reducing future accidents. But my third assignment involved, literally, piecing together smashed bodies—figuring out which foot belonged with which torso. A Cessna 206, carrying six people, hit the ground at a forty-degree angle and a speed of four hundred kph, strewing wreckage over an area much larger than you'd suppose. There was nothing on the black box; nobody knew they were about to die, and to my young self it just seemed so horrid. Lights out, just like that. No chance to make peace or contemplate one's life. The experience drove me straight into the arms of divinity school."

"Why were you selected to run Saint Joe's?"

"I wasn't. At best, I was second-in-command under Father Meagher, who until quite recently was expected to join us in the third batch of arrivals. But now he's not coming, and the seven men who were supposed to come with him are delayed at least a year, while the Church figures out how much expansion and logistical burden it actually wants to shell out for."

"You think they're not coming?" Raimy asked.

Again, Michael spread his hands. "The monastery is

already here, fully functional, and it's training students exactly per its mandate. The Church is already taking a leading role in the settling of a Second New World. In that sense, the box is checked, and further growth may be seen as extravagant. We'll see. As for why I'm second-in-command, it's because this facility was partly my idea, and I've been involved in the planning at every stage."

"You and this . . . Father Meagher?"

"That's correct."

"How were the other monks selected for service here?"

Michael laughed. "Are you picturing something like the Antilympus competition? Let me disabuse you; our pool of applicants was worryingly small. Compared with fifty years ago, only a sixth as many novices are even entering the monastic life, and only a tenth as many are actually taking solemn vows. On Earth, some ancient monasteries are actually closing, perhaps because their usefulness has been called into question. What can they offer, that's worth the entirety of a young man's life? When you start asking how many sworn monks, globally, are trained in the hard sciences, are under the age of fifty, and are willing to spend thousands of days sealed up in a can, under a black sky, never to return . . . Well, it's quite a short list, and roughly a third of us are already here."

"I see. So it's a big deal that you're functional at all? That these students came here to study your methods?"

"A very big deal, yes, although they weren't our first. The first three crew members of the Shoemaker Lunar Antenna Park stopped here for a week before moving on to their own little moonbase. It wasn't long enough to teach them everything they needed to know, but it was infinitely more than they'd've gotten from Harvest Moon, who look at Luna the way coal miners look at a mountain: with avarice and cunning, but little warmth."

"And do you have any more students scheduled to come?"

Michael smiled ruefully. "We're playing the long game here, Raimy. Even if it's years before anyone else needs us—even if it's *decades*—the fact that people know where to find us is itself important. They know we're out here on behalf of the future, and building it as we go. But I'll also say, first, that Sir Larry—sorry, Sir Lawrence—is planning some sort of large habitation project quite close to here, and has asked us if we'd like to be someday connected to it by a pressurized tunnel, at his expense. I think that answer is no, at least for the time being, but it does speak to our perceived relevance. In a more immediate sense, Andrei Bykhovski came here, at quite some risk to himself, to plead for sanctuary, which he has received. This, perhaps more than anything, confirms our mandate, which no mere murder can corrupt. But please do solve it, Raimy. In the name of Heaven, please do."

It was getting late in the day, and Raimy didn't want to disrupt the monastery's schedule any more than necessary. It had also been a very long day for him personally, but it was not yet dinnertime, and his scheduled time here on the Moon was worryingly short, so he figured he should squeeze in one more interview: this time (finally) with his top suspect, Anming Shui.

Like all of the others, Anming was someone whose Antilympus profile Raimy had studied, and whose videos he'd watched, to get a general sense of the man's character.

Right away, though, Anming surprised him: knocking on the open door, he asked, in a rather meek voice, "Detective Vaught? May I come in?"

His Chinese accent was heavy. His body language was obsequious, too; he was literally bowing, and (Raimy thought) not just out of custom or habit. On video, he'd seemed more puffed up and confident, but either that was an act to boost his ratings, or else he'd figured out he was in real danger here, and it knocked some of the stuffing out of him.

And he *was* in danger, yeah. Guilty or innocent, he was clearly the person with the most to gain from Etsub's death, and therefore the person most likely to go down for it. Even if he never went to prison, even if he never landed in court, the cloud of suspicion might well keep him from landing on Mars. It was already eroding his donations, or anyway something was.

"Come in, yes," Raimy told him. "Close the door and have a seat. This interview is being recorded."

Raimy tried to keep his mind and his voice neutral; he didn't know that Anming had killed anyone. He didn't even know for sure that Etsub had been murdered. Eight days after starting the case, Raimy was still in a loose information-gathering mode, with no solid theories. At best, he had a few testable hypotheses, which either would or wouldn't stand up.

Taking a seat, Anming said, "Brother Michael found me. He said it was my turn to answer your questions, and of course it is. I'm surprised you didn't ask me first." His hand twisted nervously at the knee of his yellow coveralls. He had the main zipper pulled all the way down to his waist, exposing a flimsy space undershirt of dark gray 3D-printed fabric. The side vents and leg vents were also unzipped for better air flow. Despite the cool, dry air in here, Anming was sweating.

Leaning forward, rocking slightly, Anming frowned and said, "Does it help to tell you Etsub was my friend? We knew each other almost a year. Did a lot of things as a team. Sometimes with Katla and Bridget, and sometimes not. We were competitors, but we judged—correctly!—that we would get more exposure working together. I came to Luna with him, even knowing it would probably help him more than me. For a long time, I was competing for second place, which is first place for the second mission. Bridget, too; you can ask her. Realistically, she could not expect to pass Katla. But we all came here together, spending half our donations. In my case, half. A little less for Etsub. But we made that money back in the first week. It was a gamble, and it worked. I would get to Mars in four extra years. I can hold my lead that long. Why not? I am a good botanist, and good enough astronaut, and smart enough to know what game I'm playing."

That was quite a data dump, considering Raimy hadn't asked him any questions. His English was better than you'd think, given the accent. The fact that Anming was so nervous didn't mean much; at this point, anyone but a pure psychopath would be. And pure psychopaths were rare even among murder suspects, and even if they could fake nervousness, they couldn't fake *sweat*. So okay, Anming Shui probably wasn't a psychopath.

Raimy asked, "You were asleep when Etsub died?"

"Yes," Anming answered.

"When did you wake up?"

"I think when Michael and Geo were in the airlock. I could hear there was something happening, but I am a guest here. I didn't think I needed to get up. But then a few minutes later I heard Bridget screaming."

"Screaming what?"

"I don't know."

"You couldn't understand her?"

"That's right. But it got me up."

"Because Bridget is your friend?"

"That's right."

"You were sharing a room with Etsub. Did you notice he wasn't there?"

"Yes."

"Did he go to bed at a normal time?"

"Yes."

"Did you see him get up?"

"No. But he often got up at night. He's a restless sleeper. He was."

"And what did you see when you left your room?"

"Chaos."

Sighing, Raimy said, "Can you be more specific?"

"There was a strange man here, in a blue-and-gray spacesuit I didn't recognize. And someone was lying down on the floor of the chapel. Everyone was crowding around; I couldn't see who it was. But Michael and Geo were in their spacesuits, and there were monks all over the place, in robes and pajamas and space underwear. Bridget was zipped into a coverall, but she was barefoot. Katla was in her underwear, too, which is not a lot of material, but she did not seem embarrassed. There was moondust everywhere, stinking like burnt matchsticks. It got in my eyes even from across the room. I said to Katla, 'What's going on?' And she said, 'I don't know. Etsub is dead.'"

Raimy made some notes. These details mostly seemed to line up with what he'd already heard, but even the slightest mismatch or inconsistency could trip up someone who was lying.

"Did Katla seem upset?"

Anming shrugged. "I think so, but it was pretty shocking. I mean, mostly she was confused."

"Were you confused?"

"Yes."

"Was Bridget Tobin confused?"

"Everyone was confused. It was just after 3:00 A.M. Most of the lights were still off, and curtains closed over the windows, which is what we do here to make it night, when the sun is not behind a hill. Even Brother Michael didn't know what was going on. He kept asking Andrei where he came from, and Andrei kept saying, 'Clementine. I come here from Clementine.' Brother Hughart was trying to revive Etsub, but when I saw his face, I thought, no, that is not going to work."

"Whose face? Etsub's, or Hughart's?"

"I guess both. Etsub was all swollen. His eyes were swollen shut, and it looked really weird inside his mouth, like lantern paper. Red and dry and crinkly. Hughart just looked grim. He got some monks to take off the top part of Etsub's spacesuit and carry him to the infirmary, so he could do an IV, but he said he could not find a vein."

"Was Bridget upset?"

"Yes."

Raimy was starting to get annoyed. Anming either said too much or too little; he didn't seem to have an in-between setting. Coupled with his thick accent, it made him a difficult witness.

"Can you elaborate on that?"

"She was crying. She said something to Michael, but I couldn't hear what. I'm not sure even Michael could understand her. After Hughart said that Etsub was dead, Bridget went back to her room and closed the door. I did not see her again until breakfast."

"And Bridget shares a room with Katla Koskinen?"

"Yes."

"Did Katla go back to her room?"

"No. Katla stayed out with everybody, just in her underwear. When Etsub was out of his spacesuit, she hugged the body, and she went with them when they carried him back to my room."

"Was she crying?"

"A little bit, yes, although everybody's eyes were watering, and noses running, because of the dust. But she's sobbing, too. Her friend is dead, very suddenly. At this point, I realize I'm sharing a room with a dead body of my friend, so I take out some of my things and I move to a different room, which is actually this room. And I go to sleep, because I am very tired."

"You moved back into your old room after the body was moved outside?"

"Yes. They said you were coming, and you needed this room."

Raimy sighed. This had all gone very badly from an evidence preservation standpoint; everything had been moved and moved again, everyone's fingerprints were all over everything, and even the dust had been cleaned up. Other than the spacesuit itself, Raimy didn't have a lot to look at.

Trying a different tack, he asked Anming, "What do you think happened to Etsub's suit?"

At that, Anming looked Raimy in the eye and said, "I hope it was an accident. If somebody killed him, I am going to get blamed for that shit. Somebody will get away with a murder, and I will go to jail. I know how this looks. I know people will think I just wanted Etsub's place on the rocket, but it's not like that."

"If you're innocent, you're not going to jail," Raimy assured him.

Anming surprised him by laughing at that. "I'm Chinese, okay? I see people go to jail. People ask me, why do you want to go to this American Mars colony? We have our own Moon stuff, we will have our own Mars stuff too. You're Chinese, you just wait, and go to Mars with us. But I'm not in the astronaut program. I was not accepted. I think I make some people embarrassed or mad when I enter Dan Beseman's contest, and even madder when I say I'm coming to the south pole of the Moon. That's the wrong pole for a Chinese man. Our stuff is north."

"What are you suggesting?" Raimy asked, not liking the direction this was taking.

Anming said, "If someone wanted me out of the program, pinning a murder on me is a good way to do that."

"Who?" Raimy pressed. "Who would kill an innocent person just to get to you?"

Anming looked nervously at the RECORDING lights on Raimy's glasses, and said, "China is a big place."

"Are you saying . . . Chinese government?"

"I'm saying it's a big place, and I piss off a lot of different people. It is pretty ironic, because there are also people saying I am a Chinese spy, and this happened so I can infiltrate Antilympus for China. That's not true, either. I'm just a botanist who wants to go to space. I do not see why that desire should get people killed. Especially Etsub, who was the better man. He was a better man than me, and I wanted him to win."

Dinner at the monastery was a surprisingly elaborate affair. The chapel doubled as a "refectory" or dining room, and its pews were cunningly designed to fold together into two large picnic tables. It took four people less than a minute to accomplish this. Only one table was necessary to hold all eleven of the monks, but it wasn't quite big enough to also accommodate three students, plus Andrei Bykhovski and Raimy Vaught, and so Brothers Michael, Giancarlo, and Hamblin left their fellows to slum with the irreligious at what Raimy couldn't help thinking of as "the kids' table."

The monks stayed mostly quiet as they passed around plates and utensils, but there was nothing particularly solemn about the ritual. In fact, these men seemed mostly to be having a good time. Raimy had been introduced to most of them by now, and though he was normally quite good at memorizing faces, truthfully he had a hard time telling them apart. They were all light-skinned and clean-shaven, for one thing, and they all wore their hair short, and wore nearly identical robes (or "habits," as they seemed to be called). None were particularly skinny or fat, so it was really only hair color, eye color, and general face shape that set them apart from one another. But even this was of limited help; Michael's hair was dusty blond, fading to gray at the temples, and his eyes were blue or hazel, and his jawline was strong. But Hamblin's hair and eyes were only slightly darker, and his face only slightly rounder. As for the rest of them, they mostly had black or dark brown hair and heavy eyebrows. Back in his Navy days, Raimy had complained that everyone looked the same in a submariner's uniform, but that was nothing compared to this.

"I wish you guys wore name tags," Raimy said.

To which Michael replied, "We can do that, if it'll aid your investigation. In fact, we certainly should. Our spacesuits have name tags, because even we can't reliably recognize each other without them. Indoors it's much easier, but yes. I see the problem. We should have thought of this before you came."

"You should do it for the benefit of your students, too," Bridget Tobin complained.

"Perhaps," Michael said. "But that's a different matter. You're here to learn what it means to live under alien skies, and it's not clear we can best accomplish that by making it easier."

"Yes, Professor," she snarked back good-naturedly, then added, "You guys just want to be interchangeable."

"We don't and we aren't," Michael replied, "but our

service does require us to set vanity aside, and practicality does require us to cross-train. Now kindly shut your pie hole."

Once the places were set, all but three of the monks seated themselves on their table's two long benches. These three, with the aid of Katla (but not of Bridget or Anming or Andrei), shuttled back and forth to the kitchen with large serving bowls and platters, which they laid down gently along the centerline of each table, being careful not to tip them in the low gravity. It was quite a lot of food, and quite a lot of variety.

"Now this is not what I was expecting," Raimy admitted.

Giancarlo chuckled at that. "It's not exactly gruel, is it?"

Michael said, "Nor should it be. Although we've vowed a simple life, we've also sworn to do our best to make Luna a place for humans. Key elements of that research include how to grow things, and how to cook the things we've grown. Also how to program the CHON synthesizer to produce substances not only nutritious and tolerably palatable, but actually delish. When we first got here, we weren't even eating real gruel, if you can believe it, but a pasty imitation blobbed out like syrup."

At this, Brother Hamblin piped in with, "CHON stands for Carbon, Hydrogen, Oxygen, Nitrogen. Those four elements are about ninety-nine percent of what your body needs to stay alive. The synthesizer can spin them into a limited number of fats, proteins, and carbohydrates."

"I think he knows that," Bridget said on Raimy's behalf.

Raimy grunted noncommittally. Most people these days knew what a CHON synthesizer was, and Raimy knew they cost a couple hundred thousand dollars and took a lot of power to run. They were not exactly something you could fuck around with in your spare time. But he didn't know how they worked or what they could do, so he said, "I don't mind a little education."

"Meaning no disrespect," Michael said, "one astronaut to another, but until you've relied on CHON to keep you alive, you really don't know how important plants and animals and trace elements have been in your life. Our synthesizer is only the nineteenth unit off the line at Nutrilutions Corp., and they haven't really had time to develop a lot of recipes yet. Here, it's nearly a full-time job for Ferris and Durm, who I assure you are more motivated than any corporate employee could ever be. We give Nutrilutions back our best creations, with the right to freely distribute, so long as the titles and descriptions credit us appropriately. It's another worldly thing we'd like to be known for. And we're already getting pretty good, if I do say so myself. I'll even challenge you to a friendly wager, to identify which elements of this meal are of hydroponic origin and which are entirely synthetic."

"Well, the salad is obviously real," Raimy said, "and the hot dogs are clearly fake."

"You should try them first," Katla warned.

"Do you culture meat cells here?"

Michael smiled. "We'll give you a tour in the morning, if you'll consent to suspend your investigation that long. Meanwhile, eat."

"It's all quite nutritious," Brother Ovid assured him, from one table over.

"And better than anything we had a year ago,"

Giancarlo added. His accent was Italian, his voice warm and slow. Ovid's was higher and more energetic, with an accent Raimy guessed was Norwegian. Both contrasted sharply with Michael's own voice, which was sonorously eastern Canadian. He seemed to be the only monk here, except maybe brother Hughart, who spoke English as a first language.

"So where are you from?" Raimy asked him, while accepting a shovelful of salad that Katla was dropping on his plate. Next followed hot dogs with what looked like whole wheat buns, and some cubes of off-white material that might be cheese or tofu. Brother Ovid handed him a gray plastic cup filled with something that looked like milk.

"No simple answer to that," Michael said. "Diplomatic families go where the wind takes them. I spent some time in England and Germany growing up, but for your purposes I'll say Cornwall, Ontario. I was born there, and I spent my last three years of high school there. I was on the debate team."

"Huh," said Raimy. "Me too. San Diego. It's good training for law school."

"And divinity school," Michael agreed.

Then Katla and the remaining monks took their seats, and conversation dropped away as everyone was eating. The food tasted better than it looked, and Raimy surprised himself by asking for seconds.

"So, what's your verdict?" Michael asked him, as he started round two.

"The meat is fake," Raimy said. "It's got a fatty, umami kind of flavor, but it's a bit flat. It's not vat-grown."

"Correct," Michael said. "It's a CHON-printed mix of four different molecules. The proteins were designed right here, by the way, thanks to Hughart and Hamblin— a physician and a chef, respectively. The trick is to find something that tastes like animal protein but is easy to assemble, so it doesn't take forever to print. This recipe's got analogs of myoglobin, myosin, and collagen, along with a fat called oleic acid. That by itself is not very convincing, but we add heme and monosodium glutamate from the drug printer, sieve the mixture into a 3D-printed mold, and cook it in the microwave. But I'm stealing Huey's glory, here; you can ask him about this yourself, if you're interested."

"I might be," Raimy said. Hughart was over at the other table, but Raimy would not have any trouble finding him tomorrow.

"It's actually my glory you're stealing," said Hamblin. "And Kurtis'."

"Well," Michael said, "You can explain it during the tour."

Meanwhile, Raimy pointed his fork at the hot dog buns and said, "The bread is natural."

"Correct. If you only knew how much labor went into a single bun! We have to grow and harvest the wheat, grind the flour, add water and yeast, knead the dough, and bake it in the convection oven. It's a treat we can't enjoy as often as we like."

"Actually," Hamblin said, "We're cheating a bit on this latest batch, by adding oleic acid and Hill protein, to give it a bit of a buttery, eggy flavor, and also some raw CHON starch to fill out the dough."

"Ah. So we're both wrong, then," Michael said.

"The milk is synthetic," Raimy said.

"Right again. And what about the white cubes?"

"Also synthetic," Raimy answered confidently.

"Nope," Michael said, smiling. "The same milk you're drinking can be blended with lupin beans and then fermented with the same yeast cultures we use to bake the bread. The result is not quite cheese, not quite tempeh, not quite tofu, and not quite hummus."

"Huh. I'll be darned."

"Is it good?"

"Yeah. Yeah it is. You guys invented this?"

"Out of necessity, yes, as a way to both stretch our garden resources and get some trace elements into our CHON. This *is* something we eat every day, or nearly. We're thinking of calling it 'moon cheese.' And while we don't have the resources to pursue this right now, Huey has told me the same process, minus the milk, can be used to make a kind of beer."

"Bean beer," Giancarlo scoffed.

"Beans have starches and sugars in the right proportion," Hamblin said. "We wouldn't be the first. Well, maybe the first to use lupins."

"Are monks even allowed to drink beer?" Raimy asked, surprised.

To which Michael said, "My friend, the best beers in the world were *invented* by monks. What do you think we've been doing these past two thousand years?"

When Raimy's rollup announced an incoming live call, it was so unexpected that at first he didn't recognize the

SpaceNet ringtone, or realize it was coming from his own pocket.

"I think you're getting a call," said Bridget Tobin.

"What? Oh."

He wasn't wearing his glasses, and the rollup hadn't been charged in days, so he had to answer by physically pulling the cylinder out of his pocket and holding it up to his ear. He had all the power settings minimized, so he didn't even have caller ID info on exterior display. It was basically 1990.

"Hello?" he said into the cylinder.

"Hi. It's Tracy. I just wanted to see how you were doing." Her voice was way too loud. He tried to turn down the volume with his thumb, but couldn't find the switch.

"Oh, hello," he said. "I'm doing fine, thank you. Eating dinner right now."

"Oh, that's exciting. Moon food! Is it good?"

"It is," he said. "Yes. Quite good, actually. Listen, can I call you later?"

"Sure, I don't want to disturb you. I'll cover the cost when you call back."

"Oh. Okay, thanks."

"Bye!"

"Bye," he said, whereupon the cylinder went dead in his hand.

Clucking with amusement, Tobin singsonged, "Somebody's got a girlfriend."

Feeling unaccountably flustered, Raimy stuffed the rollup in his pocket and said, "I don't . . . She's not my girlfriend."

"Does she know that?" Tobin asked, then burst out laughing.

"She's kind of my boss right now," Raimy tried to explain, but Tobin and Katla were smirking, and even Anming Shui seemed amused.

"I thing she likes you," he said.

"It does seem that way," Brother Michael agreed.

Annoyed now, Raimy said, "How about you guys stay out of my business? I'm not here to fraternize."

To which Tobin replied, "Yeah, it sounds like you can do that when you get back." Then she burst out laughing again.

"All right," Michael said, "let's leave our guest alone. This is a solemn occasion in a solemn place." Then he, too, snorted out a laugh. "Sorry. I'm sorry. It is funny."

And Raimy, who had run-tackled murderers and testified in courtrooms and swum half-naked out of submarines, had nothing to say to that. Nothing he wanted to say in a chapel, at any rate.

2.2
21 November

✦

Clementine Cislunar Fuel Depot
Earth-Moon Lagrange Point 1
Cislunar Space

Daniel Epureanu grabbed a pair of bolt cutters out of the
equipment locker with all the fight-or-flight energy of a
crooked policeman hauling someone out of a car. This
thing had gone too far, which ironically meant it needed
to go farther still in order to turn out well.

After a week of nothing but talk, the striking workers—
essentially the whole crew of Clementine—had gathered
early this morning in the mess hall, to speak once again
with Grigory Orlov and his management goons. (Leave it
to Orlov Petrochemical to find broke-nose musclemen
capable of commanding a space station!) That meeting
had gone poorly. Orlov had offered everyone a full pardon
and a *fifteen* percent raise (up from ten percent a few days
ago), and they had, practically as one voice, told him to
shove that straight up his rectum.

Orlov had met that response with a frightening calm,
and simply repeated his offer.

"Take it or consider the consequences," he had said grimly. People shouted at him then, and still he just hung there in space, unmoved by their suffering.

"Lockout!" someone had shouted then. Epureanu couldn't trace the voice, but it seemed to strike an immediate chord. Within moments all the workers, in their rage, were literally clogging the exits, and then fanning out into all the other modules, as each man and woman rushed to his or her workstation to lock it from unauthorized access. From *management* access, or access by scab labor. Which probably sounded good to the people doing it, except that some of those workstations controlled critical life-support functions, or the ability to safely launch spacecraft from the shuttle bay, or to recharge the batteries of spacesuits.

"Don't . . ." Epureanu had tried to say, flitting from one module to the next.

"Will you . . ." he had tried to say.

"Can you just . . ."

But nobody was listening to him, or to anyone else, and so in a triple of minutes this thing had gone from a simple work stoppage to an outright mutiny. And that was fucking serious, and people were going to get *killed* if they didn't bring themselves under control. And killed perhaps even if they did, if Orlov's goons decided to blow the airlocks or some such thing.

Epureanu didn't know whether they had that capability or not, but it seemed foolish to assume otherwise. Orlov was that kind of man, and quite frankly Epureanu might want that superpower as well, if he were outnumbered by burly Russian miners whose pocketbooks he controlled.

And so Epureanu did the only thing he logically could under the circumstances: he shut off the pumps that ran the airlock hydraulics, and then cut all the fluid lines just to be sure. Now the airlocks could only be operated by physically muscling the hatches open and closed.

And that was *really* serious—a step into sabotage as well as mutiny—but it did not make sense to cross this particular Rubicon without a good defensive position staked out, and nobody but Epureanu seemed to realize that.

Then, with basic safety under control, he started grabbing people—physically hauling them from where they were hunkered—and saying: "You, Novatny, guard the spinward airlock. Jam the hatch and keep it jammed. Don't let anyone out, and for God's sake don't let anyone in. You, Pavel, guard the hangar. Doctor Chernov, secure the medlab and prepare for casualties—we may have some soon. You, Sherval, route as many functions as you can through this terminal. *You* have access, no one else does. You understand? When you've finished, give me a list of things we control. They will be doing the same thing in Operations right now, so act quickly."

And just like that, Daniel Epureanu was in charge. He found himself snapping out orders to men who technically outranked him, and he didn't care, because this was a mutiny anyway, and somebody needed to get these fools organized, and there was not one second to spare.

People had gathered up impromptu weapons, but Epureanu told them, "No, put that away. That's not going to work. You think they don't have guns? We outnumber them, but it's our economic value that will save us. Stand down."

And that helped, but not enough, so he cut a communication trunkline and physically spliced his headset into it, granting himself override capability over every loudspeaker in the station.

"Workers," he said. "Stand down. This is Maintenance Supervisor Daniel Florinovich Epureanu. Please stand down and return, empty-handed, to the mess hall to resume negotiations."

"Who put you in charge?" asked a chemical engineer named Aronov.

"This did," Epureanu told him, covering his headset mike and brandishing the bolt cutters.

"Okay, okay," Aronov said, ducking his head a little.

"Go on," Epureanu told him.

Then, uncovering the microphone, he said, "Mr. Orlov, sir. We apologize for the disturbance. If you are willing to engage in substantive negotiations, we will hear you out. Please understand that your previous offer has been rejected, but we await your next in a spirit of camaraderie."

And so there was a second meeting, which turned out to be even shorter than the first.

Epureanu had assigned positions or tasks to perhaps a third of the crew. The rest of them flowed, in clumps and spasms, back into the mess hall. Orlov kept them waiting for fifteen minutes, though, and when he finally appeared in the hatchway, accompanied by Commander Morozov and Subcommander Voronin, and by his weird African girlfriend, the crowd was quite restless indeed.

Orlov drifted into the room, casually taking up space

so that the crowd had to fall back away from him. His goon squad backed him up.

"Sixteen percent," he said, without preamble or postamble.

While the crowd hung back, Epureanu kicked gently toward Orlov's team, stopping himself two meters away by hooking a foot on one of the tables.

"Daniel Florinovich," Orlov said, nodding politely.

"Grigory Magnusovich," Epureanu said back.

They regarded each other for a long moment.

Finally, Epureanu said, "Grigory, you once told me to know what's mine, and to take it without asking. That's advice I've followed ever since. I'm following it now, as you can see. But you seem to have locked us out of the shuttles, and even the lifeboats."

To which Orlov replied, "And you have locked me out of the hangar, and the airlocks. Very good, Daniel Florinovich. I hardly know whether to throttle you or buy you a drink."

And for a moment, it seemed a peace was possible. The great Grigory Orlov, son of Magnus Orlov and head of the largest energy company in the world, had in fact bought Epureanu drinks from time to time. Epureanu was barely a middle manager in this enterprise (and Moldovan besides!), but Orlov seemed to fancy himself a man of the people. He had taken a liking to Epureanu earlier this year, and occasionally spoke to him almost as an equal, or as a human being, at any rate.

Epureanu smiled and said, "First the one, and then—if we fail you—the other. We are not your enemies, Grigory. We came here to work. For you."

"Then do it," Orlov said without amusement.

"We will," said Epureanu, "when we are no longer your prisoners. Your generous pay raise misses the point."

"Then consider it retracted," Orlov said.

Sighing inwardly, Dona prepared for violence. She was trained in a dozen martial arts, honed and shaped by a dozen times actually fighting for her life against unpredictable humans. The crown jewel, though, was Zedo, the zero-gravity grappling style taught to her by the U.S. Space Force, back when they still thought she was working for an allied government. Back when anyone thought she was working for any government at all. Her chief instructor had called her "the most gifted micro-gee fighter I've ever seen." Except himself, he had meant, but then she had whipped him, too. Her body seemed built for it; she was immune to vertigo, immune to motion sickness and disorientation. She always knew exactly where her hands and feet were, exactly what direction her center of mass was moving, and pain did not startle or distract her. She did not suffer from the sort of empathy that kept people from winning fights. However, she had never in her life faced more than two attackers at a time, and there were twenty potential enemies in this room.

She didn't know this man who was talking to Orlov, but the name tag on his uniform shirt said EPUREANU, and apparently he and Orlov were on a first-name basis. Which was a good thing, but probably not good enough.

He was a bold one, she had to admit. But he was within arm's reach now, and the tone of this meeting—already setting off alarm bells for her—was headed nowhere but south. And so, if Epureanu so much as twitched, she was going to windpipe him. Assuming of course that Morozov didn't beat her to it. Or Orlov himself, for that matter. Voronin she wasn't so sure about, so her planned choreography simply regarded him as dead mass she could brace against for a jump.

"Grigory, come on," Epureanu said. "You are on the wrong side of this one, and surely a part of you knows it. Is this why you're so angry? Because your business model failed to take shore leave expenses into account, and now your earnings projections are garbage?"

"You presume too much," Orlov said. "You think you're a businessman now? I made you. This minor thing that you are, I made."

"You did," Epureanu agreed.

"I could have you mopping toilets in Siberia. I could have you buried."

"You could," Epureanu agreed. "But it would not serve you."

"Oh, think harder than that, little man," Orlov warned. "You've gone and made it personal. You had all better hope the public never learns the details of what went on here today. If that happens, you will all be liabilities. Ask yourself what happens to liabilities."

"This is not productive," Epureanu said, sounding less certain than he had a few moments before. Sounding like a man who had just overplayed his hand, and knew it.

"*You* are not productive," Grigory said in return, his eyes sweeping the room. "Any of you."

And that was apparently seven words too many, because the crowd bristled, drew in a collective breath, and then a dozen men were yelling and leaping, and Dona barely had time to kick off Voronin, kick off Epureanu, and grab the trillionaire in a lock hold that dragged him back toward the exit.

What followed was several seconds of confusion, as bodies traveled on the straight-line trajectories to which they had committed—some intersecting with other bodies, some with tables and benches, some with walls and floors. Nobody was where anyone else expected them to be, and everyone was shouting or crying out in pain. Over the trillionaire's violent objections, Dona got him into the hallway, her feet landing against the wall, her knees and quads absorbing the impact and tensing for another leap. Morozov followed a few seconds later, swinging out through the hatch, his hands on one side of it, white-knuckled. He was breathing hard and looking scared, two things Dona had never seen on him before. He was a tough guy, but not room-full-of-enemies tough. And then, a few second after that, Voronin was *thrown* out, so that he collided hard with the bulkhead next to Dona and the trillionaire.

"Let me go," Orlov said coldly.

"Retreat, my love," Dona advised him in a gentle whisper, directly into his left ear. "Now is not the time." Then she released him, and the four of them were launching hard and fast down the hallway toward Operations.

Thankfully, no one followed.

1.11
21 November
✦
St. Joseph of Cupertino Monastery
South Polar Mineral Territories
Lunar Surface

After dinner, Raimy was suddenly and overwhelmingly tired, so he declined an invitation to evening prayers, went back to his room, closed and dogged the hatch, stripped down to his tough, slippery, antimicrobial space underwear, and crawled into his bunk. Just like on a submarine, there was no window, although the quarters were big enough for a captain, and even had a little curtained-off restroom at one end. The bulkhead running alongside the bed was the only barrier between himself and hard vacuum, but that was all right. It was, he reminded himself, less dangerous than the deep ocean, where any serious leak could kill you instantly, like a salty sledgehammer to the chest.

If the room starts to depressurize, I'll exhale to keep my lungs from popping. Thirty seconds until I lose consciousness. I open the hatch and run out. Close the hatch behind me and dog it shut. Then breathe.

And what if the whole dormitory module depressurizes?

Same thing, just a longer distance.

And if it's the whole monastery?

Then I'll die. Okay? Happy?

Sure. Sleep tight.

He got up briefly to plug his glasses and rollup into a charging outlet for the night, then crawled under the covers. There was no voice control for the lights, but within reach of the bed were a pair of dials—one for brightness and the other for hue. Also like on a submarine, it wasn't possible to turn the lights all the way off, but he did turn them down as low as they'd go, and set them to a soothing red-orange night-light color that would help him find his way around, without keeping him up.

It was strange, to lie down in Lunar gravity. Walking around was a lot like bobbing in a swimming pool, or "bottom diving" with your buoyancy compensator fully deflated. But you didn't lie down in a swimming pool. Sleeping in zero gravity was strange at first, too, but this was different. He weighed about as much as a large lapdog, and that weight was (just barely) enough to hold him down on the bed. The thin, hard mattress felt weirdly comfortable, though, and jeez, when he moved or rolled over it was like going over a hill on a roller coaster; he practically floated off the bed. His cotton sheet and weighted blanket seemed to help, though, and anyway he was so damn tired that his mind just sort of drifted away.

4.2
21 November

✧

St. Joseph of Cupertino Monastery
South Polar Mineral Territories
Lunar Surface

Father Bertram Meagher
St. Benedict's Monastery
1012 Monastery Rd.
Snowmass, CO, USA
Earth

Dear Bertram,

It's not common to find myself less curious than you, but your question takes me by surprise, and turns my gaze outward to problems not contemplated. Your so-called "mystery at ESL1" pulls other issues along in its wake, because you're right: some hornet's nest hanging from that high limb has been knocked loose, and the buzzing (now I stop to notice) is loud. What's got them stirred up, you ask?

Let's think: they already have enough electrical power

to run a country, enough antimatter to blow one up, and enough production capability to rival a midsized city. One might think these things excitement enough, but Esley seems to take them in stride, as American children once yawned at their own exceptionalism, untouched by the black swans of true misfortune. If rumors can be believed (and you seem to have heard this before me, which again is unusual), Igbal Renz may have turned down a Nobel Prize. For what, exactly? Of his many discoveries and inventions—sprung from his own brain or else wrested from underlings and improved sufficient that his primary credit can still be straight-facedly claimed—which one stands out so much above the others as to merit such an honor? Is it the robot waiters and butlers that set him on this wealthward trajectory? The launch vehicles so brilliant at combusting their fuels and navigating a lumpy atmosphere that no one is quite sure how their calculations even work? "Deep belief motion control networks" seek the nadir of uncanny so skillfully that people no longer even find it creepy. Is that excitement enough?

Far be it from me to fawn over a man so accumulative of wealth and so unconcerned with charity. But! Fair to say he is not sitting on a pile of dollar bills two trillion high, and miserly refusing to consider the good they might do. Rather, the sweat of his brow, not so different from the sweat of my own, or any other labour addict's, has, by some strange luck or coincidence, so enriched the world that fifty-one percent of his garage startup is now worth that much. And pieces of that enterprise are harder to distribute as alms, and easier to see why it mightn't occur to him, for it would mean relinquishing control of his kingdom and placing himself at the mercy of shareholders with (let's face it) smaller dreams. Would that be a net win for the world? Or worlds, really? It's not for me to say. Could he share more of the wealth with the workers whose labour actualizes it? Of course, but already his terms are more generous than the other Horsemen's, so he can pluck away the world's most talented and industrious, or at least the most avaricious of the talented. Could he slow the behemoth's growth by paying out profits to nonprofits? Perhaps, and perhaps he should. There is no Nobel Prize in the accumulation of wealth, but surely being that wealthy, or even adjacent to wealth on that scale, must be terribly stirring, even if one must live (as we do) in metal tubes sheltered by magnetic umbrellae, and be fed by goo dispensers and sewage. So perhaps it is fair to give the Economics prize to those who have found their way to such colossal wealth, rather than those merely finding equations to describe it.

Or does the Swedish Academy look favorably on his (slight, but measurable) cooling of a sweltering Earth with that million-miles-distant parasol, thinner than a hair and broader than most of the countries of Europe? Could that be it? Or the cunning mechanisms that built said shade from the atoms of asteroidal rock, or that extract electricity from it? The unsavory aspects of his personal life are a lot to live down, or for the Nobel Committee to overlook, so we can assume they think highly indeed. They do not give out a prize for mathematics (which is certainly the backbone of a deep belief motion control network), so I'm assuming he was considered for Physics or Chemistry. Does that narrow it down enough to guess?

The antimatter stockpile itself is a possibility, for Esley Shade Station (or, more properly, the hub of the Shade itself) must surely produce antiprotons and antielectrons with one thousand times the efficiency of any purpose-built Earthly accelerator, and also, I glean, some number of antineutrons as an apparent side effect. The "wave impact amplification decelerator," as they allegedly call it, permits the fashioning not only of stable antiatoms larger than antihydrogen (quite a trick in its own regard!) but also, somehow, stable molecules of dissimilar antiatoms. The details are closely guarded, and threats released that the whole apparatus will convert to gamma rays if unauthorizedly inspected. From any other organization one might interpret such bluster as only that, but is Renz Ventures given to exaggeration?

Notably, and perhaps as a direct result, there seems to have been some sort of hostile takeover up there, hazy of detail but involving the guns of frightened governments. And frightened they should be, of such a destabilizing force as Igbal Renz! One imagines the competitors crushed under his ascent, their stakeholders crying each other to sleep at night for what might have been, if only that man had trod his heedless tread on some other corner of the global (and more-than-global) economy. There are no models or graphs for such catastrophe. There is no peaceful coexistence with an innovation wellspring that so distorts the space-time around it, and thus it is no wonder he lives so far from those who might wish him ill.

One suspects he turned down that prize for the simple reason that he fears a trap. That golden medallion, if not itself spring loaded, could well become the honest bait around which a dishonest trap might quite plausibly be sprung, which drops him into jail for sparsely defined crimes against humanity. Renz has been a reckless player, but his recent moves show a paranoia I can only think well founded, for envy runs strong among the envious.

Perhaps I do fawn, and perhaps I should stop, for there are many sins, both mortal and venal, embedded in all of this. Igbal Renz may yet burn in Hell, as could any of us, if our souls are so willfully out of alignment. Again, it's not for me to say, and perhaps even Our Father Who Art, having given such men the will to choose their own actions, is still hanging back to see what might happen! Strange things were afoot already in cislunar space, and one is never sure which rumors are crazed ravings and which are mere summary of the still-stranger facts. My simpler point, Bertram, is that whatever set those Esley hornets abuzz must be *more exciting than all of that*.

And as I pause to consider the enormity of such a statement, I find I do not have an answer to your question, or any plausible speculation thereto. Have they found a rip in the cosmic vacuum? An exceedance of light speed? A simple equation for human happiness? The last specific I heard of Esley was a whisper, stale but credibly sourced, that Igbal had been communing with metaphysical Beings and making serious mathematical inquiry into magic words of the Kabbalah. I shit you not, Bert: spoken phrases to, I suppose, vibrate the air in some quantum-mechanical manner? I'll give him this: if such a thing were true and possible (which I doubt both highly and lowly), it would be someone like him who'd discover it. But it sounds to me like a harmless hobby for a man who, fond of hallucinogens and with no real religion to prop him up, fears eternity. I do not think that's the source of their peculiar excitement, nor their even more peculiar silence.

Have they found aliens, perhaps? A voice, in foreign accent, blip-blip-blipping against the blank white hiss of the cosmos?

What has them stirred up, indeed? I shall give the matter further thought, and keep my attention to whatever eaves a man in my position might be positioned to drop. But one partial guess at least is easy to put forward: something is happening up there, or about to happen, that shocks to action men and women far more jaded than you or I could ever be. And in an unsettled time in a barely settled space, that idea sends shudders down my spine.

And so I return to my labours a bit more pale and drawn, for we still have a murder to solve, and a thousand chores besides.

Yours,
Brother Michael Jablonski de la Lune

1.12
22 November

✦

St. Joseph of Cupertino Monastery
South Polar Mineral Territories
Lunar Surface

Raimy partially woke up a few times, and struggled each time to orient himself. In the dim light and low gravity, it was hard to make sense of where he was. The sensation was oddly soothing, though, like being in the womb, so he felt no particular need to figure it out, but simply closed his eyes again. In between he slept deeply, and though he wouldn't remember his dreams in the morning, they were of a bland, calm nature, with few fantastical elements. However, when he actually woke up in the morning— roused by the sounds of activity in the hallway outside his room—his rested mind knew right away where he was.

He lay in bed for a few minutes, reluctant to start his day. Finally he got up, peed, washed his hands, and picked at his hair with his fingers because he'd forgotten to bring a comb. He did at least have a toothbrush, though he hadn't rinsed it off the whole time he was in zero gravity, and without toothpaste it was kind of nasty. Still, better than nothing. Being in space was a lot like backpacking; you just didn't bring a lot with you.

Space underwear was designed to be worn for a week at a time, so he simply pulled on his beige Antilympus uniform, including the slippers, and was magically ready to go.

Breakfast was less elaborate than dinner, and consisted mainly of orange drink and an oatmeal-like paste topped with oily pats of margarine. But it was good and hearty, and felt like it would easily hold him through lunch, at least. Once everyone had eaten, insulated sippy mugs were passed out, filled with a substance worryingly known as "brown tea." Wasn't tea supposed to be brown?

"To carry around with you while you work," said Brother Hamblin, whose first name Raimy had learned was Hilario.

Raimy, who really just wanted a cup of coffee, couldn't help asking, "What's in it?", with more suspicion and less gratitude than was strictly polite.

"Toasted chicory, wheatgrass, and dandelion root, home grown," Hilario said, his accent full of smooth, rich tones. "Caffeine from the drug printer, sucrose and milk fat from the CHON synthesizer. *Un poco* marsh thistle to broaden the sweetness, and a bit of mustard green to give it some bitterness. Kurtis and I have been refining this recipe for months, so please don't hurt our feelings."

"Can I get it without cream and sugar?"

Hilario clucked his disapproval. "This isn't a Starbucks. Just try it."

Dutifully, Raimy sipped from the spout of the mug, and found it actually not too bad.

"It tastes . . ."

"Like hot chocolate?" Hilario suggested.

"Hmm. Not . . . well, maybe."

It didn't taste like any hot chocolate Raimy had ever drunk, and it didn't particularly taste like tea, either. It certainly didn't taste like coffee. But it wasn't bad, and he could see himself actually drinking it, maybe more than once, if it was what they had here.

"The infrastructure to grow and process coffee or even tea is quite beyond us here," Michael said, as if in apology.

"What is your honest opinion? It's helpful to have outside perspectives," Hilario said.

"I like this," Raimy reassured them both. "Thank you. I'm grateful for the caffeine, actually."

"They drink it at Shackleton now, too," Michael said, "and perhaps the people of Mars, when they finally make landfall, can save themselves some trouble by following our lead. Right, Katla?"

"Um, sure," Katla answered, with careful neutrality. The monks had hauled all the dirty dishes off to the kitchen, and so she was helping fold away one of the two big dining tables, to convert this room back into a chapel.

Raimy and Bridget were the only ones still seated. Taking the hint, Raimy extricated himself from the table's built-in bench, and stood up. "I'd like to inspect that backpack now," he said to Michael.

"Right," Michael said. "Let's do it. Can we give you a tour of the grounds first, though? Consider it part of your investigation."

In point of fact, Raimy had a search warrant of sorts—a letter from the Vatican, authorizing him to access any portion of the monastery and its grounds. He also, for what it was worth, had a similar letter from the office of Sir Lawrence Edgar Killian, granting similar access to Shackleton Lunar Industrial Station. But Michael probably knew that.

Raimy said, "Sure. I assume Etsub had the run of this place?"

Michael simultaneously nodded and shrugged. "Yes. Please understand, privacy means a great deal in monastic life, even in Benedictine guest houses like this one, so a typical monastery is dominated by cloistered spaces. But in an envelope this small, it doesn't make sense to restrict the movement of our students. And Etsub was a sponge, interested in everything. He wasn't just here to learn horticulture."

"I understand. And you're right, I do want to retrace his steps. Do you mind if I record?"

"In principle I do mind, yes. But our students have been broadcasting unauthorized video the whole time they've been here, and I haven't the heart to ask them to stop, because their goals are the same as ours: to normalize life in space. And in any case, I understand this is a crime scene, and you need admissible evidence. Your need clearly supersedes our own."

Something in Michael's manner caught Raimy's attention. It was understandable that as prior of the monastery, Michael necessarily had a public face he needed to show, that was different from the private face he would use when members of the general public were not around. That much was obvious. But Raimy sensed there might also be at least one *secret* face lurking inside Michael somewhere, and that bothered him.

"Okay, then. I'm switching on."

Michael stood and spread his arms. "Well, then, let's get to it. I think you're familiar with this room already?"

Indeed, Raimy had been almost nowhere else, besides his quarters. The chapel/refectory was pretty small for a church, though slightly oversized as a dining hall for sixteen people. For a habitat module, though, it seemed quite roomy indeed, especially in comparison to the spaces onboard a nuclear submarine. It was nearly as long as a school bus, and nearly twice as wide. It had four exit hatchways: one leading into the main airlock assembly, one to the kitchen, one to the dormitories, and one leading off into a module Raimy had never seen.

Raimy said, "Why don't you describe it to me anyway?"

"As you wish. That lovely tortured Jesus up there is a medieval relic, extremely valuable. The cabinet below that is our tabernacle, where we store consecrated hosts, and in between is our teleconferencing screen, which is linked with a SpaceNet portal that lets us talk to Earth, and of course other locations on the Moon. How technical would you like me to get?"

"I don't know. How technical can it be?"

"Well, the protocol is SSL over TCP/SP, if that helps. The chapel's base module is a Harvest Moon 'high vault.' It's the same size as the dormitory modules, which are called 'rack vaults,' but it's basically hollow inside, with the standard wiring and plumbing configured basically as pass-throughs. The only services are blowers, electrostatic precipitators, and lighting; everything else is capped off. All the furnishings—the pews, the monitor, the crucifix, *et cetera*, are anchored to pawn-shaped protrusions called 'nubbins.' Here's one right here, with nothing attached. Is that technical enough?"

"Sure," Raimy said. Such details were unlikely to matter for his work, but you never knew.

Michael continued: "There were only three modules in place when we first landed here; helping HMI connect this one up was our first labor. Since that time, we've added fourteen additional modules, the most recent one just a few months ago. We've been construction workers first and foremost. It's been a strange adjustment, truthfully, to merely inhabit the place, with no immediate plans for expansion. We have seven monks still on Earth, awaiting transport, but if and when they finally get here, we can squeeze them into existing spaces, without expanding. Time will tell, but this may be it. The structure, as you see it, may stand here for decades. Or longer."

By convention, the main airlock was "west" of the chapel, whereas the kitchen was "north." Raimy didn't know whether this reflected actual compass points, or even whether compass points made any sense this close to the south pole, where every direction was "north," but anyway Michael led him into the kitchen, which was a smaller module, roughly the size of a short bus.

Raimy had looked through the hatch into this room, but had never actually stepped through into it. Brother Kurtis (also known as "Durm") was already in here, cheerfully washing the breakfast dishes in two large sinks.

"Kitchen," Michael said. He then started pointing out the various appliances: "Blender. Mixer. CHON printer. Stovetop. Combo oven. That's a microwave, radiant, and convection oven with variable internal pressure all in one. Expensive."

"It saves a lot of space," Kurtis offered without turning around.

"Yes, it does," Michael agreed. "These pipes up here are for the fire suppression system, these down here are water, and these are the return drains. Also a drain in the floor, here. They all lead to the recycler in the life-support module. There's an identical kitchen over at Shackleton, and the boys and girls over at Shoemaker Lunar Antenna Park have ordered the next one off the HMI production line. Until it rolls, they're basically eating granola bars, as Giancarlo and Purcell and I did, when we first landed here. Malinkin Base is only two people, with no galley aspirations that I know of. They have a microwave."

Hilario Hamblin walked in behind them, whereupon Michael grabbed him by the neck and actually gave him a noogie. Not hard, but still unexpected. "Hilario here, whom you've met, is our chief cook and programmer. Durm just likes washing things."

"There's dignity in labor," Kurtis Durm called out, making a rude gesture, again without turning around.

"If that's true," Michael said, clapping him on the back, "then we must all be very dignified indeed." Then, to Raimy, "Through there is the laundry. Same size utility module as the kitchen, with a small double hatch leading into the airlock. You may recall stuffing your contaminated underwear in there."

"Yep," Raimy agreed, poking his head into the module to see. There was no one in there, and the lights were off, but there was a little round porthole window through which a dim light filtered. Two washer-dryers, two folding tables, two drying racks, with an aisle running down the center. For a laundry room, it seemed pretty spacious.

"Cramped, I know," Michael said.

"Eh? You should try living on a submarine."

"Unlikely, at this point," Michael said with a laugh.

They proceeded east, back through the kitchen and into an empty classroom. Since the two of them were alone for the moment, Raimy asked, in his best investigator voice, "You have secrets, don't you?"

Michael paused, and looked at Raimy. He seemed to consider his answer for several seconds, weighing each word carefully. Finally he said, "In the sense of absolved sins I would rather not discuss, yes. You're clever to notice. Or perhaps you simply ask that question of everyone."

"I don't," Raimy said.

"Well, then you are indeed a clever man. Will you turn your camera off?"

"I'd rather not."

Uncomfortably, Michael said, "This is an interrogation, then? Very well. I have a past, yes, from before my vows. It isn't germane to your investigation."

"No?"

"No. My sins involve extramarital sex, if that helps you understand. Very few of the religious have lived completely celibate lives, myself included."

And Raimy did understand that, yes. He felt there was probably more to it—Michael was gay or a fetishist or something—but unless Raimy could link it to Etsub in some way, it really wasn't his business to press any further.

"Thank you for your candor," he said. "I don't mean to offend."

"On the contrary," Michael said. "I appreciate your thoroughness." Then, more pointedly, he added: "And discretion."

They proceeded east again, into what seemed to be a library. There were only about twenty actual books on the shelves, but there were also a pair of surprisingly large desktop computers, and a couple of empty writing desks. Another porthole, looking out onto some kind of trusswork. Michael said, "A great deal of monastic work is cerebral or academic. We don't carry rollups or smartyglasses, so many is the day one or two of us are holed up in here, finding answers to big questions and small. Outside, by the way, if you look out here, is our tower magnet, which deflects charged particles and delays the day we all drop dead of cancer."

The library had two exits, one of which led south into the dormitory where Raimy's quarters were located.

"East dormitory," Michael said. "The west dorm is over there. The two rack vaults are identical outer shells, but yours—the east dorm—is a slightly later model, with plumbing relocated in order to raise the ceilings. In the older module, we regularly bump our heads, and since it's buried here in the middle of the complex, with other modules all around it, we're unlikely to ever have it replaced, even if the Holy See coughs up the cash. It's one of those live-and-learn scenarios that are, in fact, our whole reason for being here."

To which Raimy said, "I appreciate you putting me in the newer module."

"Naturally, and you're welcome. You're also in a VIP cell, which is slightly larger and has only a single bed. The rest of us, students included, are stacked into bunks." His eyes twinkled with sudden mirth. "Please know that a normal monastery would not have en suite bathrooms in each cell, but that's how Harvest Moon designed the modules. So in this one particular, we're more comfortable than we would be on Earth, where monastery bathrooms can be surprisingly gross. Cleanliness may be next to godliness, but with enough brothers wiping their asses in the same two stalls . . . well, you get the idea."

Michael pointed east and west along the corridor formed by the two dormitory modules. Each had six dwellings, or "cells," and four exits marking the points of the compass. In a touch that was either ironic, artistic, or homesick, someone had painted stone archways over the hatches into each room and module.

"We call this hallway 'the cloisters,'" Michael said. "It leads that way into the chapel, as you see, and this way into the east airlock, which"—he opened the hatch—"also serves as our balneary, which is a schmancy medieval word for bathing room."

Raimy had never been in here. It looked a bit like the main airlock, except that the gowning area was fully open into the showers, and there was a large metal bathtub where the racks and lockers should be.

"We don't use this lock for ingress and egress, so it's dust-free. At the Marriott Stars and Esley Shade Station, each apartment actually has its own shower, but HMI doesn't love us quite that much. So it's rub-a-dub-dub, eleven monks and one tub, and whoa, that sounded inappropriate. Nothing untoward ever happens here, I can assure, or there'd be Hell and His Holy to pay. Anyway, we usually just shower, because we tend to be quite busy and a bath smacks ever so faintly of sloth. Anyway, if you find your armpits stinking, put a sock on the door handle and scrub away. These showers are not on a timer, and the water is all recycled. No Navy showers here; take as long as you like."

Raimy smiled. A Navy shower was a minute-long spray to get yourself wet, then a minute to soap up, and then a final minute to rinse off. Two minutes if you really needed it. Not one person in the history of the universe had ever found that sufficient, and one of the great pleasures of shore leave was taking a real goddamn shower, or "Hollywood shower," as the sailors sometimes called it.

"All the pleasures of home," Raimy said. "Really, this place is a lot nicer than a submarine. It's roomy, it's two-dimensional, you've got some windows . . . I don't know that I'd want to spend my whole life . . ." He paused, then said, "Sorry, that was rude."

"Not at all," Michael assured him. "I'm guessing you wouldn't want to spend your life celibate, either. We all have different callings. I'm curious, though, why you *do* want to spend your life at Antilympus."

Raimy thought about that for a few seconds, and finally answered, "Mars is a different kind of place. I mean, for one thing, Antilympus Township looks like a luxury resort or a shopping mall compared to this place. It's a lot more accommodating. But also, when you look out the windows, you see wind and clouds. Frost forming on the top of the soil. The way the light plays off the mountains, it's just . . ."

"You've seen it," Michael said, getting it. "You've looked out through the eyes of the robots there."

"Yes," Raimy agreed. "Every chance I get. Have you?"

"Oh, indeed. It's every bit as beautiful as you say, and I expect in future times, Lunar architecture will take its cues at least in part from your township. But Mars is also far away. To go there is, in large sense, to cut ties with history and start completely over with that clean slate people are always talking about. I get the appeal. I do.

"But that's the exact opposite of our mission here at Saint Joe. If I had my choice between Mars and Moon, believe me, I'd be right where I am. We're close to the Earth here—almost still a part of it—and we're here with hands outstretched to lift people into the future. Not just by ones and twos, but as many as rockets can carry. As fast as Harvest Moon can build the dwellings. We're figuring out how to live here, and I tell you, Antilympus has a greater chance of succeeding, the more it learns from our example. That's exactly why your people came here, why Etsub Beyene came here, and I hope to God and Jesus his death doesn't discourage anyone else from coming. It's expensive to get here, I know, but I tell you truthfully, it's more expensive not to. If you speak to Danny Beseman, I hope you'll extend him our invitation. The Holy See has already done so of course, but you're one of Beseman's own people, and now that you've been here, perhaps your word will carry farther than Pope Dave's."

Raimy thought about that. Michael's earnestness was

touching and infectious, but the truth was, Raimy had been here less than a day, and had learned fuck-all. And he wasn't exactly on Beseman's buddy list, so it wasn't clear he'd have any influence at all. And yet, it did make sense: next to the trillions of dollars it would take to land the colonists at Antilympus, what difference would it make if a few dozen trips to the Moon were tacked on?

"I'll talk to him, if he'll listen," Raimy promised.

Suddenly back in tour guide mode, Michael said, "This hatch leads to the east greenhouse. We keep it closed to seal in the humidity, but"—he opened the hatch and stepped through—"this is where our most pressing work takes place: growing what we need to feed ourselves."

The light inside the greenhouse was grow-light pink, and the air (humid, yes) was alive with noise. Brothers Ferris and "Bear" were in here, along with all three of the Antilympus candidates. They were just getting started with their day, not really engrossed in anything yet, but there was an energy about them that reminded Raimy of exactly why he'd wanted to come to outer space. Everything mattered. Every touch, every movement—no matter how routine—was exciting.

"These roots are getting too much phosphorus," Ferris was saying, in an accent Raimy felt he could definitively nail down as Brazilian. "This prevents other nutrients getting absorbed properly. See this yellowing around the edge of the leaves? That's how you can tell."

"A lot of things cause yellow leaves," Anming Shui protested.

"Not quite like this," Ferris said. "It's a real distinctive pattern of curling and drying."

"So what can you do about it?" Bridget Tobin asked. "The sewage being what it is."

"We add water and crushed regolith to the drip until the problem goes away," Ferris said. "Light, air, water, sewage, regolith. Once you've used up all the starter materials you brought with you, that's all you're going to have. Here, we can bring some soil components up from Earth, or make use of waste materials we can easily replace, like cloth. On Mars, you're not going to have that luxury. You want to really grow something, it's all about balance. You know all that; I'm just telling you what danger signs to watch out for. Now, if you are getting too much iron, the leaves will bronze and stipple, which is easy to do here, and probably on Mars, too."

The module was full of hydroponic racks and tanks, with all kinds of different plants growing in them. The sound of blowers—never absent anywhere in the monastery—was particularly loud in here, and the glare of pink and blue LEDs was an assault on the senses.

"We filter iron out of the water," said Bear. Raimy didn't think that was his actual name, but it was what people seemed to call him.

"Let's keep going," Michael said into Raimy's ear.

They shuffled down the aisle, stepping around people and over cable runners slotted across the floor. Michael opened another hatch on the west side of the module, and stepped through into a space that was equally pink and blue, but quieter. Raimy followed him through and then closed the hatch behind him.

"Sorry," Michael said. "Force-growing vegetables takes a lot of energy, and a lot of material flow. We're trying to maximize throughput, and it's actually pretty amazing how far we've been able to push that. It is fatiguingly loud, though. The lights and blowers are never silent. A few hours in that module will have you begging for death. I honestly don't know how Bear and Fox stand up to it."

"Why is it so much quieter in here?" Raimy asked.

The west greenhouse was much like the east one, except that the plants were smaller and more widely spaced, and the troughs were full of dirt instead of liquid. Standing at a workbench was a brother whose name Raimy didn't know. He was patiently weighing little plastic cups full of powder, in a laboratory scale with glass doors that opened and closed.

"This," Michael answered, "is the epicenter of our most meaningful task: creating new life with zero terrestrial input. Those tanks are filled with moonwater, fresh from the ice fields of Faustini Crater. Milled regolith fills the planters, along with the ground-up remains of previous generations of plants. It's quieter in here because these plants will die if you speak a harsh word to them. The lighting is on a twelve-hour cycle. Air and water circulation are on a low setting, and any handling of the plants is exceedingly gentle. The idea here is not to grow things fast, but to find those things that will grow at all, and breed them for the characteristics we want. We've found ten different food plants that will grow sustainably through multiple generations, and I'm hoping these shallots over here will be the eleventh. They take a lot of water and a lot of babying, but we've gotten enough nitrogen into the soil now that this latest generation might just pull through. It's patient work, but it's going to echo forward for generations to come."

"You sound prideful," Raimy told him. It was a dick thing to say, and he wasn't sure why he did it. He would sometimes needle a potential suspect to try and get some reaction, and this sounded a lot like that, but Michael wasn't much of a suspect. Raimy *was* becoming impatient—that much was clear.

Michael, though, simply spread his hands and shrugged. "I am prideful, and I hope it don't cometh before a fall, but it's why we're here, and I won't apologize for taking pleasure in it. Etsub, by the way, spent most of his time here when he wasn't in class. They all did. Force-growing rutabagas is less glamorous, so I'm having to make double sure they get an earful of it before they leave. There'll be a room like this at Antilympus, mark my words, and it will feed the future. But the present needs to be fed as well, and the present is a hungry bastard that doesn't like CHON."

"I didn't mean to disparage your work," Raimy said.

"And I don't mean to disparage yours," Michael replied. "I mustn't forget that I, too, am a player in this tragedy, and it's your job to watch my every move, through predator's eyes."

Raimy scoffed. "If I thought you had a motive, we'd be having a very different conversation."

"No doubt. And yet, I've been rude. Let's complete this tour with an eye toward the . . . evidence you seek."

"That would be great, yes."

Michael then led him west, into a room that looked like a cross between an operating room, a dentist's office, and a grocery-store pharmacy. The space was dominated by a med tube, which was pretty standard for medical offices these days. You climbed inside the tube, and it would do anything from routine examinations and bloodwork to invasive microsurgical procedures. The list of things a tube could do was getting longer every year, though it was still dwarfed by the list of things it couldn't. Hence the dentist chair, which looked like it was capable of stretching out fully flat, and of tilting in various directions. Behind both things were rows of lockers, and shelves full of quaint-looking pill bottles. Again, the whole thing was quite surprisingly roomy compared to a submarine sickbay. There was even a little writing desk, where Brother Hughart sat, pecking at the keyboard of a laptop computer.

"Infirmary," Michael said, pointing at various things. "Standard medicosurgical tube. Examination table. Surgical lockers. Drug printer. Drug inventory. This is where we brought Etsub, after it was a hundred percent clear he was actually dead."

"Not before?" Raimy asked. But he could see, it would be difficult to wrestle a General Spacesuit Heavy Rebreather in here. To wrestle someone *out* of a Heavy Rebreather and up onto that table, or into the tube.

"There was more room in the chapel," Michael said, "and it was closer to the airlock. If there was any hope at all, it was to lay him down and shock him with his suit's own defibrillator."

"Okay," Raimy said, looking around. "That makes sense. Why, uh . . . There are a lot of pill bottles in here. 3D printed?"

"The drug printer is *hoora* slow," Hughart said looking

over his shoulder at Raimy. His accent was Scottish. "I like to stock up on the basics, and there are a lot of basics."

"Ah. And you did the postmortem examination? In here?"

"Yes and yes," Hughart said, "and I can confidently say he died of vacuum asphyxiation. Burst capillaries everywhere. Dried blood in the lungs. It was quick, and probably rather painless, like being anaesthetized, although I can't say it was a pleasant experience. I'd guess he was conscious for about twenty seconds, and technically alive for a couple of minutes after that. By the time Andrei cuddy-backed him to the airlock, irreversible brain damage would have begun. Michael was right; there was no realistic way we could have saved him, without dire risk to other personnel. But we did try."

"How did that make you feel?" Raimy asked. It was as more a personal question than a detective one, although it might have some meaning if Callen Hughart were a serious suspect at this point.

Hughart grimaced. He was a young man, still in his early thirties, and his close-cut brown hair made him seem even younger. Though his demeanor was professional, he seemed genuinely pained. "Sir, I'd never lost a patient before. As an intern I did a rotation at an emergency department in Hull, but I wasn't directly responsible for outcomes. Other than that, I haven't exactly been on the front lines. I'm a foot doctor, and there are people who'll say you don't become a podiatrist and a tube monitor if your grades are worth a damn. Those people are correct. It came as a shock, I'll tell you. My hands still shake when I think about it."

"I'm sorry to hear that," Raimy said. Then: "What do you think happened?"

Hughart looked him in the eye and said, "All signs point to a rapid decompression. That's what I think. Etsub didn't have any enemies here, and I kind of doubt he had any at all. I think this was an accident. He was out there alone, totally against protocol, and I think he just ... did some stupid thing to his suit that we don't know about."

"Like what?"

"Lord, I wish I knew. We all use that exact same model of spacesuit, and I don't want to postmortem any more like that. Maybe he fell. I don't know."

"All right," Raimy said. "This is helpful. I may come back to you with more questions, as I fill in the missing information."

"Happy to help," Hughart said.

"Shall we move on?" Michael asked.

Raimy nodded. "Let's."

They moved west again, through a hatchway that led into a sort of machine shop, with workbenches piled high with equipment, parts bins, and pressurized gas bottles. One of the monks was here, wearing safety glasses and using a drill press to put holes in the corners of a stack of metal rectangles.

"Workshop," Michael said. "That's Brother Purcell at the drill press, or 'Puke' as he likes to be called."

"He says I like to be called that," Purcell mumbled, without visible annoyance. Raimy's ear for accents was getting quite a workout today, but he was pretty sure Purcell was Spanish. Like actually from Spain, and with a faint lisp to show for it.

"That's a lathe," Michael said, still pointing. "That's the chemical synthesizer, where your soap and toothpaste come from. Four-headed 3D printer. Arc welder. Anvil. Band saw. Table saw. That's the open space where Puke would someday like to have an induction forge and pneumatic hammer, which I don't think His Holiness would allow. I'm not sure I'd allow it myself. Perhaps, someday, an outbuilding for that kind of loud, dangerous crap. It would help offset the high cost of ordering forged parts from Earth, or begging Harvest Moon for a custom fabrication. But that's a someday problem, not a today one. Over here is our radio, because this is also the radio room, where I first came after receiving Andrei's Mayday, and where I stand every time a spaceship lands."

"Hmm. You heard the Mayday call from all the way in the dormitory?"

"It's not that far," Michael said, "and this place is quiet at night. But in fact, any traffic on the emergency channel rings a chime in every module, and traffic on the private channel rings a chime on my wristwatch, and on Giancarlo's."

"I see. So, after the first distress call, how long did it take you to get here?"

"Not long. Less than a minute, I'd say."

"Hmm."

After politely waiting a few seconds, Michael said, "That hatchway in the floor leads down to the bunker, where we hide in case of a major solar flare."

"Oh, wow. Has that happened?"

"Twice," said Brother Purcell.

"This was one of the three original modules," Michael

said, "where Geo and Puke and I lived when we first arrived here."

"Tight fit," Raimy observed, "if the bunker's the same size as the workshop."

"It is," Michael said. "Jackhammered into the bedrock and totally buried. But it's empty, and that makes a huge difference. All this stuff, this equipment and whatnot, eats up about half the volume of the module. We've so far resisted the temptation to use the bunker for overflow storage, so there's still room enough for everyone to lie down. Would you like to see it?"

Raimy would have said yes, sure, except that Brother Purcell was standing on the hatch, which had a flattened, sunken handle that fit flush with the floor. Raimy didn't want to disturb things unnecessarily, so instead he asked, "Did Etsub ever go down there?"

To which Michael answered, "Not to my knowledge. There's really nothing down there. Still, perhaps you shouldn't take my word for it. Puke, can you step aside for a minute?"

"All right," Purcell said. He stood aside and then grabbed the hatch's handle with his fingers. He lifted, rotated, then lifted again. The hatch looked heavy, but of course it wasn't in Lunar gravity, so he lifted it open with apparent ease. A ladder led straight down into darkness, until Michael flipped a switch somewhere, and the space down there lit up.

Concerned that this was taking too long, Raimy just knelt down and stuck his head through the hatch. There was, indeed, nothing down there except some foil packets of emergency rations, along with a little sink and toilet. It didn't look like a particularly comfortable spot to hang out for the hours or days it might take for a flare to subside, but okay. Bomb shelter, basically. The ceiling was a mess of uncovered pipes and wires.

"All right," he said, floating back up onto his feet. "Where next?"

"Life support," Michael said, pointing south through an open hatchway.

"Close that hatch on your way out," Purcell said. "In fact, close them all; I'm going to be welding in a few minutes."

"Very well."

There were hatches on the north and east sides of the module, which Michael dutifully closed, before leading Raimy into the life-support module and closing that hatch as well.

"If these are closed," he said, "don't shortcut through the workshop without knocking. That arc welder can damage your retinas, even from a distance."

"I'm familiar," Raimy assured him.

The inside of the life-support module looked very much like something you'd see on a submarine: big water tanks and compressed-gas tanks, heaters and blowers and pipes and electrical transformers, all connected by color-coded conduits leading straight into the bulkheads. A single touch panel on one wall seemed to function as a nerve center for the whole shebang.

Michael spread his hands. "Self-explanatory, I trust?" Unspoken: you're a submariner and an astronaut, and you know what plumbing and ventilation systems look like.

"Yes. Thank you. How many people can this support?"

Michael answered, "It's not so much the number of people as the number of hab modules, and both answers depend on how much water and electricity people plan on using. At our current usage, we could approximately double the size of this place, and the population, without adding another life-support module. But of course, the other brake on expansion is simple geometry. Right now the place is pretty neatly laid out, but any expansion would be more difficult." He pointed to a blank, rounded-rectangular plate on the east bulkhead, clearly designed to be removable so that a hatch could be installed. "If we build out in that direction, we're blocking visibility to the airlock, which is a safety issue. But if we go south"—he pointed at another hatch blank—"we turn this module into a thoroughfare, which is also potentially unsafe. Or we expand through the library, or the observatory, either of which would hinder the monastery as a place of quiet contemplation. And we can't build too close to the tower magnet, so really, to expand, we're going to have to move the east airlock. Even one more module will be a big project, tying up time and equipment from Harvest Moon. Which means His Holiness is going to have to cough up some gold. It will happen, I think, but not soon."

Next, they entered a module reminiscent of the workshop, except that instead of machine tools, it was full of microscopes and spectrometers, autoclaves and test-tube centrifuges. It looked a lot like the El Paso County Crime Lab, at the sheriff's station in Colorado Springs. On a big table, underneath a white cotton sheet, was something bulky and vaguely humanoid.

"Lab?" Raimy asked, unnecessarily.

"Indeed," Michael said. "Where I spend about a third of my waking life, along with Zachary Duppler. And if your patience is at an end, we can conclude the tour right here, as that's Etsub's spacesuit under that sheet. We can commence your inspection of it at any time, including this very moment. However, three paces to the east is a final module—our observatory—which I do think you should see, if only because Etsub himself spent time there, looking at Mars through an optical telescope."

Raimy really needed get to work, yes, on the actual evidence. He'd never had a case that pulled his attention in so many different directions! Even at the DA's office, he'd been good at investigating and interviewing people and building a case, in part because he simply didn't think about anything else.

He was, unfortunately, pretty sloppy at a lot of the other lawyer stuff. He spent too little time writing and practicing lines to recite in the courtroom, and he sort of fell apart—gripped by something akin to stage fright—whenever things wandered too far from the remarks he did prepare. But as a cop, he didn't *need* to think about anything else, beyond the investigation itself. When he spoke in court, he didn't have to make up the questions. Just answer them, with detailed descriptions of the evidence he'd so obsessively and painstakingly collected.

And yet, he was in outer goddamn space, in an actual planetary base that bore at least a passing functional resemblance to parts of Antilympus Township. Raimy might never see Antilympus with his own two eyes, but he actually was here on the Moon, right now, and so there was another strong part of him that couldn't think about anything other than *that*. So, with a little flicker of self-doubt, what he said to Michael was, "Okay. Show me."

The observatory turned out to be somewhat anticlimactic, though: a module much like the workshop or laboratory, but dominated by two desks, each with a beefy, liquid-cooled desktop computer of the sort that could do serious number crunching. Ovid and Giancarlo were in here, seated at the two workstations and peering at their respective monitors, neither of which showed a dramatic spacescape, or even any images at all. Ovid appeared to be writing code, while Giancarlo was deeply engrossed in a stack of numbers.

"Where are the telescopes?" Raimy asked.

"On the ground over there," Michael said, waving vaguely south. "Three of them, observing three different spectral bands." Raimy must have looked disappointed, because he added, "I suppose it doesn't look like much, but this was the first crewed observatory outside of Earth orbit. Which is a big deal, right? One might argue that it's less relevant, now that the Shoemaker Lunar Antenna Park is just over the hill, with three astronomers of its own, but one would be rude and wrong to say it. We're a stable platform with no atmosphere, and these two fellows are making discoveries almost every week. SLAP's claim to usefulness is that they're behind a hill, technically in the Moon's radio shadow and out of view of a noisy Earth. But the dream of putting that facility truly on the far side was shelved, in favor of the convenience of putting it within walking distance of Moonbase Larry, and so the height of the hill limits the size of the antennae to about six meters. Which is not much, by the standards of radio astronomy. And they don't have any optical telescopes, so the two of us are complementary, and close enough together that we might almost be considered a single observatory."

Raimy noticed Bridget Tobin standing in the northern hatchway, leading (Raimy thought) from the quieter of the two greenhouses.

"Hi," she said.

"Fine morning," Michael said back.

She asked, "Are you going to start soon with the spacesuit?"

"In a minute," Raimy said.

"Mind if I watch?"

"I do," Raimy said, as gently as he could manage. "You're a suspect in a possible homicide."

"As are we all," Michael said. There was an uncomfortable pause, which Michael filled by saying, "Like it or not, you're going to need three sets of hands to make this work, and Bridget has long, thin fingers which I think will be useful. Also, I assume you'll be recording the whole time, so any monkey business on her part, or mine, or anyone's, will give itself away rather quickly. Unless you strenuously object, Raimy, I suggest you let her help."

Raimy really wanted to strenuously object. Wasn't the crime scene already contaminated enough? Did he really have to let the suspects themselves assist with the physical evidence? But of course the answer was yes, he did. He might be standing next to a murderer right this very moment, and still he would have to ask for help. And if he got it wrong, then one of the first hundred people on Mars could be that very murderer, and there might be call for a detective at Antilympus after all.

"Fine," he said, unhappily.

3.2
22 November

✦

Shackleton Lunar Industrial Station
South Polar Mineral Territories
Lunar Surface

"What have we learned?" Commander Harb asked pointedly.

Tania Falstaff and Puya Hebbar were both in the mess hall, sipping Saint Joe's brown tea and trying to unwind from another long day. Harb had stepped into the beam of one of the overhead lights, casting a broad shadow across them both, and Tania thought, not for the first time, that they needed better light dispersion in these modules. Harb was looking at both of them, but the question was aimed at Tania: what have "we" learned about the activities at Malinkin Base?

The mass driver's test projectile had burned up on schedule yesterday, so this was now her primary concern.

But it was Puya who answered: "Ma'am, do you remember that nuclear rocket engine I told you about?"

Harb seemed annoyed. Puya was only here to get the mass driver working, and now that it was operational, she could pretty much go home anytime. She only reported to Harb in the sense that Harb was in charge of the moonbase; they were actually peers who both reported directly to Sir Lawrence. "The thorium-steam thing?"

"Thorium-hydrogen-oxygen, yes," Puya said, undeterred. Her voice quick as a bird, and conspiratorial. "I've been running simulations that seem to confirm my hunch, that we can get at least double the specific impulse of our best chemical rockets. Which means we can plausibly run stratospheric 'scoop' missions from here to collect nitrogen and CO_2 directly from the Earth's atmosphere."

Harb paused, her expression shifting from annoyed to thoughtful. Nitrogen and carbon were two things you really needed on the Moon. Two things not found here, and fiercely expensive to ship up from Earth. Orlov Petrochemical had stepped in to fill this void, supplying gases refined from asteroidal rock, but it was proper expensive nonetheless. And with Clementine Cislunar Fuel Depot having paused its shipments, and generally showing signs of being an unreliable supply hub, Harvest Moon could not afford to rely on them exclusively. Not to mention Grigory Orlov was a pig and all that.

"How much nitrogen?" Harb asked.

Puya shrugged. "Not sure yet. Hundreds of kilograms at the very least."

"From one robotic mission?"

"Right."

"How much ice do you have to throw away for that?" Tania asked. She was an engineer and space traffic controller, not a propulsion expert, but it didn't take a propulsion expert to see the key issue: Puya's hypothetical engine—the one she'd been talking about for weeks, when she was supposed to be fixing the mass driver— would "combust cryogenic hydrogen and oxygen over a subcritical bed of proton-baked thorium." So if you were going to use it to collect gases from Earth, you were really just trading mined Lunar ice for those gases. And ice also had a value, and so did thorium, and the labor of Harvest Moon personnel.

"I haven't fully worked out the economics yet," Puya admitted, a bit self-righteously. Then, to Harb, she said, "With your permission, I'd like to pull a couple of my engineers up here to start building some experimental prototypes."

"Using what for thorium, dear?" Harb asked, her voice now pointed again. "We've promised Dan Beseman our entire output for at least the next twelve months, and as Sir Lawrence has already pointed, out, that's quite an aggressive target. Nor, as the Americans and Russians have made quite clear, can fissionable materials be shipped up from Earth in such quantity, which is precisely why we're supplying it to Beseman. I'm afraid your request is completely out of the question. Of course, it's not me you should be asking."

"Professional courtesy," Puya said. "Obviously it's up to Sir Lawrence."

"Who is no fool," Harb said. "He'll tell you to come back to Earth and build your prototypes there."

A bit sullenly, Puya said, "The engine only works below fifty millibars' pressure, and best in full vacuum."

"Then find a vacuum chamber, or build one. You may be unacquainted with the cost of housing you here at

Shackleton, but I am not, and neither—I assure you—is Sir Lawrence. It's a very promising idea, and I'll follow your progress with great interest, but it's not a project I will willingly host at this time. Now, the EOLS capsule parked outside will be departing in three days' time, and I should like very much for you to be on it."

"Is that an order?" Puya asked.

"A request."

"Hmm."

Puya stewed, but said nothing more.

To Tania, Commander Harb said, "You're the one I came here to speak with. Can you please—"

Just then, a noisy knot of people entered the mess hall module from the adjoining workshop. One was Huntley Millar, the EVA crew chief. Another was Eldad Barzeley, a physicist—really a sort of weatherman for solar radiation—who'd come up from Earth to help with the mass driver. And last there was Stephen Chalmers, electrical engineer, whom Tania had slept with on several occasions, and might do again.

The three of them looked across at Harb and Puya and Tania, decided they didn't like the look of things over here, and laughingly sat down at a table of their own, far from whatever they thought was going on. On the very far side of the room, four of the technicians sat together (or perhaps "huddled" was the word), having some sort of quiet, intense conversation of their own. There'd been a lot of quiet, intense conversations lately. Still, the mess hall was a double-wide barrel vault—the largest module HMI had ever manufactured—and it had three tables stretching down its length. Seating for up to sixty people, in theory—more than triple the number currently on site. So yes, the room was large enough to afford some privacy if you wanted it.

"Can you please," Harb continued, "give me a very brief synopsis of your findings with regard to the men at Malinkin? I have a call with Sir Lawrence in an hour, and he's quite interested. I do trust you've been discreet?"

"As a fox in suburbia," Tania assured her. "I called them to see if they needed anything, and they said no, and so I asked them what kinds of supplies they were using most quickly, and they said food, which is not surprising because they're running on stored rations. But we don't sell food, so I asked if they needed batteries or anything like that, and they said no and then basically hung up on me. So, undaunted, I called again two days later, and finally got them to talk. I want you to know, I resent being put in that position. I didn't sign up for Esley Shade Station, now, did I?"

With its heavily female-skewed gender ratio, Esley was widely rumored to be one giant harem for its owner, Igbal Renz. And whether that was true or not, it was a useful metaphor, and Harb would know what she meant. She'd asked Tania to handle this because, when dealing with a trio of lonely men, a woman simply had a better chance of getting a result.

Harb said, "No one asked you to flirt with them."

"Didn't have to," Tania said.

There was, of course, no escaping from her femaleness here. This was true in any male-dominated environment, but it was particularly true in this remotest of outposts. Harb had enough of a commanding presence to override gender entirely, but for Tania (and probably for Puya, too), all talk was flirting, whether she liked it or not. She felt quite sure even Brother Michael noticed a pair of tits when he saw one.

However, in actual fact, Tania wasn't especially put out by any of it. Having spent three years in testosterone-drenched Antarctica, she'd come to the Moon with a very clear idea what the social dynamics were going to be like. And when she accepted this little spying assignment, both she and Harb knew exactly what she was agreeing to. Tania was pretty much just taking the piss out of Harb because she could.

Sitting down beside Tania and lowering her voice, an exasperated Harb asked, "So what did you learn from these randy young men?"

"Well, they've found a crater they quite like, with a feature called a graben, which I gather is some kind of ditch, surrounded by deep fields of dust. Apparently, the thought is, they can inflate a plastic dome in the graben and then cover it with Lunar concrete, and then simply bulldoze regolith over it and form additional concrete layers as they go. They'll need a lot of equipment and a lot of water to accomplish this, so it's good for us in any case."

"Or a drain on our resources, if we end up taking the project over. I'm not sure quite what Sir Lawrence's interest might be in all this, but I confess I fear the worst."

"That we'll soon be in the hospitality business?" Puya asked.

"Yes, and growing too quickly in the process. We've years of hard work ahead of us as it is, but a project like that could really muck things up. One thing I've learned:

you can't do everything at once, but I suppose time will tell what Sir Lawrence intends. Ms. Falstaff, did you happen to get a location?"

"As a matter of fact, I did."

Harb nodded. "Well, then. Mail me some satellite images—the highest resolution you can find—and we'll see what the big man makes of it all. It wouldn't surprise me if these civil engineers were on the Harvest Moon payroll by the end of the month."

"It's bollocks," Adam Richter was saying to his crew, on the HMI private channel. Well, not *his* crew, exactly, but he liked to think the three of them—and others—looked up to him as a kind of role model. "Pushing back our return dates and stretching out our Earthside time. Bollocks."

They were outside in one of the fabrication huts, putting the last few bolts into the outer shell of a hab module that would, in a few weeks' time, be a kitchen. It was hard and painstaking work, and although Adam wore a sweatband across his forehead, and although they were sheltered from the sun in here and the outside of his suit was at something like minus fifty Celsius, sweat was nevertheless finding its way into his eyes, as it often did by the end of a four-hour EVA shift.

"We know all about what they've done," said Blake Myneni.

He sounded weary with the topic, which annoyed Adam. The Astronaut Technicians—twenty in total, of whom ten were presently on Luna—did all the actual work around here. Shackleton was, first and foremost, a factory, where rovers and habitation modules and linear accelerator magnets were constructed in hard vacuum. This meant a lot of time in spacesuits, and thus a lot of blisters and bruises where it inevitably rubbed or dug into you. The Astronaut Technicians were all supposed to be on six-month rotation—three on Luna, three on Earth, three on Luna, and so forth. But the Management bastards, in their infinite wisdom, had, earlier this year, gone and made it four-and-four, without asking, without warning, and without any increase in pay.

"I've got blisters on my bruises, and vice versa," Adam stated, flexing his arm in an attempt to demonstrate. They would know what he meant; the elbow joint of these suits was a notorious chafing point. "Four months is too long to be at this sort of work, even in Lunar gravity. And what am I supposed to do with an extra month back home? Hug my father? You wouldn't say that if you'd met him."

"We know all about your bruises," Blake assured him. The other two, Jerry and Merv, grumbled and nodded within their helmets, without really specifying with whom they were agreeing.

"All right, well, let's get these tools put away before we get back inside. Do *not* leave them on a metal surface."

"Yes, sir," Merv said, rather mockingly.

In fairness, Adam was not, in fact, in charge. Nobody was; the EVA crew chief, Huntley Millar, had gone inside two full hours ago, leaving the rest of them to finish up. But still, if you left a tool in the wrong spot, it could sometimes just randomly vacuum-weld in place, for reasons that had never been properly explained to Adam. And then you could sometimes pop it off with a chisel, and sometimes you had to drag a vacuum torch over and cut it off, damaging both the tool and the surface in the process, and he did not want to get blamed for that again.

So they put their tools away, and then slogged back toward the airlock, their weary steps somehow heavy in the low gravity.

As they passed the portholes in the mess hall, Adam looked inside, as surreptitiously as possible. Commander Harb and her hens clustered at one end, and on the far end by the hatchway into the workshop, Crew Chief Huntley Millar sitting with a pair of *ed-you-cayted* males. Stephen Chalmers was a snot-nosed engineer several years younger than Adam himself, and Eldad Fucking Barzeley was a *dok-torr* of some fancy thing. They were not bad men, Adam judged, just as Harb's bunch were not bad women. But they did spend rather a lot of time indoors, yeah? They made four times his salary for half the work, and thought it was just fine. It was not.

"I hear the workers are striking up on Clementine," Merv said.

"Be a wonder if they weren't," Jerry opined.

"Yes, yes, and Igbal Renz has made contact with aliens," Blake told them snidely. "If you paid as much attention to your torque settings as you do to Puya Hebbar, you'd have less rework, and fewer rumors in your head."

That stopped conversation for a bit. The men looked down at their boots, just trudge-trudge-trudging across the regolith.

"She likes me," Merv finally said.

"She likes everyone," Blake said, dismissively, as he checked the pressure bleed valve and opened the airlock's outer hatch. "Wha'd she want with a bloke like you? Now, you get on a rotation with Laura..."

There were only two female Astronaut Technicians, and Laura Koble was one of them. The other, Cassey Murrain, was into girls, and married besides. But Laura had a firm rule about dating coworkers, and a bristly manner toward anyone who tried to get too chummy. Adam felt her pain on this, and didn't like the lads talking that way behind her back.

"Let's have none of that," he said firmly.

"Yes, sir," Merv repeated.

That stopped the conversation again. There were really only so many things to talk about up here. Adam looked over his crew—good men, all—and judged it time to bring them in on his news.

Once they'd repressurized and hosed off and were getting back into their indoor clothes, and were no longer speaking on an open radio channel, he said, "I've got contacted by the union."

That got their attention. All three of them looked up.

"What union?" Blake wanted to know.

"Plumbing Trades Union," Adam told him. "They've asked if we'd think about joining up."

"We're plumbers, then?" Merv said, jamming his slippers down over his enormous and vaguely misshapen feet. "I've got an associate's degree, and four hundred some EVA hours. I can assemble electromagnets with my eyes shut, literally. I've done it."

"What's some plumber know about our problems up here?" Jerry asked. "Not much, is what I'm thinking. We need our own Astronaut Technicians' union."

"Well, there isn't one," Adam said.

"Well, there should be," Merv spouted back. "We should start it."

"Oh, complicated," Blake said. "There's a lot of laws to follow, to prove you're not just, you know, shaking people down. A lot of paperwork."

"On Earth there's laws," Merv said. "Here it's just people. Workers and management. Us and them."

"Yeah," Jerry said, vaguely.

They all sat there on their benches, scratched and bruised and bone-tired, reluctant to get up and enter the moonbase proper. Right here, right now, they were among fellows who understood each other's plight, without explanation. Adam actually had been a plumber at one point in his life, which was maybe how the PTU had got ahold of him. He had then become a welder because the money was better, and then—in a strange turn of events— an *underwater* welder for the UK Docks Tyneside. And then, in an even stranger turn, an astronaut for HMI, and still not yet to his thirty-sixth birthday. Each man had followed a strange path to this place, and between the four of them they knew more about building things in outer space than any PhD ever could.

"We could just talk to Commander Harb," Adam said, in a thoughtful tone.

And they all had a good laugh at that.

Across the mess hall from Harb and Tania and Puya, Stephen Chalmers was asking Huntley Millar, "How are the technicians doing?"

Through the portholes, he'd watched four of them walk

by outside, and something in their manner had deepened his sense of concern. The technicians used to cycle through on three-month rotations, but since the naval blockade of Suriname earlier in the year it had all stretched out by a month. This made perfect sense from a management standpoint: it cut transportation costs by twenty-five percent, and also simply reduced the logistical risks associated with defying the ITAR nations. Unfortunately, HMI was basically ignoring the technicians' grumblings about the extra work, which seemed to be increasingly problematic.

Of course, Stephen was here on a twelve-month rotation, and that had gotten pushed out to fourteen months, which he also wasn't happy about. And over those fourteen months he would rack up nearly as much EVA time as the techs did in their four, which ought to count for something. But yes, Stephen did spend most of his time indoors, either in the workshop or simply sitting at a keyboard.

"They stopped eating lunch with me a few months ago," Stephen added, "but lately I've been getting some outright dirty looks."

"I as well," said Eldad Barzeley. Barzeley was only supposed to be here for three more days, but there was a possibility he could get bumped off of his flight as well, depending on what Puya Hebbar and that homicide detective ended up doing.

"Yeah," Millar said. "I spend as much time outside as they do, and on a much longer rotation, which I think helps their morale a bit, but I'm not really using my hands most of that time. Not putting my back into it, as Adam

Richter would say. I tell you, if I got to send one guy home early, he'd be the one."

"There's rumors of a labor strike at Clementine," Stephen said. "We should be paying attention to that kind of unrest, a hundred percent."

"I agree," Millar said. He held a hand up, looking upward through spread fingers into one of the ceiling lights. "I'm doing everything I can."

"Are you, though?"

Stephen, who had himself been on the receiving end of "professional management" and its casual abuses, wasn't so sure.

"What are you getting at, exactly?" Millar asked.

Stephen said, "For a start, imagine yourself in their shoes. I know you work shoulder-to-shoulder with them, but imagine if you had their pay structure."

"Don't tell me what to think," Millar said mildly, but with an edge of that same blue-collar hardness.

Well, yeah. Millar had his own problems, Stephen was sure, just as Eldad Barzeley must. But Stephen himself had taken some big knocks that nobody here knew anything about—he had once been fired from a company he'd started himself!—and that kind of thing never really left you.

"No offense intended," Stephen said, also mildly. "But if it's a problem for them, it's a problem for all of us."

Back in graduate school, Stephen had gone by the nickname "Edison," because he'd invented a new type of light bulb. Unlike LEDs, the Magnetic Induction Illumination Device took in alternating current directly, and produced a full-spectrum illumination without a hint of flicker, while converting an astonishing 99.3 percent of input power into visible light. The utility lines that fed it were more wasteful than that. At the urging of his advisor and with the help of the university's tech transfer office, he'd filed for worldwide patent rights and formed a corporation. Then the venture capital money had found him (really not the other way around), and he'd let himself be demoted from CEO to Chief Technology Officer. And he'd been content, working in his well-equipped laboratory with a team of skilled researchers, and occasionally flying to exotic locations like Johannesburg and Macau and Shenzhen to explain the technology to interested parties. But then came the board of directors— old money types from Oxford and Cambridge and Harvard Business School. And then, just when things were starting to go really well—just when Magnetic Light was breaking ground on an actual factory, on British soil no less—they'd suddenly informed him they were eliminating the CTO position and "moving to a more production-orientated business model." And suddenly, just like that, old Edison was out of a job.

And then—then!—they'd created "a new class of specially priced voting shares, with liquidation preference" that had diluted Stephen's own shares into oblivion, leaving him with essentially nothing. Even if they sold the company, he would not see a penny of the proceeds until those bastards had sucked out the first billion pounds for themselves, if there were even a billion pounds to be had.

"Imagine the proceeds of every fourth month have been taken from you," Stephen said. "Just for a moment, stop rationalizing and just feel that."

"What am I supposed to do?" Millar asked, a bit defensively. "No laws are being broken."

"No?"

It might be true, but that was hardly the point. It might have been true of what happened to Stephen, too. He'd been enough of a twat to believe those Old Boys were his friends—that they were cheerfully inducting a new member into their little millionaires' club. But no, they were squeezing him like a grape, fermenting his juice and then drinking it right in front of him without really thinking much about it. Naturally, their version of events sounded rather different: Stephen was immature and difficult. Stephen's actual contributions were minor and early, and it was his team that had really invented the thing. Stephen's technical missteps had burned up millions, and yet Stephen also spent too much time peering into an oscilloscope to understand how the business actually worked.

Some of that might even be partially true, but did it matter? Human beings were entitled to profit from their own ideas and labor. Taking that away from them—even in small measure—was so inherently wrong that he'd thought even the most flint-hearted members of the investor class could see it. Stephen's misfortune was no different than anyone else's, who'd ever been swindled and then told it was fine.

"There's also karma to consider," he said.

"Karma is not a thing," Barzeley said. "Studies find no evidence for it."

"Then they're looking in the wrong place," Stephen told him.

When Stephen was gone from Magnetic Light, the Old Boys had flown the company straight into the ground, because they didn't even know that additional technical problems would inevitably crop up in the shift to production. They didn't know that some off-the-shelf idiot couldn't simply step in and do all the millions of things Stephen had done to bring the company and the product into existence. So they crashed and burned, and although they walked away unscathed, protected from consequence by their wealth, Stephen felt sure that their pride and reputations had suffered a wound or two. Other members of the Old Boy network would be a bit less willing to trust them in future, and deservedly so. They deserved to fail, and so they had.

Meanwhile, Stephen had lost his house and his car, along with his starry-eyed innocence. He had not deserved that, so maybe Barzeley had a point. But still, he felt increasingly guilty, that he was just standing by while HMI shook the coins out of its astronauts' pockets.

When things went south for him, he'd still been young enough to start over. He took a shitty apartment and a shitty job at Harvest Moon, which had eventually led to his managing their magnetics R&D lab, which in turn had led him here to the Moon. Nobody here called him Edison, or cared about what had happened to him in his past. His staff at Magnetic Light had also gotten screwed—their shares worthless, their long hours chucked down the drain—and he knew that kind of thing happened to frontline workers all the time.

But did it really have to happen here? Did Stephen really have to let it?

"We need to raise this issue with the commander," Stephen said.

"I have," Millar assured him. "Repeatedly."

"We need to do more," Stephen insisted. "If Sir Lawrence won't increase their bonuses, we should be offering them a portion of ours."

"Hold on, now," Barzeley said, looking alarmed. "That's half our pay you're talking about."

"Nearly half," Stephen agreed. "A portion of that. But hear me out: we bring that offer to Harb, she's going to pass it up the chain, and it's going to shame Sir Lawrence, and he's going to do the right thing."

Truth be told, Stephen wasn't at all sure of this. Sir Lawrence was well liked by nearly everyone who worked for him, but there could well be an Old Boy lurking back there behind that kindly mask. Even an Old Boy might do the maths and determine that the right thing would cost less in the end, but that assumed a certain degree of rationality. Stephen wasn't at all counting on that happening. He was simply trying to get Millar and Barzeley on his side for this. If he were going to do the right thing, he didn't want to be doing it alone.

"And if it doesn't?" Barzeley demanded.

"If it doesn't," Stephen said, "then at least we're doing the right thing. *Someone* has to. These blokes' workload really has increased, and they deserve to be compensated for it."

"They do," Millar agreed, with a visible show of reluctance. "It's not fair if that has to come from us, but the situation's already not fair. How big a percentage are we talking about? Covering their losses would be . . . hard."

"Even a symbolic amount would mean a lot," Stephen said confidently, "but I'm thinking we give up twenty percent."

"Ten," Millar suggested.

"Fifteen," Stephen said.

"But these jobs are glamorous," Barzeley said. "And the men are replaceable. I like Adam. I like all of the men, but each of them has a million others waiting to replace him. I could get higher pay myself, yes? I could build reactors for an energy company. I could buy and sell real estate for a profit. But Lawrence Killian has chosen me as his solar radiation guy, his space weather guy, and I get to come to the Moon for a while. So I accept the deal, as they did."

"Your deal hasn't changed," Stephen said. "Theirs has."

"Well then perhaps we should be focusing on recruitment. Aren't they always saying we need more women up here?"

"I've brought that up, too," Millar said. "And I don't think it's exactly news to Harb. But it isn't that simple. Half my guys were underwater welders or underwater concrete masons in their past life, and the other half were mechanics in deep-shaft mining operations, doing the kind of work a robot simply can't. There aren't a million qualified applicants for these jobs. There aren't two dozen. And do you know any females in those occupations who want to try something even more dangerous and less comfortable? Because I don't. And the women who are qualified get snapped up by Renz Ventures, who pay a lot better, or they're competing for Mars, which apparently is a lot more attractive. If I get some more solid female candidates, believe me, I'll hire them, but that still won't address the issue Stephen's talking about."

"No, it won't," Stephen agreed. "And Jesus wept, even if we're absolute bastards, it's still not in our own personal best interest to cheese these blokes off any worse than they already are. What would happen if there was a strike here at Shackleton? Not generous bonuses for you and me, I'll tell you that. But a small gesture can go a long way. With your permission, Millar, I'll go talk to Harb right now."

"Hmm, maybe not right now," Millar said, nodding over to where the three women sat, talking very seriously about something. "But if you see an opening in the next couple of days, then I suppose so. Are you on board, Barzeley?"

Barzeley looked uncomfortable. He'd only been on the Moon a couple of months and would hopefully be leaving in a few days, and Stephen was not clear on exactly where he'd come from or what his deal was. There were plenty of places in the world where people who worked with their hands were very openly looked down on by people who didn't. Twenty-first-century England at least pretended to not be one of those places, but Barzeley seemed perfectly comfortable drawing a salt line between the officer and enlisted classes, so to speak. Stephen didn't like that one bit, but he had to work with the tools at hand, even if they were tools, so to speak. But perhaps Stephen's argument had struck home, or else Barzeley had simply succumbed to peer pressure, for although he frowned and looked displeased, he nodded.

"Yes, all right. Let these poor men have their share."

Choosing to ignore the condescension in Barzeley's voice, Stephen said, "Right, then: a stand for basic human decency. And trust me, I do sincerely hope Sir Lawrence doesn't call our bluff."

1.13
22 November
✧
St. Joseph of Cupertino Monastery
South Polar Mineral Territories
Lunar Surface

The backpack of a Heavy Rebreather was normally covered by a layer of tough, polymer-wrapped mesh. Brother Michael had removed this, and also separated the back cover from the backpack itself.

"The outer sheath is held on with Velcro at these four corners," Michael said, pointing to black Velcro circles on the heavy plastic of the backpack. "It comes off in one piece, and when I first removed it, I did not observe any damage to it, other than normal wear and tear."

The inspection table had a powerful, illuminated magnifying lens clamped to it on an articulated arm. Raimy used this to study the sheath, once Michael had handed it over to him. He wore a set of black nitrile gloves to avoid contamination, although the sheath had already been touched by the bare fingers of at least three monks—first when they were trying to revive Etsub, and again when they were removing him from the suit. Brothers Michael, Purcell, and Groppel had each completed a General Spacesuit Certified Maintenance Technician course before coming to Luna, and so the three of them had personally inspected the suit a few days ago, sending pictures down to GS for analysis. But they'd been wearing gloves at the time, so the only real risk was that they might have smeared the fingerprints from the previous handling.

However, Raimy's glasses were police issue, and had preinstalled on them a remarkable app called Fingerprint Finder. There was no need for powders or sprays or ultraviolet light; something called a "deep belief network" was able, somehow, to pick up even the faintest or smudgiest fingerprints from an ordinary video stream. And there were definitely fingerprints, all over the thing! These flashed red, one by one, in Raimy's vision, and then green as each print was matched to a known suspect.

These days, everyone surrendered up their genomes and biometric data, including fingerprints. It was a condition not only for space travel, but for getting married, getting a job, getting a license to operate motor vehicles in manual mode, etc. Raimy could consult remotely with a number of global databases, but that could take hours and cost many thousands of dollars. Instead, he had preloaded the algorithm with the prints of everyone who might ever have come in contact with the suit. That meant, literally, everyone at GS, Spaceport Paramaribo, Transit Point Station, Shackleton Lunar Industrial Station, and of course, Saint Joe's. Studying the display now, Raimy found no surprises; the sheath had been handled by Etsub Beyene, Michael Jablonski, Purcell Veloso, Eliaz Groppel, and Daniel Ramirez—a name Raimy didn't recognize, but which was flagged as belonging to a GS quality control technician.

None of his prime suspects had left any prints. This didn't mean they were innocent. It didn't mean that they hadn't touched the cover of the spacesuit backpack. It only meant they hadn't left fingerprints. He also didn't see any signs of sabotage on the sheath itself—no rips or cut marks—but he wouldn't have expected to. It was only ever Velcroed on.

"What do you see?" Bridget asked.

"I can't discuss it," Raimy said.

He repeated the process with the back cover of the backpack, which was made of a rigid gray plastic, about three millimeters thick, and there he did find some tool marks on one side. Putting them under the magnifier, he captured video and still images: a centimeter-wide band of streaks, and a crease or dent in the heavy plastic. A few centimeters away, a similar but larger marking.

"I tried to open the backpack with a screwdriver," Michael explained. "I couldn't get enough leverage, so then I used a crowbar. That popped it right open."

"I can corroborate that," Bridget said. "I was in here when he did it."

"Wonderful," Raimy muttered.

"What?" she asked, sounding as though her feelings were hurt.

"I realize you're dealing with a very contaminated crime scene," Michael said sympathetically. "Every witness a suspect, every exhibit tampered. For all you know, Bridget and I killed him together. And yet, someone has to help you. It must be maddening. Perhaps they should have sent an entire team of investigators."

Raimy had nothing to say to that. Instead, he said, "I'm going to need to have a look at those tools."

"Of course. Now?"

"Later is fine. Technically I should take them back to Earth with me as bagged exhibits, but I don't want to endanger your facility by carting off critical equipment. I can make do with pictures; I just want to verify that the tools and markings match."

"Understood," Michael said.

Next, they pulled the sheet off the spacesuit itself. It was in two pieces—the pants and the coat—facedown on the table so that the open backpack was exposed. Raimy didn't have to look very hard to find the burst air hose; it was as thick as his thumb and as long as his outstretched hand, and looked like it had been attacked with a hatchet, or shot, or both. Really, both.

On his glasses, Raimy pulled up the 3D model given him by the CTO of General Spacesuit. Its clean lines overlaid with the jagged ones of the actual hardware, confirming that yes, indeed, the air hose was no longer in factory condition.

"There's a missing bracket," Raimy said. He pointed. "It should be here, holding this hose and this cable to this"— he read the part name on his display—"vertical spar."

"Indeed," Michael agreed. "I think it's down at the bottom of the backpack. There. Do you see it?"

"Yes. Right, yes, that's the right shape. Did you detach it?"

"No, it was like that when we opened the pack. I'm guessing it fell off when the hose blew out."

"Hmm."

Looking at the shape of it, Raimy wasn't clear on how that could have happened, and he didn't care to speculate just now. Especially he didn't care to listen to someone else speculate, but he parked that thought for now. His attention fell on the rupture itself. Dong Nguyen had told him to look at the metal wires that formed the hose's outer braid, to see if they were severed or stretched. It was hard to tell, even under the magnifier, but it kind of looked like the answer was "both."

"I need a closer look at these braids," Raimy said, pointing. "Can we get a microscope on this?"

That proved to be harder than it sounded, because the lab's microscope—a high-end binocular model with lots of knobs and lenses—was configured for tabletop use, and in fact securely bolted to the table. Between its stand and the bottom of the objective lens, the tallest object that would fit was about fifteen centimeters. The spacesuit was rather larger than that, and although the backpack by itself might have been maneuvered into that gap, Michael said it would be several hours' work to detach the backpack from the actual suit.

"It wasn't ever meant to come off," he said, "and we might damage your evidence in the process."

"We could take the microscope apart," Bridget suggested. "Look, it screws down to the base, here and here."

"And here," Michael said, pointing to the back of it. "But you're not going to see anything, holding it freehand."

"Can we clamp it to the sides of the backpack?" Raimy asked.

"I think we very well could," Michael said, "though we'll need to fabricate an appropriate fixture."

This involved dragging Brother Purcell over from the module next door, to take measurements and study geometries. "Yes," he said, in a voice both cheerful and slightly annoyed. "This can be done. You want it now? *Merde.* Give me, I think, ninety minutes. Michael, will you assist? You have steady hands."

"Certainly."

The two of them hustled off into the workshop, leaving Raimy and Bridget alone with the suit. Raimy reminded himself that a man had died in this thing. He reminded himself that he only had three more days to solve the crime, unless he wanted to wait two weeks for the next scheduled EOLS departure. He reminded himself that the nearest crime lab technician was four hundred thousand kilometers away, and so he was going to have to be really, really careful to get clear images without messing anything up.

"I'm a little out of my depth," he confessed to Bridget, perhaps unwisely.

"Eh? How so?"

"My victims are usually killed in their homes, or stabbed in a bar fight, or sometimes run over by cars, although that's getting harder to pull off. If there's a firearm involved, I send it to ballistics. If there's a knife or a rock or a samurai sword, we've got experts for that. I'm not a spacesuit expert."

"But you were in the Navy," she said. "You were, what, a diver?"

"That's right."

"So you've seen an air hose before."

"Yes. That's not really my point."

"What are you looking for, with the microscope?"

He explained to her about braids and tool marks, and then added, "That's not something I would normally tell a suspect. This is a very strange investigation."

"I'll keep my hands where you can see 'em," she said, half-jokingly. "But you know I could've tampered with this hardware any time before you got here. In the dead of night, with everyone else asleep. Who'd know? There are no locks or security cameras here."

He sighed. "I'm aware of that, yes."

"Well, then, shall we continue your investigation? What about that bracket of yours?" The bracket, actually an "upper clamp bracket" according to the plans, was nestled behind tanks and wires, up against the bottom of the backpack.

"I can't get my hand in there," Raimy said. He looked at Bridget's hands, which were slender and long, barely filling out her lab gloves. "Can you reach . . ."

"You want me to touch it?"

"Yes," he said. "If you can reach."

She tried, but although she was able to touch the bracket with the tips of her gloves, she couldn't actually get a grip on it.

"We're going to have to tilt the suit," Raimy said.

"Or I could get some tweezers. Or a magnet."

Raimy thought about that. "A magnet is less likely to scratch it."

He air-touched the bracket on the AR plans hovering

over the suit, and confirmed that it was made of stainless steel. "It should work. What did you have . . ."

Rummaging in a drawer below the lab table, she came up with a sort of telescoping probe, like a pointer or a dental probe, with a little round magnet on the tip. "I saw Michael use this to pick up metal shavings," she said.

"Okay. Have at it."

But the probe also wouldn't grab the bracket. The magnet seemed not to affect it at all.

"I'm not sure stainless steel is magnetic," Bridget said, still fussing with the thing.

"My refrigerator is stainless," Raimy said, "and it's got magnets all over it."

"So is mine, and magnets won't stick to it at all. You can try asking Andrei. He's some sort of metallurgist."

"It would be better to ask General Spacesuit."

"Yeah," Bridget said, "probably." Then: "Aargh! I give up. This thing's not working." Defeated, she set the probe down on the countertop.

So yes, they did end up having to tilt the suit. And shake it. And have Bridget reach her fingers in there again to jiggle the clamp bracket out of its hiding place. Finally, in Lunar slow motion, it tumbled out onto the table. They set the suit back down, and Raimy put the magnifier over the bracket. It was scratched all to hell, which he supposed wasn't all that surprising if it was wrapped around a braided hose while it exploded. Still, it wasn't *bent*, and something in the pattern of scratches didn't look right; they all formed perfect little synchronous loops. Or so it seemed; he really needed to get it under the microscope for a better look.

"Do you see anything?" Bridget wondered.

"Maybe."

He picked up the bracket in his gloved hand, and tried to fit it back over the blown-out portion of the hose and antenna cable, where the AR diagram said it should go. It wouldn't fit, though, so he tried a little lower, on the smooth, intact portions. Still no dice.

Interesting.

"Doesn't fit?" Bridget said.

"No," Raimy said. "It doesn't look like it *can* fit, without bending it."

"So bend it," she said.

"You don't understand," he told her. "If it was blown off the hose, it should be bent open already. It isn't."

"Oh. Wow. What does that mean?"

"I don't know," he said. "Maybe nothing. I'm going to send a picture to General Spacesuit and see what they can tell me."

With a few air gestures, he did this.

Then he was out of moves.

"Let's take a break," he said. "Until Michael gets back with that part."

"Sure."

Taking a break in Lunar gravity was pretty easy; you didn't even need to sit down. You just stopped what you were doing and stood there, much like you would in a swimming pool.

"So you were also a lawyer?" Bridget asked, filling a long moment of silence.

"Prosecutor, yes. It was a waste of time; I didn't like it, and I'm still paying off the student loans."

She twirled her hair around a finger, and then released it.

"Why didn't you like it?"

He snorted. "I don't know. Too many plea deals. Too many badly constructed cases, where the city simply couldn't overcome reasonable doubt. I let five murderers walk who were clearly guilty, along with hundreds of burglars and thieves and child molesters, and finally I just couldn't take it anymore. Plus I didn't... It just wasn't a good fit for me. Of course, some people would say I traded that job for an even uglier one, but I don't know. As of this month I've got a ninety percent conviction rate, which is pretty good for a homicide detective. Makes me feel like the good guys are winning."

She nodded, thinking that over, and finally asked, "What's it like to arrest someone?"

He looked her over, trying to decide if there were ulterior motives to that question. Did she fear arrest? But no, she simply looked curious, and maybe a little bored.

She also—it had to be said—looked good. It was getting a little stuffy in here, and she had responded at some point by unzipping her coverall to the top of her shiny-gray space camisole. She'd also unzipped and rolled up her sleeves, and she'd had her trouser bottoms cuffed the whole time. She wore her moon slippers without socks, and while it seemed strangely Victorian to be attracted to a woman's ankles... Well, there you had it.

"It's very confrontational," he told her. "Very in-your-face. They hate your guts—even the ones who go quietly—and you're touching them and restraining them and controlling their movements. Nobody likes that. And a lot of them don't go quietly! You have to be ready to fight. Really, you have to be ready to fight to the death, because some of these guys are armed, or just willing to choke you to death the first chance they get. So you have to control them in a way that provides no openings. It's basically combat, every time."

"Well, aren't you a chancer? You seriously like that better than being a lawyer?"

"Yeah. I do. I'm not sure I want to spend the rest of my life on it, but right now, yeah, I've never felt more useful. Justice is . . . Well, you know. Very important. Even if the victim was a dirtbag, they still have families, friends, coworkers. You rip someone out of the world like that, and it's just very damaging. A conviction lets everyone start to heal."

He weighed his next words more carefully: "For someone like Etsub, it's even more dire. If it wasn't an accident, and if it goes unsolved, it's going to leave a black mark on, what, four different organizations, and three planets? Plus all the people he's left behind. I'm sorry, I know he was your friend."

"He was," she said wearily. She seemed to have more to say, but the wind had gone out of her. Instead, she nodded glumly, and made one of those faces that said, *I have no idea what to do with any of this, so what can you say?*

After another long moment, she asked, "How many of them fight you? What percentage?"

"Oh, less than ten percent. But that's because we show up with overwhelming force, hopefully in public, and hopefully with the element of surprise. Catch them with their pants down, sometimes literally. But about half of them are thinking how they could try it."

"Huh," she said. "What's the scariest thing that ever happened?"

"To me? On the force? I mean, I got stabbed in the leg once. That sucked, especially because I'm pretty sure he was aiming for my femoral artery. If I hadn't've blocked it, it could have been fatal."

"That's awful," she said. "It must have been terrifying."

"Not as bad as escaping from a submarine," he said, "but yeah, pretty bad."

"You did that? Escaped from a submarine? Like, underwater?"

"Yeah, deep," he said. "Very deep. Once with scuba gear, once with an inflatable escape suit, and once with basically just a plastic hood. That was scary. I also crashed a motorcycle once. On a closed track, but still pretty hairy. Oh, and I had a couple of close calls as a diver. Also deep underwater. Somebody once knocked my helmet loose from its collar, so it flooded. I had to rip it off and grab the spare regulator—which is called an octopus—and breathe with my bare face in freezing black water. Saltwater really burns in your eyes, so I had to close them. I had to climb back into the torpedo tube like that, which is how we got in and out. I suppose that was probably the scariest single incident."

"Jesus, Raimy."

"Why, what's the scariest thing that ever happened to you?"

"Nothing like that. Nothing like any of that. I'm not brave enough to put myself in those kind of situations."

"Says the astronaut headed for Mars."

She snorted. "Yeah, I suppose. I mean, it's scary going EVA in a spacesuit. Especially now."

She waved in the general direction of Etsub's suit, as if wishing all her anxieties onto it. Then she reached for her coverall zipper, pulling it down another few centimeters, and fanned herself with her hand. "It's hot in here. The sun is out, and I don't think we're getting quite enough airflow in here."

"There's a thermostat," Raimy said, pointing to a primitive little analog control on the wall. It wasn't particularly hot in here, but Raimy's Antilympus uniform seemed to handle a broader range of temperatures than Bridget's Harvest Moon one.

"We're not allowed to touch the temperatures," she said. "Michael's very fussy about it. But yeah, when he gets back I'll ask him."

Then she leaned toward the west hatchway and called out loudly, "Hey Michael! Hurry it up!"

Apparently, she was just clowning; Michael was on the other side of the noisy Life Support module.

"I don't think he can hear you," Raimy said.

"Well, I'll yell louder."

"Please don't."

She pulled her zipper down still further, now past the bottom of her camisole, revealing an inverted triangle of pale, pale skin that exerted a magnetic pull on Raimy's gaze.

"Don't go getting ideas," she said, with what might have been a playful tone.

Raimy surprised himself by answering, "Ma'am, I've already seen you naked."

"So you have," she agreed. Then: "Tell me something else about you. Not scary, something else."

"Like what? I grew up vegetarian. Actually, I grew up *vegan*, but that's just not realistic for Mars. I had to train myself on printmeat and vat cell cultures."

"McDonald's?" she asked.

"Actually, yes. The Ethical Mac was my introduction to animal protein, and I've never looked back. As long as it doesn't come from actual animals."

"Huh. Okay. I guess that makes sense."

They chitchatted like that, and time slipped by rather easily, until eventually Michael and Purcell came back with the microscope, now outfitted with a 3D-printed clamping mechanism. This was fitted over the edge of the spacesuit backpack and then screwed into place. Then, after messing with a couple of clip-on LED lamps around the sides of the backpack, Raimy finally got a close look at the wire braids of that hose.

They were . . .

Well, his initial impression was right; the braids absolutely had been cut through in some places, and had stretched like taffy in other places. Raimy looked at where the clamp bracket was supposed to fit, and concluded that the bracket itself was the cutting instrument. Which didn't make a ton of sense, because it didn't have any obvious sharp edges, but he supposed any corner could be a cutting instrument if you put enough force behind it. Force from where, though?

He captured some pictures, for later annotation and inclusion in the case file, which was finally starting to have some real heft to it.

"What do you see?" Purcell asked.

"I see what cut the hose," Raimy answered, holding up the clamp bracket, "although I don't see how."

He let Purcell look through the eyepieces.

"I see what you mean," Purcell said. "Although it's a good question where that torque come from."

"May I see?" Michael asked. So Raimy let him, and then (very much against his best judgment) let Bridget look as well.

"Oh, wow," she said. "It just pushed right against it, right there, didn't it. That's amazing. What could cause something like that?"

"That's the question," Raimy agreed. It didn't look accidental to him; when he did his best to fold the braids back into place, and fit the broken ends of the antenna wire together beside them, there was a perfect little crease along the right side of both hose and cable, right where the top of the clamp bracket would have sat. But there was nothing else around it—nothing that could press or twist or explode, forcing the clamp hard to the left like that.

Raimy looked, and looked again, and looked some more, and got no closer to figuring it out.

"I don't know," he finally said. "I don't know. I guess the damage must have happened in Florida. I guess we knew that anyway, because of the lack of tool marks on the lip of the backpack. But what are we talking about, here? Someone jammed a crowbar against this thing and pulled really hard, to weaken the hose?"

"Put a crowbar where?" Purcell wanted to know. "Braced against what?"

Raimy shrugged. On the left side, there were a couple of places that might provide the necessary leverage. But the damage was on the right, and that region of the backpack interior was pretty empty. Also, there were no tool marks anywhere along the plastic. Like, zero.

"I don't know," he said. He didn't even really have any theories at this point, and it seemed like he ought to. He was on the verge of saying it was time for another break— time to look at other evidence and just let this stuff percolate for a while—when his glasses chimed, and a message icon appeared in his field of view. From CTO@generalspacesuit#com, with a header that said simply, ????

He touched the icon, and the message unfolded into a photograph and a block of text.

Hello, Mr. Vaught. I'm a bit confused by the pictures you sent, because this here is our hose clamp bracket.

The attached photo showed a part that was similar to the one in Raimy's black-gloved hand, but shinier on the outside surface, and lined on the inside with a couple of millimeters of black rubber.

I don't know where you got the piece you showed us, but it's sure not one of ours.

2.3
22 November
✦

Clementine Cislunar Fuel Depot
Earth-Moon Lagrange Point 1
Cislunar Space

"Is that your entire report?" Orlov asked quietly.

"It is," Commander Morozov confirmed, managing to sound, all at once, stiffly formal, deflated, and furious.

"And do you have a recommendation?"

Dona wondered, briefly, whether these two men were about to come to blows. Orlov because he couldn't stand losing and needed to take it out on someone; Morozov because he'd been put in an impossible position. Both men were hard-pushed, and both capable of violence.

Morozov and Voronin had gone back into the mess hall, the morning after the conflict. They had stayed in there ten minutes, talking and listening. Now they were back in Operations, with Dona and the trillionaire, regrouping.

"Hiring scab labor isn't going to work," Morozov said. "Neither are strike breakers."

"No?" Orlov replied.

Morozov said, "I know it's a satisfying thought, but

anyone we bring up here will have to be comfortable operating in spacesuits, in zero gravity. They will need to bring cutting tools with them. They'll need to breach one of the airlocks, and then install a new outer hatch, before they can even enter the station. There is likely to be interference, and perhaps violence, over which they will need to prevail. And then they will have to operate all of our equipment, or force our own people to do it. There are not enough people in the world willing and qualified to do all of that. Not enough to fill a shuttle, Grigory, and world opinion was already against us, based solely on Andrei Bykhovski's complaints. Which frankly pale in comparison to the shit we've stepped in since then. If you're unwilling to meet the workers' demands, then our best move is to fire them all, send them home in peace, and then hire a replacement crew handpicked from the ranks of Orlov Petrochemical. If we do it right, we'd be down for less than three months."

Dona watched Orlov react to that, and thought again that Morozov was risking violence by speaking like this.

"You have no imagination," Orlov said. "Dona may be the only person in this room who doesn't know how to use a cutting torch."

"I do," Dona said.

Orlov looked at her. "What?"

"I know how to use a cutting torch. It's been a long time, and I've never done it without air, or gravity. But I know how." She'd learned it at *Commandement des Opérations Spéciales*—not how to weld or do anything useful, but as part of a two-week course called *Comment Ouvrir les Choses*, or "How to Open Things."

"Good for you," Orlov said darkly. The Operations center was lit by the green and red and yellow of graphs and Cyrillic lettering on video displays, and this glow made a mask of his face.

Uneasily, Voronin said, "Sir, what are you getting at?"

Orlov snorted, saying nothing.

Dona answered for him: "An accident."

"Unacceptable!" said Voronin. "However angry they may be, these are our own people."

More reasonably, Morozov said, "The workers are surely aware of that possibility, and will be taking appropriate steps to avoid it. If they're frightened enough, we four are at greater risk from them than they are from us. And even if we succeeded, the optics would be poor. What story would you tell the world?"

When Orlov didn't answer right away, Dona said to him, "Morozov is right. It's wise to move things back into in the administrative realm."

She watched Orlov think about that one, too. His father's company, Orlov Petrochemical, had thrived amid chaos in large part because it did not follow that rule, and never had. But when unsavory things happened, there was at least a thin veneer of deniability that let the relevant authorities off the hook. Dona herself had made a career of coloring well outside the administrative lines, and Orlov knew that, and seemed unpleasantly surprised to find her backing away from it now.

But her operations for *Commandement des Opérations Spéciales* had always been covert and, yes, deniable. She'd cleaned up her share of crime scenes, none of them involving thirty-six bodies and global scrutiny. And it was well past the time when she could plausibly have infiltrated the strikers and worked them from inside. She'd been too busy working the trillionaire himself, trying to shore up her tenuous position. Not looking outward, not smelling this larger trouble until it was too late. She kicked herself inwardly for the lapse, for letting the situation get so far ahead of her, but here they were.

"Can we at least find out what they're saying to each other?" Orlov grumbled.

"At this time, no," Voronin said. "I'm sorry, but they've got IT on their side. I can't even access the security cameras."

An uncomfortable silence settled over them.

"Three months is too long," Orlov finally said. "Three days is too long."

Voronin said, "It's a violation of international law, sealing the lifeboats. Assuming we can even keep them sealed."

"Unlikely," said Morozov.

"So we're on borrowed time?" Dona said, unhappily. It was her least favorite kind of time. If control of these events was about to slip even further from Orlov's grasp, then he was compelled to act now, selecting from an ever-shortening list of options.

"We are," Morozov confirmed.

"Well, then," Orlov said with sudden and suspicious good cheer, "we must kiss their cheeks and invite them back to the bargaining table. Unlock the lifeboats at once, Voronin, and blame the lapse on Ms. Obata, who is ignorant of these matters. Apologies, Dona, but you're the only one who can take the fall for this."

"And if the workers all evacuate?" Voronin asked.

"The four of us would be hard-pressed to keep the station habitable for very long," Morozov warned.

"Anyone who evacuates will forfeit all wages, past and future," Orlov said. "And we'll bill them the replacement cost of the boats."

"Okay, that's the stick," Morozov said. "What about the carrot?"

Orlov was holding a rollup in one fist, and at this question he hurled it, hard, against the hatchway behind Morozov, where it broke apart and tumbled away, trailing its screen like a tattered gray flag.

"Idiot!" Orlov said. "Have you never seen an Internet meme? Or political cartoon? The carrot is suspended from the stick by a string. The stick protrudes from the collar of a donkey. The donkey, being hungry and stupid, walks toward the carrot, thinking he will reach it. But he never does, because the carrot moves with him, step by step, dangling always out of reach. And so he walks forever, pulling a plow or turning a wheel, until he drops dead from exhaustion. This is what grown-ups mean, when they say 'carrot and stick.' Perpetual motion! Labor without cost! A simple visual metaphor, understood by the wise and always mangled by idiots like you, who cannot be trusted to run a simple petrol station."

No one had a reply to that.

Finally, it was Dona who spoke: "They want yearly shore leave, Orlov, and you're going to have to give it to them. *Seeming to* is not enough—these are highly intelligent people, not donkeys. And the world is on their side. But why not force them to bundle it? Send them down one full shuttle at a time, and make the workers themselves figure out who goes when. All the weddings and funerals and graduations are their problem, not yours. Until they fill a shuttle, no one leaves, and until that shuttle returns, everyone else is on extended shifts. Make them share the cost and the headache, down in the fine print of the agreement they sign. It's too late to be magnanimous, but quite frankly, they expect you to be transactional."

"You're speaking English," Voronin complained.

"Shut up," Orlov told him. To Dona he said, "So now you're a negotiator?"

Someone has to be, she thought but did not say.

Orlov looked closely at her, and said, "You're a clever woman; you know when to slip in the knife, and how. Is that what's happening here?" Without waiting for an answer, he continued, "You also know when to run. You ran here, because you feared what would happen if you ran home, a burnt asset who betrayed her masters. But from here, where can you run? Who would ever trust you? Nobody. This place is the end of your road, unless you deign to lose yourself in Africa, living in a tin shack until everyone has forgotten you. You need for this enterprise to succeed—to flourish—or you *will* be going home. Where someone else will slip in the knife."

Without a trace of irony, she said, "This is why I love you, Grigory." Of all the people she'd ever met, the trillionaire was the first to really understand her. Effortlessly, it seemed.

He continued his scrutiny for several more seconds, and finally said, "Now you are my own asset, ah? You have a point—several, actually—and your dogshit plan may just end this madness. Your ambiguous position here even gives us the opportunity to save face, because no one knows who the fuck you are."

She said nothing, because what was there to say?

Orlov continued, "You will go back in there and speak to them. Apologize for the lifeboats. Tell them it was a mistake—your mistake. Tell them it was all your mistake. Then make your ridiculous offer, and whatever threats you deem appropriate. These idiots"—he nodded at Morozov and Voronin—"have failed twice, and I myself have failed once, because we underestimated the enemy's conviction. But you cannot afford to fail."

Again, she said nothing, simply waiting to see if he was done.

"I misspoke," he said, then. "It was caution, not fear, that kept you from going back to Earth. I am not sure you are capable of fear."

"I am," she said.

"But it takes more than that, ah? It takes more than this. You were never afraid of me."

"No," she agreed. She had broken into his safe, rifled through his encrypted files, slept next to him. Slept next to him, yes, the most dangerous man in the solar system.

"I'm not sure I am capable of love," he said to her, heedless of Morozov and Voronin. "At least in the sense other people seem to mean it. But I think it's a good thing you came here. I think it's good you are my asset."

"I think so, too," she said, now impatient to get on with it. The situation was far too dynamic; she preferred to move, silently, through a world of other people's scripts and routines, but they were "off book" now, as people said in her business. They needed to get back on book, fast, and right now she didn't care how much money or embarrassment it cost Grigory Orlov.

"You may regret my methods," she warned him, "but I will solve your problem."

"Is this wise?" Morozov demanded, eyeing Dona with something like resentment. He knew more about her than most, but still basically nothing. She could see he didn't trust her, and that was smart. She was not to be trusted.

"Our interests are aligned," she told him, because that much was true.

"Go," Orlov said. "I want us operational by nightfall. Make that happen, and what love I can muster is all yours."

"Always a charmer," she said, touching the back of her hand to his cheek with genuine warmth, because in all the rough-and-tumble years of her life, all she had ever really wanted was that kind of honesty.

1.4
22 November
✧

St. Joseph of Cupertino Monastery
South Polar Mineral Territories
Lunar Surface

The next few hours passed in a fog. Raimy wandered through the monastery, looking at everything and seeing nothing. Just mulling the evidence, trying to make any sort of sense of it.

Who, what, when, where, why, how?

Who: That's the question, isn't it?

What: Sabotaged Etsub Beyene's spacesuit, leading to his eventual death. HOMICIDE.

When: Prior to launch. During QC testing? During fitting?

Where: General Spacesuit assembly plant, Cocoa Beach, Florida. Feel pretty good about this part of it.

Why: Open up a slot at Antilympus Township.

How: Replaced a bracket inside the backpack, AND SOMEHOW MAGICALLY CAUSED THE SUIT TO FAIL FOUR WEEKS LATER????

✦✦✦

It didn't make sense, and no amount of rolling it around in his mind seemed to change that.

"Can you analyze the metal?" he asked Purcell at one point.

To which Purcell replied, "I can measure its density and resistivity, and if you give me and Groppel a day or two, maybe permeability, which is an electrical property. But I'm thinking that will not tell you much. There are a million different alloys, and even if you knew which one, how would that help?"

"I don't know," Raimy admitted.

"Take it back to Earth with you," Purcell advised. "Find a lab that can tell you where it came from. But I will tell you, anyone with access to a 3D drawing program can order up a custom metal part, from a hundred different online services. It's like making a T-shirt, or coffee cup. We've even done it here. Our fabrication ability is limited, but I got a special drill bit made, and a plate for attaching the drill press to the printer table. Only the shipping is difficult."

"Great," Raimy muttered.

At another point in his wanderings, he came across Andrei Bykhovski, studying in the library.

"I am learning Catholic," Bykhovski explained sheepishly. "I think seriously about staying on Moon, but this requires permissions and approvals. And who is Andrei Bykhovski? What is Russian Orthodox Church? Harvest Moon will not want my skills, which are different from their skills and knowings. And Catholic will not want me, because this is also different. I think I must become true seeker, or they will soon revoke sanctuary and send me back to Earth. I have risked too much to just throw away. It was not easy to get here! Most people could not do this. I am real spaceman, useful. Is better to live here than die on Earth, I'm thinking."

"Hmm," Raimy said. He didn't know what to think about that, and frankly didn't care very much at this moment. Right now, the only thing that mattered about Andrei Bykhovski is that Raimy could cross him off the suspect list. Bykhovski had never been to Florida, and while his spacesuit was a GS Light Orbital, GS had not been not responsible for fitting it to Bykhovski's body. That had apparently happened at an Orlov Petrochemical facility in a place called Baikonur, in Kazakhstan. "Most likely," CTO@generalspacesuit#com had said, "they just matched him to a size M, let the joints out a little, and handed him some moleskin to cover the spots that chafe."

So Bykhovski had been nowhere near Etsub's spacesuit backpack, at any of the times it could have been sabotaged. Neither had Geary Notbohm; he'd been on Transit Point Station the whole time. Neither had any of the monks. So actually, he could cross thirteen people off his suspect list.

Of course, there were thousands of GS employees and contractors who could have done it, but why? They had means and opportunity, but not motive. That really left only three people.

WHO: Anming Shui, Katla Koskinen, or Bridget Tobin.

He jotted this in his notes, and then underlined Anming's name three times. Raimy didn't have enough evidence for a conviction, or maybe even a grand jury indictment, but if the suspect pool was down to three people, and he was the one with the most to gain . . .

"For what it's worth, I'm taking you off my suspect list," Raimy told Bykhovski.

Bykhovski simply shrugged. "Okay. I am already knowing I didn't do."

And that, right there, cemented it for Raimy. Only a truly innocent man, with truly nothing to hide, would so casually shrug off that particular news.

"Well, good luck with your studies," Raimy said. "Even aside from the fear of reprisal, I can understand why you'd want to stay here."

"Is meaningful," Bykhovski said.

"Yes, exactly. I get that." And now that Bykhovski was no longer a suspect, and Raimy could suddenly see him as a complete human being, he said, "Things must have been pretty bad at Clementine."

"Our lives were not in danger," Bykhovski said, shrugging. "Only freedom. But this is enough reason to escape, yes? We are working, and not benefitting from work, and not free to leave, and not free to complain to any authorities. Someone must do something about this. And so I have. Complaints have been heard everywhere, and Orlov cannot continue doing as they have done. There is no law in space, but Orlov's assets on Earth are inside of countries, yes? And so, laws will find a way to touch him. This is why I am qualified to be monk: because already I risk my life for my fellow mankind, and succeed. My, how do you call, my character is proved. The rest is only ceremony, and this I can learn."

"Ah." Raimy had to agree, that was a hell of a résumé. The monastery would have to be crazy to turn him away. And then, because Bykhovski actually was some sort of metallurgist, Raimy asked him, "Is stainless steel magnetic?"

Again, that shrug.

"Sometimes yes, sometimes no. How much nickel is in metal?"

"I don't know."

Raimy handed him the clamp bracket, which had already tested negative for fingerprints.

Frowning, Bykhovski opened his hand to accept the part. Hefting it, he frowned more deeply. "This is light. Too light for steel. This is, I'm thinking, titanium alloy. Where did you get?"

"This came out of Etsub's backpack."

"Oh," said Bykhovski, handing it back as though it were poisonous.

"It's not the right part," Raimy said. "It's a fake, and it was somehow used to sabotage the air hose and antenna cable. I don't know how. There were no tool marks in the vicinity, and nothing pushing against it."

"Oh," Bykhovski said again. He shrugged a third time, looking uncomfortable. It seemed to be the end of the conversation.

"Well," Raimy told him, "good luck with your conversion. I have no doubt you'll make an excellent monk."

He then resumed his wandering, through the empty classroom and into the dormitories. He found himself standing in front of the room he knew had been assigned to Anming Shui.

Raimy had authorization to search whatever he liked, and he was tempted to simply open the hatch, walk right in, and toss the place. But something stopped him, some instinct of decorum or interplanetary diplomacy. Or even . . . safety? Did he fear a booby trap? Etsub Beyene had died from one, after all. If Anming Shui was responsible for that, then maybe Anming Shui should be in the room while it was searched.

Feeling like he might really be onto something, he opened the hatch into the greenhouse, and stepped into pink light and noise.

"Anming!" he called out.

Three monks and three students looked up from their vegetable trays, their eyes on Raimy.

"Anming, come with me!" Raimy told himself he was shouting to be heard over the blowers, but he just sounded angry, even to himself. Righteously angry.

"What is it?" Anming asked, in a much quieter voice.

"I need to search your room," Raimy answered gravely. "I need you to come with me." In the many pockets of his two-piece Antilympus uniform, Raimy had both handcuffs and zip ties. He was prepared to make an arrest if necessary. He was prepared to fight for it.

I won't turn my back, Raimy told himself. *If he tries to hit me, I'll block it and take him down. If he tries to stab me, I'll block it and take him down.*

Anming seemed an unlikely suspect, and really unlikely to resist arrest. Not only because he was small and bookish and mild, but because where the fuck could he escape to? Nowhere. Even if he somehow got away from Raimy and into a spacesuit and outside the hull of the monastery, what would he do? Walk to Shackleton, commandeer the *Pony Express* and somehow fly it all the way back to Transit Point? And then what? Nothing. There was no getting away from this.

Still, Raimy was careful not to turn his back.

With the watchful eyes of three monks and two students upon them, Raimy followed Anming back into the dormitory.

He stood by while Anming opened the hatch.

Nervously, his Chinese accent deeper than ever, Anming said, "You want me to step in?"

"Please," Raimy said. "Then I want you to start opening drawers, and very carefully removing the items."

"Okay. Just me? Nobody else?"

"Just you," Raimy confirmed.

There were three drawers set into the space under the bed, and Anming immediately opened the bottom two of these, to show they were empty. He even felt around the front and top of each drawer, with nervous slowness, and Raimy was vigilant for him to pull out a weapon. Which he didn't. The top drawer contained an extra coverall, in Harvest Moon yellow, and a set of space underwear, a pair of socks, a pair of slippers, and an ordinary rollup cell phone.

"Turn it on," Raimy instructed.

Anming did so, asking, "What is this about?"

"Hopefully nothing," Raimy told him.

The phone turned on normally, and reported that it had local network access, SpaceNet access, and (surprisingly) one bar of signal strength for the cell phone network back on Earth.

"It's a space-capable phone," Raimy said.

"Yes. I knew I was coming here, so I got it. The battery life is not very good."

"Hmm." Raimy turned the phone off—all the way off—and pocketed it for evidence. He didn't have the know-how to search a person's phone; that would have to be done by a crime lab, once the arrest had been made.

Next, Raimy searched the three drawers himself, and found nothing new. He asked Anming to strip the pillows and sheets and even the thin, waterproof mattress off of the bed. These were dutifully searched, and found innocent.

That left only the material lying in the open: Anming's phone charger and wristwatch charger, his hairbrush and toothbrush, his sleep mask. A couple of personal effects: a moon rock, a little metal sculpture, and a squeezy-handled spring of the sort that people used to exercise their hands.

"What's this?" Raimy asked, pointing to the sculpture. It was an atom: three stiff loops of shiny metal wire, each with a spherical dot attached, and each with a little stalk connecting it to a shiny metal nucleus at the sculpture's center.

"A toy," Anming said. Then: "May I pick it up? I'll show you how it works."

"Go ahead. Slowly."

"What is this about, Raimy? Did something happen?"

Grimly, professionally, Raimy told him, "You were always the number one suspect."

"Okay," Anming said, meekly. He picked the little atom and dropped it into the palm of his left hand, and then just sort of froze.

"What am I looking at?" Raimy demanded.

"Just wait," Anming said. "It takes a few seconds."

And then something odd happened: the metal jumped and shuddered in Anming's palm, the wires and spheres of the atom suddenly folding themselves into the shape of a Valentine's Day heart. It happened in an eyeblink, and with such force that the whole thing seemed to have been spring-loaded all along.

"What is that?" Raimy asked.

"Just a toy." Anming set it back down on the metal desktop, silver against enameled white, and after a few seconds it jumped again, jolting itself back into atom form.

"How does it work?" Raimy asked, forgetting himself for a moment and simply marveling. He'd never seen anything like it.

"I don't know," Anming said.

There maybe wasn't all that much to know; the thing had no room for gears or motors or springs or electronics. It was just three pieces of wire.

"Where did you get it?"

"It was a gift."

"From whom?"

Anming seemed about to answer, but then a look came over his face: startled, then horrified, then guilty. Or rather, caught.

"From whom?" Raimy demanded.

"I don't know," Anming answered, in such a way that even a five-year-old would know he was lying. "It came in the mail."

"From where?"

"I don't know."

"Did you save the packaging?"

"No."

"How long have you had it?"

Anming seemed to consider carefully, before answering, "About a month and a half. It arrived a week before I left Shanghai."

Raimy felt his frown deepen. "Left for where? Paramaribo?"

"No, Florida," Anming said. "I met my friends there, and we all went to Paramaribo together."

When Raimy was close to solving something, he often passed through a moment of feeling unnaturally stupid, because he could feel the evidence dancing right in front of his face, but he couldn't yet make sense of it. This didn't always happen, but it was often enough to be a thing. And he was definitely feeling it now.

Sensing some importance in this little valentine atom, he picked it up and set it in his own right palm. He kept a finger on it, though—determined to feel it while it transitioned.

"Be careful," Anming warned. "It's—"

The warning came a moment too late; like a heart-shaped mousetrap, the thing snapped shut on Raimy's finger.

"Ow! Fuck!"

Reflexively, he flicked his hand, hard, several times. The thing didn't budge.

"Fucking, fucking . . . Ouch!"

"You have to let it cool off," Anming said, with what sounded like genuine concern.

Raimy kept flicking, though, and pawing at it with his

other hand, until he finally dragged it off his finger, taking a good square centimeter of skin along with it.

It fell with a ping to the metal decking of the floor, bounced once, sprang back into the shape of an atom, and settled.

"Fuck," Raimy said, a final time.

"You have to be careful," Anming said. "I should have warned you."

"Pretty dangerous toy," Raimy said.

And then he had it. He knew how Etsub Beyene was murdered.

He pulled the clamp bracket back out of his pocket, carefully, and compared its color and sheen to that of the valentine atom. They were nearly identical. Nearly.

"Tell me who sent that to you," Raimy said, pointing at the valentine atom.

Anming did not reply. Barely reacted.

"Tell me where you ordered it," Raimy tried.

Again, no reaction. Anming looked miserable. Scared. Caught.

"You're under arrest," Raimy said, fishing now for his handcuffs.

"I know," Anming said. "I know I am."

And then he began to cry.

5.2
22 November

✦

H.S.F. *Concordia*
Moored to Transit Point Station
Low Earth Orbit

"I think you two are going to have to catch me up," said Carol Beseman. Still wearing her pressure suit, she floated in one of the docking modules of Transit Point Station, having arrived with a shipment of dry goods and produce.

"I think I'd better stay in here a while," she added, holding a hand to her stomach. She was one of those people who always needed a couple of hours to equilibrate after arriving in zero gee. Her helmet was already stowed on *Concordia*, along with the rest of her gear, but she hadn't felt up to removing the suit quite yet. Miyuki was sympathetic, but could not really relate, having taken to space the same way she'd taken to water as a toddler: with an almost instinctive gusto.

"We've been thinking more about terraforming shortcuts," Beseman said to his wife.

"I'd gathered that much," Carol said, with remarkable patience considering she'd just arrived, and was already being bombarded with his work crap. Twelve hours ago, Miyuki knew, she was hosting a fundraiser at West Beseman House in Portland, and thirty-six hours before that she'd been in Iceland, trying to hammer out some trade agreements with the European Union, who were still balking at the sheer quantity of goods being imported through their borders by Enterprise City. "It's not our fault your people want to buy our stuff," she'd told them— a quote picked up by every tabloid and news service in the world. But of course it was more than that. Enterprise City was where everyone went to buy everything—a fact that had been raising eyebrows around the world for decades. Governments had long seen this as a threat, albeit one that was hard to quantify or pin down. Bad for small business! Waste of packaging! Waste of energy and infrastructure! EC should source local ingredients and labor, rather than shipping products all over the world! But lately those same governments had started moving from empty rhetoric to actual legislation, specifically written to disadvantage the Besemans. Because the Besemans were making too much money—in fact, pumping money out of every country in the world, in exchange for "crap no one needed." Except they did, obviously, and Enterprise City was also the single largest philanthropic entity on the planet. If it gave just half a percent of its income to charity, that was still five billion dollars a year! But that was the old debate. The new, more urgent one, was that the Besemans were using that money to leave the Earth behind entirely. Unthinkable!

"You know what a von Neumann machine is?" Beseman asked her.

"The computing architecture?" Carol asked. Reasonably, Miyuki thought, because Quantum Von Neumann Complete, or QVNC, was the platform her husband had originally used to build their retail empire, and was still the backbone of their hyperweb services business.

"The self-replication architecture," he said, positively radiant with excitement.

"Oh, dear," Carol said, as if she knew what was coming. "Nanotechnology again?"

"Almost," Beseman said.

"I need a drink of water and some Tums," Carol protested. "Let me get my bearings, come inside, get some clothes on . . ."

Miyuki handed her a squeeze bottle of chilled water she'd been planning to drink herself, and then launched herself out into the corridor in search of Tums. By the time she got back, though, the Besemans were in animated conversation.

"What about the gray goo problem?" Carol wanted to know. "What's to stop your replicators from eating the whole planet?"

Beseman seemed about to answer, but then looked up at Miyuki and made a gesture that said, "You explain this better than I do. Please, come here and take over."

Handing four antacid tablets to Carol, Miyuki said, "I'm not sure what he's told you, but we're not talking about little machines. They don't have arms, or legs, or wheels, or mouths. It's more of a crystallization process, although admittedly the unit cells are quite complex. About the size of a free-culture ribosome."

"Who came up with this?" Carol wanted to know.

"R&D department," Miyuki said. Which didn't exactly narrow it down, because R&D was a quarter of the Antilympus Project's overall budget, and employed tens of thousands of people worldwide. And those budgets had lately gotten even fatter; when news got out that the project was actively manipulating the Martian atmosphere, donations tripled overnight (mostly earmarked for terraforming research), and remained at that high level. Let the United Nations whine all it wanted; the people of Earth had spoken with their wallets. They wanted a new planet, and were willing to buy it outright, now that Beseman was willing to sell it to them.

But the answer seemed to satisfy Carol, who said, "How long would it take these . . . crystals to consume the entire planet?"

"A long time," Miyuki told her. "To coat the surface to a depth of one millimeter, about half a million years, if we don't intervene. But the Martian atmosphere would be breathable long before that happened, because every unit cell replication frees up one CO_2 molecule and ten oxygens. Oxygen molecules, I mean, not atoms."

Carol *hmmed* and nodded at that, and then said, "Safeguards?"

"Numerous," Miyuki assured her. "First of all, the unit cells—we don't have a fancy name for them yet—aren't capable of pulling CHON atoms out of organic material. They're not pathogens, or even decomposers. They're more like lichens: they're powered by sunlight and they eat rocks, very slowly, liberating oxygen in the process. Unlike lichens, they can survive in hard vacuum and hard ultraviolet, which is critical for us. They can also eat dust particles, which is likely how they'll spread, although our primary intention is local. If we spread these over the floor of Antilympus Crater, then within a few years we'll have patches of greenish-white all over the place, with less soil mobility and an elevated local concentration of oxygen."

"How elevated?"

"Half a millibar partial pressure, if R&D's calculations are accurate. Less, when the wind blows through."

Carol chewed that over for several seconds. Miyuki could see the calculations happening—the same ones she'd made herself when P.K. Rao first brought this proposal to her. Half a millibar of oxygen was a negligible fraction of a breathable atmosphere, and it would react furiously with the lithosphere, finding any free iron or other metals and rusting them. But the planet was already mostly rusted, so eventually the oxygen would start to build up. Slowly. From a near-term colonization standpoint, such a project was ridiculous, and would have no value beyond the purely symbolic. But what a symbol! If Antilympus had two ongoing projects to modify the Martian atmosphere, then the average man or woman in the street would start thinking they might actually be able to live on Mars someday—not in a dome or habitat tube, but in a house, under an open sky. It didn't matter that that wasn't true. It wouldn't matter if Enterprise City and the Antilympus Project went on public record saying it wasn't true. People would latch onto the idea, as enthusiastically as they'd latched onto the colony project itself, the moment the Besemans announced it. Who else could say they'd raised a trillion dollars in voluntary donations in a mere five years? Nobody.

"And how do you know it's not a pathogen?" Carol wanted to know.

"They put a sterile mouse corpse in a beaker with the stuff, and nothing happened. So they put a live mouse in, and still nothing happened. Finally, the developers took a shower in the stuff, literally. Got it in their eyes and everything. That's how confident they were."

"And how long ago was that?"

"Five days."

"And are they quarantined right now?"

"Yes, although they were planning on exiting tomorrow."

"And they're in some sort of containment facility?"

"Yes. They're sleeping on the floor of a BSL-3 laboratory." Biosafety level three, meaning the room was maintained at negative pressure, laminar flow at all times, and any exiting air had to pass through a 0.3-micron HEPA filter. Basically a giant fume hood, with antimicrobial coatings on every surface. The only higher level was BSL-4, for pathogens that could literally end civilization if they got loose. Setting up a BSL-4 required a lot of time and red tape, and attracted a lot of attention. And it would have been overkill for something like this.

It would not be quiet in that BSL lab by any stretch; those blowers were *loud*. Also, the piled-up foam mats the research team were sleeping on were of a special fluid-proof, non-particle-entrapping design that did not look comfortable. She had to admire their dedication.

Carol mulled that over a moment before saying, "My husband's throttle is always stuck at full, and most of the time, you're his enabler. Or vice-versa. But I sit on the board of directors, and they need to know somebody's got a foot on the brake pedal. I'm sorry for their comfort, but let's keep these eager beavers locked up for a full month. How many are there?"

"Five. Three women, two men. Playing a lot of Dungeons & Dragons, apparently."

"Okay," Carol said, "I like the optics of that. We'll send in pizza, and if they don't mind a camera drone we'll put them on their own publicity feed. Maybe set up a press conference."

Looking at Beseman, she said, "With your permission, dear."

"Please do," Beseman said.

"They might not like the camera," Miyuki said, her thoughts clearly running more prurient than Carol's own.

"We'll ask 'em," Carol said. And then suddenly barfed.

After Carol took some medication and started to feel better, she changed out of her pressure suit and into her Antilympus coveralls. Then they all went down into Transit Point Station to visit with some of the crew, who knew Carol pretty well at this point. Without invitation, they entered the Traffic Control module down at the Earthward-facing end of the station's towerlike structure.

"Mrs. Beseman," said Geary Notbohm, looking up from a display screen with evident gladness. "Welcome aboard. Are you feeling better?"

"Thank you, Commander. I am."

These were commonly exchanged words here on TPS, almost rote.

"Hello," said Paul Young, the lead space traffic controller. Who did not look up from his screen, and who clasped a hand over his headset's microphone when he spoke.

"Was your journey pleasant?" Geary asked.

"Never," Carol said with a laugh.

Miyuki knew the feeling; even though Enterprise City ran some of the gentlest crew-launch profiles in the business, it was still a violent ride, topping out at 3.5 gee and with a lot of heavy vibration around the stage-separation events. EC also had only a handful of human-rated launch vehicles of their own, so a lot of crew transfers were through purchased tickets on the crew flights of Renz Ventures or Harvest Moon or even, God help you, Orlov Petrochemical. But Carol co-owned the EC launch vehicle fleet, or rather, shared a majority stake in the publicly traded company that owned the fleet, so as long as it didn't conflict with critical operations, she could have an entire booster to herself if she wanted to. Which was exactly what she'd just done. Miyuki tended to ride with Beseman, often crammed in with six or eight other people, so that was a luxury she envied.

"I understand," Geary said.

"I need quiet in here," Paul complained. "I've got two flights incoming and one about to depart."

"Of course," Geary said, leading them all out into a neighboring module, currently configured as a simple corridor—its walls and floor and ceiling a bright enamel white, with black trim and brushed-steel fixtures. Most of the modules of TPS were configured that way most of the time. However, they could also, fairly efficiently, be unpacked into crew quarters or, with greater effort and planning, laboratories and light manufacturing space. The Antilympus Project had rented both things, many times, during the early phases of building the H.S.F. *Concordia*. Now of course they had their own space onboard the ship itself, and plenty of it, but it wasn't that long ago Miyuki had operated these brushed-steel latches and levers to reconfigure stuff. She was oddly tempted to fiddle with them now.

To Beseman, Geary said, "I keep hearing rumors about ESL1 Shade Station."

"Uh huh," Beseman said.

"They are building something."

"They're always building something," Beseman said.

Geary looked annoyed at that. He and Beseman were good friends at this point, so finally Beseman relented and said, "Neither of these two have heard it yet"—he nodded his head first toward Miyuki and then toward Carol—"but Igbal Renz is building a spaceship."

"They are always building spaceships," Notbohm said, his voice a bit snippy.

"This is different," Beseman said.

"Different how?" Carol asked. And now she sounded annoyed as well, because she didn't like Beseman keeping secrets from her. Nor did Miyuki herself, for that matter.

"He offered me a trillion dollars for *Concordia*," Beseman said. "Cash, outright. I turned him down, of course, so then he offered me half a trillion for just the blueprints, including weekly updates as we actually finish construction."

"That's a lot of money," Miyuki observed. A trillion dollars was in fact probably the entire cash reserve of Renz Ventures, whose entire value was probably not more than triple that.

"Yeah," Beseman agreed.

"Are they going to Mars?" Carol asked, sounding mildly concerned.

"We don't own the place," Beseman said, "but no, I don't think so. He said he was going to modify the cockpit and drive sections. There'd be no reason to do that if he was going to Mars."

"So, where's he going?" Carol asked.

"I don't know," Beseman said. Then, after a significant pause: "But it's apparently very important to him."

Carol and Geary both looked concerned at that, and Carol finally said, "Do you get the feeling things are slipping away from us? It used to be so simple, but things have gotten so... secretive. Even you." And here she glared at Beseman.

"There are more players than there used to be," Beseman said. "And more variables. Murders and skullduggery and invisibility cloaks. Igbal Renz has always been a nut, but he's been a public nut. Now he's holding his cards close. Even Killian's acting shifty. He's got confidential projects of his own, but I think there are people keeping secrets from him, too. And I expect he doesn't like that. And Orlov—Jesus Christ. He straight-up *has* lost control."

"What about us?" Carol asked. "Are we going to be carrying a hundred hidden agendas to Mars with us?"

Beseman sighed. "Probably. Hopefully not an actual murderer, but people are people. There's no telling what's going on inside some of them. We may own the equipment, but we don't . . ."

"Own the hearts and minds?" Miyuki suggested.

"Not automatically, no. We've made a show of Mars being a democracy, but I'm thinking the whole project might need to be. Not just the people who go, or even just the candidates. Maybe everybody who's involved, at any level."

"Maybe now is the time to start," Carol said. "Poll the top hundred about your . . . lichen crystals? My God, Miyuki, why don't these things have a name?"

Miyuki laughed a little. "In their official reports, the development team has been calling them STROVs, which stands for Self-Templating Reductive Viroids. Informally, they call them 'oxygen bugs,' but I told them both of those were nonstarters."

"How about 'Lichenoids'?" Carol suggested.

"That's less terrible," Beseman said. "But you're right: let's let the candidates decide it for themselves. It's their home we're proposing to contaminate."

1.15
22 November
✦
St. Joseph of Cupertino Monastery
South Polar Mineral Territories
Lunar Surface

After explaining the arrest to the knot of onlookers behind him, Raimy asked someone to fetch Brother Michael, and then left Anming temporarily in his care. He then went off to talk to Andrei again.

"What is this thing?" Raimy demanded, holding out the valentine atom in a gray ceramic coffee mug.

"Is coffee cup," Andrei said dryly, then noticed the valentine atom and stopped. "Mmm."

Raimy dumped the thing into his palm and demonstrated its transformation: atom to valentine. He then dumped it back in the cup, where it sat for a few seconds before popping back into its original shape, with a clatter like a dropped coin.

"Is shape memory alloy," Andrei said confidently. "Probably titanium nickel alloy. We say Nitinol in Russian. I do not know American word for this."

"Explain," Raimy said. "As though I've never heard of it."

Andrei shrugged. "Is forged in two shapes. Cold shape and hot shape. People use this metal to make eyeglasses that fix themselves if they are bent. Also little medical robots that move without motors, or a hermetic seal between two pipes, very strong. Is pretty old technology. Actually molecules of this metal can have six different structures, so perhaps this kind of object could be six different shapes, but I have not seen this. Usually it is two. This is probably medical wire, with *perekhod* temperature, uh, *change* temperature, close to body heat."

Raimy very carefully pulled the bracket clamp out of his pocket, and held it out in his open palm. "What about this thing? Could it also be memory alloy?"

Andrei furrowed his brow and said, "You thinking this is *orudiye ubiystva*? Ah . . . murder tool? Weapon? Yes . . . yes, it could be." He picked it up and seemed to measure its weight again.

"Be careful," Raimy said.

"You have held this thing all day," Andrei observed. "It is not switching shape from your body heat. But it could be shape memory alloy, yes, with higher switching temperature."

"How much higher?"

Andrei shrugged. "Could be anything. How hot is spacesuit backpack in full Lunar sunlight? Could be maybe eighty, ninety degrees centigrade."

"Can we get it that hot?"

"We have kitchen," Andrei said, as though it were obvious. Which of course it was.

The kitchen was only two modules over from the library, but Raimy and Andrei took the long way around, through the cloisters and the chapel and the infirmary and the workshop, where they picked up Purcell.

"I can heat it up with a torch," Purcell offered, once the situation was explained to him.

"I prefer something less destructive," Raimy said. This was going to be one of the exhibits presented to a jury, and he didn't want any extraneous scorch marks on it.

They then went back through the chapel again, where Michael and Giancarlo were now keeping watch over Anming.

"What's going on?" Michael wanted to know.

"I want to heat this thing up on the stove," Raimy said, holding up the now-familiar clamp bracket. "I have reason to believe it's going to change shape."

"Keep him here," Michael said to Giancarlo, with a nod in Anming's direction. Then, to Raimy: "Let's run your plan past H.H. before we start messing with his equipment. Are you thinking that's some kind of shape memory alloy?"

"Yes," Raimy said.

"Probably Nitinol," Andrei added. "Based on weight."

"I see the logic," Purcell agreed. And so they all shuffled into the kitchen, where Hilario Hamblin (who had overheard through the open hatchway) said, "How can I help?"

The stove was basically just an induction hotplate that would only activate if a metal pot or pan were placed on it, so Hilario placed the clamp bracket in the center of a frying pan, and turned the heat up to a temperature, suggested by Andrei, of one hundred and twenty degrees Celsius.

"That will not melt or damage," Andrei explained, "but should exceed backpack temperature."

They all crowded around, waiting for they knew not what. And they waited. And they waited some more, until, suddenly, the clamp bracket jumped and clanged in the pan, clattering to rest again in a different shape. And right away you could see how this thing had popped the hose and severed the antenna cable, because in its hot configuration it was a tight spiral with a nasty, pointed tip.

"Boom," Raimy said. This thing had heated up inside Etsub's backpack until it suddenly coiled into a cutting, puncturing instrument. And then, when he'd fallen into shadow and the backpack started bleeding its gas and heat into the vacuum of space, the clamp bracket had released its death grip and fallen away, its evil task complete.

"You appear to have cracked the case," Michael said, in a tone that managed to be both admiring and sorrowful.

"A nearly perfect crime," Raimy said. "I never would have figured it out if he hadn't brought a sample of the same technology to the goddamn Moon with him. That's usually what trips people up. They leave their clues, never imagining . . ."

"I am not stupid," Anming said. Because somehow he was there at the back of the crowd.

"Get him out of here," Raimy said, to no one in particular. Then, to Hilario: "Let's turn the heat off."

Hilario did so, and after a much shorter delay, the clamp bracket clanged and clattered back into its original shape, as though nothing had happened at all.

"Oh my God," said Bridget, who was somehow also there at the back.

"Where did you get this?" demanded Katla, who was also there.

Everyone was there. Everyone wanted to see.

"Damn," said Raimy, who had never once had control over this crime scene.

To which Michael said, wearily, "Can I beseech you, all of you, to stop taking the Lord's name in vain?"

Fifteen minutes later, Michael and Raimy were alone in the chapel, a handcuffed Anming temporarily in the custody of Hilario in the laundry room.

"How certain are you about this?" Michael asked.

"About what?"

The question seemed to surprise Michael, who said, "That you've identified the killer in our midst."

Raimy processed that for a few seconds. It was a completely logical thing for a layman to ask. Superficially, it was the whole point of any criminal investigation, right? But it did kind of miss the point.

"We have a suspect," he said carefully, "with motive, means, and opportunity. By Etsub's death, he stood to gain an entire planet. Just him—no one else. He clearly had access to custom Nitinol fabrication services. He was at the GS plant in Florida, where Etsub's backpack was sitting unsecured, before it was sealed and fitted to its user. We've found the murder weapon, and a second piece of physical evidence that ties Anming to it. It's circumstantial, but unless we find DNA or fingerprints somewhere, it's what we have, and it's more than enough for a prosecutor to build an airtight case. Actual guilt or innocence is for a jury to decide—*not* me—but in procedural terms this one is open and shut."

But Michael was frowning. "That's not what I asked."

"There are always loose ends," Raimy said, and here his voice sounded a little condescending and a little defensive, even to himself. But damn it, he'd spent eight years lawyering and ten years policing, and he didn't need some civilian telling him how to do his job. "Some of these we'll tie up once I get back to Earth. I'll try to figure out exactly where those metal parts came from, and who placed the order. But there are easy ways to conceal your identity online, and Anming is not stupid, so I'm not expecting to find anything. And some of these ends are going to dangle forever, because we just can't know everything that happened. And we don't need to."

He paused then, looking at Michael, who managed in his monk robes to look both sternly authoritative and utterly naive. Raimy realized that answer was not going to fly, so he tried another:

"You know, people think I'm supposed to be some kind of mind reader, studying the faces of everyone who's acting weird"—and here he gestured with his hands holding them up around his face and wiggling them slightly—"but everyone acts weird when they're under suspicion, and even good cops make bad lie detectors. The ones who try to run it that way have low solve rates and low conviction rates, which drove me *crazy* as a prosecutor. There is no magic to this job; a good detective needs tangible evidence to show who did what to whom, and why. It's a lot like science: you present your hypothesis, you collect evidence, you prove it beyond reasonable doubt. And still it's called a theory, not a fact."

Unimpressed, Michael repeated, "How certain are you?"

"Ninety percent," Raimy said. "Which is as certain as I ever am about anything."

The prior's face softened, then. "All right. I suppose congratulations are in order. And gratitude."

"Just doing my job," Raimy said, with transparently false modesty.

Michael side-eyed him a bit, not liking that. But what he said was, "We have no way to confine him, so we're going to have to figure out sleeping arrangements. You can't watch him 24/7, and I'm assuming you don't want to sleep next to him."

"True," Raimy said. That concern had been hypothetical up to this point, but there simply wasn't anywhere to lock up a prisoner. Not here, and not at Shackleton, or the other little bases, either. "And I'm assuming we can't, you know, stuff him in the bunker and pile weights on top of the hatch?"

"I thought about that," Michael said. "It's got a sink and a toilet. But a lot of our plumbing and wiring runs right across the ceiling, unprotected. Even restrained, he could sabotage the whole complex. In retrospect, it's a design flaw, but who knew?"

"Hmm. Could we maybe maroon him in a separate module, out on the Lunar surface, with no spacesuit?" Raimy had already asked Tracy Greene to run that question up various flagpoles, and none of them had come back with answers at all, much less affirmative ones.

"Even with advance planning," Michael said, "that would cost a hundred million dollars. We're going to have to keep him under constant supervision, which means we'll need to watch him in shifts."

"At night we are," Raimy agreed. "I can cover him during the day. Except, you know, when I need bathroom breaks and such."

"You seem to go to bed early," Michael observed.

"On the Moon, anyway," Raimy said. But it wasn't just on the Moon. He still thought of himself as a night owl, but if he really thought about it, that had mainly been back in the thirties, during the great renaissance of coffeehouse culture, when he was freshly out of the military and trying to figure out who he wanted to be. And in fact, since he'd turned forty, there were more and more nights where he'd lost his steam by 9:00 P.M., if not earlier.

"We can cover for you from, say, 8:00 P.M. to three o'clock in the morning. That should leave you enough time to get six or seven hours of sleep."

"Sold," Raimy told him. "But who's going to watch him?"

"I'll ask for volunteers," Michael said, "but I'm guessing Andrei will want to do it. His fear of leaving makes him eager to please. Probably also Brother Purcell, because he's a firm believer in sleeping twice per night, with a wakeful period in between. He's into lucid dreaming, too, by the way."

"Okay," Raimy said, unsure what to do with that. Then, changing the subject entirely, he said to Michael, "Your secret is safe with me, by the way."

"Oh? What secret is that?" Michael asked calmly.

Lowering his voice, Raimy said, "You don't want the men to know you're gay. Or were, rather."

Still calm, Michael said, "What gives you that idea? Past homosexuality is not forbidden, by the way. The church has strict codes of conduct, but they do not extend backward in time. Statistically, at least one of us here is bound to have something like that in their past."

"You and Purcell," Raimy said. "Though not with each other. You have a . . . person of interest back on Earth, who also keeps the secret."

"What gives you that idea?" Michael said again, his face mild.

"In Purcell's case, it's . . . well, I'm sorry, but it's the way he moves. I saw it right away."

"I thought you weren't a lie detector," Michael said. "Are you saying you have some infallible gaydar?"

"Not infallible, no."

Michael stood impassive for a long moment, then sighed. "What gave me away?"

"You really want to know?"

"I do."

Carefully, Raimy said, "It's the way you say the word 'church.' Like it was a person. Specifically, a . . . beloved mentor, maybe? Once I noticed that, I got an electronic search warrant and stalked your deleted social media profiles."

"Why?"

"Because you were a suspect."

"Ah."

There was a long pause. Then, quietly, Michael said,

"Nothing ever happened. I want to be perfectly clear about that."

"Understood. And none of my business."

Then, ruefully, Michael said, "That's extremely flimsy evidence, isn't it? I never said anything online. I hugged some men in photos, maybe. Until a few seconds ago, all you had was a hypothesis."

"Correct," Raimy said.

"You've trapped me. To illustrate how your job works."

"Also correct."

"Well, consider me illustrated. The police are lucky to have you, Raimy. I expect the Navy was, as well."

Dinner that night was a subdued affair. That Anming had to be watched every moment was not a problem, because all eyes were on him, and he seemed to feel it keenly. Whether he was a serious threat to anyone's safety was hard to say; he'd already killed one person, but for a clearly definable reason. Now that he was well and truly caught, it seemed unlikely he had anything to gain by hurting anyone else. Raimy consented to re-cuff him with his hands in front, so he could eat and drink and such. He seemed very sad, and disinclined toward conversation. Nor would he meet the eyes of his classmates, although he looked hard at Raimy a few times.

"What I can't figure out," Bridget was saying, "is why that thing didn't pop off the minute Etsub stepped outside? He went EVA a lot. It must have been a near thing."

"Maybe it did," Purcell said. "Maybe multiple times, weakening the hose each time."

"A little luckier and he might have made it all the way

back to Earth, none the wiser he was ever in danger," Katla agreed.

To which Michael opined, "If it's true the Lord works in mysterious ways, then the universe by definition cannot be mere clockwork. There's an uncertainty about things, and it's there we can look for his handiwork."

To which Bridget said, "Why would God want him to die at that particular moment? Why would God want him to die at all?"

To which Giancarlo replied, in his thick Italian accent, "Ouch, Bridget. Yes, everyone dies, unpleasantly. It's unwise to think we know the mind of God, or can know it, but this much has always been true, and likely always will be. It's hard not to feel victimized."

Several of the monks had responses to that:

Ovid: "Mathematics shows us the mind of God. The how of creation, at least, if not the why."

Groppel: "Teilhard de Chardin agreed with you, and wrote a lot about the prevalence of exponential growth in nature and in human affairs. He was actually the first to believe in a Singularity as a heaven of man's own creation."

Bear: "No he wasn't, and no he didn't."

Purcell: "*Merde*. Roger Bacon and Francis Bacon both said empirical evidence is the standard by which all knowledge should be measured. Detectives, both of them, among other things. They would say, until your singularity arrives, it's not real. Unlike death."

Groppel: "Bacon's advice is not relational. Are we machines or men?"

From there, the conversation grew both more esoteric and more overtly Christian, to which Neither Katla nor

Bridget nor Raimy had anything to add. Raimy had grown up Baptist, but had stopped going to church the minute his parents stopped making him. He had sometimes attended the chaplain's services while he was aboard the U.S.S. *Jimmy Carter*, but that was as much out of boredom as anything else.

However, after another twenty minutes of chatter, Anming effectively ended the discussion—and the meal— by saying, "In my religion, murderers also go to Hell. And liars. And we sometimes say, those who love badly are in Hell already, and have nothing further to fear." He said nothing more after that, and once the dishes were cleared away and the tables folded back into church pews, he stuck around with Andrei, who had indeed volunteered to watch him. Anming seemed inclined to sit there all the way through "vespers," which is what the monks called their evening prayers.

Raimy took the opportunity to return to his quarters and call Tracy Greene, to let her know the case had been solved, and how.

"Congratulations," she said with apparent sincerity. "I knew you would, though. You have a ninety percent solve rate."

Raimy couldn't help calculating: as of today, it was actually more like ninety-two and a half. He let it go, though, and simply thanked her, then hung up when it looked like she was going to start asking personal questions. After that, he typed up a little report and emailed it to her, then watched some cartoons, listened to some music and, at some point, drifted off to sleep.

❖❖❖

He was a light sleeper, so when his room's hatch opened later on in the night, he was aware of it, and instantly opened his eyes to a silhouette in the doorway. Female. Wearing only space underwear. She came inside and gently closed the door behind her, and from her smell and the sound of her breathing he could tell it was Bridget.

"What are you—" he started to say in a quiet whisper, but she laid a finger vertically across his lips. Hush. Then she got into bed with him.

He thought for a moment that she was there to seduce him, or reward him, or whatever, but instead she simply snuggled under his arm. And that was better somehow, warmer and more soothing. "I just want to be close," she said, in a very quiet whisper even he could barely hear.

Her smell was intoxicating. It was funny—right?—how every woman smelled different, and how some of those smells just crawled inside you and set up camp. And she was not a suspect anymore, and he was not on the clock, and so he adjusted his position to make room for her, and she adjusted to settle her shape into his. It was good, and they stayed like that for a long time, until Raimy fell asleep again.

Some hours later she slipped out from under his arm. Slipped out of bed and out of the room, quiet as a feather in vacuum, leaving only her scent behind. Raimy breathed it in deeply, surprised at himself for deriving so much pleasure from so chaste an encounter. And then fell back again into dreamless, virtuous slumber, until his rollup chirped its 3:00 A.M. wakeup call.

1.16
22 November

✦

St. Joseph of Cupertino Monastery
South Polar Mineral Territories
Lunar Surface

The news media—already alive with chatter about Etsub's death—went bananas when they found out Raimy had solved the crime. To hear them tell it, he was both "a charismatic detective with roots in the U.S. Navy" and "a would-be astronaut with almost childish aspirations to Mars." He had "cracked" or "untangled" or "blundered into a solution for" something that was either "the crime of the century" or "a fiendish plot to steal one percent of a planet," or simply "nerdmurder." He was being "paid a hefty sum" by a "shadowy group of Horsemen's footmen," or he was just doing it "for the exposure" in this age of "faux celebrity roughly as convincing as a 3D-printed pizza." He was from Colorado Springs or San Diego or else he was a transient who moved around a lot. He was a failed lawyer or a failed cop or a Navy washout, or he was "a Renaissance man who's tried his hand, successfully, at more career paths than a cat has lives."

He tried not to read it, and when that failed, he tried not to obsess over it. And when that also failed, he simply tried not to spend whole days on it. He was the ninety-first person ever to set foot on the Moon, and he had only another two days at Saint Joe's before the H.S.F. *Pony Express* returned to pick them all up, students and cops and perps. Whatever the vlogs and tabloids might say, he was no publicity hound. He lacked the tongue for it! And yet, only an idiot would waste an opportunity like this. With the most critical part of the investigation complete, he was technically at liberty to record and post videos of his Lunar adventure, and basically take free advantage of a free trip to the Moon. The same trip had cost Bridget and Katla a hundred million dollars apiece—not out of pocket, but from their Antilympus funds, with the donors' approval. They'd made their money back immediately once the news got out, and had doubled it once they actually started vlogging from the Moon, so in that sense it was very much a winning strategy. But he was getting his for free.

The publicity didn't seem to work so well for Raimy, though; in those first two days, while the news was fresh and the iron was hot, he netted barely fifty million in additional donations. This was not even quite enough to move him from third place into second, so basically it meant nothing at all. The kindest interpretation of this (and the one Bridget and Michael favored) was that people had trouble seeing how a murder investigation (even if successful) related to the task of settling a new world. It was a fair point. The somewhat harsher view (espoused by Katla and Andrei and even a few of the monks) was that Raimy was truly shit at vlogging, and it was shocking he'd gotten as far as third place for the uber-competitive Male Administrator slot.

The darkest view, held publicly by many reporters and privately by Raimy himself, was that people simply didn't want him for the job. Maybe not so much because of his personality (although maybe, yeah), as because he'd never actually administrated anything. Up against CEOs and congressmen and the head of goddamn National Geographic, he'd never really stood a chance. But he wasn't good for anything else, either; Mars needed mechanics and doctors and hydroponic gardeners. It needed pilots and construction crews and people who could drive a big vehicle over rough terrain. What it didn't need—what people didn't want it to need—were cops, lawyers, or military guys, of which Raimy was all three. So yeah, maybe it was simply never meant to be.

That was only in his darker moments, though. The rest of the time he was watching Moon people do their Moon jobs, and learning everything he could, and helping out where he was able. If this was his one and only trip to space, well, it was an incredible experience that was (visibly and audibly) the envy of millions. Certainly, no one at CSPD (not even the Air Force veterans, of whom there were several) could boast of a better vacation. God, could he go back to CSPD after this? Turning over ice-cold corpses with his foot, to see the look of horror on their faces? If Mars wasn't an option, then yes, that was probably his highest calling. But it occurred to him that he might very well try his hand at something else, and meanwhile, he had the Moon.

Every day there was an elaborate breakfast and an

elaborate dinner—different and surprising each time. Lunches, where they occurred at all, were hurried affairs, because everyone was busy during the day, so Raimy learned to really load up at breakfast—enough food to carry him entirely through the day. Which was an adjustment, because he was generally a big fan of big lunches. But here on the Moon, everything was different and required adjusting to, so he just rolled with it.

He and a still-handcuffed Anming even spent a morning in the kitchen with Hilario and Kurtis (or Hamblin and Durm, or H.H. and Dewey), learning how to work the CHON synthesizer, the induction stove, and the weird combo oven that immolated foodstuffs with simultaneous microwaves, radiant infrared, and superheated air, flashing them to baking or broiling or frying temperature. Officially a "Hammerschmidt Combination Oven," it was colloquially referred to as "the hammer," and cooking food in it was called "hammering."

"This thing is expensive like a small airplane," Hilario explained, "much more than the six appliances it combines. But it saves space, and it saves mass, and so it's actually way better than shipping six things up here. But for a foodie it does limit options. I miss choosing to air-fry one thing whilst microwaving another."

It was a bitch to operate, too; never intended for consumer use, it had separate control menus for each heating feature, and no macros or recipe controls to tie it all together. Slow-baking a potato in forty-five minutes was straightforward enough, but flash-hammering one in ten minutes, without exploding or charring it, required a PhD in thermodynamics.

"And yet, we have a lot of people to cook for, and different dishes at every meal. So it has to be fast."

"You get good at it," Kurtis said, with the patience of a monk.

The CHON synthesizer was even more complicated, although it did at least allow you to dial up preprogrammed food simulants from a series of menus.

"By itself this stuff is *cosa muy pegajosa*," Hilario said of a manufactured protein paste. "Basically glop. But so is miso, or Vegemite, or"—he looked up at Anming—"rice congee, and people eat those things. Today we're going to put this in chicken nugget molds and then starch the outsides. Tomorrow, maybe blend it into broth, and never let the brothers guess it's the same ingredient. Cooking well is a tricky skill up here."

Raimy was nowhere close to mastering the equipment by the end of the breakfast shift, but he at least understood the basic principles. He had no idea if there'd be ovens and printers like this at Antilympus, and anyway he had even less qualification as a chef than he did an administrator. But like any real student of the monastery, he was learning how to live in space.

"I burned the biscuits," he told his followers in a poorly edited video, with Anming lurking dolefully in the background, "but I printed out some decent glop."

He spent the afternoon in the workshop, "helping" Brother Purcell repair an electrostatic precipitator from the floor vent of one of the dormitory cells. His contribution consisted mainly of fetching tools and holding a work light, while making sure Anming didn't get anywhere close to anything he could use as a weapon. But still, Raimy got an idea of how the precipitator was put together, and how it worked.

"The charge pulls air past this plate," Purcell said. "And the dust sticks to it. But the ozone filter's bad, and without that, the whole thing's *no bueno*, more harm than good. Ozone's also bad for your lungs."

Fixing the ozone filter involved putting on paper masks, using compressed air to blast moondust out of a little brick of pumice-like material, and immediately sucking up the dust with a little vacuum hose, to keep it out of the monastery's atmosphere. The brick was then sprayed down with some sort of anti-static solution from a 3D-printed plastic spray bottle.

"Now we put the filter back in its slot," Purcell said. "Now we close the housing and screw the grating back on. Now we charge the plates and turn it on, to confirm it's *funcional*, which it is. Now we put it back where it came from, and go to the next to-do item on the punch list."

It wasn't exactly the most fascinating work, but again, it taught Raimy something important about living and working on an alien planet.

He spent the evening in the library, skimming through Harvest Moon's maintenance and operator's manuals for the hab modules and their various subsystems. Verrry dry reading, but it helped him make sense of the equipment all around him, on which his life depended. It was all quite different from the systems onboard a submarine— especially because they were designed so that new plug-and-play hab modules could be snapped into place with minimal fuss. And these were undoubtedly different from the robot-built modules at Antilympus, but maybe not that different, because how many different ways could there be to move air and water and electricity around?

Anming seemed particularly bored here in the library. He tried reading magazines on one of the computers in here, but finally gave up and just sat there, looking accusingly at Raimy. And Raimy did feel somewhat bad for this murderer, because he should have been processed into a jail by now, or (less likely) out on bail after pre-trial hearings. Being dragged around like a parcel was surely humiliating, and it wasn't Raimy's job to humiliate anyone. But the alternative was for Raimy himself to sit around bored along with Anming, and he simply wasn't going to do that, when he had a whole moonbase at his disposal.

The second night Bridget came to his bed, she did so less innocently. They let their hands roam over—and then under—the slippery-stretchy fabric of each other's space underwear. But only for a while, and only in an exploratory capacity. She then curled up next to him and fell asleep, and when he woke up a few hours later, she was gone. But that was fine. They had another full day here together at the monastery, and then . . . who knew?

1.17
24 November
✧
St. Joseph of Cupertino Monastery
South Polar Mineral Territories
Lunar Surface

Raimy and his prisoner spent the next morning in the greenhouse, watching Bridget tend to her herbs and vegetables. He supposed technically they were Michael's herbs and vegetables, but Michael was off on some other business. Probably administrative, Raimy noted jealously; he was the "prior" of this place, and ultimately responsible for its smooth functioning. Perhaps, instead of treating St. Joe's like it was Disneyland, he should be asking Michael to mentor him on what it was like to administer a space colony. But when Michael did check in at the greenhouse—once to make sure Bridget was properly monitoring the urea levels in the dripwater, and later to poke his finger into the dirt trough in several places—he seemed distracted in a busy way, and uninterested in talking to Raimy. He was, however, very intent on feeling the texture and moisture level of the "starter soil," which (according to Bridget) was actually a combination of regolith, human waste, chopped-up cloth, and a weirdly spongy Earth mineral called "vermiculite." And some actual Earthly potting soil, yes, although that made up less than a quarter of its total volume.

This was the east greenhouse "working garden," from which most of the monastery's food sprang.

"It's vitally dull in here," Bridget declared at one point. "We don't want anything interesting happening, and so it never does."

Anming looked incensed by that comment, but otherwise kept it to himself. Even handcuffed, he seemed more at ease in this module than anywhere else Raimy had seen him. From his chair in the corner, he studied the plants and the mechanisms around them, nodding occasionally. Still studying a craft he would never again put into practice.

"It is dull," Raimy agreed. It seemed important to get a sense of what went on in here, and he was doing that. But yeesh, this was definitely not the job for him.

The routine was only broken when H.H. stopped by to pick up some turnips and hot peppers for that night's dinner stew.

"Are you gentlemen and ladies behaving?" he asked, leering a bit at the way Raimy was standing so close to Bridget. Not like he knew anything—more like he was full of shit and wanted to share it with the world.

"No business of yours," Bridget said, though, in a tone virtually guaranteed to make him think it was.

"Well, *te dejo a ti*," he said, tossing the harvest into a bag. "I'll leave you to it."

And that was their morning: dull and more dull. The real action was of course next door, in the west greenhouse "experimental garden," where Earth matter was forbidden, and food was grown from seed, using only Lunar water and Lunar regolith and electricity generated from Lunar sunlight.

"Is that what Katla's doing this morning?"

"I don't know," Bridget said. "Katla's been scarce. I think the thing with Anming has her glooming pretty hard. The two of them were . . . you know, close."

Another glare from Anming. Ignoring it, Raimy said, "I didn't realize that. I thought she was just avoiding me."

Katla took her meals with everyone else, but sat as far from Raimy as she could. Although, perhaps she was just trying to stay away from Anming.

"She's avoiding everyone," Bridget said. "It figures she'd be sad. I guess we're all sad, but . . ."

"I understand."

If he thought about it, Katla didn't say much at meals, and answered in monosyllables when asked a question. To Raimy's eye she seemed more troubled than sad, as if plagued by unpleasant dreams, but he supposed it all amounted to the same thing in the end. And yet, he did still kind of think she had a problem with him, specifically.

"Not much food comes out of the experimental garden," Anming said.

"That's true," Bridget said. "Not a tenth of what we get over here. But it's a fine thing to figure out what the Moon farms of the future can really grow, when they haven't got potting soil to fall back on."

"Will those same plants grow on Mars?" Raimy asked.

"Don't know," she said. "It's partly about what'll grow in nutrient-poor soil, which is, you know, useful knowledge on any planet. Fixing nitrogen is a chore even on Earth; when there's not enough turkey poop to go around, organic farmers have to grow legumes or buckwheat, which are nitrogen-fixing crops."

"Alfalfa," Anming said.

"Or that, yes. But even when you solve the nitrogen problem, Mars and Luna both have too much iron, and not enough sodium or potassium. That's a similarity, and really not so different from the deserts of Utah. But we don't grow crops there, even with irrigation. Luna's also got excess calcium, and Mars has toxic levels of chlorine and nickel. That's different, and bad. We can do some of this development work on Earth, and we have been. But as Michael could tell you, you never really know until you're there. The first group on Mars is going to make a lot of mistakes."

"Learning experiences," Anming said.

To which Bridget said, rather cruelly, "Not for you."

Raimy spent an afternoon flitting between the life-support, lab, and observatory modules, not doing any real work or even asking good questions, but simply watching the work that the monks were doing. There was a lot of it; the work of teaching and the (profitable) side hustle of made-to-order astronomical observation seemed, collectively, to take up perhaps twenty man-hours each day, spread out across five or six individuals. Prayers and such took up another two hours of each monk's time, as did communal meals, with another hour or so reserved for

hygiene and such. But the upkeep on the monastery itself
was serious business, and was something for which they
all pitched in. Sweeping the floors, wiping down the walls
and ceiling, dusting the fixtures, checking and rechecking
the quality of each module's air and services...

One thing that continually struck Raimy was how *new*
this place was; not one module here had been inhabited
for more than a year. By contrast, the U.S.S. *Jimmy Carter*
had been over thirty years old when Raimy was stationed
aboard, and that age showed on nearly every surface.
Some spots had been worn smooth by contact, ten
thousand times over, with hands or sleeves or shoes or
pant legs. Others had been painted so many times the
rivets barely showed, and still others were scratched and
scraped and dented in ways that might never be repaired
in the lifetime of the boat. Glass instrument covers were
cracked, and display screens of obsolete types had streaks
of dead pixels on them that you just stopped noticing after
a while. Old Jimmy had been worked hard, that was for
sure.

But here, everything shone. It looked new, it *smelled*
new, and the monks seemed determined to keep it that
way. Which, given the abrasive nature of the ubiquitous
moondust, was no easy task.

The brothers also spent a lot of time checking up on
each other's moods and mental health. They were mostly
a pretty taciturn group of people—Michael and Hilario
and Purcell notwithstanding—but when they did speak,
there was a surprising amount of intrusive gossip, which
seemed to consume a lot of their mental energy. Raimy
suspected, for example, that most of them knew what he

and Bridget were doing at night. And why not? This was their home, and Raimy was an invited guest. Bridget, too.

Each monk was also responsible for the upkeep of his own spacesuit, which some seemed to take more seriously than others. But when Michael and Giancarlo went outside to receive a shipment of gas bottles space-dropped from Clementine Cislunar Fuel Depot, they each spent a good half hour going over the seals and gauges on each other's suits, making very, very sure everything was working correctly.

"Hey, can I come out with you?" Raimy asked.

He was standing in the chapel, looking through the hatchway into the airlock module's gowning area, watching the two of them perform their checks and begin to suit up.

"The airlock only takes three at a time," Giancarlo said.

"Also," Michael said delicately, "I understand you want to get the most out of your Lunar adventure, but the men are starting to complain about the imposition."

"I thought they liked teaching," Raimy said.

"Oh, indeed, most of them very much do. But none of us ever signed up to be jailers. I'm sorry to ask, by which I mean, I'm sorry you're forcing my hand and *making* me ask, but would you please take proper charge of your prisoner? It's really not appropriate to stand him in the corner like that"—he waved in Anming's direction—"while you goof around. I understand the position you're in. I do. You're excited, in a new place, burning with curiosity. We all understand this, and can indulge you up to a point."

"But we've reached that point?"

"Perhaps," Michael said, smiling warmly. Then shut the airlock hatch in Raimy's face.

Never one to miss a hint, Raimy ducked his head into the kitchen to apologize to Hilario and Kurtis, whom he had inconvenienced perhaps more than anyone else in the monastery.

"There are a lot of sharp objects in here," Hilario agreed. "If you're asking, I actually would rather you not bring a murderer in here."

"Yep," said Brother Kurtis, who was wiping his hands on a white towel. "But it's mostly Eliaz who's been complaining. You should maybe go apologize to him."

"I see. Where can I find him?"

"Usually the library."

Suitably chastened, Raimy cut through the empty classroom and into the library, where he found Eliaz Groppel, along with the defector Andrei.

"Finally he shows his face," Andrei said. "Are you here to make us watch this murderer while you play spaceman?"

"Murder suspect," Raimy corrected. "And no."

"Good," Andrei said, holding up two fingers, pinching the empty air. "I am this close to asking one third your salary."

"It has been a lot for the brothers," Eliaz agreed, with a sort of dour skittishness, as if afraid of fully speaking his mind.

"I am sorry, Eliaz," Raimy said sincerely. "I didn't mean to inconvenience anyone. I've never had custody of a suspect for more than a few hours at a time, and I'm afraid there are no procedures for it."

"Call me Groppel, please. My brothers call me by my first name as a kind of teasing. Where I come from, we don't use them so much." Where he came from was certainly European, Raimy thought, but he couldn't pin it down any more specifically than that. Dutch? Belgian?

"You can stay in here if you like," Groppel continued, "but I'm quite busy, so you'll have to be quiet and keep a close eye on him." He gestured at Anming, with poorly concealed contempt. "I come in here for the quiet. This is a monastery."

Eliaz Groppel was an automotive electrician by former trade, Raimy had heard, but he also seemed in some ways to be the monastery's second-in-command, at least in a paperwork sense. He spoke flawless English, and seemed to spend a lot of time talking about "the accounts" and "the records" and "the stores"—usually in harried tones. He struck Raimy as the least monkish of the monks, who never seemed to look quite at ease or at home. Raimy wondered, suddenly, whether Groppel was actually going to cut it here, long-term, or whether he'd eventually give up and request a transfer back to Earth.

Looking annoyed, Groppel said to Raimy, "Don't judge me."

"Excuse me?" Raimy said.

"Nothing. Never mind."

Anming said, "He's been complaining about you when you sleep."

"Well, that's fine," Raimy said, taking his lumps. "I'm in his home, and apparently not a very polite guest. Maybe we should take you to the chapel."

"He says you talk too much," Anming continued. "He

says you stare too much, and look around too much. You categorize people. I think it makes him nervous."

"Everything make him nervous," Andrei said, not unkindly. "He needs brother like me, who never get worried about anything. Yes?" He clapped Groppel on the shoulder. "But he is correct, you are suspicious man. Always looking around you. What are you looking for?"

Escape routes, Raimy almost said. *Enemies. Hiding places. Makeshift weapons that could be used against me, or that I could use to defend myself.* A diver's eyes were alert to dangers in the environment, and a cop's were attuned to the people around him. But that was maybe a little too much honesty, so instead he said, "I'm sorry if I've upset anyone. I'll take my prisoner and go."

To which Groppel said, "Apology accepted," and turned his back.

Huh. Okay. Raimy was getting a lot of that today.

3.3
24 November
✧

Spaceport Paramaribo, Eastern Made Peninsula Paramaribo, Suriname Earth

"What you're saying is incredible," Lawrence Killian told his Director of Launch Services, Puya Hebbar.

"It's quite true, though," Puya told him, a bit breathlessly. And he supposed it was. Puya spent perhaps too much time worrying about things other than her job, but she was brilliant, and Lawrence trusted her.

She was on a monitor screen, because she was still up on the Moon at the moment, and Lawrence envied her that. He couldn't help touching the aching incisions on his chest.

"Are you all right, sir?" Gill Davis murmured into his ear. Gill was Lawrence's assistant—what in older days might have been called a steward or valet or butler, though his duties ran also into the technical and administrative.

Lawrence and Gill were in an air-conditioned trailer

with beige everything, that reeked of burnt coffee and
thic-nic vape. They were surrounded by young men
Lawrence didn't know, who all seemed quite busy at their
tasks, pretending not to be awestruck that the owner of
the company—the trillionaire, the Horseman—had
dropped by unannounced. Because Puya had said she had
an emergency, and needed to talk to him ASAP on a
screen larger than his rollup.

"Fine, fine," Lawrence murmured back to Gill,
although he wasn't. Four days ago, in secret, he'd visited
with the best heart surgery team in the United Kingdom
to have a "flexible piezoelectric film" implanted. The
surgery had been manual rather than robotic, but the
instruments were cunning, the incisions surprisingly
small. The whole procedure had been done in an
examination room rather than a hospital, and they hadn't
even needed a general anesthetic beyond dental-grade
laughing gas. "You'll be on your feet tomorrow morning,"
the surgeons had assured him several times—a prediction
that had proven accurate. He'd had no trouble flying back
to Paramaribo, where he found himself now.

Those pinprick incisions ran deep, though, and
touched him literally to his core, all the way to his heart,
which, at the age of seventy-nine, had somehow lost its
ability to keep a steady pace on its own. Because
Lawrence was "too old for foolishness, now, and too old
for pride," as the lead surgeon had unceremoniously put
it. The pride of insisting that he was as stout and strong as
ever. The foolishness of seeking an adrenaline high,
whether in a freefall jump or on a motor track or running
with the bulls in Pamplona. "Your life's far from over,"

they'd told him, "If you follow a few simple precautions." Which amounted to giving up everything he'd ever held dear. Eleven years ago he'd lost his beloved Rosalyn, and never sought the company of another woman. And since then he'd lost his lock on the tralphium market, and with it his lighter-than-helium airship. And now it seemed he must lose everything else. Except perhaps the Moon itself.

The irony that he'd never actually been to space was something he'd always meant to correct, and never quite got around to. And now perhaps he was too late, for anything but a one-way trip. But not to Shackleton, not to Saint Joe's. Another irony: he spent most of his time trying to convince people to live in habitats exactly like those. To build communities of them—to *live on the Moon*. And yet the truth was, Lawrence himself didn't want to live that way. If he were going to retire on the Moon, he must first build a place there, that he would actually want to inhabit. A posh retirement community, spacious and well lit, where withering bodies could breathe free at last, unburdened by Earthly gravity. And he needed to do it quickly, lest he be too old for even that terminal venture!

This is what he wanted to talk about—not with Puya Hebbar, but with her peers up at Shackleton, and down here on Earth, who could begin making that community a reality. But Commander Harb only wanted to talk about labor issues, and only reluctantly turned her attention toward Lawrence's latest project, which she seemed to regard as a distraction. The first real civilian settlement on the Moon, a distraction! But he needed to present Marriott with so refined a design and business plan that they would immediately hand over everything they knew, and the project could get started, and for that he needed her help.

"Give the workers whatever you think is fair," he'd told her. "Leave me out of it, put this issue behind you, and then bring me your undivided attention." But she still hadn't, and this annoyed him greatly, because she was the person he most needed to talk to. Right now, truthfully, he didn't want to talk to Puya at all.

He knew what Puya wanted to talk about, too. She'd been pestering him for days, something about a thorium-powered rocket engine. To her credit she had developed, before coming to him, both a clear description of the technology and a clear business case for deploying it. Which was all well and good, but he was quite busy enough with other things, and her project didn't mesh with HMI priorities, and she didn't like that and clearly wanted to invest a lot of energy into changing his mind.

So neither of them wanted to be talking about *this*. And yet, cycling on the screen next to Puya's face was the looped, grainy telescope video of a Harvest Moon booster, wobbling suddenly as it rose up through Earth's atmosphere. Wobbling and recovering.

"It's a very close call," Puya said, "from something directly in our flight path."

"So this could happen again?" he asked her.

"It could," she said.

On the video, the rocket was thundering along, minding its business, more or less centered in the frame of the tracking telescope, when a blurry gray object struck it from above, fast and hard, and then spun away out of view. Or rather, the rocket struck the blurry gray object, which had—Puya said—been vertically motionless at the time. Coasting along horizontally with the equatorial Hadley cell winds at perhaps thirty kilometers per hour, but vertically motionless. Then the rocket lurched, wobbled, and recovered. Barely.

"No one was hurt?" he asked her.

"No, sir. Unmanned cargo launch. But the launch vehicle is worth half a billion dollars, and the payload very nearly as much. We're going to have to replace that fairing as it is."

"And that object definitely wasn't a balloon?" he asked her, for the second time.

"No, sir. As you can see in the video, it's quite solid when struck. A little bendy, perhaps, but it springs back into shape after the collision, like a block of very strong rubber."

Her words came out quick as birdsong, or the gasps of a drowning woman. When Puya Hebbar had something to say, the actual saying of it seemed a great inconvenience to her, best gotten over with as quickly as possible. She also sounded, most of the time, as though she were, in confidence, relaying secrets of a sensitive nature. Which might in this case be true, but was wearying nonetheless. She'd've been happier, he thought, whispering to him in a corner, her lips safely behind the barrier of a hand held vertically at her cheek.

"Is it disc-shaped?" he asked her.

"We believe it's hexagonal, actually, but it's flat, yes. And its electromagnetic cross-section is so minimal that it literally didn't show up on our tracking radar at all."

And that was, as he'd said, incredible. A solid block of

radar-invisible material just floating around in the air? Getting struck by rocket ships on ascent? It couldn't be held up by antigravity, because that was impossible, and also why would it be vertically motionless at that particular altitude? That implied something buoyant, like a balloon. Except it was solid, and apparently quite robust. When struck, it didn't explode or swirl or flutter; it bounced away, hard.

"Where did it come from?" he demanded. He wasn't in the habit of demanding things, not anymore, but these were extraordinary circumstances. "Heads will roll for this, I assure you."

"We knew you'd ask that," she said. "The video is actually quite good—two hundred fifty-six frames per second—which is how we were able to determine the initial vector of the object. The impact was over the Atlantic, most of the way to Africa, and if we trace that trajectory back along the equatorial winds, there are no land masses. This object did not originate from South America."

"A ship in the mid-Atlantic?" he asked.

"Not quite," she said. The rocket video was replaced with a map, showing the edges of Africa and South America, and in between them a little island chain called Cape Verde. The path of the rocket was shown as a dotted line, and a very familiar one, because it was the path traced out by most everything launching out of Paramaribo. Southwest of the islands and north of the dotted line, by what looked like several hundred kilometers, was a flashing red circle.

"At this location we found a floating platform, about a hundred meters across. It really wasn't easy to find, sir—

it looks like it might be deliberately camouflaged. It also appears to be anchored in place."

The image changed again, zooming and zooming toward that circled location, until Lawrence could see a vessel or platform of some kind, set against the ocean's gray-blue with a slightly darker gray. The shape of it didn't make immediate sense, perhaps because the satellite image had been captured at a poor angle, from a long way off, and through quite a bit of atmospheric haze. It was basically a grainy smudge, neither circular nor rectangular nor streamlined like a ship.

"What is it? An offshore facility of some sort?"

"Not in the sense you mean," Puya said. A cursor appeared on the screen, tracing invisible circles around an even fainter smudge. "This is its shadow."

"How's that possible?" he asked her. It didn't make sense, because the shadow of any object at sea should be attached to the object itself. Unless . . .

"The platform," Puya said, "is floating midair, a full kilometer above the ocean's surface. It also appears like a flattened hexagon, which would not make sense for an inflatable structure this large. Colorimetry indicates it's the same material as the block that struck our rocket. Apparently, a solid piece of this solid object just . . . broke off and floated away, like it weighed less than nothing."

Lawrence's mind set to work right away. If this had happened, then they could put aside any question about whether it was possible, and start focusing on how it was done. And by whom. And for God's sake, why? Where was the gain in such a thing, and why had he never heard so much as a whisper about it?

"Find out everything you can," he told her.

"We will, sir. We are. But we're at a loss for leads to follow, if you see what I mean."

"Sir," said Gill, handing him one of the cold packs the surgeons had given him, "Will you please sit down?"

Lawrence waved him off. To Puya he said, "Get IT involved. Tell them to train a deep belief network on these images, and pay SearchNet for a full scour of anything similar that's been posted, anywhere, ever. Show it to R&D. Show it to everyone. Collect guesses about what this might be, and then train a deep belief network on *that*, and scour SearchNet again."

"Sounds expensive," Puya hedged.

"Cheaper than losing a launch vehicle," he said. "And possibly a lot cheaper than being the last one to know what's going on here."

1.18
24 November
✦
St. Joseph of Cupertino Monastery
South Polar Mineral Territories
Lunar Surface

Raimy sat across from Anming at dinner. There was nothing unusual about this; he'd done it the past two nights as well, not only to watch him but also perhaps hoping to get some sort of confession out of him. He was as laconic as the monks, but dinnertime was when they opened up, if they were going to. Perhaps the same for Anming? Perhaps he would let slip some sort of explanation or excuse? It always bothered Raimy, because most murder victims were killed by someone they knew— someone who was, at least theoretically, a friend or family member. But what would drive someone to kill a friend? Well, in this case it was Mars, obviously, but what actually went through Anming's mind while he did it? This crime was meticulously planned; he'd've had a lot of time to contemplate his feelings. Some killers didn't have any, of course, but Anming was no sociopath. Most murderers weren't. Most murders were crimes of momentary passion, barely planned at all.

Anyway, as usual, Anming had nothing to say on the subject, and not much on any other subject except "pass the salt." Anming seemed to have a bottomless appetite for the stuff, which the monastery seemed content to indulge, despite the exorbitant cost. Also as usual, Anming looked more frustrated and heartbroken than guilt-ridden. Which was also not unusual for a murder suspect—whether or not they regretted their crimes, murderers invariably regretted getting caught. A lot. Anming was no exception, but something about it seemed out of place on him. He often looked like a man who wanted to explain himself, but didn't dare.

"You can talk, you know," Raimy said to him in a low voice. "If there's something you want to get off your chest."

"I think I need a lawyer," Anming murmured back.

"Oh," Raimy said to him, "you definitely need a lawyer."

"I'm voting for *Folly Beach Folly*," Brother Hughart said, in a much louder voice, and apparently out of the blue. Doctor Callen Hughart, whose official title was Infirmer.

"Again?" said Zachary.

"Tomorrow night is movie night," Giancarlo explained, mainly to Raimy. This made sense, because *Folly Beach Folly* was a TV dramedy series from the thirties, set in North Carolina or some such. About off-season life in a tourist-trap beach town, where everyone was sleeping with, stealing from, or selling drugs to everyone else.

Raimy didn't have much appetite for that particular kind of trash TV, but a lot of people seemed to watch "FBF" over and over again, not caring that the series had wrapped a decade and a half ago.

"Yes, again," said Hughart. "I want to find out what happens to Sarah and Kate."

"Look it up," Zachary suggested.

"*Folly Beach* is fine," said Groppel. "Anyone opposed?"

No one spoke up or raised a hand, although a few looked less than pleased.

"We won't be here for it," Bridget remarked. "We're going home tomorrow."

"Yes. How do you feel about that?" Michael asked.

"Mixed," Bridget said. "I'll miss you fellers. I'll miss the whole experience. And it's very strange and sad that Etsub will be riding back in the cargo hold. I think . . . as long as we're still here, it doesn't quite . . ." She cleared her throat, her eyes suddenly full of tears, and said, "This place always felt a bit unreal to me, doubly so after the accident. As long as we're here, his death . . . doesn't count? But they're going to *bury* him in a few days. In the ground."

"I understand," Michael said.

"But life goes on," Bridget said, straightening. Wiping away the tears. "Isn't that what they say? It's time to get back home, and get back to our work."

"Clowning for ratings?" one of the monks asked under his breath. Raimy thought it might have been Groppel, but he wasn't sure. It was a shockingly unkind thing to say, under the circumstances.

But Bridget answered warmly enough, "Doing the research that makes me relevant to a Mars colony, and the publicity that brings in funding for it. If that's what you mean, then yes."

"Five of us crammed in that little spaceship," Katla said, wrinkling her nose.

"With a killer," Hughart said.

"Yes," Katla agreed. The idea seemed to make her nervous, and a little angry. Raimy could understand that. Jeez, it was hard enough just riding in a taxi with your ex, or finding yourselves at the same party. How much worse, if the party were days long, and that ex had murdered a mutual friend?

"I would like to take a shower after dinner," Anming said.

"You have the right to," Raimy said. Showers seemed to be relatively uncommon here. Sometimes a module would heat up if the slanting sun hit it just right, but mostly (as on Transit Point Station), the air was kept a few degrees below room temperature. Mostly, a one-piece coverall or multilayered monk's habit was comfortable to wear without sweating, and although the quarters were close here, they weren't *that* close. People weren't all up in each other's armpits, the way they would be on a submarine. Consequently, the social pressure around hygiene seemed much less intense than in the Navy, or even normal civilian life. He was guessing the monks bathed maybe once or twice a week.

Also, except for the monks' clean-shaven faces, there wasn't much of a culture of personal appearance here. Even the students looked, for the most part, pretty relaxed about their grooming; Bridget held her hair back with elastic bands or plastic clips, and sometimes seemed to be wearing some kind of eyeliner that probably took about five seconds to put on. Raimy hadn't noticed any other makeup. Katla's hair was too short to pull back, and spiky in that way that barely seemed to need combing.

Raimy had sometimes seen someone headed toward the "balneary" with a towel and a 3D-printed squeeze bottle, but he'd never been there himself, except when Michael showed it to him. It was two whole modules out of his way, and he'd already fallen into a rhythm that kept certain parts of the monastery fresh in his mental map, and other parts remote. There really was a lot of space in here! But he did remember it had a closable hatch that could afford genuine privacy.

"It should be much easier than a submarine," he said, somewhat incongruously.

"I can show you how to work the shower," Katla said. "I was going to take one tonight, anyway."

"I could actually use one myself," Raimy said, thinking of that journey back to Earth, crammed into the *Pony Express* with Eduardo Halladay and Bridget and everyone else.

"I could take mine," Katla said, "And then show you how to work the controls. Then I can watch Anming for you while you take yours."

"No," Raimy and Anming said simultaneously.

Raimy was going to say, "That would be a conflict of interest and a security risk. I can't turn a prisoner over to the custody of his ex-girlfriend. No matter how innocent she seems."

But since Anming had spoken, Raimy kept his yap shut just to see what happened next.

"I don't want to be alone with you," Anming said to Katla. Then, to Raimy, "I don't want to be alone with her. Personal reasons."

"Understood," Raimy said.

Then Andrei volunteered to watch Anming, "To save you embarrassment of showering with your prisoner. That's got to be problem, right?"

And several of the monks seemed to find that funny for some reason, and then the conversation turned to the ways in which this particular monastery afforded less privacy than the ones they'd each come from back on Earth, and then to the more esoteric tradeoffs between privacy and community, and between community service and self-reflection. It was actually pretty interesting, but Raimy didn't have much to say about it, and neither (it seemed) did Bridget or Katla, who passed the rest of the meal in thoughtful silence.

"Unlike the airlock shower," Katla was saying, "this one has both cold and hot. The control is . . . here . . . and . . ."

She tried to demonstrate by taking an actual shower right in front of them, but Raimy stopped her. There were several big things wrong here. First of all, she was naked, and now glistening with beads of water. Her short hair was wet and unkempt, and she had a towel with her, but instead of wrapping it around her body, she simply held it in her hand and gestured with it, like it was a floppy brown laser pointer. That seemed entirely unnecessary to Raimy, not least because she was carrying her coverall and space underwear under the other arm. Nudity might be necessary during ingress from the Lunar surface, but it certainly wasn't necessary here.

Second, the shower controls were entirely self-explanatory to anyone over the age of twenty. Instead of a digital controller, this shower had a hot water knob (marked prominently with a big red flame icon) and a cold water knob (marked with a blue snowflake). Like most people, Raimy had grown up with faucets like these, and still occasionally encountered them in the older or cheaper hotels.

Thirdly, this very definitely *was* an airlock shower. The balneary sat on the opposite side of the complex from the main airlock, and the sign on its hatch said:

BALNEARY
EMERGENCY AIRLOCK
EXTREME CAUTION IS WARRANTED

Unlike the main airlock, this one didn't have a separate locker room, shower room, and actual airlock. Instead, they were all together in one chamber, roughly half the size of the main airlock module. So, yeah. Every module in the monastery was snuggled up against the vacuum of space, but they didn't all have a door that opened out directly to the Lunar surface. This one did. He supposed it was no more dangerous than the emergency exits on an airliner, but those got his attention, too, because any idiot could walk up and try to open one, decompressing the cabin and killing everyone on board.

So, as was his habit, Raimy was more interested in scoping out the emergency locker and the seals and levers of the outer hatch than he was in listening to Katla's yammering.

In fact, there was something weirdly performative about her whole deal. Not just the faucets. She seemed to be upsetting Anming, who was understandably less than delighted about watching her prance around naked. That might actually be her intent, to upset him, but then again that would be an awfully petty act, given the gravity of recent events here.

"Please," Raimy said to her. "Just go. We'll figure it out."

"I already know how it works," Anming said, sounding just as puzzled as Raimy.

"See?" Raimy said, "He already knows how it works."

"Okay, okay," Katla said. "I'll be outside if you need anything."

"Great," Raimy said. And then couldn't help watching her leave. He wasn't attracted to her, exactly, but she was a fit human being, very naked, and his eyes did not slide away from her smooth back and buttocks, pale as the veins in a block of Himalayan salt. She shut the hatch behind her, though, and latched it, and that was that.

"I need you to take off the handcuffs," Anming said.

"I know how that works, too," Raimy said, his voice testy and unnecessarily loud.

Which didn't make sense, because Anming hadn't done anything. Except murder, obviously.

Raimy took the cuffs off and then watched with casual suspicion as Anming got undressed, folded his clothes neatly on the metal bench, and started messing with the shower knobs.

Damn it, Raimy smelled a rat. Something wasn't right here. Katla was acting weirder than usual, and that meant . . . something. She'd been intimate with Anming, obviously, not just here on the Moon but back on Earth as well. It was one of the loose ends he still needed to follow up: When had they started, and how serious were they? He'd planned on asking Katla these questions on the long trip back to Earth.

"The cold water doesn't work," Anming said.

"Then take a hot one," Raimy snapped.

And then immediately felt bad about it, because Anming seemed so sad. Not angry or guilty or contrite, but genuinely heartbroken, and it had only gotten worse with Katla's little stunt.

Why heartbroken? Did he miss her that much? She didn't seem to miss him—at least, not in the same way— but she did seem angry. Angry and suspicious and strange and . . . selfish? Resentful? Did that make any sense?

"It's too hot," Anming complained.

Raimy ignored him, because it seemed suddenly important that Katla and Anming had been together on Earth. Suddenly important that they would both have known—known!—that Mars would tear them apart. Katla was going, and Anming wasn't. But with Etsub out of the way . . .

It suddenly seemed important that Anming hadn't confessed.

It occurred to Raimy, all at once, all in a hammer-baked moment, that if Katla committed that murder, she'd get to take her boy toy to Mars with her. And if her schemes failed but it was her boy who went down for the crime, she would simply let him take the fall. She was the type, yes, she definitely would. And if he loved her more than she loved him—which he clearly did—then he might indeed be willing to take that fall for her. *Go to Mars, my love. Live for both of us.* But oh, it would break his porcelain heart when she let him do it. *Go to prison for me, yes! Show how much you love me!* Jesus, that would break anyone's heart.

And all at once, Raimy knew he'd gotten it wrong.

"It's too hot!" Anming said again, in a much louder voice, and Raimy turned and saw steam, actual boiling steam shooting out of the shower head.

And then, instantly, he knew they were in danger— himself and this innocent plaything. He suddenly knew what all that heat was for: phase change.

"Turn it off," he said. "Turn it off! Anming, turn it off!"

Raimy leaped for the knob, too late.

What happened next was recorded clearly by a maintenance camera mounted to the mast of the tower magnet, pointed down, eternally unblinking, at the back side of the little moonbase.

One sees a curious puff of vapor, like a sausage sighing on a hot grill. For a moment, that's all, but then the outer hatch of the emergency airlock simply blows off its hinges, traveling twenty-six meters across the powdery regolith before finally skidding to a stop. Behind it spills a tangle of clothing and towels, along with two human beings: one naked as the day he was made, the other dressed rather neatly in two-piece Antilympus stretch-khakis. One sees them tumble and roll, flailing their arms in confusion and fear. The event happens fast, and you can see in their body language that it has caught them so completely off guard that they don't even have time to protect their faces from impact.

They leave long skid trails in the gray dust before they, too, slide to a halt. One sees their sunken rib cages, empty of air. One sees their mouths gaping in horror, and one can very nearly make out their bulging eyes, unaccustomed to the kiss of vacuum. Rarely have two people ever looked deader.

And yet, clearly visible in the unblinking eye of the camera, they get back up again, both of them, and start crawling back toward the shredded-open space of the emergency airlock.

1.19
24 November
✧
St. Joseph of Cupertino Monastery
South Polar Mineral Territories
Lunar Surface

Raimy knew right away what had happened to him: he'd been blown out the fucking airlock. By Katla. By some kind of shape-memory gizmo jammed into some critical edge of the outer hatch.

He was shocked and terrified and badly disoriented, but his diving instincts kicked in before he'd even hit the ground. He didn't panic, because panic was death. He didn't hold his breath, didn't let the overpressure explode his lungs, but rather let the vacuum of space whoosh the air right out of him. He burped violently as well. It was a lot like ascending from a submarine escape lock: an upward rush through ever-shrinking pressure, your lungs and stomach emptying, your eardrums screaming with pain. Raimy's eyes wouldn't focus, and he couldn't breathe, and he *couldn't fucking breathe*, but still he didn't panic.

Crawling feebly, he took a fraction of a moment to collect his bearings, and then he pressed his hands against the ground in a push-up motion that bounced him unsteadily to his feet. Turning, he spotted the dark blur of the exploded airlock against the white blur of the modules around it. He leaned forward and ran, in dreamlike silence, scrabbling for purchase on the dusty soil.

His skin felt curiously dry and slippery against the vacuum around it. He could feel the moisture on his eyes and tongue fizzing away into space, leaving him mummified. The low sun, impossibly hot and impossibly bright, shone like a death ray on his hands and the right side of his face, for what felt like a long time, before he found his way into the cool shade of the module. The shower was still running, silently sputtering out a stream of liquid that evaporated into nothingness halfway to the floor.

Thank God he had memorized the position of the emergency locker, or he might not have recognized it in the blur. Overpressure had blown open and shattered its glass door, but that was fine. That was fine. He groped inside, knowing exactly what he was feeling for: a ring of heavy polymer, with a disc of crinkly plastic film strung across it. A goo suit. For a terrifying moment he couldn't find it, and he couldn't find it, and he was starting to buzz and faint and die, and maybe this was it. Maybe rummaging in this locker was the last thing he would ever do.

But then his hand closed on that ring, and with hardly a thought he pulled it out and, with both hands, jammed it firmly down over his head. The film, rolled up inside the ring, unreeled down over his face and neck, until the ring jammed firmly against his collarbones and spine. It didn't matter which end was up; these things were designed to be used in a hurry.

What happened next was airbag-quick, an explosion far too rapid for human senses to perceive. The ring sprayed out a fine, soaking mist that became a liquid that became an expanding foamy gel, and then a rubbery solid, fiercely hot. The goo easily penetrated clothing, but sealed firmly against human skin, creating a sort of rubber collar beneath the ring—theoretically airtight. Then a separate set of nozzles injected gas—mostly pure oxygen—into the bag of plastic film that contained Raimy's head.

For Raimy, there was simply a bang and a punching sensation on his chest and face, and then he was magically wearing a baggie-shaped space helmet. Or dive helmet, or escape hood to get you out of a burning building, or whatever. All he knew was that the fucker was *hot*, and the bubbling goo had stopped just a few millimeters short of covering up his nose and mouth.

And he was alive. He took a breath, and it felt like knives and paint remover, but it worked. He inhaled a lungful of reeking gas, and nothing had ever felt so terrible and wonderful and strange. He exhaled and then breathed again, hearing the rasp and click of the thing's little regulator, trying to deliver a constant pressure that wouldn't suffocate him and wouldn't explode his lungs, seeking that knife edge of survival that might not exist at all. But he could breathe. He'd been exposed to vacuum for something like fifteen seconds, and yet here he was. He was going to live another second, another five seconds, another minute.

Sweet Jesus.

Probably not longer than a minute because he could hear and feel the hiss of air escaping through microchannels in the collar, where it couldn't quite seal around the fibers of his jacket and undershirt. Because that's how it was with goo suits: they were very dangerous and worked only in a very approximate sense. Bad medicine; they were what you tried when you were going to die anyway.

And he *was* probably going to die, and the screaming animal part of his brain had to be wrestled into submission about that, because panic was death.

He looked at the inner hatch, and realized there was no way to open it. Even if he were willing to depressurize the entire monastery, the hatch opened inward, against the air pressure within, and it would take thousands of pounds of force to get it open even a crack.

Shit.

He realized he could see again—not perfectly, but better, and his eyes hurt less, so that was something, but he also realized he had exactly one chance to get out of this alive. And it was in the main airlock, on the exact other side of the monastery complex.

Shit and shit.

He spared a momentary glance at Anming, who was sprawled in the dust, unconscious but possibly not actually dead yet. He had crawled half the distance back to the airlock, and that was all.

No way. Anming Shui might be an innocent man, framed by his girlfriend, but there was *no way* Raimy was slapping a goo suit on him and carrying him to safety. His own chances were slim to none as it was, and anything that further reduced them was out of the question. The moment seemed to last a long time. Then he took off, running gracelessly in the low gravity, but he seemed to move in slow motion, while his mind raced. Sorry, Anming. *Sorry, sorry. I'll say a prayer for you, I'll light a candle for you, I'll name a scholarship after you if I can, sweet Jesus, just get through this alive.* Then the moment passed, and he was hopping his way through a ninety-degree turn, and then rounding past the library module and turning again, threading between the library and the spindly-tall tower magnet, and then past the classroom and kitchen and laundry modules, and around the corner again.

He couldn't hear his feet skidding on the dusty regolith. His breath—a shallow/fast hyperventilating pant—was pretty much the only sound, other than the clicking of the regulator and the hissing away of his meager air supply. Best case, a goo suit had maybe two minutes of fresh air, and then maybe another two minutes of breathing your own filth before the CO_2 levels knocked you unconscious. With a bad seal off-gassing like this, he wasn't sure he could count on even one more breath, so he ran, sweet Jesus he ran, and finally he was at the main airlock.

Which was pressurized, of course, because there wasn't supposed to be anyone outside right now, so he slapped the red EMERGENCY INGRESS button.

For a long moment, nothing happened, and he knew from his reading that this was because the inner hatch was closing under hydraulic control. Then he was rewarded with an upward blast of silent white gas—the precious atmosphere of the airlock venting irretrievably into space. And then the lights went green and he was undogging the hatch, pressing down and pulling outward with the handle, and then the hatch was opening which was good because he was out of air, exhaling again into hard vacuum, and the bag helmet was sagging and deflating around his head and face. But he was inside and he was closing the hatch and dogging it shut, and the airlock's emergency logic knew what to do.

Air howled into the chamber, pressing in painfully on his eardrums and flattening the bag helmet firmly against his face, and he was shrink-wrapped for sure.

Now, the thing about a goo suit was that it could just as easily suffocate you as save your life, and so one of its awful design compromises was that you could claw through the bag with your fingers. Yeah, it was that fragile. So Raimy poked a hole through it over his mouth, and then clawed the whole thing away from his face altogether, and then . . .

And then he was safe.

Raimy sat on the bench in the airlock for a long several seconds, contemplating mortality. Anming was certainly dead by now, and Raimy was to blame for that, albeit incidentally. Maybe Raimy could have saved him. Maybe. More to the point, Raimy himself had just come as close to death as it was possible to get. Much closer than he'd ever been before, and he'd had some close calls! The Grim Reaper's scythe had touched him, for sure. Heck, he still might not survive this; everything hurt, from the hair follicles on the top of his head to the nail beds of his toes. The human body was never designed for explosive decompression, and he might well have a lung embolism or a blood clot or a brain aneurysm, or any of a thousand other decompression injuries. Who knew? His hands were shaking so badly he half-suspected a neurological tremor, and his vision still had not returned to normal. The signs on the airlock wall were written in large print, but Raimy could barely make them out. He might need glasses from now on. He might need a lot of things.

Truthfully he might have sat there for a long time—for hours, for days—but of course the monks came rapping on the inner hatch, calling out, "Hello? Hello? Is this safe to open?" And then opening it anyway.

Raimy could see where they were coming from on this: there they are just standing around doing monk stuff, when suddenly the emergency airlock blows out. And they're scrambling to look out the windows, trying to figure out what's going on, and maybe some of them are struggling into their spacesuits, either as a safety precaution or to go outside and assess the damage, and the casualties. But then, barely a minute later, someone is rapid-cycling into the main airlock, and just how could that be? How indeed?

The handle on the inner hatch turned, and the hatch itself swung outward, into the shower room. Hilario Hamblin stood there in his monk's habit, looking bewildered.

"Raimy? How are you . . . What happened?"

"The goo suit works," Raimy said. What else could he say?

"*Merde*," Hilario said, somehow making a blasphemy

of it. It was as if he'd said "I take the name of Jesus H. Fucking Christ deliberately in vain!"

"Anming is dead," Raimy added.

"Yes, we know. We thought you were, too!"

Raimy pictured it: from the east window of the library, or for that matter, the east window of the cloisters, Anming's corpse should be clearly visible, along with a mess of debris and scuff marks, and the emergency airlock's outer hatch, sitting far away. The fact that Raimy's own corpse wasn't visible would not have told them much; they'd have no reason to think he wasn't out there, too— just too close to the building to be visible. Or hung up on something in the balneary, or whatever.

"Happy to disappoint you," Raimy said.

"What happened?" Hilario said again. "We know there was an explosion, but why? Was it the explosive bolts?"

"Maybe," Raimy said. "I didn't see where the device was planted."

"Device?"

"Yes. Where's Katla?"

"I don't know."

Standing behind Hilario was Brother Hughart, who said, "Raimy, we've got to get you to the infirmary."

"Later," Raimy said, levering himself up into a standing position. This should have been easy in Lunar gravity, but he felt Earth-heavy.

"You look bad, my friend," said Hilario as Raimy stepped through the hatch.

"Excuse me," said Raimy. "I need to get past."

Practically the whole monastery was standing behind Hughart, and as Raimy brushed past them on his way through to the gowning area, they said things like, "Are you all right?" and "Good lord!" and the ever popular "My goodness!"

Raimy stepped through into the chapel, aware that he was covered in toxic moondust but really beyond caring at this point.

Michael stood there in front of the pews, looking worried, and behind him, in the hatchway to the infirmary, stood Katla, holding a scalpel.

"Sanctuary!" she cried out. "Brother Michael, please, grant me sanctuary!"

"You're under arrest," Raimy told her, "for the murders of Etsub Beyene and Anming Shui, and the attempted murder of myself. You have the right to . . ."

Actually, here on the Moon, she probably didn't. Under maritime law there was virtually unlimited power vested in the captain of a vessel or, by extension, the prior of a Lunar monastery. In that sense, Katla had hardly any rights at all. By agreement, the Church had already ceded Raimy the power to arrest and interrogate, and that power was also, in principle, unlimited. But also easily revoked.

"What's going on?" Michael demanded, in a voice at once loving and stern.

"She sabotaged the balneary's outer hatch," Raimy answered. "Anming didn't kill anyone; she did. And then she killed Anming to cover her tracks. That's our killer, right there."

"He's crazy," Katla said to Michael.

Just then, Bridget Tobin appeared in the cloisters hatchway, looking this way and that way, assessing the situation. She was out of breath, and had her glasses on, recording.

"Raimy?" she said.

"I'm alive," he confirmed, his eyes returning to the scalpel in Katla's hand.

"If Raimy is mistaken," Michael asked Katla, "then why have you armed yourself?"

Katla didn't seem to have an answer to that. She started to say something, but then stopped herself. Started to say something else, and stopped again. Because yeah, what could she say? Honestly.

"I need to take her into custody," Raimy said.

"How?" Michael asked, with something like amazement.

"I actually still have zip ties in my pocket," Raimy answered.

"That's not what I meant," said Michael.

"Sanctuary!" Katla pleaded. "Michael, please."

"Oh, I think not," Michael told her. "And what's your purpose with that knife, exactly? Are you going to stab your way to safety? You'd have to kill every man here. And then what?"

"And woman," added Bridget.

In the kitchen hatchway, Kurtis Durm stood, holding what looked like a meat tenderizing hammer.

"Don't you touch me," Katla said. Not specifically to Michael or to Raimy, but to everyone here assembled.

"You're breathing our air," Michael told her. "You've eaten our food and drunk our water. Many gallons of which just bled off into space, by the way, at staggering cost. The nearest place you could hide is, oh, far away. Not here. Whether you're a murderess or not is for God and a jury to decide, but your arrest is foregone and concluded. A moment's thought should confirm, you're in custody already."

"I can take her," Raimy said.

"That won't be necessary."

For several uncomfortable seconds, nobody said or did anything.

Then Katla sighed loudly, dropped the scalpel, and kicked it out among the pews.

To Raimy, Michael said, "You're bleeding from the eyes, my friend. You're pale as a toffee. Will you allow one of us to arrest her for you?"

"No," Raimy said, stepping between the pews and walking purposefully toward Katla. As purposefully as Lunar gravity allowed, at any rate. "She tried to kill me."

Reaching her, he grabbed her roughly, spun her around, and pulled her hands together so roughly her feet left the floor. With his other hand he pulled out a zip cuff and slid it over her wrists.

"Police brutality!" she cried out.

"Save it," Raimy said, jerking the cuff tighter. Then, leaning in close to her ear, he murmured, "If you hadn't dropped that knife, I'd've killed you with it. You give me a reason, I still might."

1.20
24 November

✧

St. Joseph of Cupertino Monastery
South Polar Mineral Territories
Lunar Surface

In what seemed a distinctly un-monkish move, Purcell and Groppel printed up some nylon cord and, after letting Katla use the bathroom, tied her securely to a chair, stuffed her in the airlock, and then tied the airlock shut for good measure. Even if she somehow managed to free herself, there wasn't much harm she could do in there with her bare hands.

"She could bludgeon the pressure controls with the chair," Michael worried.

This possibility was discussed—right in front of Katla—and eventually dismissed, on the grounds that the likeliest outcome was her own death by suffocation, and even if she somehow damaged the controls so the airlock couldn't depressurize properly, she'd only be trapping herself in the monastery. And then a repair crew from Shackleton would come on over with a whole 'nother emergency airlock module, and she'd be shipped back to Earth right on schedule.

"I'll check on you every few hours," Purcell said, in a concession to basic human decency, but his tone suggested he was doing this more for God's benefit, or his own immortal soul, than because Katla deserved it.

"Sleep well," Groppel called in to her, just before the inner hatch was sealed.

These brothers were angry.

And no wonder: Katla had killed two people under their care, and gravely injured a third. She'd also blown up one of their modules, wasting precious air and water in the process.

"It's appalling," Michael said, "that our noble grounds should be put to such wicked use, so early in our history. This is not what we've given our lives for." Then he turned his glare on Raimy, and said, "You, sir, will submit yourself to the infirmary, forthwith and posthaste. I won't stand for any more deaths this month, so under the Articles of War, you may consider that an order."

"Under the what?"

But Michael was simply pointing toward the infirmary, his face as stern as Raimy had ever seen it.

And so he spent the night in the autodoc tube, with an IV drip in his arm and a catheter up his wiener. Sealed in at one full atmosphere of pressure—nearly twice the ambient pressure of the monastery itself—he wore a freshly printed hospital gown with some sort of clown pattern on it. Thus humiliated, he endured the scrutiny of Brother Doctor Callen Hughart, who hovered nervously, peering in through the tube's window and, via the intercom, asking questions like, "Do your eyeblinks feel normal? Do you feel a need to move your bowels?"

Truthfully, Raimy felt a lot like he'd been kicked half to death and then sandblasted, but Bridget kept stopping by to shoot video for his feeds, and nearly everyone else at the monastery stopped by to check on him at least once. In the face of that kind of public scrutiny, he was not about to admit weakness. Thus, he kept answering, "I'm fine, I'm fine."

"Your heart rate is nae fine," Hughart glowered. Indeed, according to Raimy's monitor it hadn't once dropped below ninety beats per minute, even after two doses of something called Fear Away, a "third generation calmative." The stuff did take the edge off his jitters, but that was mainly a physical effect; it didn't do much for the waves of emotion still rolling through him.

In a quieter moment, Hughart told him, "Your blood pressure is coming back up. We're getting you rehydrated, so don't be surprised if there's some puffiness or even edema here and there. I can't do much about the bruising, I'm afraid."

"Do I look bad?"

There were no mirrors in here. In fact, there were no mirrors anywhere in the monastery, except the VIP guest rooms, so Raimy had not seen himself. Oh, he could see his arms and (if he craned his neck) his legs from the knee down. They looked all right to him—a perfect acorn brown. But his face felt swollen, and he couldn't open his eyes all the way, and his nostrils and ear canals were itchy with a crust of dried blood.

Ducking the question, Hughart said, "You'd be better off if the decompression had happened more slowly. As it is, you're fortunate we keep our atmosphere at six hundred millibars, and the partial nitrogen at two hundred. If we'd been running a full Earth atmosphere, your injuries would be a good bit worse. I still don't know why you're not deaf."

Raimy snorted. "I'm a diver, Callen. It's not the first time I've busted both eardrums. But I've got good eustachian tubes."

Meaning, the tubes that connected the inner ear to the throat—critical for pressure equalization, and a diver's best friend if they were in good working order.

"Are they draining now?"

"Yeah," Raimy said. "Like a mother."

"Hmm."

"Can I get something to drink?"

"Absolutely not. You're getting fluids through your arm until I'm certain there are no hemorrhages in your digestive tract. We'll reassess in the morning."

Finally, after a long time, Hughart got tired and laid himself down, fully clothed in his habit and slippers, on the examination table beside the surgical tube.

"Just resting a moment," he said. But within a few minutes, he was snoring.

It was late—nearly midnight—but Raimy felt wide awake. He'd refused sedation, and now he was paying the price, stuck in a tube and wracked by a combination of guilt and relief and fear and boredom.

Fortunately, by a stroke of good luck he'd had his rollup in his pocket when all this went down, and he'd insisted—

over numerous objections—on bringing it with him into the tube.

He could not resist checking the headlines on HNN. His name was there, along with Anming's, and Katla's. SECOND MOON MURDER NEARLY CLAIMS ARRESTING OFFICER—DEVELOPING STORY. The facts were sparse but mostly accurate. More detail was promised as it became available. He wondered if Brother Michael had given a statement, or planned to, or whether that duty was reserved for higher church officials. The article didn't say anything about how he'd arrested the wrong person, how he'd gotten Anming killed for no reason. How the monastery had suffered hundreds of millions of dollars in damage because of him. In fact, the word "heroic" was used more than once, as was "miraculous."

Though his eyes ached and burned, he could not resist also checking the Antilympus leaderboard, and found, with mild surprise, that surviving in the actual vacuum of actual space had moved him up into second place. He'd squeaked—just barely—in front of Tim Long Chang (of National Geographic fame), but the billionaire Ian Doerr was still ahead of him, by a wide margin. He didn't begrudge it; Doerr was not only capable of sponsoring himself, and more capable than Raimy of attracting additional supporters, but he was probably also the better man, or at least the better administrator. He wasn't a cop and a lawyer and all that Earth bullshit, and he hadn't gotten himself blown out an airlock through sheer stupidity. And Raimy's lead on Tim Long Chang was slim, and already shrinking, and he didn't begrudge that either, because who didn't like Tim Long Chang?

A wave of peace settled over Raimy: he simply wasn't going to Mars. He'd been so stressed about it for so long—had sacrificed so much toward that goal, and pursued so little else—that it shocked him how easily he let it go. Having come so absurdly close to death, he suddenly felt lighter and freer than he had in a long time, or maybe ever.

His next thoughts were of Bridget, and rather than ruminating or waking up Hughart and asking to see her, he silently opened up the message interface on his rollup and sent her a good old-fashioned text message, which kicked off a whole exchange.

RAIMY: Was going to 😫 we can't see each other 2nite.

BRIDGET: Tht's ur biggest concern right now? Srsly?

RAIMY: I was going to 😫 we can't see each other, but its mch bggr than that. It sddenly occurs to me, UR 🚀 to Mars. Definitely 100%

BRIDGET: Be lying if I said that wasn't my 1st thot. As soon I knew U were safe. As soon I knew Katla was guilty. It's going to be me and Geary Notbohm, from Transit Point Station.

RAIMY: & definitely not me.

BRIDGET: U don't know that. Theres still time.

RAIMY: It's fine, Bridget.

BRIDGET: Well damn. I kind of hoped we had a future. Can I interest you in two 😡 years, followed by an awkward 💔 ?

RAIMY: And watching U on 🌐 📡 , falling in 🖤 w/ someone else? It's tempting.

BRIDGET: You almost 💀 tonight.

RAIMY: Yeah. All thngs considered, I feel amazing. I'm in the bonus round, now. Evrythng in my life frm now on is bonus.

BRIDGET: I thought you were dead. For several minutes, that's what I thought. And it made me so upset, Raimy. So sad I couldn't.

BRIDGET: ...

RAIMY: Couldn't what?

BRIDGET: Couldn't have you as my consolation prize. If neither one of us went to Mars, we could at least have been together, or tried. But now... I don't think I want to get any more invested in you than I have been. The offer is retracted. I'm sorry. The heart knows what it wants, and I don't want to get mine broken, for pursuing a dream that's in my grasp. I'm so sorry.

RAIMY: RU breaking up with me by text message?

BRIDGET: Were we ever togethr even? Oh Raimy. God damn.

RAIMY: It's fine, Bridget.

BRIDGET: We could have been good.

RAIMY: We could have been great. We will be great, in other ways.

BRIDGET: Do U hate me?

RAIMY: Quite th opposite. It's all fine. Very beautiful to be alive. I'm @ peace with the world, and wish U UR best life. And me mine, whatever that may bring.

1.21
25 November

✦

St. Joseph of Cupertino Monastery
South Polar Mineral Territories
Lunar Surface

Callen Hughart reluctantly released Raimy in the morning, in time for him to get suited up and leave on schedule.

"Drink lots of fluids," he advised sternly, "and get plenty of rest. No joke. You should be in that tube another three days at least."

Then he hugged Raimy goodbye, and said, "I hope you've learned something from your time here." And then all of the monks were saying goodbye, and it was surprisingly emotional. They'd only known Raimy for a few days, but in close quarters, and with a lot of drama.

"I wish," H.H. said to him, "for your next investigation to go easier."

"And I do hope you get to Mars someday," said Purcell Veloso. "Lord knows you deserve it."

Last to say goodbye was Michael, who told him, "Outer

space requires a degree of self-reliance rarely seen in other environments, but it also lays bare a truth that's otherwise much concealed: we survive only through a web of mutuality. Without Orlov Petrochemical my brothers and I would be dead in a year. Without Harvest Moon, in a month. Without each other, in a day and a half. This is no less true on Earth, and if you learn nothing else, I hope this at least you'll carry with you. I'll bid you farewell, my friend, assured that 'well' is exactly how you'll fare. But do please write letters. Life up here is not always so interesting, and we'll follow your adventures as closely as your feed permits."

"Thanks," Raimy replied, unsure what else to say. "I definitely will."

Meanwhile, things were awkward with Bridget, who avoided eye contact and barely said twenty words to him all morning. "Hi" and "yes" and "thank you," and in an unguarded moment when no one else was listening, "The summer before I went away to college was the hottest of my life." Raimy wasn't quite sure what she meant by that, or what to do with it, and given the situation he wasn't going to have the privacy to ask her about it for a week at least. Assuming it was even ethical to follow up on that particular lead. He might just let it go.

And of course things were really awkward with Katla who, once stripped to her underwear and enclosed in her spacesuit, had her hands zip-tied together in front of her, and then roped to her ankles with an A-shaped arrangement worked out by Andrei, that would allow her to walk in Lunar gravity.

"You suck balls," she said to Raimy, more than once.

She said it to Andrei, too, and then finally let loose with something like an explanation.

"I loved Anming, you know. You bastards think I didn't? But there was no way to save him. I loved Etsub, too—he was one of my favorite people. We would have done well at Antilympus. I and he, teammates until we died. It would have been just fine. But I wanted better. For my whole life, for the whole rest of my life. It has to be what I need."

She paused, then said, to no one in particular, "Oh, don't give me that look. Like you're all so much better? You do it, too. We all do. We all make that choice, to live the life we want, not the one that's handed to us, or we'd all still be in villages full of sheep. That's what separates—"

"Shut your hole," Andrei said to her mildly, and then latched her space helmet down, effectively stifling her.

"Radio check," Bridget said into a headset. "Check, check. Katla, if you can hear me please respond. Roger. Roger that."

"Get fucked," Katla said, loudly enough that Raimy could hear it both through Bridget's earpiece and through Katla's helmet bubble.

Bridget winced and took the headset off. To Raimy she said, "The network is active."

"Okay," he answered. As satisfying as it might be to leave Katla sealed up without a radio, it was too much of a safety risk, and inhumane besides.

"I could go with you," Andrei said to Raimy, in a tone suggesting otherwise. He was still in his novice's robe, and looked wholly unprepared to put on a spacesuit.

At that moment, Raimy was pulling his own suit top down over himself, and trying to mate it with the waist ring of the bulky pants. This was surprisingly difficult to do, and, seeing his struggle, both Bridget and Andrei leaned in to help. Bridget held the pants in place, while Raimy pulled the coat down and Andrei worked the rotary latch. Finally, they got it.

"There's room for you on the ship," Bridget agreed.

"Yes," Andrei said, "and Harvest Moon has offered me Anming's seat, already paid for. All the way back to Earth, if I want. If I dare. But I think I stay. It takes years to become monk, did you know? Many chances to change mind, to back away before making vows. I wait here while heat dies down and people forget about me, and I figure out what I want."

Raimy reflected on that. He'd never quite thought of Andrei as a genuine suspect, and yet, now that the matter was concluded, he was not quite able to think of him as an innocent, either. Andrei had done a strange and daring thing, and an illegal one by almost any measure. With good reason, yes, but still. How many people, faced with those circumstances, would respond in that way? Could someone that restless really be satisfied by someplace so . . . restful?

"I hope you find your peace," Raimy told him sincerely.

"And I hope you find yours," Andrei replied, lowering Raimy's helmet into place and sealing the latches.

2.4
25 November

✦

Clementine Cislunar Fuel Depot
Earth-Moon Lagrange Point 1
Cislunar Space

This is too much macho bullshit, Dona thought.

"Drink," Orlov commanded.

Obediently, Daniel Florinovich Epureanu, the Moldovan nobody from the station's middle ranks, shot the syringe full of medical-grade ethanol into his mouth and swallowed. He then immediately shoved the stopper end of the syringe into the bottle, and withdrew another fifty milliliters.

The two men hovered, alone together, in the spinward airlock, observed by the crew on every video screen in the station.

Orlov lurched momentarily in the direction of the red EVACUATE button—a schoolyard bullying tactic that would have worked a lot better in gravity. But here at L1, in the zeroest of zero gravity, he hadn't actually braced his foot to launch his body that direction, and so it looked as much like a dance move from some twentieth-century film as it did a genuine attempt at murder.

Epureanu didn't flinch.

Epureanu smiled.

Epureanu handed the syringe over to Orlov and said, calmly, "Drink."

It was macho bullshit, and yet, Dona had to admire the purity of it. After the contracts had been signed and thumbprinted, there'd been three days of uneasy relations between workers and management, neither side willing to put any real trust in the other. Finally, Orlov and Epureanu had come up with this ridiculous scheme to end it: a peace summit with very high stakes indeed. They were in the spinward airlock, on the side of the station most likely to be hit by meteoroids and debris. Each man wearing only space briefs—showing off muscles and scars and tattoos, showing there was no physical weakness here. Epureanu's hair, long and brown, was pulled into a rather severe topknot. Orlov was older, and it showed in the texture of his skin, the moles and tufts of graying hair on his back. He was also perhaps a bit smaller, but the look on his face said he was more wicked than Epureanu, and more capricious.

Each man within reach of the red button that would evacuate the airlock and blow them both out into space. Each man within reach of a grab bar that could keep him inside, if he grabbed it soon enough. Each man within reach of the goo suit—the one and only goo suit—that could keep one and only one of them alive. If he fought the other man for it. If he kept it sealed over his head, unripped, long enough for the other man to die.

"This American policeman has shown us up," Epureanu had said, waving the goo suit at Orlov in naked challenge. "Are we less capable than he?" And so they had somewhere located a spacesuit glove and solemnly slapped each other with it, and then gone into the airlock with their bottle of drug-printer *khuligan*, with all the station watching them on screens tapped into the security feed. Dona herself was sequestered in Operations, ready to seize control of the station should this venture go awry. Which it very easily could; Orlov was known to be a mean drunk, and Epureanu a bold one.

Orlov drank.

"Few men are brave enough to test me twice," he said, reloading the drink syringe.

"With good reason," Epureanu agreed.

Indeed, where the enemies of the trillionaire's father, Magnus Orlov, had tended to quietly disappear from the face of the Earth, Grigory Orlov's tended to meet with very public accidents. Epureanu surely knew this. It was no small thing, for him to place himself in such peril, at the hands of such a man.

"Drink," Orlov said, handing over the syringe. Then, grudgingly, "Your people were wise to align behind you. Had a lesser man confronted me, you might all be breathing vacuum now. Or rendered into component atoms and sold."

Epureanu smiled and said, "It was logical, Grigory. People fear you, but they don't like you. They like me, and they know I fear nothing." And then he drank.

"You're a fool, then," Orlov glowered. But in a friendly way. "Twice a fool, and blessed with luck."

"You're very certainly more ruthless than I," Epureanu said, "and probably smarter. But are you quicker? Do you even know how to close and refill the airlock, should you survive?" He paused for effect, and then said, "Ah! That glimmer of doubt in your eyes. See? Bet your money on the ones who do the work, Grigory. Even if you remember the emergency ingress instructions, can you follow them with no air in your lungs, after half a liter of this stuff?" He shook the bottle, and then refilled the syringe from it.

Continuing, he said, "I'll tell you what would happen: you'd slap that button, then grab for the goo suit and miss. You'd see it flying out the airlock, and your hopes of survival with it. And then I would calmly work the controls, close up the hatch and blow a tank of air into this chamber, saving both our lives. Assuming your lungs hadn't exploded, which they very well might. Drink."

"You're quite a prick," Orlov observed.

"And yet, they like me better," Epureanu said.

Orlov's frown deepened.

"I am not your enemy," Epureanu said quickly. Dona judged that the Moldovan had, yet again, overplayed his hand with the trillionaire. But he was a canny fellow, and recovered quickly. "As you know, sir, I am actually quite an asset. You accomplish nothing without your people— remember that, please—but this place attracts strong ones, who want strong leadership. Like teenagers, they push against the boundaries set upon them. And like teenagers, they secretly feel those boundaries as a hug from loving parents."

"Hmm," said Orlov, sounding (at best) partially

mollified. This was blatant flattery and half-truth, but sincere in its way.

"They watch us drinking together," Epureanu said, "in the barrel of a loaded gun. Think how we look to them now, you and I. Who will dare not to love you? Who will dare not to fear me? Who will cross either of us?"

"Mmm."

Orlov eyed the red button, and the other airlock controls, and the hatch, and the grab bar, as if working out a specific plan of action. As if working out whether there were any slight advantage in murdering Epureanu at this moment. Through the video screen, Dona thought she detected a flutter of nervousness in Epureanu then, though he hid it well.

"Add me to the list of people who like you," Orlov said, drinking. Taking the bottle out of the air and refilling the syringe from it. "But I've liked a lot of people who got in my way. Ask them how well it went. No, Daniel Florinovich, what you need to be is *useful*. Everyone here needs to be useful." He seemed to muse on that for a moment, and then said, "Not just here. People throughout the world would do well to remember it. Husbands, wives, children, parents. Retired old grannies. It's the useful ones who keep what they desire. Drink."

"I'll keep it in mind," Epureanu said, and drank. "But perhaps it applies to you as well. Perhaps that's why we finally came to terms."

"Mmm," Orlov said. Then: "My father owned a palace in Minsk, every room striped with rare stone and endangered wood. Striped! He owned a yacht the size of a World War II battleship. He had another little mini-palace in a cargo container, that could go on a train or the back of a truck, or in an airplane, so he could have his rare wood wherever he went. Me, I gave these things to my sisters. Even as a form of intimidation, luxury is a fool's game. I think it was his greatest weakness, and the first thing I ever dared to challenge in him. I do sometimes miss the smell of the wood."

"My father was a bastard," Epureanu said. "Drink."

"Mine was a killer."

"Ah, yes. He was. I've been tempted to say, you and I are not so different, but it isn't true, is it? I couldn't do what you do. You could learn my job well enough, but I do not think I could learn yours. The nuance, the posturing, the following through. The math! It's like watching a man smash bricks with his fist. He must commit to the act so completely. If he doubts himself for a moment, then it's his hand that will break. I wasn't born to any of that."

"Nor I," Orlov said. "*Papochka* beat it into me, and called me weak until the day he died. And yet, his company could fall, unnoticed, within the rounding errors on my balance sheet. Is vengeance mine? Do I piss on his grave? I bring him flowers, Daniel. I thank him for the education no other man could have provided. As for you, I see one important bit of wisdom you've acquired: when to back off a challenge and flatter your boss like a little bitch."

"To flatter my boss, yes," Epureanu agreed.

Dona could see him eyeing the bottle as it hovered absolutely motionless in the air, placed there skillfully by the trillionaire, as if on a shelf. "But tell me, Grigory, if we do not pull the trigger on this gun and fight each other to the last breath, then this is merely a drinking contest. How will we know who won? This teensy bottle is not enough to knock the heart's-piss out of me. Nor you, I think."

Orlov smiled then, with surprising warmth. "If we finish this teensy bottle and you can still pronounce your own name, then you and I will go together to the mess hall, and knock the piss out of anyone who dares to oppose us. And then we are both winners, ah?"

It was macho bullshit, Dona thought, but it served a purpose. On the schoolyard, the wisest boys fell in line behind a bully, while the idealists who stood up to them left the playground in tears. And the wisest bullies knew how to lead the boys who fell in behind them, and then they grew up and ran the world. Dona was pretty sure she could whip Orlov if he were drunk, and possibly even Orlov and Epureanu both. But if they did indeed make it back to the mess hall still conscious, she would hug them both, and kiss their cheeks, and call them her heroes, and drink with them until she passed out or puked.

Because God damn it, this place was home, and she'd never loved anything more.

3.4
27 November
✧

Business Center, Hotel Playa Blanca
Paramaribo, Suriname
Earth

"Another emergency?" Lawrence Killian said to Puya Hebbar.

The hotel's business center had a gigantic video display on the back wall, currently showing her face so large Lawrence could count the pores. Lawrence was holding a sweaty hotel glass filled with ice water, and mopping his brow with a paper napkin. Gill Davis by his side, as nearly always.

"We have to get the hell out of Paramaribo," Lawrence had said to him a few minutes ago. But a lot of things were moving quickly—flying bricks and grumbling workers, arrests and airlock blowouts. And a Lunar graben that the men at Malinkin Base seemed to feel was definitely suitable for a Marriott Hotel! Or, if Lawrence had his way, a jointly branded retirement community. There was all that, on top of the usual minutiae of any large multinational corporation, and it left him no time to escape.

He could, in theory, handle all of this work from anywhere, including his personal jet, but a solar coronal mass ejection—detected late and moving fast—was due to strike the Earth sometime today. The EOLS capsule, returning from Luna with the detective and his prisoner, had fortunately slipped ahead of the storm into the safe harbor of Earth's magnetic field, so at least Lawrence did not have to worry about *that*. However, the ionosphere would be a mess for the next several days, endangering any signals passing from ground to orbit, or vice versa. With good equipment (and Lawrence of course had the best), this would merely limit bandwidth, but even that was intolerable. He dared not stray from the physical fiber optic lines linking device to device and continent to continent, and he dared not let too much distance fall between himself and the giant uplink antennae that could shout above the noise. He dared not leave Paramaribo, in other words, and so he flitted from site to site in this miserable city, attending to business in person where he could, and on video chat when he couldn't. His cyborg heart ticking out an artificially steady rhythm, reminding him he was technically too frail for this kind of thing.

As if Gill would ever let him forget.

Puya shrugged enormously. "You said, find out what we could."

"And?" Lawrence was already impatient with her—impatient with basically everything today. From the scene behind her he could see she was still on the Moon, having apparently declined to hop onboard that EOLS capsule, though it had had a seat reserved for her. But perhaps it was just as well. Perhaps she did not want to be in transit, onboard a spaceship with no privacy, while working on a problem they'd both agreed was urgent. But it annoyed him nonetheless, because Puya was easily distracted, and he wanted her back here on Earth, in her actual office, bombarded all day long by her actual duties.

"I've got good news, bad news, and strange news. And background information."

"Let's start with the background," he said.

Gill pulled up a chair for him, silently urging him to sit. Which, after a moment of pointless resistance, Lawrence did.

On the screen, Puya said, "The object that struck us was a hydrogen-filled graphene aerogel."

"I see." He'd suspected something like this, because there really were very limited other things it could possibly be.

The video screen split in two, the left side holding Puya and the right side showing what appeared to be a browser page, for a company called SkyBric. It included, prominently, a photograph of a rectangular, brick-sized block of material, pressing upward against a human hand, with an out-of-focus chemistry lab in the background. The block was dark gray in color, and hazy-looking in a way Lawrence immediately associated with nanostructured materials. The hand that held it was Caucasian, probably male, and sharply in focus, so one could see that it was the brick itself, not the photograph, that was blurry. But the page was also full of dead links and unreachable images.

And text, including (also prominently): CURRENTLY SEEKING INVESTORS.

"We pulled this off an archive site. The web page went up about two years ago, without fanfare, and was pulled down again within a couple of weeks."

"So, they found their investor," Lawrence said. Someone with deep pockets and a penchant for secrecy. "Do you know who?"

"Nobody we know," Puya said. "It's something called the Aphrodite Group, ostensibly operating out of the Cayman Islands, although we couldn't find a physical address there, or anywhere else."

"And what about the platform?" he asked.

"That's the strange news," she said. The video screen now divided into quarters, one of which was blank, and one of which showed an image of what Lawrence could only think of as a flying island. This time the resolution was good, and even included a short, three-frame video loop as the observation satellite overflew this object. It was roughly hexagonal in shape, and made up of smaller hexagons in a pattern that seemed incomplete, as though the island were still under construction. A sense of scale was provided by a helicopter parked near the center of the large hexagon, on what looked for all the world like a painted helipad, surrounded by gray buildings made, apparently, of the same stuff as the "ground." There were people down there—three of them that Lawrence could make out—and near the uncompleted edge stood a sort of crane or robot arm, white and orange against the gray.

Puya circled her cursor around the robot arm and said, "From the coloration we believe this is a Printech architectural 3D printer, or made to look like one. If so, it's heavily modified, as you can see from these tanks and hoses here, here, and here."

"What's it doing?" he asked. The answer had already popped into his head, or half an answer at any rate, but he wanted to hear her say it, with the full weight of the IT and R&D departments behind her.

"It appears to be additively manufacturing the base of the platform. In other words, printing out the aerogel directly, filling it with hydrogen, and extruding it onto the platform's edge. It appears to be drawing the mass directly out of the atmosphere, through these intakes here and here, and powered by this quite ordinary-looking solar array over here. This . . . well, this is probably a gas compression and sorting assembly so they can separate out CO_2 and water vapor, and then crack off just the carbon and hydrogen. The whole platform may be nothing but carbon and hydrogen, cleverly arranged."

Lawrence grunted and paused a moment, thinking about that. Aerogels simply weren't that easy to make, much less to join together like that, so the technology involved was impressive in its own right. There had to be twenty or thirty distinct chemical steps taking place inside that machinery, all in real time. It was all kinds of clever, and Lawrence admired it at once. But . . . why? What was the purpose of a flying island that could make itself larger, like a lily pad slowly growing on the surface of a pond? What end required such elaborate means?

"That's, uh, remarkable," he said, temporarily at a loss for words. Then: "What's the bad news?"

Puya cleared her throat, looked uncomfortable, and

said, "The Aphrodite Group purchased a black-box heavy-lift rocket launch, paying extra to provide only the dimensions and mass properties of their payload. Departed last week, while we were busy thinking about the mass driver and the monastery."

A black-box launch, by itself, wasn't particularly unusual. The government of Suriname didn't give a hoot what people launched, as long as it was headed away from their country when it left the ground, and companies like HMI, RzVz, Orlov Petrochemical and even Enterprise City were happy to oblige if the money was good. Which it always was, when keeping secrets was important to someone.

"What's bad about that?" Lawrence asked, suddenly not so sure he actually wanted to know.

"Well, sir, from those dimensions it's clear the payload included an interplanetary booster stage, apparently manufactured by Good Luck Industries Shenzhen. That appears to be the only link between Aphrodite and the Chinese, but I thought I should mention it."

"So it's a probe, then?"

"Not exactly, sir."

"My dear," Lawrence said, as patiently as he could, "let's not do this all day. Bad news. Out with it."

"We went back through our radar logs, and found this:"

A fourth image appeared on the teleconference screen. An object. Not blurry or grainy this time, but a gray-white computer-animated blob, against a blue-gray arc representing the horizon of Earth, and a darker background representing the vacuum of outer space. Clearly, an AI's attempt to reconstruct an object's shape from radar echoes alone. The object, already in orbit, separated itself from the stout cylinder of its second-stage booster. For a moment, it looked like pretty much any interplanetary probe in launch configuration, until a measurement ruler appeared beside it, showing its overall length, including the third-stage interplanetary booster, at just over twenty meters. Quite large for a probe. Too large!

On the screen, the object began to unfold itself, which was not unusual for a satellite of any type. Gray blobs that looked like antennae and solar panels began to unfold, bringing the object to life. But then other shapes began to appear: a conical nose shield of some sort; a trio of inflatable bubbles around the object's middle.

"What am I looking at?"

"I'll jump the video ahead," Puya said. The time codes at the bottom of the screen skipped ahead by eighty minutes. Presently, a little cartoon flame appeared at the tail end of the booster stage. The view pulled back, now showing the Earth as a full, shaded blue sphere, with stylized cartoon continents. A dotted line appeared, showing the object's trajectory. "Here the object is headed out of cislunar space entirely. Toward Venus. In fact, as of today it may already be out of Earth's gravitational sphere of influence and into interplanetary space."

"And it isn't a probe?" Lawrence asked, unsure why Puya was showing this to him.

"No, sir. It's, we believe, a colony ship, carrying equipment like this." She circled her cursor again around the hardware setup of the floating island. "Set to arrive in a hundred and twenty days."

"To colonize Venus?" he said. "Impossible."

Even the highest point on the surface of Venus—the top of Maxwell Montes—had an air pressure of forty-five atmospheres and a temperature of, what, four hundred centigrade? Hot enough to melt at least a dozen different metals. Fancy aerogels weren't going to change any of that . . .

He figured it out at the same time she said it:

"Not the surface, sir. The upper atmosphere, above the cloud tops. At fifty-five kilometers altitude, it's quite Earthlike, except for the composition of the atmosphere. If you can keep yourself from falling, I mean."

Lawrence could picture it: Earthlike temperature, Earthlike pressure, a sun hanging brightly in an azure-blue sky. The planet itself rotated on a scale of months rather than hours, but the trade winds zipped right along, circling the planet's equator in just a few Earth days. So one could have a day-night cycle, too, sailing from the light side to the dark side and back again, as fast or as slowly as one preferred. And if one lived on a floating platform *made from the atmosphere itself*, why, there was no real limit to how much "ground" one could choose to occupy. For free, basically. They'd need to crack their hydrogen from H_2SO_4 rather than H_2O, but that was quite a minor problem compared to all the others they'd already solved. Perhaps one could also fashion diamond scoops, and lower them to the ground, far below, to scrape up farmable dirt and refinable ore as the hills and valleys of Venus whizzed by. Also for free—easier than asteroid mining! He could imagine whole cities made of clear, hard diamond and dark, spongy graphene gel, inhabited by millions. Self-sustaining, dependent on no one.

"Oh," he said quietly, suddenly glad he was sitting down. This was serious.

Harvest Moon Industries already had quite enough competition from Danny Beseman, thank you very much. The lure of Mars—however distant, however unreachable—always somehow made the Moon seem shabby by comparison. Just a few days away from any beach or jungle or city one cared to visit, and yet shabby. Even Lawrence thought so! But how much more difficult would it be, to convince space-bound people to live like the monks of Saint Joe, if they could live under a blue sky instead? Walking outside with just an oxygen mask?

"I'm sorry, sir," Puya said, with apparent sincerity. She'd apparently figured it all out, too, she and her team. "A fifth Horseman has entered the fray. On quite a tiny budget, I might add. We estimate the Aphrodite Group could settle a hundred people in the Venusian atmosphere for less than one percent of the cost of the Antilympus Project. And sooner."

"I see."

"The flight package wasn't human-rated," Puya said, "so presumably it's just going to set up some sort of minimal habitat that the actual settlers can land on later. But that could happen before the end of next year."

For a moment, Lawrence simply felt stupid. For another moment, he felt angry. Why this? Why now, at this moment, with his pacemaker scars still aching? All the resources at his disposal, all the geniuses in his employ—how had he been blindsided like this? He permitted his failing heart a moment of self-pity. Just a moment, and then his mind set to work.

So did Gill Davis', for he said, "We have quite a head start on them, Sir Lawrence. And a number of other advantages, besides. A luxury dome just two days from Earth? If we move quickly, there's no reason Aphrodite's plans should have any impact on our own."

"If we move quickly," Lawrence agreed. To Gill he said, "Get Fernanda Harb on the phone, immediately. Tell her we break ground on a new project in thirty days, or she's fired, and I do mean that."

"Understood, sir."

"I can get her for you," Puya said. "She's in her office right now; I can just walk over there."

"Please do so," Lawrence said.

"Is this about your hotel?"

"Not a hotel. A retirement community. But it's about the survival of the company, Puya. Let's focus on that, shall we?" Then: "You never told me the good news."

"Oh," Puya said. "Well, the Aphrodite Group seems to have bought most of their equipment, including the launch, from us. So we've made some pocket change, at any rate."

1.22
18 December

✧

Peakview Apartment Complex
Colorado Springs, Colorado, USA
Earth Surface

As it turned out, Raimy never did go back to the Colorado Springs Police Department. The story of his narrow escape from a blown-out airlock had gone viral, and then pandemic, and by the time he touched down on solid Earth he was fielding interview requests from dozens of talk shows, and product endorsement requests from Innotex, the manufacturer of the goo suit that had—twice, now—kept him alive in deadly environments.

He found it difficult to say no to any of these—especially the ones with free travel and even cash offers attached—and so he was kept busy for weeks, flying all over the world.

None of this seemed to affect his Mars rankings—most likely because he still looked like an idiot on camera. A highly accomplished idiot, perhaps, but he rarely volunteered information, and he answered questions with a jumble of sentence fragments that only the most talented interviewers could make him feel good about. And he always looked nervous, and always sat or stood like he had anal beads up his butt, and why the hell should the Antilympus sponsors shell out their own personal hard-earned money for that? He didn't expect them to. It was all good.

In good humor, he actually told all this to one of his final interviewers—Howard Glass from *Mars Today*—in what proved to be his most authentic video appearance of the whole run.

"It's not a skill I'd need on Mars," he'd joked, "but it's a skill I would need in order to get there."

"I see the predicament," Glass responded. "I hope you don't mind my agreeing, but you really do need some help. You should hire an image coach."

"Is that a thing?"

"Oh, very much so. Very much so, yes. I don't use one myself, but they're very common among media personalities, and especially among aspirants. And the world is full of aspirants, isn't it?"

"Is that what I am?" Raimy asked.

"Isn't it? This is getting pretty far afield, but let's go with it. It's clearly something you need if you're going to keep trying, which it sounds like you're on the fence about. Just take my advice, and don't try to cheap out on it. Coaches are like lawyers; the good ones are worth a lot more than they cost. Who knows? Their influence may already be playing a decisive role in the Antilympus competition."

Raimy thought about this for a few days afterward, but

finally took the advice, and hired a woman who charged more for an hour of her time than Raimy earned in a whole day at CSPD. But she prepped him for the Innotex commercial, which happened at the end of his talk show run and actually went quite well indeed. He looked and sounded better than he ever had, and of course the product spoke for itself.

"It's not something you ever want to need," Raimy told the cameras, "but it's not something you ever want to be without."

That message seemed to resonate, and so once its paid placements had run out, the ad lived on for a time, boosted along by viral sharing not only among firefighters and space enthusiasts, but also divers, spelunkers, coal miners, natural gas workers, and anyone else who worried about suddenly running out of breathable air.

And so Raimy's fifteen minutes of fame got extended a little longer.

It still didn't really help his rankings, but that was fine, and to his surprise it did result in more offers to travel to outer space. Did he want to spend a week at Transit Point Station, training people in his survival techniques? Could he spend the week after that at the Marriott Stars, shooting some TV commercials for them?

He said yes to both things, barely pausing to check how much they were offering to pay him, because of course the travel costs would be in the high tens of millions of dollars, and he'd be happy if a thousandth of that landed in his pockets. And as it turned out, they were offering a bit more than that.

So he cleared his schedule and was preparing for

another trip to General Spacesuit, to get fitted for something a little lighter and more flexible than a moon suit.

He was packing for the trip when his rollup chime announced an incoming video call. He'd been fielding a lot of these, lately, and didn't think much about it as he pulled the thing off his nightstand, unrolled it, and answered. Only then did he remember he was dressed in his plain old Earth underwear.

"Hello?" he said, angling the phone up toward his face.

"Good morning, sir," said an old white man with a gruff British accent. "Do you know who I am?"

Raimy didn't for a moment. And then he did, but couldn't believe it. And then, after staring for three whole seconds, he blurted out, "Lawrence Edgar Killian?"

Raimy's mind couldn't quite take it in, but somehow his mouth went right on speaking. "What can I do for you this fine afternoon?"

Killian chuckled at that. "I seem to have caught you in the middle of something, Mr. Vaught. Is this a bad time?"

"Not especially," Raimy said, with a kind of calm now settling over him. He was in Bonus Round, and the world was full of surprises.

"Well, then, may I call you Raimy?"

"Sure."

"Good. Please call me Lawrence, and I mean that. Now, I understand you used to race motorcycles. That's something you and I have in common. I'm also a deep-sea diver, though not as accomplished as you. Sir, I'd like to start by saying how impressed I am, that you managed to survive that airlock incident. You displayed quick thinking, and quick action, under a level of duress most of us will thankfully never experience."

His accent was odd. Not upper-class English, or at least not completely so; there was a regional working-class lilt at the back of it that Raimy figured was a holdover from Killian's parents. Too, his voice had coarsened with age, becoming slow and grainy and blurred in a way that transcended ethnic and national origins. A citizen of old age.

"Thank you," Raimy answered sincerely. "I regret I wasn't able to save Anming Shui."

"Oh, goodness," Killian said, without judgment, "if you had tried to do that, you wouldn't be alive to have this conversation with me. This is partly what I mean about quick thinking. The American Navy must train its people very well indeed. Either that or you're a born astronaut, which is fine, too. I'd like to thank you for solving this crime."

"Not well enough or soon enough," Raimy said.

Killian tsked at that. "Once again, Raimy, Mr. Shui's death was not your fault. He could have exonerated himself and laid the blame on Katla Koskinen at any moment. But he chose not to. Love is a funny thing, isn't it? Even knowing she'd betrayed him, he held his tongue. She must have had quite a hold on him."

"Yes. I've thought about that a lot."

"And if not for your unlikely survival, she'd be guilty of three murders and still on her way to Mars. One wonders how many bad actors might be in space already. Of course, some would say I'm one of them."

Which was an odd thing to say because Killian had

never actually been to outer space, and of the Four Horsemen, he also had the gentlest reputation. Igbal Renz was a drug addict and a womanizer. Grigory Orlov, a straight-up robber baron. Dan Beseman was tone-deaf in his determination to make Mars his own, and Raimy was among the people who half-expected him to declare himself King of Mars once he got there.

But aside from a flair for the theatrical and (in days gone by) for the physically daring, Sir Lawrence seemed harmless enough. A sweet old man, ten years a widower and still wearing the ring.

"I wouldn't say that," Raimy told him. And then, because he was in Bonus Round and had nothing to lose or gain, he added, "Opinions vary, but I've always kind of liked you."

"I'm glad to hear that," Killian said, sounding genuinely flattered. "Because I'd like to offer you a full-time job. On the Moon."

Raimy, who was done turning corpses over in the rain, and who was not going to Mars and was not romantically involved with Bridget or with anyone else, simply shrugged and said, "I accept."

4.3
24 December
✧
St. Joseph of Cupertino Monastery
South Polar Mineral Territories
Lunar Surface

His Holiness Pope Dave, PP.
00120 Via del Pellegrino
Città del Vaticano
La Terra

CC: Father Bertram Meagher
St. Benedict's Monastery
1012 Monastery Rd.
Snowmass, CO, USA
Earth

Dear Dave,

Being aware that I have made strange and costly requests of thee in the past, I fear thou wilt, upon seeing my letterhead, roll thine eyes and sigh, and wonder what now, what next from this most annoying of thy remaining monks? On Christmas Eve, no less! And the contents of this letter will, I fear, not disappoint, for I've received an Invitation, the exact nature of which I am not sure, for it accompanies a nondisclosure agreement I have not signed (and, I think, cannot sign) without a co-signature representing the highest approval our Church can grant. Namely, yours. With me so far?

The invitation comes encryption-stamped via the internal blockchain of Renz Ventures, and bears the return address of ESL1 Shade Station. Yes, I know: the place where wanton women allegedly barter themselves into haremic servitude for a chance to live and work in space, although I hear and suspect that's not entirely true. Not a promising beginning, you may think, and I daresay I cannot disagree, for the letter purports to be from Igbal Renz himself. Yes, I know: the skinflint profiteer whose past ravings about extracorporeal Beings are indelibly tied to his consumption of illicit substances. One mightn't be surprised if you stop reading at this point, and want nothing further to do with this matter, and if so, I do truly understand, for our Church can accomplish nothing without reputation, hard-won and easily tarnished. But I beseech you: hear me out, for you have not yet heard the strangest part, nor the most wonderful.

The NDA is also encryption-stamped, and appears to be what practitioners refer to as a "living contract," incapable of alteration and enforced by an indelible linkage of accounts. I am no expert in these matters, for the contract is legalese rendered as formal source code, and quite impenetrable to casual inspection. Nor dare I consult such experts without authorization, for reasons obvious enough, but it appears that any breach of the nondisclosure, detected by the aforementioned code, is automatically enforced by a vast transfer of funds and, I think, generation of a secured debt contract to cover any shortage. Serious business, you'll agree, and one cannot help but wonder what wonders merit such strong concealment.

The letter itself is brief:

Dear Brother Michael: In recognition of your impressive role in settlement of space, and your unique education and leanings, you are cordially invited to serve as chaplain and spiritual advisor to ninety-nine persons onboard a research mission. Mission will last two years, during which at least some passengers will hibernate at least part of the time. There will be danger. There will be discovery. I realize you're a busy man with obligations, and I wouldn't ask you if I did not think you'd allured [sic] by the prospect. Please sign attached NDA for details.

This by itself is intriguing sufficient to tie my dentate gyrus in knots, for that's the part of the brain that governs curiosity—itself a part of the hungry hungry hippocampus, which governs memory. I pressed so hard for a Lunar monastery for the simple reason that I thought it best for the Church to play a role in this frontier, as it did in the frontiers of yore, and also best for humanity to be so guided. Better than an endless Godless blundering from one destination to another, yes? And for a man so widely thought immoral, or amoral, to come to us for guidance (or at least the outward appearance of guidance) is quite exactly the hoped-for effect. We, in a word, matter.

I *do* have obligations, to you and my Brothers and to the green shoots of Lunar habitation, and I'll confess that any acceptance of this invitation would vex me considerable, so I will suggest that it needn't be me, per se, who'd fulfill the contract if accepted. But whatever may or may not be going on here, is it not better that it go with the help of our beloved Church? You begin to see, I hope, why I dare once again to disturb your many labours and entreat your brief attention.

If I may, Your Holiness, speculate on the matter a bit, I will note in more than passing that ESL1 is in possession of enough antimatter to power a spaceship to quite tremendous speeds. Two years is not enough time to reach a neighbor star, nor even a fraction of the distance thereto. And yet, such a span is quite oversufficient to reach any known point within the solar system, and so I conclude that the expedition is to some extrasolar place or object or event or substance known only to Renz and his people. I have conferred, briefly and vaguely, with Brothers Giancarlo Marino and Ovid Šćekić (either or both of whom you may recall as former Vatican astronomers) about the possibilities, and they have said there might be a brown dwarf out there, or an icy or gassy planet of considerable size, that's nevertheless difficult to detect by conventional astronomic observation. Do either of these possibilities merit such cloak, dagger, and cypher? When further pressed, both Brothers became more curious than I cared to entertain, and so I withdrew from said discussion. Suffice to say, it's not merely my own imagination that's beggared by the prospect.

Perhaps what Renz proposes is merely a shakedown

cruise for a ship with longer destinations in mind at some future point. Indeed, humanity did not settle the Moon the first time one of its rockets burned a parabola that tall! No, there were missions upon missions, carefully expanding our reach. Mars is a bit of an anomaly in that regard, for the only shakedown cruises H.S.F. *Concordia* will enjoy will be jaunts—first partially loaded and then fully laden with slumbering contest winners—within cislunar space itself. Tooling 'round the Moon and buzzing the Esley Shade are no real practice for the much longer and more velocitous journey to Mars. And yet, to burn sufficient to reach that planet, one might as well go the distance, for it's only a few months additional.

On a journey to the stars this would not be the case, for that transit needs decades, or more than decades. Are we even one-tenth ready for such a venture? I can scarce believe it a possibility, for we haven't even watched the mistakes of Antilympus, to learn us what's what! And so, yes, a shakedown cruise is certainly in order, though it cost a pile of antimatter worth more than all the gold there ever was. (Sell gold, by the way, Your Holy; its recent price drops are nothing compared to what's in store, as Orlov Petrochemical inches toward producing that substance as well. The Church's holdings of bullion and coin, saving of course the priceless relics, will do more good converted to quick cash than hoarded 'neath the floorboards!) And yet, were mere shakedown the goal of said mission, why bring along eight dozen and three frozen researchers, and a spiritual advisor besides?

No, it must be bigger than that. It must be big indeed, this extrasolar whatsis, and two humble servants of our beloved Church—being your own self, and mine—are offered to be let in on the secret. It might be a tame black hole, Dave. It might be little green men!

An RSVP appears mandatory; the robe will not open, so to speak, until the invitation is accepted. And so if this be a bluff, the cost of calling it is high. If it be something true and wonderful strange, as it certainly appears, then the cost of folding our hand may be higher still. If we are made in God's image, then surely the curiosity that bit Eden's apple is merely (and wonderfully) His savoring, through us, the sweet agony of *not being omniscient*. To quote my American granddad, it sounds like hobo hootenanny, and I think it would be disappointing to disappoint the cosmic consciousness by missing the boat.

Are there potentially unsavory entanglements and conflicts of interest lurking in the wings here? Assuredly, yes. Is there a possibility of bodily or reputational harm? I'm quite certain there is, or are. Is it the opportunity of a hundred frozen lifetimes? Igbal Renz certainly seems to think so, and I will opine, sir, that he is no easy man to impress. I have prayed for guidance to Our Father Who Art, and though I find it quite impossible to distinguish His answers from my own base thoughts, I fortunately know that it's *your* counsel and assessment I actually require. Shall we meekly but wisely inherit the world that hangs above the Earth, or shall we boldly and perhaps foolishly carry forward, premature and all that, into the darkness beyond? Your thoughts on the matter are humbly (and, I confess, impatiently) awaited.

>Yours,
>Brother Michael Jablonski de la Lune

Appendix A
Dramatis Personae, in order of appearance:

Andrei Bykhovski: Metallurgist and asteroid mining specialist at Clementine Cislunar Fuel Depot.

Etsub Beyene: Hydroponics specialist, first in line for the Male Hydroponics slot at Antilympus Township.

Brother Michael Jablonski: Prior of St. Joseph of Cupertino Monastery. Has a master's of divinity from Fuller and a master's of physical chemistry from MIT. Former airplane crash analyst. Canadian.

Raimy Vaught: Homicide Detective for the Colorado Springs Police Department. Former prosecuting attorney, Navy diver and submariner. Third in line for the Male Administrator slot at Antilympus Township.

Carol Beseman: Wife of Dan Beseman, in charge of public relations for the Antilympus Project.

Tracy Greene: Assistant to Carol Beseman.

Bridget Tobin: Hydroponics specialist, second in line for the Female Hydroponics slot at Antilympus Township.

Ian Doerr: Billionaire CEO, first in line for the Male Administrator slot at Antilympus Township.

Tim Long Chang: Astronomer, author, former Dean of Sciences at Princeton University, and currently CEO of NationalGeographic. Second in the running for the Male Administrator slot at Antilympus Township.

Dona Obata: Twenty-eight-year-old operative from France's *Commandement des Opérations Spéciales*. Grew up in Brazzaville, Republic of the Congo. Stole an RzVz shuttle to escape from Transit Point Station to Clementine Cislunar Fuel Depot. Allegedly has two siblings, both in Europe, and two living parents in Africa, although it might be a cover story.

Grigory Orlov: Founder and CEO of Clementine Cislunar Fuel Depot. CEO of Orlov Petrochemical, founded by his father, Magnus Orlov. One of the Four Horsemen.

Andrei Morozov: Station commander of Clementine Cislunar Fuel Depot.

Christina "Tina" Tompkins: President of the United States, successor to President Yano.

Iqbal Renz: Founder and CEO of Renz Ventures. Inventor of deep belief motion control networks and many other technologies. One of the Four Horsemen.

Lt. Commander Geary Notbohm: First Officer of Transit Point Station. Number three in line for the Male Hydroponics slot at Antilympus Township.

David Ling: SLEO pilot for Harvest Moon Industries.

Luke Hopken: Fluid management systems expert for General Spacesuit, fourth contender for the Male Hydroponics slot.

Fernanda Harb: Commander of Shackleton Lunar Industrial Station.

Tania Falstaff: Flight controller and radar engineer for Harvest Moon Industries.

Stephen Chalmers: Electromagnetics engineer for Harvest Moon Industries.

Sir Lawrence Edgar Killian: Founder and CEO of Harvest Moon Industries, and a major financial backer of St. Joseph of Cupertino Monastery. One of the Four Horsemen.

Dwight Bratton: Civil engineer stationed at Malinkin Base.

Chie Rongish: Civil engineer stationed at Malinkin Base.

Dong Nguyen: Worker and astronaut at Transit Point Station.

Dan Beseman: Founder and CEO of Enterprise City LLG, and owner of both the Mars colony ship H.S.F. *Concordia* and the soon to be populated Mars base known as Antilympus Township. One of the Four Horsemen.

Miyuki Ishibashi: Personal assistant to Dan Beseman, and Mars colony applicant. Physicist. First in line for the Female Administrator slot at Antilympus Township.

Father Bertram Meagher: Abbott of St. Joseph of Cupertino Monastery, but stationed permanently on Earth. Has a master's of divinity from Fuller.

Brother Eliaz Groppel: Electrician, administrator, and second-in-command of St. Joseph of Cupertino Monastery. A member of the second wave of monks to settle there. Belgian.

Brother Purcell Veloso: Machinist and maintenance engineer of St. Joseph of Cupertino Monastery. A member of the first wave of monks to settle there. Spanish.

Eduardo Halladay: EOLS pilot for Harvest Moon Industries.

Shonda Vaught: Mother of Raimy Vaught. Resides in San Diego.

Katla Koskinen: Finnish botanist, first in line for the Female Hydroponics slot at Antilympus Township.

Brother Giancarlo Marino: Former Vatican astronomer, and resident of St. Joseph of Cupertino Monastery. A member of the first wave of monks to settle there. Italian.

Anming Shui: Chinese botanist, second in line for the Male Hydroponics slot at Antilympus Township.

Brother Callen Hughart: Medical doctor and Infirmer of St. Joseph of Cupertino Monastery. A member of the second wave of monks to settle there. Scottish.

Brother Hilario Hamblin: Head kitchener of St. Joseph of Cupertino Monastery. A member of the second wave of monks to settle there. Argentinian.

Brother Ovid Šćekić: Former Vatican astronomer, now a resident of St. Joseph of Cupertino Monastery. A member of the second wave of monks to settle there. Montenegrin.

Brother Ferris Dis Santos: Resident of St. Joseph of Cupertino Monastery. A member of the second wave of monks to settle there. Brazilian.

Brother Kurtis Durm: Assistant kitchener of St. Joseph of Cupertino Monastery. A member of the second wave of monks to settle there. German.

Daniel Florinovich Epureanu: Moldovan maintenance supervisor at Clementine Cislunar Fuel Depot.

Doctor Sergei Chernov: Physician onboard Clementine Cislunar Fuel Depot.

Brother Marcus "Bear" Bryant: Resident of St. Joseph of Cupertino Monastery. A member of the second wave of monks to settle there.

Brother Zachary Duppler: Resident of St. Joseph of Cupertino Monastery. A member of the second wave of monks to settle there.

Puya Hebbar: Head of Launch Services for Harvest Moon Industries, with a PhD in aerospace engineering.

Adam Richter: Astronaut Technician for Harvest Moon Industries.

Blake Myneni: Astronaut Technician for Harvest Moon Industries.

Jerry and Merv: Astronaut Technicians for Harvest Moon Industries.

Huntley Millar: EVA crew chief at Shackleton Lunar Industrial Station.

Eldad Barzeley: Harvest Moon's chief solar radiation scientist.

Mikhail Voronin: Subcommander of Clementine Cislunar Fuel Depot.

Paul Young: Lead space traffic controller for Transit Point Station.

Gill Davis: Personal assistant to Lawrence Edgar Killian.

Howard Glass: Interviewer for *Mars Today*.

Appendix B
NOTES

Notes for Thread 1

Gravity Gradient: The difference in gravitational acceleration between Transit Point Station's center of mass and its endpoints is small—just 0.17 micro-gee or, more specifically, 0.001683 millimeters per second squared. The distance traveled at a fixed acceleration is given by $d = 0.5at^2$, so after twenty-six minutes hovering in midair, Raimy's car keys will have traveled about two meters.

Launch Window: Technically, the period of days or months when a Hohmann transfer is possible between Earth and Mars is known as a launch "period," not a launch "window." A launch window is a period of hours or minutes when conditions are acceptable for launch (for example, due to time-of-day restrictions, i.e., an orientation of the Earth with respect to the celestial sphere, a position of the vehicle along its orbit around the Earth, etc.). Space industry professionals may recognize the error, but the incorrect use of "launch window" has firmly embedded itself in the public vernacular, probably because it just sounds better. So I'm assuming that as more and more private citizens make their way into space, common usage will overwhelm twentieth-century engineering jargon.

St. Joseph of Cupertino Monastery is loosely based on St.

Benedict's Monastery in Snowmass, Colorado, to which my wife has been a frequent visitor across several decades, and with whose members she's formed many close friendships. The idea of a monastery on the Moon occurred to me during a visit there.

Timelines for Raimy: He graduated high school at nineteen. He spent one year in dive school and submarine school, three years onboard the U.S.S. *Jimmy Carter*, three years in law school, five years as a prosecuting attorney, three years as a patrolman, and seven years as a detective. Ahead of him in the Mars rankings are world famous billionaire Ian Doerr and world-famous astronomer/author/Ivy League dean Tim Long Chang (now the CEO of National Geographic). Note: *Concordia* will fly in 2055.

Notes for Thread 2
Andrei Bykhovski was able to hitch a ride to the Moon for the simple reason that carbon and nitrogen are almost totally unavailable in the Lunar regolith. Thus, any permanent habitation on the Moon, however sophisticated, will necessarily be dependent on imports of these two materials. Hydrogen is also quite rare, except in shaded craters of the polar regions. However, since that's where St. Joseph of Cupertino Monastery is located, its availability is not a huge problem. Because carbon and nitrogen can be found in near-Earth asteroids, at up to seventy-five times their concentrations in Earth's crust, asteroid mining will likely be a cheaper way to supply these materials than shipping from Earth.

Notes for Thread 3
Thorium Reactors

Depending on the reactor design, a critical mass of thorium is around 1000-3000 kg. However, it's possible to excite a subcritical reactor with a particle accelerator and thus get by with a lot less fissionable material. How far this technology can be pushed is an interesting question, but 300 kg is a value seen in plausible reactor designs, so that's what I've used in this story.

Mass Driver

The HMI mass driver is ten kilometers long, and has to accelerate its 1000-kg payload to a speed of 2.37 kilometers per second to reach Earth. This requires an average acceleration of 28.1 m/s^2 over a period of 8.4 seconds. However, since the acceleration is actually driven by one hundred individual magnets, it can't be constant. Rather, it's a "scalloped" curve with one hundred upward-facing peaks. Travel time for the payload is 4.9 days, after which it burns up in the Earth's atmosphere. By this time, thanks to acceleration from the Earth's gravity, it's moving at about ten kilometers per second, so if it's aimed directly at the Earth's surface, rather than a grazing shot into the atmosphere, it could reach the ground largely intact, producing an impact crater about forty meters wide and knocking down buildings as much as three hundred meters away from the impact site, with an explosive force equal to about twelve tons of TNT. So while a single mass driver projectile is not as dangerous as even a small nuclear weapon, it's equivalent to four or five good-sized truck bombs. That's more than enough of a security threat to make Earthly government nervous, even if they have access to countermeasures.

The main purpose of the mass driver is to get the payload up to Lunar escape velocity. If it has even a small rocket engine, the payload can then be nudged to pass through virtually any point in cislunar space. Actually stopping (or matching orbits) at any point in space is also possible, although the fuel requirements are larger.

Antigravity Bricks

Most aerogels are basically open-celled foams made of glass (or other materials) that are mostly empty space, or rather, mostly air. As such they're translucent as smoke and incredibly light, though not terribly strong. You can easily crumble a sheet of silica aerogel in your hand, although you need to be careful, because the dust consists of microscopic broken glass. Also, because the material is mostly air with a little bit of glass mixed in, it's still heavier than air.

But! Imagine if that brittle, open-celled glass foam were replaced with a flexible, closed-cell diamond or graphene one. Such (charcoal gray) gels can be made with densities of just one hundred sixty grams per cubic meter (which is barely any mass at all!), but let's make ours a bit more robust at, say, six hundred grams per cubic meter. This would be more than strong enough to support the weight of a human being (see, for example, www.nanowerk.com/spotlight/spotid=52741.php).

Now imagine that instead of air, the structure is filled with hydrogen, with a sea-level buoyancy or lifting force of about twelve hundred grams per cubic meter.

Graphene and diamond are both "sticky" to hydrogen molecules and have been used to store them in bulk (see www.researchgate.net/publication/235637852_Hydrogen _Storage_in_Diamond_Films and link.springer.com/article/10.1134/S1995078020030027), so we can assume most of the gas won't leak out immediately. However, just in case, let's add a thin, impermeable, inelastic shrink wrap to hold it all together when compressed.

The result is an "antigravity brick" that's strong enough to build things out of, and yet "weighs" negative six hundred grams. It would literally fly up into the sky if you let go of it, and one hundred and fifty of them glued together would be enough to lift a good-sized person, clothes and all.

Notes for Thread 4
Earth-Sun Lagrange Point 1 Shade
The Earth-Sun Lagrange 1 (ESL1) Shade has a radius of two hundred sixteen kilometers. Since it's only a fraction of a millimeter thick, there is not room for a lot of fancy photovoltaic layers, so its initial photovoltaic conversion efficiency is only around one percent. However, this is still sufficient to generate 1.47 terawatts of continuous electrical power—more than the entire United States circa 2022. Unbeknownst to anyone outside of ESL1 Shade Station, ongoing improvements to the Shade, in the form of additional coated layers, are improving this efficiency as time goes on. As seen from Earth, the Shade subtends an angle of 0.158 degrees (roughly three percent of the width of the Sun), and blocks 0.1 percent of the

solar energy that would otherwise strike the Earth. Eventually, observers on Earth and elsewhere will begin to notice the shade is becoming more opaque.

Igbal Renz's Spaceship
Brother Michael is correct that Renz Ventures has more than enough antimatter to reach any point in the solar system, and return, within the specified two-year mission duration. However, a mission headed outside the solar system first has to answer one question: where exactly is the outer edge? The orbit of Neptune is roughly thirty AU ("astronomical units") from the Sun. The Kuiper Belt—a very loose swarm of comets in elliptical orbits—spans between forty and sixty AU. The "bow shock," where the solar wind begins to be affected by the galactic wind, occurs at one hundred AU, and the heliopause, where the solar wind stops altogether, occurs at about one hundred twenty-five AU. However, if you cross the heliopause, you're still not there, because the Oort cloud (an even looser swarm of comets orbiting the sun really, really slowly) begins at around ten thousand AU (or 1.7 percent of a light-year), and continues all the way out to one hundred thousand AU (or 1.58 light-years). If you're headed toward Alpha Centauri, the light from that system will be brighter than the light of Sol once you've reached a distance of about 1.0 light-years, and if you're headed for Sirius, it will become brighter than Sol at about 1.5 light-years. In other words, the solar system has a number of different "edges," some easier to reach than others.

Let's say, for example, we decide to go to the inner edge of the Oort cloud. A quick back-of-the-envelope calculation shows that (for example) a starship weighing one million kilograms, accelerating continuously at 1 m/s^2, could get there in roughly seven months, at an ending velocity of six percent of the speed of light. Assuming total conversion of antimatter into kinetic energy, you'd need 1.9 tons of the stuff for the outbound journey, and an equivalent amount to turn around and come home.

Notes for Thread 5

The effects of the MSL1 magsat are perhaps the most speculative element of this story. From the distance of Mars-Sun Lagrange Point 1, it should actually be fairly easy to deflect a significant portion of the solar wind; the Earth does this with a fairly weak magnetic field of 3×10^{-5} Tesla (or ~3 gauss). By contrast, the electromagnet in an ordinary MRI scanner can be up to three Tesla (thirty thousand gauss), though it's generated in a much smaller volume of space. The Earth generates its field with gigantic layers of molten iron flowing past each other at different speeds, so the field geometries are really not that similar, especially close to the planet. However, the field strength of the Earth's dynamo drops off with the square of the distance, just like Miyuki's fusion magnet, and still manages to keep our atmosphere from being stripped away by charged particles. The MSL1 magsat could potentially have an even stronger effect.

Blocking the solar wind would in fact cool the outer regions of Mars' atmosphere, which right now sizzles with energetic collisions. At this time there's no evidence this would have a dramatic effect on the atmosphere's deeper layers—I made that up—but the Martian atmosphere is so thin that very small absolute changes could still wind up having large percentages attached to them. Now, according to the ideal gas law, a thirty percent reduction in the volume of Mars' atmosphere, with no pressure increase, should result in thirty percent higher temperatures as well. However, as we've seen here on Earth, real atmospheres are not ideal gases, but complex systems that can produce head-scratching results. Alien atmospheres will no doubt have surprises of their own, especially if we start artificially mucking with them.

By the way, this would be a remarkably easy experiment to perform. As space exploration budgets are increasingly decoupled from risk-averse national governments, it seems likely that someone will eventually try it.

Acknowledgments

✦

Lakewood, Colorado, USA
Earth Surface

I'd like to thank Toni Weisskopf for taking a chance on this series, and the whole team at Baen for making it a reality. The following people are, directly or indirectly, responsible for the ideas that became this story: Gary Snyder, Aaron Cotter, Wayne-Daniel Berard, and Evangeline Jennifer Hoyer McCarthy. Early drafts were endured by Marie DesJardin, Ember Randall, Glen Cox, Ron Holser, Pat Smythe, Peter Sartucci, Eneasz Brodski, Thea Hutcheson, and Ronnie Seagren. I'd also like to thank the actual Horsemen who, despite the barbs of a fickle public, are presently building the aerospace infrastructure that may someday make events like these possible. Any mistakes you may find in this book are, I think, caused by information leaking in from alternate universes.

About the Author

Engineer/novelist/journalist/entrepreneur Wil McCarthy is a former contributing editor for *WIRED* magazine and science columnist for the SyFy channel (previously SciFi channel), where his popular "Lab Notes" column ran from 1999 through 2009. A lifetime member of the Science Fiction and Fantasy Writers of America, he is a two-time winner of the AnLab award, a one-time winner of the Prometheus Award, has been nominated for the Nebula, Locus, Seiun, Colorado Book, Theodore Sturgeon and Philip K. Dick awards, and contributed to projects that won a Webbie, an Eppie, a Game Developers Choice award, and a General Excellence National Magazine award. In addition, his imaginary world of "P2/Sorrow" was rated one of the ten best science fiction planets of all time by *Discover* magazine. His short fiction has graced the pages of magazines like *Analog*, *Asimov's*, *WIRED*, and *SF Age*, and his eleven published novels include the *New York Times* Notable *Bloom*, Amazon.com "Best of Y2K" *The Collapsium* (an international bestseller) and, most recently, *Antediluvian* and *Rich Man's Sky*. He has also written for TV and video games, appeared on The History Channel and The Science Channel, and published nonfiction in half a dozen magazines, including *WIRED*, *Discover*, *GQ*, *Popular Mechanics*, *IEEE Spectrum*, and the *Journal of Applied Polymer Science*.

Previously a flight controller for Lockheed Martin

Space Launch Systems and later an engineering manager for Omnitech Robotics and founder/president/CTO of RavenBrick LLC, McCarthy now writes patents for a top law firm in Denver. He holds patents of his own in seven countries, including thirty-one issued U.S. patents in the field of nanostructured optical materials.